SNOWLEG

Nicholas Shakespeare

A Harvest Book
HARCOURT, INC.
Orlando   Austin   New York   San Diego   Toronto   London

Requests for permission to make copies of any part of the work
should be mailed to the following address: Permissions Department,
Harcourt, Inc., 6277 Sea Harbor Drive, Orlando, Florida 32887-6777.

www.HarcourtBooks.com

First published in the United Kingdom by The Harvill Press.

The Library of Congress has cataloged the hardcover edition as follows:
Shakespeare, Nicholas, 1957–
Snowleg/Nicholas Shakespeare.
p. cm.
1. British—Germany—Fiction.   2. Children of immigrants—Fiction.
3. Fathers and sons—Fiction.   4. Dissenters—Fiction.
5. Germany—Fiction.
I. Title.
PR6069.H286S63   2004
823'.914—dc22   2004047543
ISBN-13: 978-0151-01146-9   ISBN-10: 0-15-101146-X
ISBN-13: 978-0156-03046-5 (pbk.)   ISBN-10: 0-15-603046-2 (pbk.)

Text set in Monotype Sabon

Printed in the United States of America

First Harvest edition 2005
A C E G I K J H F D B

To Niko and Brit

My memory of your face
Prevents my seeing you

—RUMI

On that night without sequel
You realised you were a coward

—BORGES, *Snorri Sturluson*

CONTENTS

PROLOGUE

THE SCREECHING OF A blackbird, flying through the icy branches above the hut, tore the peace.

Early Sunday morning and the snowflakes tumbling again over the deserted gardens. In the middle of this grey city, the snow brightened everything. The narrow allotments were flannelled with it, the pruned pear trees glittered with it, the garden ornaments looked holy with it. Only the gnome on its back seemed out of place, the flakes drifting into its wide-open mouth and the wire poking from its feet.

Two men, one leading an Alsatian, tramped in haste towards the hut. They were dressed the same, in kidney-coloured jackets and "Present 20" trousers. The cold had reddened their ears and noses. The dog-handler was about twenty-five, ginger-haired, with insolent, protruding eyes. His younger companion was a foot taller, more educated-looking, and held up a bespoke case made of black plastic.

They didn't speak, picked their way with care. A wildcat frost had hardened Saturday's snow and the puddles had refrozen with points on them that pricked into the men's bootsoles. Even the sure-footed Alsatian found walking treacherous, and slithered over the frosted furrows with its nose low and the day in its eyes sparkling cold and bright from the iced-over pools.

The man with the case noticed the footprints first. "Kresse, look," pointing to the bottom of the wooden gate.

The dog-handler stared in fury at the two sets of tracks, while his hound, distracted, criss-crossed the path, wanting to go the other way.

Again the blackbird. In the silence that followed Uwe heard Kresse humming to himself. Kresse always hummed, he noticed, at moments when he himself would have sworn like a sailor.

Anyone approaching might have supposed Kresse happy until they saw those eyes. They seemed to share the property of one of Uwe's chemicals at the Runde Ecke. An acid that burned on contact.

"Come on, boss!" With a gesture of impatience, Kresse drew his pistol from his holster and unlatched the gate, and together they followed the footprints coming towards them all the way to the hut.

It had a lime-green door. The gnome that had guarded it lay upturned on the path. Something about the ornament attracted the Alsatian, which started whining at full stretch of the lead, but Kresse, ignoring it, nodded curtly to the gnome as to a superior, and kicked open the door. He erupted inside with the frustrated energy of a man who had badly wanted to arrest two young people lying in bed.

A silverfish streaked across the matting and under an open fridge.

Kresse opened his mouth, revealing a gap at the side of his teeth. "Shit," and dropped the pistol to his side. "They've gone, boss."

Thank goodness, poor bastards, Uwe thought. Standing in the dark behind the angry wrecker, he breathed in. The hut was musky from passion and squirrels, but his nostrils picked out other scents. Damp firewood. Burnt dust from a heater. Incense from a cone.

His glance darted about the room, his eyes adjusting, and he saw under the low window an unmade bed. Whoever had spent the night here had departed in a hurry. A Formica table and three white garden chairs. Uwe clacked open his case on the table and drew from their tight velvet lair two glass jars of the sort used for storing honey. He unscrewed the lids.

Something moved across the floor and Kresse stamped on it. He advanced on the bed like a miner towards the rubble his explosion has detonated. His pace was too slow for his dog. The Alsatian lunged from his grasp and made a dash for the thin mattress. It leaped around, barking, then gave a confused yelp and pawed at the sheets, leaving muddy marks, and Uwe knew that it was smelling one scent and then another and that the scents were competing.

"Get that dog off!" Uwe said sharply, and once the Alsatian had been ordered to the floor, he knelt beside the bed. His gloved hands separated blanket from sheet and soon found what they were looking for. He walked to the table and rubbed his fingers until the hairs dropped into their respective jars. The girl's pubic hair was dark.

Another stamp shook the hut. Kresse dragging the Alsatian from the bed had caught his boot on something. On the worn matting, a woman's cerise silk shirt.

Uwe moved swiftly to retrieve it – old-fashioned and fragile, oriental dragons stitched into the fabric. He spread the shirt on the table and with a pair of tweezers laid a strip of yellow felt, about 4 inches square, on the armpit. He covered the felt with a sheet of foil and onto the foil he pressed one of the lead weights that he carried in his case.

Meanwhile, Kresse had spotted, over the back of a chair, a blue woollen scarf. He thrust the animal's muzzle towards it and watched for a sign that the trails were not confused, that the Alsatian would detect a single scent. The Alsatian sat down, confirming the trace.

"Good boy." Kresse turned. He looked wild and unreasonable. "His?"

Uwe lifted the scarf, noting the British label, and nodded.

"Reckon they'll come back tonight, boss?" There was a speck of dried blood on the undertip of his nose.

"Maybe you can still find them, Kresse," Uwe said in an even voice. "Maybe they haven't gone far."

Kresse walked his dog to the broken door and looked out. The light reflected on his bulging eyes. They smiled tightly at the footprints that fled from the hut, beginning to fill with snow.

"There's a good boy, go find," snapping off the leash.

The Alsatian bounded away.

Uwe checked his watch: 9.17 a.m. Because of the intense cold it would take two hours for the felt to absorb the body scents. He went down the steps to deal with the gnome.

Afterwards, he plugged in the heater and turned on a tap. No water – and he remembered that the Schreber gardens didn't open for another week. He scraped back a chair and was on the point of sitting down when he saw, spine up on the seat, an English book. The cover showed a flock of swans and, suspended between them, the figure of a boy. One glance and he knew the book was illegal. He picked it up and tucked it into his case.

He was glad the couple had escaped. Yes, he had hoped to find them inside the hut, but now he was relieved. His eye fell on a smear on the matting and, like a crushed thing that he wanted to rescue, a thought squirmed up. To what end am I doing this? He didn't ordinarily care to open the door to this sort of reflection. His was a science, a pursuit of the silverfish in order to understand how it scuttled – not to trample on it. He hated to think of his work ending up in the hands of a mammoth like Kresse.

At 11.17 he lifted off the lead weights, tweezered the felt strips into the jars, screwed shut the lids and wrote down details on a label: date, location, name. He licked the second label and the raw taste of adhesive on his tongue reminded him of Morneweg's storeroom, floor to ceiling honey jars, in every one a body scent trapped at a specific moment. A damp and sandy track, Uwe knew from his experiments, held the smell for twelve hours; an overgrown path away from the sun for 24 hours; but a sample in one of these jars – he still didn't know how many weeks, months, even years, it retained a person's body-scent. Certainly until such time as the order was made to pluck down a name, unscrew the lid and offer the contents to Kresse's Alsatian, in the special villa which the animal enjoyed to itself, saying in a caressing tone: "Good boy, go find."

He crushed the thought, and peeling the label from his tongue he pressed it to the glass.

4

PART I

England, 1977–9

CHAPTER ONE

SHE LED THE WAY along the bridle path, through a field of black-spotted stones and blackberry bushes that glistened with rain. Peter's favourite walk.

They climbed in silence. Near the summit they came to a steep chalk verge dotted with yellow and red bee-orchids – "one of the few places in England where they grow", according to his father. Once, taking a specimen to draw, his father had found embedded in the chalk a twisted scrap of aluminium, the relic, he maintained, of the Heinkel that had blazed into the ridge in the last months of the war. He kept it on a shelf in his studio, a precious metal flower.

At the lookout on the ridge – which Peter for ever after dubbed "Revelation Hill" – his mother paused.

The Friday before, Peter sat in Mugging Hall waiting to hear his name.

"Liptrot?"

"*Sum.*"

"Leadley?"

"*Sum.*"

"Hithersay?"

"*Sum.*" His presence confirmed, he drew the tangerine curtain of his "toyes", the wooden stall – a jumble of horsebox, Arab tent and cupboard – that encompassed his private world away from home. He was meant to be writing an essay on Henry VIII's secession from Rome in preparation for History A level. Instead, he listened, on headphones, to *Morrison Hotel*, while his eyes drank in the freckled young woman with a thin fox's face pinned to his wall. The first woman to catch his fancy.

Peter had boarded at Southgate House since the age of twelve. It had taken him until this, his fourth year, not to feel alienated by its customs and chronically homesick. His school – St Cross College, outside Winchester – had its own confusing language in which something desirable, such as the image on his wall, was known as "cud". Parents were "pitch-up", and when walking between his House and classroom it was compulsory to wear a "strat", a straw boater bought at phenomenal expense from Gieves & Hawkes in Winchester that served as a barometer, according to its state of disintegration and width of hatband, of a boy's seniority. Then there was the "tub-room", with its high-backed Edwardian tin baths of a sort Peter had never seen outside the school except at a plasterer's in Salisbury. At St Cross you measured your progress towards manhood also by your ability to lift – and tip out – the weight of your dirty bathwater. When he was twelve, Peter had needed both hands. Now, at almost sixteen, he could empty his tub with one finger.

On those first Sunday afternoons, to escape the torpor that descended on his House and sharpened the smells of instant coffee and rancid milk and locker-room mud and the thick grey whiff of masturbation, Peter would wander beside the Itchen with no sense of connection. Four years on, this fretfulness had diminished. He had grown to admire the flint and brick buildings which he could see from the riverbanks, the beauty of worn stone and ritual, the emerald playing-fields which extended into water meadows that Keats had written a poem about. On these days he felt at one with St Cross, involved.

Only later did Peter appreciate the depth and saturation of the school's Englishness. When he did at last consider it, he realised there were hardly any boys from outside the southern half of England, let alone from overseas. One exception was Tweed, a Greek boy in his House whose parents were so desperate to join the English Establishment that they had changed his name from Nikoliades. Apart from Tweed, a wealthy mathematician with weirdly blond hair and a loud voice, Peter had encountered few foreigners.

His own parents weren't well-off. His father's distress at the sight of a bill made Peter overly conscious of the fact that had he not won a scholarship they couldn't have afforded the fees. Certainly they weren't able to afford the same kind of school for

Rosalind, who, not being "academically minded" as they put it, attended the local comprehensive together with her friend Camilla Rickards.

"'At first flash of Eden, we rush down to the sea, / Standing there on freedom's shore.'"

One part Rimbaud and two parts nonsense, it still gave him a buzz. Eyes closed, dreaming of Camilla, he didn't hear the curtain snap open. Seconds passed before Peter was aware of Mr Tamlyn. Briar clamped in mouth, his housemaster surveyed the wooden stall.

"Sir!"

Peter struggled to turn off his tape recorder while Mr Tamlyn's waxy gaze roamed over the "Abolish the House of Lords" sticker, took in the electric filament in his mug and moved up the photographs stuck on the toyes wall: Jim Morrison, Steve McQueen in *The Great Escape* – and the women he craved to sleep with. Like Camilla, whose meek response on learning that Peter went to St Cross – "You must be clever" – inspired the wild grain of hope that she would be the one to ease his sexual desire.

Out of place at the centre of this gallery was Peter's No. 1 hero, and the most prosaic. St Cross owned a copy of the Malory manuscript, and this explained the presence on his wall, next to a tanned young woman in a rubber swimsuit advertising Lamb's Navy rum, of a reproduction of a Victorian painting of Sir Bedevere, last Knight of the Table Round and scourge of the Germanic hordes who had dared to threaten England.

Peter was drawn to the knight whom the dying Arthur entrusted with his sword. He recognised elements of himself in Bedevere, someone who was not a natural leader but who had pockets of this quality which allowed him to advance and retreat. He envied Bedevere his experience of the miraculous: the hand dolphined out of the water – brief confirmation of a calm and secure order – before it sank back into the depths, to vanish for ever. He loved the story and sometimes wished he might come across a dragon-threatened damsel so that he could display a courage which his surface hid.

9

Rosalind mocked his obsession. She preferred Bedevere as played by Terry Jones in *Monty Python and the Holy Grail*, a film which their parents had taken them to see at Christmas. She was twelve, but considered it juvenile of her brother to have "a comic-book fart as a pin-up".

And yet if Peter believed in anything, it was in the paternal spirit embodied by King Arthur and his chivalric knights. The fact that the school – itself founded in the fourteenth century – had custody of the manuscript which told their stories consoled him hugely.

Without divulging by one facial muscle his opinion of bold Sir Bedevere, Camilla Rickards or the desirability of the House of Lords, Mr Tamlyn removed the damp pipe stem from his mouth.

"Your mother's on the telephone, Hithersay."

Peter followed his housemaster down the red-tiled corridor and through a studded swing door. Into the only part of Southgate that resembled a normal house.

"Take your time," Mr Tamlyn said, his voice kind. It was always stressful to receive a call.

Peter went into the study. The telephone on the desk reeked of "Malvern mixture".

"Hello?" uncertain whether to sit in his housemaster's swivel chair.

"Darling, it's Mummy. Your grandfather's not very well." She spoke quickly. "Don't worry, he's absolutely fine at the moment. But instead of us taking you out on Sunday, it might be better if you came home."

He started to ask for more details, but she cut him off. "I've spoken to Mr Tamlyn and he agrees. It would give your grandfather enormous pleasure if he could see you on your birthday. We can have a lovely picnic."

Peter was walking back into Hall when a curtain twitched and a face stuck out: close-set eyes, jutting nose, the corners of a mouth raised in an expression of crafty hope.

"Anything wrong?"

"No, Leadley."

"Well, Hithers? What was it about?" Leadley persisted. His family owned a substantial estate 3 miles from Peter's parents. "Your pitch-up OK?"

"If you must know, I've been invited to a really smart party."

He continued towards his toyes, a short Achilles tendon causing the bounce in his step that people sometimes mistook for good cheer.

For the two days following his mother's call, Peter lost himself in the curriculum. Routine pulled him back from introspection. Worries about his grandfather faded.

On Saturday he played cricket on Lavender Meads, his favourite pitch. He took three wickets and scored 54 with the Slazenger bat his father had given him for Christmas. An hour after being caught at slip, he was sent out as a temporary substitute for an injured fielder and in the very next over sparked thunderous applause when a ball he threw in from the boundary hit the stumps. Delighted to have run out Leadley, he retreated to his position on the edge of the river, "saving four", as the visiting school captain had instructed him to do.

The Itchen here was known as Old Barge and this was a dream of long waving weeds, the occasional trout lying like a torpedo in the depths, particularly under the bridge beside the playing field. Standing in the weeds, an untidy figure cast out a line in an effortless harmony of rhythm and balance.

"Brodie!"

Brodie, eyes on the water, didn't hear.

Back on the pitch, a new batsman occupied the crease. Peter knew that he ought to walk in, but he lingered to watch Brodie cast again. Emboldened by his unexpectedly accurate throw, by six centuries of chalk streams and certainty and Englishness, he looked at where the plump trout flared against the current and tried to work out where he would pitch the sword.

"How's school?" His father stood by the ticket gate. Curly grey hair, deep-set eyes, yellow cravat at his throat.

"Good," said Peter, who felt a rush of affection as soon as he saw him. He had inherited certain of his mother's looks and bothered gestures, but felt closer to his father. "I got a fifty yesterday."

"Oh, that's splendid. But you aren't going to snare me into another Fathers' Match?" Last time, he was out first ball.

"I'll find an excuse," grinned Peter, and put an arm around his father's shoulder, breathing in that familiar, encompassing smell, a blend of printer's ink and hopefulness.

Rodney had to stand on tiptoe to return his son's embrace. "Happy birthday." And then, a little regretfully, "Taller than ever."

"Where's Mummy?"

"Making you a cake."

"Rosalind?"

"She's dying to beat you at Scrabble."

Not until the Rover turned out of the station did Peter ask about his grandfather.

"He's not awfully well. Last Sunday, your mother found him lying on his floor. He didn't know who he was. He's been quite confused since then. But yesterday he got up and talked about going to the pub. Doctor Badcock thinks it's time we started thinking about putting him into some sort of care."

"And?"

"Well, you can imagine. He wants to die in his own sheets and your mother has promised. Anyway, see for yourself. He's coming for tea."

They drove up Tisbury High Street and as a roof flashed past Peter couldn't help thinking of the old man lying in bed. His grandfather had been born at a time when if anyone living beside this road fell seriously ill, straw would be scattered thickly outside the house to dull the noise of horses' hoofs and wagon wheels. This morning, opposite the shoe-shop, two men sat on their motorbikes and adjusted the straps on their helmets.

The Rover turned right after the post office and headed east towards Sutton Mandeville. Narrow lanes and tall hedgerows opening at intervals into wide downs where his father took him bird-watching. The Nadder glinted at the bottom of a shallow valley and in fields on either side the chalky soil glowed up through grass and lines of beech. Walking with his father on the edge of that river, Peter had come across his first plover's nest. "See, the eggs are all pointing towards the middle. That means the chicks will soon be hatched."

He turned to look back at the river. On the rear seat was a camera case and tripod. "Dad, what's that camera for?"

"Ah, yes, well. Didn't Mummy tell you?" As was his habit when under pressure, his father scratched at the large, inflamed bump that the cravat concealed. He called the unsightly goitre his "Derbyshire neck" and attributed it to the limestone in the water around Tansley where he had grown up.

"No," said Peter. "She hasn't told me anything."

"I've become a photographer. Nothing fancy. Weddings, portraits, that kind of thing. But it makes a lot of sense – if I'm doing the invitations. Two birds with one stone and all that." He gave a sad, light laugh. "Guess who I'm photographing next week?"

"I'm no good at guessing, Daddy."

"Port Regis."

"The school?"

"The whole school. Tell Mr Tamlyn. Maybe he'd like a House photo of Southgate. Tell him I'll give him a discount."

Minutes later, the Rover turned through gates Peter had never seen closed, into the white gravel drive, and stopped outside the house.

His parents didn't have the means to live in London after Peter was born and moved to the "Wet country", as Rodney dubbed the rain-soaked countryside south of Salisbury. Here, in a stone tithe-barn, Rodney clung to the lifeline offered by commercial art, earning a living of sorts designing letterheads and bookplates and invitations to parties, weddings and funerals.

Despite a coolness in the air, the French windows were open. From inside came the sound of a piano.

Peter rolled up his window and they sat for a moment, neither seeming to want to leave the car. Large insects moved in and out of the foxgloves and everywhere it was green and lush. His eyes tracked a hobby across the lawn and the sight of the swing suspended on blue ropes from the chestnut tree brought back another birthday. He was eight when his father had put up the swing. Suddenly, now, he wanted nothing so much as to feel a hand on his back, propelling him into the sky.

The hobby flitted to the roof of the stable that was his father's studio, paused on the gutter, and flew off over the fields to the steep ridge beyond. The long hill, stretching from Salisbury to Shaftesbury, had a Roman ox-drive along the top. Peter didn't know its name, but on summer days, when the wind was right, they would go up there and reel out a kite.

"Doesn't look too promising." His father, hand on door, glanced at the dark clouds bunching over the summit, and got out.

And still the music poured from the living room. His mother had hung on to the piano after she stopped singing. She was a first-rate pianist from her family's point of view, but she was never going to sing again.

"I do hope Grandpa recovers," Peter said to his father over the car roof. "Poor Mummy sounds seriously tense."

"Go and talk to Ros," said his father in a tender voice and went to put away his camera.

In the kitchen, Rosalind stirred a pot. Peter crept towards the stove. On the antique oak table where his mother's pots had rested and burned circles, there were marks left with a blunt knife that mimicked his grandfather's face.

But she heard him and spun around, and in a Monty Python voice said: "And that, my liege, is how we know the earth to be banana-shaped." She licked the wooden spoon and made a mus-keteer's lunge at his chest. He parried the spoon, seized her about the waist.

"Has Mummy told you? I have a Holy Grail to whit to woo, too." She pulled away, smoothed back a stubborn blonde curl, and said, very seriously: "I'm going to become a gourmet chef."

"Of course you are."

Being at home, Rosalind was first in line in the epic food battle with their mother.

"Happy birthday, Bedevere," giving him an asparagus-scented kiss.

From next door came their mother's staccato rendering of the Goldberg Variations. Her voice might have gone, but her music was unstoppable.

"She's bought you a present you won't forget," Rosalind teased, with the same inflexion as their father.

"What is it?"

"Not exactly something you can take back to school with you."

"Have you heard from Camilla?"

"Yes," slyly. "She sent you a message."

"Well?"

"She wants to invite you to a party with Luke."

"Luke?"

She wiggled her index finger in a way calculated to irritate. "Her BOYFRIEND."

"Peter!"

Peter hadn't heard the music stop. His mother wore a long saffron dress, a hand-me-down from one of his nannies, and her man's watch, always slipping on her thin wrist.

"How long have you been here?" looking with a puzzled expression at the watch. Peter had given up asking why she insisted on wearing it. Never for a day had it kept the right time.

"Only a minute."

They kissed. He put his hand on her shoulder and she tensed, drawing back to look at him. "Happy birthday, darling," she said a little sadly, the same regretful tone as his father. She smelled of the French perfume that she always put on for special occasions, and he wondered for one ghastly moment if she had invited Leadley's parents to lunch.

"I just hope it doesn't rain, that's all. What do you think, Rodney?" She placed all her faith in picnics.

He had just come into the room. "I don't think it'll rain," and turned his inattention to the window. Next second, the heavens opened.

They had Rosalind's vichyssoise in the dining room, then an asparagus quiche. His mother had chosen his favourite food, spoiling him, and he drank too much red wine.

He felt his father watching. He was aware of a quiet unrest in him and, when he thought about it afterwards, a premonition of something final.

The rain went on until they were eating strawberries and then the sun came out.

"Darling," said his mother, rather nervous, as if testing a blade. "Can I show you something?"

"Mummy, the cake! Don't forget the cake's in the oven," Rosalind said.

"Oh, God."

His mother went into the kitchen and moments later he heard her going upstairs. When she came back she was clutching a photograph album he had never seen before. She sat beside him at the table and opened it: calf-bound, blue, full of images stuck down with white triangles, all of an odd-looking boy. Holding a cricket bat in a communal garden. Leaning from a pram. In christening robes.

"Look at those eyes – huge – always watering."

He yawned. Why was she doing this?

From somewhere up in the house came a yap.

She moved her chair closer. Turning the wide pages, she told Peter that the boy was him. A fearer of dragons who had to ask their permission to get up in the mornings. The sun wasn't yet hot enough for her face to be trickling with sweat. Some sort of expectation was making her nervous.

She went on speaking, but in a voice he hadn't heard before. What she was telling him was beyond the furl of his under-standing. Peter found the images far from reassuring. This was not a person he recognised, the boy with huge eyes. And why had his mother hidden this album all these years? He felt intruded on.

"Mummy!" he protested, and struggled against his mother's arm around his shoulders. It was probably the cake making her morbid. She hated to cook, and had spent the whole morning preparing it.

"Wait." In the same strange, needy tone she told him that he had been born one tea-time during a cold summer shortly before the Berlin Wall went up.

Pretending to look at the album, Peter studied the watch almost at her elbow. Even allowing for a spectacular margin of error, his train didn't leave for another three hours. "You ought to get a new watch," he said.

"I'm quite happy with this one, thank you."

"Who's that?" He craned forward, interested for the first time.

"That's me in the Wigmore Hall, the year I went to Leipzig." She had trained as a singer in Manchester and was poised for a career with the BBC when something happened, Peter wasn't sure what. The photograph showed a frizzy-haired young woman, firm shoulders in a long piqué dress, singing with an expression that she had lost.

In an otherwise crotchety cosmology, his mother had certain areas of tolerance. Unusual for one of her generation, she had a soft spot for Germans. The reminder of Leipzig gave her a second wind.

"Do you know what they called the Wigmore Hall before the First World War?" she went on tenaciously. "The Bechstein Hall. It was founded by Germans for German musicians." She made a finger-crossing gesture. "That's how close we used to be. Anglo-Saxons! I don't care what Grandpa says. For centuries, the Germans have been England's natural allies in Europe."

"And didn't the Connaught used to be the Coburg? And didn't America very nearly choose German as its official language?" said his father helpfully, a hand burrowing under his cravat.

She exchanged a grateful glance, but it was Peter she had to convince. "You simply cannot imagine the Germanophobia," she said, her enthusiasm shifting from the album to encompass in one bound a nation. "Even in the '20s, Schubert Lieder, when sung in London, were sung in French." She touched his arm. "And to think that we owe them our Royal Family, our religion, to say nothing of our music."

"Come on, Peter." The conversation was boring Rosalind. "Let's play Scrabble." And tugged at his hand, eyes plaintive under the stubborn curls.

Another yap.

"Why don't we go for a walk?" Flustered, his mother brushed a lock of hair from his temples in the way that used to infuriate him as a boy. "And then you can have your present."

"I'm not going for a walk," said Peter.

"No, he's coming with me," piped up Rosalind.

"Rosalind!" From the end of the table, their father's tone categorical in a way that Peter hadn't often heard.

"Dear, maybe you could begin the washing-up."

"Peter never does the washing-up," Rosalind complained, spitting a strawberry onto her palm. "Ever."

Rodney looked at Peter. "I think you should go. Do this for me." And to his wife: "Henrietta. I really think. Now."

Peter burst out: "What's going on? It's something about you, isn't it? You're having an affair. You're getting divorced. You're ill. Does Rosalind know?"

"I'm not ill. No affair. Just go for a walk. Go with your mother."

Often at night when he couldn't sleep Peter sifted his English childhood, beginning with the dragons under his bed and proceeding to the walk along the ox-drive and his mother's revelation. A life-altering secret smelling of blackberry bushes after rain and causing a beating in his blood as if a large bird was taking off in the burrow of his chest.

In his memory, they climbed towards a summit fuzzy with rain. Towards the wreckage of the aeroplane and a body never discovered, just an iridescent slick for the Nadder mayflies to hatch on. But the sun, as it happened, was shining.

When they got to the top, she applied lipstick and adjusted her scarf, buttoning every single button of her coat.

"It's turning into a lovely afternoon, but so chilly. Are you covered up? Look at that open neck of yours. Why didn't you bring your scarf? I hope you don't run around St Cross like that."

A flint road led like vertebrae over the cornfields. She had been stumbling along it for five minutes when she stopped, already breathless.

"As you so often point out, I do have a knack for filing away things I prefer not to think about." She fixed her watery green eyes on the sky. Her words flat and giving the impression she had rehearsed them. "You could describe it as a blockage of some kind. Or an inability to grapple with 'personal issues', as Rodney calls them. But I'm starting to talk about myself, and you need to know about Peter."

She's speaking of me as if I'm not here, he thought. Is she going nutty like her father? He yielded to an irritable blankness: "What do I need to know?"

"Not you, my love, not you," she murmured. She rotated the watch on her wrist in a purposeless way and said: "Rodney's not your father."

Peter was aware of a bird's shadow on the damp grass and something tearing inside.

"Your father's someone else."

"You mean I'm adopted?" he heard himself say.

"No, no, I'm your mother. In every other sense Rodney is your father. We met when you were six months old. Here, let's sit down. I can say it better sitting down."

They found a patch of grass where she began to explain that Peter's father was not the affable and diffident Englishman to whom she had been married for 15 years, but an East German political prisoner whom she had known for hardly a day.

CHAPTER TWO

No-one remembered what the young man had said, not even he himself any more. But he was overheard and sent to Bautzen, a prison known as Yellow Misery.

He lived in a 3-metre cell until 1960. A smallpox epidemic resulted in a move to Waldheim and then to a temporary prison south of Leipzig outside a town called Dorna.

On the day he was due to return to Bautzen he was marched with a line of inmates through the prison gate, along a narrow cobbled street until he came to a main road. People were going to work. The man ahead of him stumbled and through the sudden space he saw a pale young woman with frizzy hair hurry out of a garden.

When the line turned the corner into Breitscheidstraße he noticed the guard looking at a bread van in the opposite direction. He saw his chance. He kept going, across the street, and took the woman by the arm.

"*Hilf mir*," he said and continued walking. Strolling on. Not exchanging a word. Walking her into a park. Expecting a shout.

In silence, she let him guide her through the park and out the other side. Workmen were putting up electricity lines along a road to the lake. The buildings beyond were open and unfinished, stopped in mid-conversation. She could see an ancient forest in a dark green wedge on the far bank.

"You'd better go."

But still his fingers held her arm and his voice sounded cavernous, as though he hadn't spoken in a while.

"I'm sorry," she said, "but I don't understand. I'm from England."

She came from a valley 5 miles west of Clitheroe. A roll of wild country that funnelled into the Trough of Bowland. She had no particular interest in Germany, but singing was her overriding passion. She wanted to stand up and sing and it didn't matter whether her audience was a field full of Lancashire cows or a hall in Leipzig packed with Communists.

What little she knew about Germany she had learned from her music teacher in Manchester. Joachim was an East German refugee who worked tirelessly to create a partnership between the Leipzig he had fled and his adopted city, both much destroyed in the war. In Cheetham Hill he started the local branch of the Free German League of Culture and founded a choir that sang in an old Methodist Mission hall. He encouraged local singers to join who had no links with Germany.

In 1960, the Gewandhaus honoured Joachim's dedication with an invitation to send one of his pupils to compete in the Bach festival. His first choice falling ill, he called on Peter's mother.

She didn't win. In fact, her performance was a disappointment. But something in her performance appealed to the assistant director. He asked what she would most like to see in Leipzig. "The countryside," she replied without hesitation, after three days cooped up in a city that depressed her intensely. It wasn't a common request, but the assistant director enjoyed good contacts with the Party. He arranged for her to spend a week in a cottage near Leipzig and provided her with a hamper of food and fruit, part of a consignment sent by the new government in Cuba.

On the second day of her stay, her hostess announced out of the blue that she had to go for the rest of the week to Jena. Her English guest would be collected, as agreed, on Monday morning. Meanwhile, she was to treat the house as her own. A number of recommendations were made as to how she might pass the time and she was introduced to a girl of her age who, if she liked, would take her on an excursion to a medieval hunting forest.

It was the time of autumn when the cherry trees looked their barest. The half-timbered house was a five-minute walk from the Friendship Theatre. It was noon, she was bored and she was on her way to the cinema to see *The Mystery Airship* – "I was wondering how much of it I would understand" – when the young man walked across the road and took her by the arm.

———

They stood a while at the edge of the park, a girl who didn't speak much German and a strange man in another country.

"This is an interesting area, round here." He spoke in English. The precise accent of a schoolboy.

She raised her eyes. Glanced at his striped shirt, his grey fingers gripping her blouse, and was on the verge of speaking.

"Look at that flowering lavender," he went on. He might have been speaking from a phrase book. "Soon it will be time to put out the beehives."

"Bees?" she snorted. "In October?"

"Can you help me? I need somewhere to stay."

She assessed him. He had an open face. "Are you running away?"

"Yes."

"Where have you come from?"

"Do not let us talk about it here."

She started to walk away. A boy with stuck-out ears paused on his bicycle. The young man reached for her hand. Fumbled for it. Missed. And then she stopped and held it out and they walked to the house together.

"Are you hungry?"

"Yes."

"Stay here." She went into the larder and ransacked the hamper. When she came back the radio was playing. He sat at the end of the table facing her. Large forehead. Thin neck. Late twenties. Slanted olive eyes sooted with fatigue.

She cooked him a meal on the blue tile stove and watched as he ate. When he chewed he became repulsive. His face went the colour of fodder-beets and his cheeks became a series of lumps. Everything she served him he ate: rolled beef, red cabbage, fried Baltic herring, mashed potato and an orange.

He stretched for the second orange, but she moved it out of his reach. That one was hers. "What did you eat in prison?"

"Watersoup." He used to see the bottom of his bowl through it. "Who owns this house?"

She told him.

"What about her husband?"

She pointed to a cast-iron weathervane in the shape of a gun

22

dog on the floor. "That's what fell on him," and grimaced. "Just think of surviving two world wars and being killed by a weathervane."

On the radio a record came to an end. The room was cold. A log popped in the stove. He moved his eyes from the floor and she looked down. On one of his ankles a wristwatch.

She made up a bed on the sofa and he spent the morning asleep. She washed his clothes and hung them close to the stove to dry and in the afternoon she sat on a chair beside him while his chest rose and fell and she read a history of polar exploration that she had begun in Clitheroe. After an hour she heard a noise and her attention stumbled from the cold south seas, the icy drizzle, the gulls beating against her cheeks, and she felt him leaning over her shoulder, alert olive eyes, reading the same page.

He hadn't read a book in 18 months. The only words he had seen were in the newspapers used to wrap the sausages his parents sent at Christmas, stained in blood. Mostly what he read were advertisements. "Linaugran: this highly valued health aid will give your bowels an education in regularity." His shoulders cast a shadow on the page and she could tell that he was biting his lip.

In Bautzen, he taught himself to banish language. He picked his words with care, neutralising them, blanching them of colour, shape, meaning, until the day came when all he would say was Yes or No – often by a shake of the head – and nothing that he was overheard saying was worth repeating, not even his name.

She closed the book. Stood up. Held out her hand. "I'm Henrietta."

He wiped his eyes with the back of his hand. When he squeezed, his knuckles cracked. "Peter."

They talked until evening. They lay beside each other on the sofa, his thin legs across her knees. He had learned his English from a tutor in Thuringia. He wasn't allowed to study in the GDR because he was "landlord class" and so his father arranged for private lessons. The same tutor taught him French, Latin and Greek. He looked nearly thirty, but he was twenty-two.

She listened to him describe his childhood in schoolboy English: the Protestant parents, the large estate, the house occupied by the same family since the seventeenth century. Following Germany's defeat, his father, a paediatrician, was one of a handful of aristocrats who elected to stay on even after their lands were confiscated. The new Communist government permitted him to remain as a tenant in the house, but the estate had dwindled to a moat of grass on the outskirts of the village where he practised as the general physician.

She asked, fingers playing piano on his ankles: "Why didn't he leave?"

Peter described the incident with an expressionless face. He was five at the time. It was almost his first memory. A hot day in 1943. The smell of pear blossom. The family having lunch outside. They had arranged their chairs around a blanket under the pear tree when a man, probably a Jew, was brought from across the field and hanged in front of them. He wore a dark green suit and two SS soldiers pushed him from behind.

It happened quickly. The older soldier grabbed the chair Peter's mother was sitting in and stood on it to tie a belt over a stumpy branch. The man in the green suit fixed the family with a nervous apologetic expression. The younger soldier punched him so that his face crumpled and the two soldiers lifted him, still wheezing, onto the chair and slipped the belt over his head. Their prisoner was tall and the branch selected not quite high enough so that when the chair was kicked back at the second attempt his feet brushed the ground. He strained on tiptoe to keep balance and the two soldiers had to kick his ankles several times until he suffocated. Then the younger soldier undid the trousers and groped inside. He grinned at Peter's mother who was colicky from gulping her glass of Kalterer wine. Too late she hastened to cover her son's eyes.

He blushed when he told Henrietta what he saw.

"Look," the man snickered, unbuttoning the dead man's flies and fondling the stiff penis. "It's true." He spoke with a Bavarian accent.

Peter's father was a German from the worn soles of his Salamander shoes to the crown of his bony head. He had served

24

in an ambulance unit in the First World War. Had been a member of the National German Party, even though he thought the Kaiser was a clown. On an equally hot day in July 1940 he had stood at the radio to hear of France's capitulation and acknowledged a charge of pride. But in this moment three centuries dissolved. He turned his back on his country and eight months later shambled into the drive, arms raised, to greet an American jeep.

"My father couldn't tolerate the thought of his only child growing up in this culture."

His childhood wasn't all dour. There were days on which his life sparkled. His happiest moments were those when his father sat at the kitchen table and called for a spool of thread.

"He asked me if I wanted anything mended," she said 17 years later, on the damp grass among the bee orchids. "I thought it was odd, especially from a man. Then he revealed he wanted more than anything to be a surgeon. He was anxious to show me something his father had taught him."

They were sitting on the sofa when he lifted his legs from her knees. "Get that other orange. And a needle and thread. And a knife," he shouted after her.

He cut the orange in half. It was green and fibrous and good for juice, but not much else. "A grapefruit would be better," starting to suture together the two pieces.

She watched his deft fingers zigzag the needle in and out of the pith.

"In surgery," he told her, "the knot is everything."

Afterwards, he held it up, reciting: "Its feet were tied / With a silken thread of my own hand's weaving."

Because of his father he was forbidden to go to Humboldt University to study medicine. "You come from the class of yesterday," was the attitude of the authorities. The universities of Halle and Kiev also rejected him as a class enemy.

After the Soviet 20th Party Congress in 1956 he hoped that greater democracy would come to East Germany. He joined a small demonstration at Humboldt University calling for the Social Democratic Party to be legalised. The leaders were imprisoned for ten years, but he escaped arrest. "Probably because I wasn't registered as a student." Thereafter he avoided showing his face in Berlin.

Without some professional training he could gain no full-time employment. He worked as a messenger for an X-ray lab in Ludwigslust and for a forester whose brother was a border guard in Boizenburg and finally on a pig farm. Within two months his shoes fell to pieces and the farmer lent him another pair, but the hard leather didn't bend around the toes and he began to walk in the lilting gait of a pack animal. One day a lean snobbish girl visited. She wore a stylish grey dress and busied her fingers in a purse full of cosmetics. After lunch, she walked to where he was feeding the pigs and stood around smoking good cigarettes and the smell of the grey smoke tortured him.

He decided that his only chance of studying medicine was to escape. Once in the West he hoped to enrol at Hamburg University where his father had a good contact. He told his parents and his father wept and his mother just nodded. They had become lonely in these last years. His father had no more friends while his mother's circle had shrunk to four women who visited once a week for coffee. He implored his parents to accompany him, but his father declined. He was a doctor. He was old. And he was needed. "I can't change."

Wary of leaving through Berlin, on a cool cloudy day in April he took the train to a village on the border. The guide, a former patient of his father, waited on the platform. Peter held a large cast-iron key from the house as a signal. The man saw it and approached: "Follow me."

They walked several kilometres. Wooded hills on either side and in the gaps between the trees the copper-coloured rooftops of a small town. They reached a fork and the man said: "Go this way. It will take two hours."

He walked at his special lilting pace for two hours along a narrow path overgrown with ferns. After another hour he worried he had taken a wrong turning or was walking too slowly. The sun set and he panicked. In the night there were Russian soldiers on patrol with orders to shoot. He walked on in the dark and 40 minutes later arrived at the edge of a town. He saw a billboard advertising Juno cigarettes and knew that if the wording on the cigarette packet read "Juno – long and round", then he had left the GDR, and if the words read "Juno – thick

26

and round", then he had not. He walked impatiently towards the billboard.

"I was so full of hope and happiness. I thought, now it's Go. I was free, I told myself."

He read the words "Juno – thick and round" and exclaimed something out loud. He never knew what, but a woman was passing who heard him. Within a short time he was stopped and taken to a small room next to the police station and charged with slander against the state. It was the time of Ulbricht's paranoia. The mildest objection was a pretext for imprisonment.

"The accused delivered the remark in such a manner as to mock the noble aims of the revolution," declared the prosecuting judge. When his name was discovered on a list of members belonging to the banned Social Democratic Party his sentence was increased to five years.

That was 18 months ago. He had been a prisoner ever since.

"It seems anyone who lives here has to fool themselves in everything they do." She picked up the orange he had stitched back together with blue cotton. Pressed it to her nose. Smelled it.

He scratched his cheek with the back of his thumb. He hadn't shaved and his thumb made a rasping sound. "Come here."

She put down the orange and walked towards him, stopping a foot from his chair. He looked into her eyes and without taking his eyes from her face he lightly sawed his hand between her legs. He removed his hand. Looked at it. Began to lift it to his nose. "I'd better leave."

She moved behind him and touched his neck. He did nothing for a while, feeling the pressure of her fingers. Then his hand reached slowly up and clasped hers and their fingers intertwined.

He stayed that night and in the morning they came for him.

She was standing in the front room without her shoes on. "La-la-la," she hummed. "La-la-la."

He looked at her, then back at her book.

"La-la-la."

He tried not to look up this time. She saw him blush.

"La-la-la." She was singing now.

He looked up. Half smiled. Shook his head to himself.

"La-la-la."

"What are you thinking about?"

The door burst open. Out on the street the boy with stuck-out ears was laughing.

CHAPTER THREE

QUICKLY, NOT LOOKING AT Peter, his mother finished. "They bundled me out of the country. I stayed with friends in London – I couldn't face going back to Lancashire. When I found out I was pregnant with you, I wrote to say I wouldn't be coming home. You were born the following summer. I met Daddy at a firework party in Notting Hill. We were married by Christmas."

Three pigeons flapped from the verge. Peter watched them fly off, feeling a chill in the back of his arms and in his kidneys.

"You'll get to my age," she said, rotating the watch like an amulet, "and you'll learn there are things you cannot speak about right away. They need to be salted and packed in ice."

Still she avoided his eyes. "The awful thing is, I've never been able to discover what did happen to your father. If the West Germans paid for his freedom or if he's still in prison or if he died. Believe me, I tried. I wrote to the prison authorities in Dorna, Bautzen, Rottstockbei, Berlin, Leipzig, Dresden, Bützow, Ludwigslust, Waldheim, Torgau . . ." The recital had the desperation of her piano-playing. "But without a name – hopeless. And then the Wall went up. Not that that stopped me. Joachim, my music teacher, made persistent enquiries through his contacts in the Party. As did the Foreign Office. Nothing. Not a lead. I tell you, when your father was dragged out of that door, he vanished. But I doubt a single hour passes when I'm not aware of his face looking back at me."

She started to undo the watch-strap. "I remember every useless thing he said. But I never knew what he was called apart from Peter or where he came from – or if he told me I can't remember. All I have of your father is this."

In a daze he put on the watch. Only now was she able to look at him through eyes she might have been rubbing. "You can make a life in a night, but that doesn't mean –"

"Oh, Mum," and put his hand on her shoulder.

"It's all right," she murmured in a low pressed voice, as if he was a child again. "I don't have a photo, but you are very like him."

"How?"

"Your eyes, darling. And the corner of your mouth goes down just like his."

He felt her chin on his head. Looking down towards the radio mast in Sutton Mandeville. Her arms wrapping him. Endeavouring to keep something from falling apart. "I always thought that if he could, he would have got here. Absolutely, he would have got here. But how was he going to find me? He never knew I was pregnant."

"Daddy knows all this?"

"Yes. If your father . . . if Rodney had had his way I would have told you many years ago, but – I'm going to start crying here – knowing how much he loved you I couldn't bring myself to because he *is* your father and he will always be your father, and I think you'll have to accept that this day is sadder for him than it is for you."

This was too much for Peter. He burst into inconsolable tears. He didn't work out then, not immediately, how much grief it had cost her, how much anguish she and Rodney had been through on the road to deciding when to tell him; nor that he was weeping not least because nothing had changed with his mother.

How long they sat in their peculiar embrace, he didn't know. At some point, his mother stirred and when she spoke again he was reminded of how much he had inherited from her. Including a very English ability to tidy away. "You know, I think Rodney's right," slapping the grass off her damp yellow dress. "It's not going to rain any more."

He felt strangely suspended as he followed her back through blackberry bushes on which spiders had left their webs and towards the group sitting under the chestnut tree. In the far corner of the lawn, the sun shone on a straw hat.

"I suppose Grandpa knows all about it?"

"Your grandfather's been an infernal pest all these years. It's been very difficult –"

"Peter!" Rosalind's voice floated to him. She was on her feet, hurtling over the grass. "Grandpa's told me!" and threw her arms around his neck.

His mother glared at the old man sitting cross-legged on the beach mat. "Dad, what in God's name have you done?"

Weathered and grey like a cemetery angel, he looked up. There was a brief benign smile. "Peter."

"How are you, Grandpa?" and kissed him on his flaky cheeks.

"Well? Well? Well? Has she told you or hasn't she?" His questions smelled of beer.

"Do shut up," said Rodney, and to his wife, "I'm sorry, but there's a limit."

The air was livid with his mother's concern. "You told Ros? How could you?"

"Of course I told her," the old man grizzled in a voice slow but lucid. "Just like you should have told the boy years ago. He was perfectly capable of dealing with it at twelve. Don't know why you had to wait until his sixteenth birthday. Anyway, where's the cake? Rodney, get the cake."

"For once in your life, father-in-law, will you piss off. Just this once." His neck was inflamed and he was trembling.

"Easy for you to say piss off," staring at Rodney in a baleful way. "Didn't fight the buggers. In battle. Bastards. Not like us."

He removed his panama, with its regimental hatband the colour of purple carbon, and fanned his face with it. Everyone knew what Milo Potter thought of the Germans. As an army doctor, he had fought against them in Egypt. Seen them blow up monasteries in Italy. Lost friends to them in the North Atlantic. The war continued to upset him.

"Dad, you're a tiresome old baggage," said his daughter, distressed. "That's the past. We're moving forward now." She was trying not to cry and her face looked twisted with the effort. "Stay here," to Peter, "I'm going to fetch your present."

Moments later a golden retriever puppy ran across the lawn.

"She's called Honey," said the woman who had orphaned him. Her eyes, still red, fastened on him and waited for his reaction, smiling gamefully.

He looked at the puppy. Went inside.

———

31

Twenty minutes later, Rosalind came into his room and found him sitting at the window, a book open on his lap.

"Tea's ready."

"I'll come in a moment."

"Does that mean no Scrabble?"

"What? No." Then: "Just set it up. I'll be right down."

She wanted to say something. "It's brilliant!"

"What is?"

"Your being German," almost proudly, staring as though at a steaming dish of lamb shanks.

He threw down the Malory. "It's not brilliant. It's not riveting. It's not even interesting. It's absurd. Everyone hates the Germans and so do I. So do you."

Rosalind hadn't seen him crying since they were small children. She stared at him with eyes wide open and ran from the room. Only then did he look into the mirror, and look away.

Outside on the lawn the palaver of tea. Of his stepfather's distress. Of a cake sunk in the middle. His mother had forgotten to remove it from the oven and the disreputable heap lay on a green Tupperware plate, the 16 unlit candles like a bed of nails.

"I still say you shouldn't have gone to Leipzig," his grandfather said crossly – and Peter understood Milo Potter's lapsed attention towards his daughter, his grudging acceptance of her baskets of washed laundry, of the meals she brought to his spartan flat above the shoe-shop in Tisbury. The more she did for him the more he looked west, to Canada, where his two youngest daughters lived somewhere on the prairie. Viola and Ruth only came home for the big events, but he talked about them in a different voice. A voice in which his Lancashire accent all but disappeared. They wouldn't have gone singing in Germany.

She drew up her knees under her and started to saw. "Here, Dad," she sighed. "Sink your teeth into this."

"What about the candles? He needs to blow out the candles."

"Don't worry about the candles," mumbled Peter. He caught a whiff of Rodney's Patum Peperium. Already it smelled oddly different.

"Then give that slice to the boy. It's his birthday."

A quarter of a century later, Peter could still taste it. The mess of dense banana-flavoured sponge and the dreaded fizz of baking powder.

Towards the end of the afternoon, Peter went into Rodney's studio. The kind, jolly man he had, until now, called "Daddy" sat at a slanted desk making sketches for a wedding invitation.

Rodney didn't glance up. He leaned over his drawing board and rubbed out a pencil outline calmly, with no excitement, the way Peter had seen a fisherman on the Yorkshire coast scrape the bottom of his boat. A vicar's son from Tansley, Rodney had escaped the Church to study art at Camberwell, but he struggled after college to live off his paintings.

"Say what you like," he said, speaking to the cherub, "I always thought of you as my son. I always will."

"You'll always be Daddy," Peter said uselessly. "Always."

"Your mother never told me who he was, nor did I ask. I adored her. Still do." He examined the edge of his eraser with a fierce look. "But I can tell you the moment when I fell for you." At a bonfire party in Elgin Crescent, the same evening that he met Peter's mother. "She was holding this dark-haired baby and both of you were watching the flames. You stretched out your hand to me and kept on stretching it out. That's when I had the feeling you could be my child."

"I am your child, Dad," and cast his eyes at what, until this afternoon, had been more fixed than any compass point. The maple-framed watercolour of a Derbyshire vicarage. The lime-washed floors. The tray of nibs that always had seemed an extension of his father.

"Just remember you are exactly who you want to be at any moment of any day – you have the opportunity. Remember that."

"I will, Dad."

At last it was time to go to the station. His mother insisted on driving.

Rodney tapped on the window for him to wind it down. "If you want me to, of course I'll play in the Fathers' Match."

"Thanks, Dad."

"Darling, will you tell Rosalind we had to leave?" called his mother across his lap.

"Bye, Peter," bending down, his voice infallibly gentle. Behind, the blue ropes of a motionless swing.

"Bye, Dad."

"See you in 20 minutes," said his mother.

The car filled with her perfume as they drove towards Tisbury, filling the silence until she could bear it no more and started to lament the fact that her father had become senile. "It's a pity you didn't know him when he was practising."

Two days later, there was a note from Rosalind to say that she had waited for him. She had laid the whole game out, prepared the score sheet. "But when I came to look for you, you were gone."

CHAPTER FOUR

IT SHOCKED PETER TO return to St Cross. His mother's revelation had removed him to a ridge a continent away from his previous life. As he walked from the station past Southgate Cinema, he noticed a poster for *Where Eagles Dare* and caught his breath. Richard Burton in Nazi uniform.

In Mugging Hall, the roll-call had begun. Like the *Appell* at Colditz.

"Tweed?"

"*Sum.*"

"Sibley?"

"*Sum.*"

"Rood?"

"*Sum.*"

Numbly, he sat in his toyes and drew his curtain tight. He felt fragile, exposed, like a fruit cut in half and stitched back together. He wanted to jump in the Itchen. He didn't care if he never spoke to his mother again. What had she left him with as his identity? How was he to deal with Rodney?

"Liptrot?"

"*Sum.*"

"Leadley?"

"*Sum.*"

In a way, it would have surprised Peter less to discover that his mother was not his parent. Everything he was she had shattered and, all his solidity gone, he felt a complicated hostility towards her. This afternoon she had not simply lost him the father he thought he had, but she had given him one that was foreign. A German.

"I lithersay?"

Until he followed her onto "Revelation Hill", the only German Peter had given much consideration to was a charred corpse in a cockpit. Beyond the pages of *The Colditz Story* or the Commando "trash mags" that circulated the dormitory, he had no vivid picture of the place or of its people. Germany, so he understood from his grandfather, was somewhere to escape from as soon as you humanly could, a blank region on the map over which his concentration skidded to the warm blue Mediterranean. East Germany was a greater blur. He had barely considered it.

"Hithersay?" repeated the testy voice.

Peter sat up. "*Sum*," he called. I am. But now who was he?

That night, he attended evensong in Chantry, and singing the Nunc Dimittis he had a sense of what it must feel like to be excommunicated. The service drove home how English everyone was at school. He studied Tweed in the front row, tie tight-knotted, dressed in a new herringbone jacket of the same grey-green as the medieval glass. His voice bellowing for the Lord to let His Servant depart in peace. And all at once understood Tweed's eagerness to fit in.

Among his friends at St Cross, the one Peter admired most was Brodie, a shambolic extrovert two years older, who spent his every spare moment with a split-cane rod on the Itchen. Brodie had, for all his bumptiousness, a side that was gentle and considerate, and Peter trusted him.

On the following Wednesday he and Brodie were taking a short cut through the War Cloisters when Peter found himself reading for the first time the words from *The Pilgrim's Progress* carved into a stone plaque. "THEN SAID HE MY SWORD I GIVE TO HIM THAT SHALL SUCCEED ME IN MY PILGRIMAGE AND MY COURAGE AND SKILL TO HIM THAT CAN GET IT." On pale columns the colour of his breath in the cold were plaques dedicated to fallen old boys in two world wars. A separate plaque was inscribed with two German names. "Members of the college who also died for their country. Here in equal honour." The words provoked in Peter a feeling of such despondency that he couldn't think straight. He blurted out his story.

"Well, you know the first thing you've got to do?" said Brodie in his sympathetic but firm voice.

"What?"

"Learn German."

"You're joking?"

"Seriously, Hithers."

His French master queried him, surprised by the request, and Peter explained.

One afternoon Leadley clicked his heels in the tub-room. "Heil Hithersay!" He snapped out his arm and started to goose-step across the white tiles. "A Hun – and a Prussian at that!" Suddenly, he had the preoccupied smile of a baby filling its nappy. "Oh, I think I'm going to fart. Schnell, schnell!" He cocked his leg and something plopped out. Peter stared in mystified fascination at a mole-coloured turd.

Leadley's instinctive slur wounded him. Peter didn't know what it was to be German, hadn't a clue, but Leadley had firm ideas: the Germans were an aberrant race with no culture, strange food and an ugly syntax.

"Germans are our enemies," declared Leadley, casting aside the *Hurricane* comic, the two of them alone in the dormitory.

"Don't be a prick. The Russians are."

"You're wrong, Hithersay," and leaped up on the metal-framed bed and aimed his arm. "And unless you admit you're a filthy Bosch, I'll shoot you."

The drama of Leadley's turd took precedence over the novelty of Peter's German ancestry, but not for long. By the end of term everyone at St Cross knew. Thereafter his Germanness became a badge. It defined and labelled him and he couldn't escape it, not even in the Australian outback. In English they were reading *Voss* by the Australian Nobel-prize winner Patrick White. "'Uggh!' said Mary Hayley. 'Germans!'"

Initially, Peter tried to pretend away his new identity as something to be suppressed and fought against. At the same time, it tallied with a feeling he had inside him of being odd and incomplete. He had often wished to be someone else. Now he was.

"Prepare to die, Schweinehunde!" yelled Leadley one night, and from his vantage point on the coarse blue blanket he sprayed Peter's stomach with a double-fisted rat-a-tat-tat.

Soon a fresh set of faces stared from his toyes wall. He replaced Steve McQueen with a portrait of Bach. He took down Camilla Rickards, the "I'm backing Britain" sticker, the House of Lords poster. The only survivors were a tanned half-naked model with a sandy elbow, and Sir Bedevere.

CHAPTER FIVE

THE NOTION THAT HIS mother would tell a difficult story straight was, of course, absurd. First time round, in her choppy and defensive way, she had given a watered-down version. At the start of the summer holidays, to fill in the shadows, he walked up Tisbury High Street and pressed a bell saying "Milo Potter".

Peter enjoyed a close relationship with his grandfather. Unlike Rosalind, who had always been tricky with him. She hated his smell. Screamed if he tried to kiss her. Ran out of the room as soon as he embarked on one of his six war stories. "I can stand the blood and guts – but it BORES me."

But with Peter something happened: Milo Potter lost his accusatory tone. All the warmth he couldn't offer his daughter or granddaughter, with both of whom he shared a temperament, he concentrated on his grandson.

Consequently, Peter was the one his mother would take on visits. Peter never minded listening to him. It pleased his mother and it pleased the person he listened to. Old people, he learned early on, liked to talk.

He once heard his mother enthuse to the vicar: "Peter's wonderful with my father. He never complains when he repeats himself." Nor when his grandfather farted as he sat down in his wing-back chair. Or mislaid his teeth. Or soiled himself after a morning at the Black Dog pub.

Peter's shyness helped. It was a kind of shyness, after all, not to want to hear your own voice. But it was more than shyness that made him draw out a crusty old man about his experiences with the Royal Army Medical Corps in the Adriatic or, after 1945, as a general practitioner in Clitheroe. It took Peter off from himself. Relieved the unease that sometimes he felt when he looked in the mirror.

His mother remarked that his eyes gave him warmth. Hers were pale green, the colour of her favourite herbal tea. Peter's on the other hand were dark and slightly slanted, the irises as black as his ropy hair, and photographed well. His skin was dark, too, a shade of oloroso that marked him out from others at school as well as from his parents and sister – and which his grandfather attributed with a knowing chuckle to a French sailor in the family. Peter took it for one of his stories.

Like anyone who has fought in a war, his grandfather was full of stories. Alone with his grandson, he told Peter about the places he had seen. The train station in Trieste. The enemy flag he had captured from a castle. His adventures.

Milo Potter. Terse, tricky, a good hater of Germans and a lover of pale ale and the dark chocolate he kept in his freezer. Who shared his daughter's stubbornness, but not her hope that Peter would grow up to be a medical man like him. "I don't know why your mother wants you to become a doctor." Or rather he did know, but wasn't telling. "Just because doctors cure people, it doesn't mean they're good. Don't be fooled into thinking *that*."

At his grandfather's flat the curtains were drawn in the living room, which stank of stale breath and urine. Peter walked into the small kitchen and called in a loud cheerful voice, "I'll get you a beer."

His grandfather had returned to his chair. He sat in his favourite woollen sleeping cap, knitted for him 62 years before by the Baptist women of the Shepherd's Bush Tabernacle. Peter handed him the glass and kissed him on the cheek, slipping something onto his lap and whispering, "I've brought you some Bournville."

"Dear boy, how are you?" sitting up, with a squeezed expression, revived by the sight of the beer. A week before, driving to Port Regis, Rodney had been alarmed to see him shuffling in his slippers towards the Black Dog. "You know, you're very sweet to come and spend this time with me, particularly since I've been such a pain to your parents." He unwrapped the Bournville. Pinched blue eyes, skin the colour of horseradish and a dent in his forehead that might have been left there by an exploding cork. "Tell me about school. What are you doing?"

"I'm studying German."

"You're not studying German! You're English, for God's sake."

"I have a German father, Grandpa."

"I want you to forget about your so-called father," he said angrily. "Here you are, English mother, English stepfather, English upbringing, and you're at an English public school. It's just one of those things that happened."

"Put yourself in my position. What would you do?"

"What do you mean, 'do'?"

"If you discovered you were German."

Silence.

"Go on, Grandpa," and Peter egged him on, breathing through his mouth to avoid the smell, all his concentration on the figure who rocked in his chair and struggled to snap off a square of chocolate.

Milo Potter folded his lips and chewed. And stared at the sisal floor. Forced by his grandson to see the English officer lying between his slippers. Watching himself leap from the jeep to attend the groaning man. "Maybe when you're older," licking at the dark rim on his lips. And telling him anyway. "If I discovered I was German, I'd top myself. It's simply the bottom end of the scale. Let me tell you a couple of things about Germans . . ." and gulping his beer, he started to talk with a fluency that he couldn't bring to the recent past.

Later, Peter stood on the pavement where he and Rosalind used to play hopscotch. My God, he thought, am I capable of slitting throats?

CHAPTER SIX

INSTEAD OF THE DOORS he listened to punk. *Anarchy in the UK. Bodies. Pretty Vacant.*

"Filthy Boche!" chanted Leadley, chewing his ear. His voice lazy and larval and powered by inherited money. "Achtung, Spitfeuer, aargh!"

In March went the last of his moorings. Amid acrimony and controversy, St Cross had sold the Malory manuscript to the British Library and his favourite history master resigned. Encouraged by this master and also by Rodney, Peter had set his heart on reading history at Oxford.

His German father became the sword he drew against those who approached. To stop the dissonance in his life he thought of him obsessively. He wanted to know about the man. To see and to touch someone who was his blood, who looked like him, who might understand him.

"*We* know our fathers' names, where we come from," whispered Leadley, heatedly stroking Tweed under the blanket. "What we want to know is: What's *your* father's name?"

"Oh, go screw yourself," but reading in Leadley's eyes the horror of his deformity.

While Mr Brodribb, the replacement history master, stuttered through the dissolution of the monasteries, Peter sat in the back row and imagined his father in a toyes-sized cell. Scrubbing himself beneath a cold shower. Sweeping the hair from his eyes (was that his habit too?). Sometimes he reflected on the sentence uttered by his father that had caused him to be imprisoned. Could there be a comparable formula to bring him back, to undo the spell?

Then, in the summer term of his lower-sixth year, a Hamburg academic contacted St Cross to enquire if there might be a boy willing to improve the English of his daughter, a member of the German Winter Olympics team.

Peter volunteered and was accepted, but waited until half-term before approaching his parents to pay for the journey. His instinct being to treat them separately, he asked his mother first, seeking her out in the living room where she sat at the walnut piano. She had played it all weekend: Mendelssohn, Beethoven, and more and more Bach. Eschewing Chopin, Scarlatti and Borodin in favour of German, German, German music.

Now it's out in the open, he thought, there was bound to be a reaction.

He explained that he wanted to spend the summer holiday in Hamburg. "Mum, this is what I really want to do. I just want to look like somebody. I want to see someone walking up the street who looks like me."

"Darling, I understand," and her expression said: Look at my life, the way it has been made. There's no way I can go to Germany to find your father. But I am moved to see you studying German, and it's perfectly natural that you should one day go looking for him in the city where he wanted to be. "It's just that I don't know if Daddy can afford it. Things are rather tight right now."

In his studio, Rodney was replying to a letter.

"Dad?" and Peter watched his stepfather turn stiffly to greet him. Feeling the first spike of worry. The first glimpse of Rodney's frailty.

Rodney listened carefully. "Of course, you must go. No question about it." He would just have to take a lot more photographs, that was all. He gave a ghost of a smile. "And maybe this will bring in some money," holding up a strange letter he had received. An old school-friend – someone he hadn't seen for many years – had written from North Africa with a business proposition.

Only Rosalind didn't understand. "Teaching a *speedskater*? Why would a speedskater need to speak English?"

For three weeks Peter stayed in a turn-of-the-century white stucco house in Ottensen with wide windowsills and full of pot plants. He had never left England before. At every step he came to know the meaning of the word "foreign". He scrutinised the giraffes and marmots in Hamburg zoo, the watch shops in Gänsemarkt, the windows stacked with cakes and furs and smoked meats. He thought, Is this where my roots are?

His postcard home read: "I am enjoying myself very much." But he was miserable. He regretted more than he could say the waste of Rodney's money. The pot plants. His pupil.

Kirsten was a tall blonde German speedskater who had an uncomfortably open relationship with her parents. At his introductory meal with the Viebach family she told Peter about her first kiss and Peter was asked to supply the words in English. Her father nodded and smiled while her mother grew red-faced and said: "Sssh, Kirsten." Even though she didn't speak much English, Frau Viebach was aware that her daughter had gone too far.

Away from her adoring parents, Kirsten was less full of herself. One night Peter collected her from the rink in her father's Mercedes-Benz. He watched the athletes, most of them older than he was, loitering animal-like before they disbanded, having completed their two-hour *fartlek*, a Swedish word, Kirsten explained, that meant "speedplay – a combination of running and intensive callisthenics". Lazily, the girls zipped up their vivid warm-ups and dispersed on bicycles, eyeing Peter. And he couldn't help seeing himself through their eyes in his borrowed car, his English flannels, his stiff, non-athletic body. A different species.

"Goodbye, Kirsten," shouted one of them, refastening her pony-tail. "Be a good girl!" she added in English, and her words injected into the car the atmosphere of a nervous first date.

Kirsten's parents were out for the night. She suggested they stop for a hot cocoa. They ended up drinking beer and then on the way home she directed him along Hafenstraße and into a parking lot beside the Elbe where workers for the shipyards caught the ferry. After a nervous conversation, she let him undress her. She smiled distantly as he peeled off her layers, beginning with the warm-up pants and ending with a sheath of navy Lycra. He saw the stars through the rigging and became senseless with panic. His anxiety and desire so great he could hardly breathe. At St Cross he used to pray that he wouldn't die before this moment. When the moment came, he yelled in pain and grabbed at his calf.

Kirsten knew better what the problem was and that he was an innocent in the country of sex. "You're having a cramp. Magnesium deficiency. You should eat more bananas."

At the end of their next lesson – to which she arrived very late – he asked in a significant way if they could go back to the parking lot on Hafenstraße.

"Oh, no. I can't. I'm meeting a friend. Bye."

"Tomorrow, then?"

Kirsten shook her head. "No, Peter," in a faraway voice, as if it wasn't his tongue that had circled her breasts a few hours earlier, or her calves that had stiffened against his neck in the seconds before his unfortunate and disturbing seizure. "You are here to teach me English."

So instead of undressing Kirsten again, in the afternoons when she was training at the oval, he walked through Hamburg. Up the Reeperbahn, down through the port, along the Alster. Only the stucco buildings in Eppendorf had resonance for him, their tall windows and tidy front gardens reminding Peter of photographs in his mother's blue calf album of a house in Notting Hill. And Sierichstraße: a street down which the traffic flowed one way until noon – and for the rest of the day in the opposite direction.

In this mood – fluctuating, rejected, homesick – he had his first glimpse of East Germany.

One Saturday morning, early, he boarded a train to a small harbour on the border. A fisherman stood by the water's edge, surrounded by cormorants, while on the marina a father and son unstudded the tarpaulin from the deck of a speedboat with an English name, *Follow Me*. The father, a pipe-smoker with a sunburnt face, in narrow black jeans, ducked inside and emerged with a duvet decorated with an enormous strawberry. He was laying it out on the rails to dry when Peter called down to him.

They had a conversation after which the man tapped his pipe against his palm and gave Peter directions.

He didn't attempt to cross into East Germany. On this morning it was enough to stand near a wire fence and gaze at the forbidden country. He had no inkling of the whereabouts of his father's

45

village, but he composed in his mind a white-turreted house and a tall-ceilinged corridor hung with the portraits of previous Junkers. (A week later, his German master dismissed his reverie as absurd. After 1950, and Ulbricht's collectivisation of the farms, whatever life the family led would have vanished. "Besides, Hithersay, there were no Junkers in Saxony.") He stayed an hour, then walked back towards the toothpick masts. His head boiling with the same questions. Was his father still in prison? If not, what had happened to him? His mother had believed in him utterly, but what if his grandfather was right and he was not to be believed? *Let me tell you a couple of things about Germans . . .* Could he have been "re-educated", become a functionary in the Communist regime? Or had he achieved his ambition and made it to the West? Become like the man who pointed him towards the border, a successful surgeon with a speedboat he had restored, turning lobster-red in the sun and smoking Dutch tobacco?

Peter searched for the sleek black hull of *Follow Me* and thought of the pipe-smoker's reaction. "Watch out! The only liberty East Germans have is to sail without any clothes on!" The speedboat had slipped her berth.

He stared into the empty space and found himself looking for the first time through Eastern eyes. The smooth water of the harbour amplified each sound. The distant yell of the fisherman. The cormorant that plunged, croaking, towards whatever scraps were being tossed away. The bark of a dog on the opposite bank. Someone shook their raincoat, but it was a swan taking off.

At the end of August he said goodbye to the Viebachs. He had sat out his remaining meals trying to avoid seeing in their expressions a sign that he had become dinner-party fodder.

"You are welcome here any time," said Kirsten's mother solemnly.

Next day found him in Holland. In a bakery, overhearing his accent, a man mistook Peter for a German and spat in his face. A small part of him was relieved: his German must be getting better.

He had not found the language easy to learn. His schoolroom

German wasn't the German he heard spoken in Hamburg. But his desire to communicate with Kirsten had had a liberating effect and in the following term he rose to near top of his class. Nervous of Peter's sudden fluency, his teacher – a frilly, Gothic script of a man who had until now insisted on calling him Höthersay, thinking he was doing Peter a favour – stopped singling him out.

His German master wasn't alone in observing a change. He had returned to St Cross more dissatisfied and confused. More defiant. One evening after "namers" Mr Tamlyn took Peter aside. "Is everything all right at home?"

"Everything's absolutely fine."

"It's good to talk about these things."

"Really, sir. Everything is fine. Couldn't be better."

He retreated deeper into his toyes, spending his last pocket money on a subscription to the German soccer magazine *Kicker*. He covered the walls with team photographs of Hamburger SV and at their centre pinned a poorly taken snap of Kirsten after a race, her suit of silver Lycra barely distinguishable against the snowbank.

Until he was sixteen, he had assumed he would marry an English girl. Had built a picture of her in his mind, a sort of composite model of a young woman on a beach who happened to be one of Rosalind's friends. But now? With each passing week, he sensed himself divided from his fellows, even Brodie. His German summer had taught him that there was a European culture and he was not part of it. In England, he felt small and restless. At the same time, his experience in Hamburg had led him to fear, even to dislike, a part of himself he couldn't know.

To vanquish this dragon he determined to ride out to meet it. As Bedevere might have done.

He settled into his studies, making himself into a German and also qualifying himself to escape. If his decision to go to Hamburg marked the first jutting of the jaw, the second was demonstrated by his choice of university. He would become what his mother wanted, but that was incidental as it was also what his father had wanted – and now what he wanted, too.

Eighteen months since his 16th birthday and he was ready to make the break. To go against every grain. To find himself by taking not Leadley's obvious path through an Oxford quad and dark panelled rooms to an institution in the City, but the route which led in the opposite direction, among a people whose language he falteringly understood, past the rough streets of the Reeperbahn where he had heard shots in the night, past the grim housing projects, to the teaching hospital.

His mother couldn't contain her joy. "Medicine? But how wonderful, darling. Where will you go? Oxford or Cambridge?"

"Hamburg."

"Hamburg?" she said and looked down at her book – she was reading *Maurice Guest*. "That's a good university, I'm sure. If you can do it, you can do it." What else could she say?

The Universitätsklinik Eppendorf, or UKE, was not Peter's first choice. He had looked into studying medicine in Leipzig, but the process was full of red tape and after contacting the new East German embassy in Belgrave Square he couldn't see a way, at least not until he graduated. And so he decided on the city his father was aiming for when he was captured and where he himself had first tasted Germany.

Thanks to Mr Tamlyn's efforts, an interview was arranged at UKE in the Easter of Peter's last year at St Cross. Over a leisurely meeting he was tested for his knowledge of the German language, biology, chemistry and Latin. The admissions tutor was an Anglophile with a reedy voice who kept insisting that medical education was so much better in England. Nonetheless, he was prepared to accept Peter's four A levels in lieu of an Abitur, the offer conditional on his results and on his agreement to spend the gap year improving his German. "University study is free. Accommodation you will have to pay for."

"Tremendous news," said Rodney. "Of course, I'll foot the bills."

Feebly his mother said, "You do realise, darling, Hamburg is a very different place from Leipzig."

Rendered more and more incoherent by Alzheimer's, his grandfather told Peter his opinion. His mind was perishing and he fuddled through his days and nights without recourse to the Black Dog. "Walter Hammond was the finest cover fielder that England has ever had. You can take Bradman out and pee all over him."

48

CHAPTER SEVEN

ON THE EVE OF Peter's departure for Germany, Rodney's old school chum Joseph Silkleigh came to dinner. Rodney had been a little startled to hear from him. He had only the dimmest recollection of Silkleigh at school. Nor could Peter's mother understand why they had to entertain a virtual stranger on Peter's last night.

"I've never heard you mention his name before."

"I tried to put him off," said Rodney, defensively, "but he's in England only till tomorrow. He has some wheeze to sell printing-machines in North Africa."

His mother had wanted the occasion to be a special one, but Silkleigh's arrival threw her into such turmoil that she burned the sprouts. Not that Silkleigh minded. "I say, Mrs Hithersay, these are splendid."

Despite the fact that Silkleigh didn't draw breath all through dinner, Peter was at a loss to understand what he did. He seemed to spend a lot of time frog-diving off a Spanish enclave named Abyla ("a place of contradictions where anything can happen"). He was also writing a book about his life. He had stalled on this for several years while the title eluded him, but now he had it.

"I'm well into volume one, old soul. Well in. The whole thing's going swimmingly."

"What's it called?" asked Rodney politely. He pushed away his plate.

"*Pain Has No Memory*."

Peter wondered if Silkleigh was joking, but he didn't seem to be. When Rosalind giggled, Rodney asked swiftly: "And you have a publisher?"

"Not yet, not yet. As a matter of fact I was rather hoping, following this sumptuous repast," winking at Peter's mother, "you might point me in the right direction. You see, Abyla's a little out of the literary loop. So I racked my brains and I remembered you,

49

Rodders. I have to tell you, young Peter, your father was a bit of a poet at school, weren't you, old soul?"

"Were you, Rodney?" asked Peter's mother with a dubious look.

"I did write one or two poems," he admitted, "but I seem to recall they were pretty dire "

"Oh, but one had to be kind to one's young self," said Silkleigh.

Rodney dredged up the name of an editor in Donhead St Mary who many years before had commissioned a book jacket. His offer to write on Silkleigh's behalf brought a beam to the face of his guest.

"That's the marvellous thing about school chums, Mrs Hithersay. Never. Let. You. Down. Your husband and I, we share the same moral compass. Always have. Which is why I've come here tonight with a little old *proposizione*," and raised his glass. "Anchors away!"

His mother plainly thought Silkleigh insufferable, but Rodney was tempted to believe every word. Peter see-sawed between the two.

Only when discussion turned to Peter's departure for Germany did Silkleigh's face take on a sober aspect. "Rodders did mention your German connection," and then to the undiminished horror of Peter's mother, Silkleigh went on confidingly: "I know these East Germans. Infuriating lot. Eavesdrop on each other from dawn to dusk. It wouldn't get off the ground here. Have you any idea where they put their cameras? They put them in the ruddy gnomes! Can you imagine anything stupider?"

"You've been to East Germany?" asked Peter, very interested.

"Oh, yes, I've been. Ruthless place. Quite the vilest regime in the Communist bloc." He helped himself to more singed sprouts, his appetite for them contributing to a demented look. "Everyone turns a blind eye to what's going on, but you don't have to be a Fellow of All Souls to see that it's a police state. Most of their lady shot-putters have penises. And the dogs they get over there! We had one retired to North Africa once. Astonishing creature. He could smell out almost anything. Kept him in the laundry, so when anyone lost their knickers I could say: 'Oh, Mrs Herbert, is this yours?' And you know, it always was."

"Darling, could that be your pudding?" asked Rodney.

Once Peter's mother had disappeared into the kitchen, Silkleigh plucked at Peter's arm and said in a hushed voice: "Going back to your father, young Peter, a note of Silkleigh caution. It's perfectly natural that you should think him a romantic hero and all that, but have you ever thought he could be working for the other side? For all you know he could be the chief of the dark forces."

Peter was still at that stage where it was hard for him to believe bad things of his father's country, or of his father. "You're just making that up."

"I'm afraid I've rather overcooked the next course," said his mother, coming back into the room and fixing Silkleigh with an expression of marked antipathy.

"Course I am. Course I am."

After dinner Rodney took Silkleigh off to his studio. They reappeared an hour later.

"Don't worry, old soul, I'll make my own way out," said Silkleigh, wrenching open what he thought was the front door and sailing with tremendous brio into the saucepan cupboard – "Why have all the stars gone out?" – after which Rosalind had to be escorted to bed.

"He's barking," giggling so violently she was weepy.

"I suppose he is," said Rodney, who kept it secret for several weeks that he had tentatively agreed to go into partnership with him.

"He's not coming back?" asked Peter's mother.

Next morning Peter flew to Hamburg.

He was leaving with the express idea of trying to see whether, partly in response to his grandfather, he couldn't sacrifice himself to the memory of what Germany had meant to England. He refused to become like Milo Potter or Tristram Leadley. He didn't think like that. He had never thought like that. He was going to be like one those two old boys at St Cross who had given their lives to their country. In his visored vision he was anxious to accept both England and Germany. At St Cross he had become aware of the great Protestant Alliance and of the chivalric links that had existed between both nations. He wanted to exemplify the bridge, the alliance, the best of each tradition. He had spent his first 18 years as the son of an English mother. It was time to swing into the saddle and discover his father's culture.

He spent his gap year in Hamburg. Speaking German more fluently. Becoming less and less English.

His grandfather died in the summer and was buried in his wool cap. Peter couldn't afford to be there for the funeral, Rodney having only been able to pay for a single ticket. He wrote, he telephoned, but for years he never went back to Wiltshire. Instead, he read Musil, Canetti, Fontane and looked up words like "Eisenwaren" in the dictionary. And learning about Emperor Barbarossa who sat alone for a thousand years on Kyffhäuser, and Christian Rosenkreuz, founder of the Rosicrucian Fraternity, who lived to 106 and whose body was discovered 120 years after his death, untouched, it was said, by decay. Reading a twelfth-century poem by Wolfram von Eschenbach, he came across another hibernation – "half-death, half-asleep" – ascribed to the King of the Grail. He learned a lot, but not about himself.

One Sunday afternoon, feeling a sudden loneliness and a fear that Germany might not assimilate him, he telephoned Kirsten. Her father answered. "Ah, the boy with cramp! Sorry, Kirsten's in Insel. Training. Yes, I'll pass on your regards."

The campus was situated in a dead corner of Eppendorf. A week before the beginning of term, he read on the department pinboard that a group of students in Eimsbüttel were seeking a room-mate. Two days later, he moved from the Youth Hostel to Feldstraße: a brown-painted building converted from a piano-maker's factory, with low ceilings and no front garden and a second building in the small back yard where his room was, and which he decorated with a few objects from England. A cricket bat, the Blu-Tacked print of Bedevere, the antique oak table from Tansley.

Thenceforth Peter was alone. His childhood was a well from which he feared to draw, and he had very little to cling to. Only the thought of his German father sustained him. He had a mechanical hope that sooner or later he would meet his father. Whether as head of a teaching hospital or part of the vilest, most repressive regime in the Communist bloc.

PART II

Germany, 1983

CHAPTER EIGHT

ONE NIGHT IN HIS third year at university, Peter was working late when there was a knock and through the door came a thin-framed young man with long, prematurely grey hair.

Teo, who boarded in the room above, was a Konservatorium student who had given up the violin in favour of composition. (He once demonstrated to Peter, by twisting a knife in a cabbage, how to imitate the sound of someone's head being battered with a club.) They didn't know each other well, although once a week they played in the same soccer team.

"Look here, Peter. I know it's not the right moment, but an amazing opportunity has turned up."

Peter cleared the pile of books from the sofa and Teo sat down. "I see Anita hasn't been in here," grinning.

"Banned – till after my Physikum."

"How would you like to go to Leipzig?"

"Leipzig?" He went over to close the curtain. It was hard to work in this cold. The snow wanting to fall. But his chest was beating.

Quickly, Teo explained. He was part of a group of student actors who had been invited to perform in East Germany during the week of the Leipzig Trade Fair. This afternoon their stage-manager had pulled out. "You can open and close a curtain? It's that simple. Otherwise, it's a matter of taking a few props on stage and fiddling with some lights. Teach you in an hour."

"I don't know anything about theatre," Peter said guardedly. One of his least favourite experiences at St Cross had been to hold a lantern as a nightwatchman in *Othello*.

"It's not strictly speaking theatre," said Teo, skating over his reply. "It's mime."

"Mime!" Even worse. Conjuring images of audience participation and Marcel Marceau.

"You wouldn't be expected to act, you oaf." Teo's face had the expression it wore when he was about to pass the ball. "Why don't you come with us? We just need an extra body, Peter. It's hard to visit East Germany unless you have connections. You could dig out your father, extend the search."

"Let me think about this," said Peter.

Teo tilted back his head and regarded the poster of Johnny Rotten, his eyes skirting over the upside-down Wehrmacht insignia safety-pinned to Rotten's waistcoat and coming to rest on the coloured print of Bedevere above Peter's desk. "Listen, if you can't pull it off I know someone I can ask."

"Wait, when is this?"

"Leave Thursday, back Monday morning. We can sort out the visa tomorrow."

Peter glanced at the five textbooks – one chemical, one zoological and three botanical – that he planned to have read by Monday. "Oh, shit. I couldn't – even if I wanted to. This is the weekend of Anita's wedding."

Anita, Peter's German girlfriend of two years, was playing bridesmaid for her colleague, a teacher at the same kindergarten. All month she had attended fittings and returned with Polaroids of herself holding up yards of salmon-coloured satin. Peter pretended to be interested, but the whole business bored him to death.

"Oh, right," nodded Teo, "the wedding where Anita will catch the bouquet, hell or high water?"

"She's already caught the bouquet," sighed Peter. "It's in a vase beside her bed."

Teo chuckled and stood up. "You don't stand a fucking chance. Listen, I refuse to get in the way of your audition. I'm going to find a free man instead."

"No, don't!" The invitation to bolt, to leave behind Anita and the wedding feast in Blankenese was exhilaratingly tempting. "I'll go. I can do it."

They looked at each other. "Are you sure?" said Teo. "I don't want to be held responsible for what Thomas and Michael might do . . ." Anita's hulking elder brothers, crew-cut engineers, played in the same soccer team.

"They're OK. I'll just have to figure out what I'm going to tell Anita."

56

Teo opened the door and stopped. "Remind me – who's that?"

"Sir Bedevere."

"King Arthur stuff?"

"The guy with the sword."

"Oh, that guy."

Long after Teo had left the room, Peter continued to look at the face of the medieval knight. As he brushed his teeth, he murmured to the mirror in English:

"What saw you there? said the king.
Sir, he said, I saw nothing but waves and winds."

Minutes later he switched off the light. If he could do this, obviously he didn't love Anita. If he loved her, he wouldn't consider abandoning her on a day when, as she had made very clear, she needed him. But German girls were stoics. She wouldn't make a fuss. She would understand about his father. It was a while before he slept.

Following his anatomy class next morning, he went with Teo to a studio on the corner of Bellevue, on the top floor of an old house overlooking the Alster. A large light room of blues and yellows fitted with a stainless-steel counter and with an upstairs gallery reached by a spiral staircase.

The room had been cleared to make a stage. Two actors, sitting on stools, rehearsed before a cubicle assembled from sheets of corrugated plastic and hung with a green curtain. Peter leaned against the wall to watch, but what they were doing seemed incomprehensible to him.

A dog's basket lay at his feet, and tidied onto a davenport-style desk with barley-sugar legs were the traces of a woman's presence. A bright orange bra. A straw boater like one he used to wear at St Cross. A silver-framed hand-mirror. He was wondering, Which one is she sleeping with? when Teo nodded at the shower-shaped cubicle. "That's where you'll be."

The scene over, Teo introduced him to Sepp who was the director and principal actor. It was an extreme face that Peter looked into. Harelip. Beak of a nose. And above the sparse beard cheeks clear and pink as if hand-coloured.

Sepp leaned from his stool, extending his hand far out over the floor. "Thanks for helping out at short notice."

Peter began to apologise, "Anything to do with theatre, I'm an idiot," but Sepp held up his hand. There was one rule only Peter had to remember. It applied to tragedy and to comedy as it did to mime and to life. "True drama is when there are no more chances. This is it and how it will be."

The statement flummoxed Peter and his apprehensions of the night before came tumbling back. Was the man serious?

Before Peter could find his footing, Sepp turned to his companion, a severe-faced man in tortoiseshell glasses, and raised an invisible glass. "Marcus. To our fourth member."

Marcus responded with a series of hard, brief noises hammered out on a wooden gong.

Sepp next lifted his imaginary glass to Teo, who had taken up a position behind the counter and was crouched over an apparatus with rubber and metal tubes coming out of it and resembling an oxygen mask.

The director pretended to drink Peter's health. Instantly, the studio filled with a loud swallowing as of liquid gurgling into a vast stomach. Peter recognised the sound. All term, he had heard it coming through Teo's floor.

The pipes and valves were Teo's invention, the product of a temperament that delighted to catch people by surprise. Blowing into his machine, Teo conjured sounds to announce themselves in the most unlikely places, like a coin behind the ear, so that no-one who had their eyes fixed on Sepp was likely to associate his raised glass with a stooped figure 20 feet away.

Teo abandoned the counter and piloted Peter into the cubicle, drawing the curtain. The curtain gave them invisibility, and that made it palatable. So long as he could see out and not be seen he was fine.

At 11.00, Teo had to go to the Konservatorium. Aided by an occasional prompt from Sepp, Peter operated various lights and pulleys until he reached the end of the script.

"See?" said Sepp. "Easy."

So relieved was Peter that instinctively he started to clap, but Sepp once again held up his hand. "Oh, didn't Teo tell you? We don't applaud."

"Why not?"

"That way the audience is forced to keep their energy with them. To carry it out of the theatre."

Something else Teo had forgotten to tell Peter, who was reminded of how little, really, he understood the Germans. At the end of the third performance the Permanent Representative of Federal Germany was hosting a reception at Leipzig's Hotel Astoria. Peter, as part of the group, was expected to attend. "Bring a jacket and tie, would you?"

Anita was not stoical. Not at all. "I thought you loathed the theatre. How can you do this to me?"

"Not all theatre."

"I've never heard you say anything positive about it."

"There are a lot of parts of me you don't know," said his voice rather high.

"Like what? Like this desire you have to see the GDR?"

"Anita, it's where my father comes from."

She didn't understand. "And what about your exams?" through her teeth. "I thought you had no spare time."

"Look," he said, "I'm sorry. I'm going."

"I can't believe you're doing this," her eyes brimming. "Don't you care about me?"

"Of course I do. But it's not your wedding."

She drove him to the station anyway. He hadn't asked her to do so, but he was grateful for the ride. She walked along the platform in unaccustomed heels and a brown jersey dress. Afterwards, she was going on to the church for the rehearsal.

"I know you don't like presents, but everyone says how cold it is in Leipzig."

She unzipped her bag and withdrew a dark blue scarf and a matching Masaryk hat. She tugged the hat over his head. Not looking him in the eye, but glad that it fitted. "You're really lucky to get this from me, you know."

Her fussiness suffocated him. What were they doing together, the two of them, on this platform? He foresaw a lifetime of such departures. Anita, this talkative, motherly, totally inappropriate woman packing him off on trains. Bestowing on him gifts he didn't want, woven from Scottish lambswool.

And then she was offering up a little brown paper bag and he felt his heart sink further. Another claim. "The train food's terrible," she said, "and who knows when you'll next get to eat – and you'll like the sandwich, I promise."

He took the bag. Kissed her. Squeezed her arm. "Monday, then. And thanks."

She tried to laugh. "I've got a wonderful night of torture planned – the Polaroids of the wedding."

He was happy to get into the sealed train.

CHAPTER NINE

ONLY AT THE LAST minute – thanks to the intervention of Sepp's father, a paint manufacturer who did business in East Germany – had Peter been issued with a five-day visa. Marcus was confident that he could explain the consul's jittery behaviour when he opened his newspaper on the train. He made Peter read the article, about three East German border guards who had shot at a woman crawling across no-man's-land. When the men reached the body they found a partially dissected corpse stolen from a morgue in West Berlin. The young woman they were firing at had been twitched across the concrete by a long black rope, attached to her wrist, that disappeared over the wall.

While the train waited at the border, it fell to Marcus to take Peter aside and deliver a pep-talk. "We've been to Leipzig before. This makes it all the more important we behave. So don't consort. Don't get pissed and don't potter off the beaten track. Otherwise, do what you like. But if you're not there on the dot of 1 a.m. Sunday morning we'll have to leave you behind. And don't think your Foreign Office will bail you out!"

"I'll behave," Peter promised.

It had been decided that Peter should take charge of the dressing-up box, a wickerwork trunk resembling a large laundry basket that contained Marcus's wooden gongs as well as Sepp's costumes. Three hours later they reached Berlin and Peter hauled the trunk from the rack. He stood behind Teo in an S-shaped queue in the underground at Friedrichstraße, waiting a second time to show his papers. A policeman stamped his passport and made him change his money into a useless and derisory currency that was tossed into a large box when he recrossed the border three days later.

"Admission fee," joked Teo, as if they were entering a zoo.

They caught the next train. Then more border police came on and the train stopped and nothing moved for half an hour. A tension passed along the carriage bound up with their progress through it. One policeman removed Teo's newspaper. Another asked Peter where he was born. They couldn't have shown less interest in his trunk.

Shortly before 3 p.m. they reached Bahnhof-Lichtenberg from where their train left for Leipzig. Not until it pulled out of the station did Peter begin to feel the excitement of having crossed the border.

Ever since coming to live in Hamburg he had expected at some point to visit East Germany. In the languorous fashion of his generation he had been gathering himself to go. Not putting it off exactly. More like setting aside a book he wanted to read in order to savour the expectation of it. Until now his studies had kept him busy. Four days in Leipzig, breathing its air, might bring him a step closer to answering a question that had lain under the fingernail since his sixteenth birthday.

He spent the next two and a half hours staring out at the countryside. Piled along the track were earth-removal machines for brown-coal extract. They passed an opencast mine and Teo pulled a trollish face and murmured something to Sepp. It was obvious they found the landscape ugly and polluted. Peter didn't join in their remarks. His throat wrapped in Anita's blue scarf, he pressed his face closer to the window.

The fields and woods wore the pallor of Sepp's leather jacket. The leaves had blown from the trees so that Peter could see birdnests in the branches. Here agricultural practices hadn't destroyed the wildlife or the sense of a Germany from the nineteenth century. The train ran through villages where the architecture implied that the inner-German border was older than the Warsaw Pact and matched a more ancient division between civilisations. There were storks in the chimneys and cobbles on the roads. It was the land of someone's childhood. Not his, but his father's maybe. He looked out, drowsily searching the fields and villages, until his breath misted the glass.

"And," said a short, coarse-featured man, speaking in a Dutch accent, "if they don't publish this novel, I am prepared to sacrifice all my other books," and tapped in a significant way on his brown attaché case. "Every. Single. One." With that, he tossed his head, bade Sepp farewell and receded in busy steps towards the buffet car.

Peter sat up. Looked around. Marcus was reading. Teo asleep. "Who was that?" rubbing one gummy eye, then the other.

Sepp gave a laconic smile. "Our joint guest of honour."

Although Peter hadn't heard of the author, Sepp assured him that he was a figure immensely popular with East German teachers on account of his potted scientific histories. "He's probably the most famous writer in the West as far as they're concerned. But it's not what he wants."

"What does he want?"

"He has a desire to be regarded as a novelist."

The author had taken Sepp into his confidence, infuriated that his publishers in Leipzig showed polite indifference to his fiction. In order to urge them to change their minds he had clandestinely brought along in his attaché case several copies, in English translation, of his first novel.

"He's got it into his head that because it's been translated this will impress them."

"What's it about?"

Sepp's voice was a touch mocking. At the same time he was respectful, as a fellow artist, of the author's ambitions. "I understand it contains a lot of swans."

CHAPTER TEN

They arrived in Leipzig at night. A cavernous station of dark ribs and dirty glass. Sepp was first onto the platform. He lifted his long nose and sniffed. "The air tastes wrong."

Marcus passed Sepp their bags while Peter helped Teo with the large metal case containing his tubes and valves. He went back to fetch the wickerwork trunk and shoved it on top of Teo's case. "Jesus, you could put a body in that."

At the end of the platform a clock told 7.25. Under its red-rimmed dial a young couple kissed, the girl's right hand clutching a letter to post. Just then a young man – smallish, lots of black curly hair and brown coat flapping – ran puffing through the malarial light. He introduced himself. A student, sent by the director of the Rudolph Theatre, who sent his apologies.

"Do you mind a short walk?" catching his breath. This being Fair time, all hotels and university hostels were full. "You're booked into a room at a private address."

He organised a porter to wheel Teo's case and the dressing-up box to the left-luggage office. "They will be collected in the morning."

The four of them followed him into a time warp. Cobbled streets with no advertisements. An overhead grid of sagging tram-lines. One or two cars belching smoke. Peter's first impression of Leipzig: potholes, fumes, rigid faces.

Their lodgings were in Erich-Ferl-Straße in a house painted up to the first floor but no higher. Their guide pressed the bell and spoke his name into a combed grid, adding: "The group from Hamburg." A large tidy woman opened the door and before they could enter a man in a vest shambled past.

The landlady led them to an attic room with porcelain taps and two bunk-beds. She wore a carp-green cambric frock and every time she smiled her lips parted on long white teeth. When they came downstairs she asked them to sign a visitors' book.

"You from Hamburg, too?" turning to Peter.

"No," he said instinctively. "England."

"Ah, England." And showed him a postcard she had once received from Winnipeg.

They ate downstairs. There was a tiled oven in the corner of the room and as they began their meal the man in the vest carried up from the cellar a bucket of black octangular bricks and one by one fed them into it. On a corner shelf was a stone struck by lightning, and beside it an aubergine cut to reveal a message from God that the landlady had preserved in a brown solution.

"What's the message?" asked Marcus, tremendously interested.

"I don't know. A Fair guest gave it to me. It's in Arabic."

She settled by a lamp in the corner and watched everyone eat. They shared the room with a gay couple from Lake Como who had brought their own supply of spaghetti, tomatoes and olive oil, and who sat at a separate table and conversed in low whispers. At the end of each course, she creaked to her feet and collected their plates. She served them a salad of tinned asparagus and a dish she called Toast Hawaii consisting of ham, pineapple and cheese, and finally a metal cup of vanilla ice cream smothered with egg-liqueur. When Peter thanked her for a delicious meal she misheard and told him that her teeth were made in Hungary.

Dinner over, the couple from Lake Como said goodnight and soon afterwards Sepp and the others filed upstairs. She called out as they climbed the staircase: "Do you want to be woken if you're not awake?"

"Why not?" said Sepp, his extreme face visible between the banisters.

"What about you?" to Peter.

"I don't feel like going to bed." The pineapple had furred his tongue and he had a hankering to see this city that he had waited so long to visit. "I'd like a walk."

She produced a key to the front door and told him to leave it in the visitors' book.

Peter wrapped Anita's scarf around his neck and headed down Erich Ferl Straße and into a small park. There was yellow foam in the river, and along one bank, surrounded by the filth of unraked leaves, the trees stood out against the streetlamps. He picked up a twig and peeled it and threw it away and picked up another. A dog loped past. Its front paw was hurt and every time it put down that foot its right eye closed. Peter called out and extended a hand, but the dog ignored him.

His throat soon hardened to the acrid taste in the air. He crossed the park and walked down an alley one side of which was boarded up. Smell of fermented hay and animal shit and from over a tall fence the growl of something wild. Down the alley and out the other side to a ring road. Squeal of trams and one or two grey Wartburgs.

A car went by, the driver low in his seat. The headlights caught Peter's walking shape and lofted it against a wall and the light raked slowly over a door and over windows so rimed with dirt it was impossible to conceive what might be visible through them. His shadow grew thinner and longer until it stretched over the buildings ranged before him monotonous and grey, carious facades of dark sandstone against a darker sky, and he imagined that he saw pass in the windows the images of all that had brought him to this place.

He walked more quickly, sucked down the street. Feeling as never before the vacuum of his absent father. Drone of a factory. Out of a clanked-open gate a stream of bowed men and women, many clutching plastic bags. The late shift, he guessed. They tilted towards him. Faces harried and dead-looking. Clothes garish and ill-cut and made of some synthetic material that had never reached the West.

Peter searched their features as they walked by. He thought, Could one of these be my father? A cousin?

He passed a shop. Painted on the wall above was "Eisenwaren", the old word for ironmonger. A woman stared down from a single window. Her arms leaning on a cushion. A soot stain under the window as though a flame had been stamped out. She called out something, but he couldn't make out what. He turned and walked back.

The moment arrived when he realised he was lost. He waited at a junction and everything stretched away undifferentiated, a grey prairie of streets and pavements and sky. He heard a muttering and out from a concealed passage between two houses emerged an old man in a long quilted coat the colour of hare's fur, tattered and haggard and grisly. White curly hair to his shoulders. Talking to his dog. Thin and angled as a Danish buoy.

Peter approached to ask directions. At the man's groan, the dog darted from between his legs and Peter recognised the lame animal he had seen in the park. The man drew his coat around his shoulders and shuffled away, still speaking to himself in the way of someone whose memory was confused and dimensionless.

At the next corner, Peter spied the entrance to the zoo and hurried home.

He spent the morning at the Rudolph Theatre. The wickerwork trunk had arrived from the station and Peter unpacked it: costumes with ruff-necks, enormous false noses, paraphernalia for the cubicle. By 11 a.m. he had rigged this up. Assisted by a taciturn electrician, he cabled the lighting keyboard to a lamp on the edge of the stage. Then he asked Teo to run through each prop and explain it again.

At noon, the director appeared and took them to a one-room bar called the Tagesbar Bodega, run by an elderly couple, where he ordered a bottle of Romanian wine and toasted their success. They sat at a shared table and ate frankfurters while he discussed with Sepp the advanced state of East German theatre.

No matter how much Peter tried to concentrate, his inattention mastered him. He kept looking outside. The street drew him like a magnet. He knew that his quest was fruitless and silly. That he was never going to find his father among these strange, resilient faces. Even that he was enacting his own pantomime, the parody of the lost son. But he felt powerless to fight the impulse. At the end of the meal he excused himself.

The director glanced up. His trousers were too short for him and he was visibly agitated.

"Make sure you're back by seven," called Marcus, looking more than ever like a Lutheran priest. "And remember – be careful."

"Listen, off you go, off you go," said Teo.

In a light rain of lignite ash he drifted with the crowd towards the centre. Soot had settled everywhere. There were slashes of it in the sky like something crumbled into water and even the pigeons clustered along the aerials seemed coated with it.

He came to the end of a street, and feeling the raw cold he paused to wrap his scarf tighter about his neck. An icy wind blew from behind and he started forward into the square, following the tail of his scarf towards a grimy basilica of carbon-smeared stone.

Not until he was halfway across the square did Peter notice the uniformed men. Six of them, standing close to the church wall and enthusiastically kicking a man on the ground, in the kidneys and in the back. One of them, pale-faced and stumpy with reddish hair, held a frenetic dog on a lead and spurred on the others as if he didn't remotely care that anyone might be looking. And no-one was looking, even though plenty of people were in the square. Everyone diverted their eyes except Peter, who watched the man, hardly able to walk, being dragged to a van with a fish painted on it. Peter could see six cages inside. An unvarnished floor, bulb screwed into the ceiling, no window. The man was locked in one of the cages. Then the men in uniform climbed in and the van drove off.

Sprayed across the outside of the church was the uncompleted graffito: "SORRY, KARL MAR".

Peter continued towards the entrance, shocked by the awful violence he had glimpsed. Still fresh in his mind was a vision of East German guards on the Wall, willing to shoot a young woman who had crashed through no-man's-land and prepared to leave her dying in agony on the cold concrete.

He walked up four steps and pushed his way through a blanket the colour of moss. The interior smelled stale, suggesting the church was not often aired. Lamps cast a yellowish glow on the grey octagonal pillars and on the red flagstones, and above him a choir was singing. He could make out the choristers and the organist's head and in the side gallery a row of young men and women sitting engrossed.

Knees moved to let him through. He sat in a pew, smelled the polish. The church wasn't full. A few rapt pensioners turned their heads to the gallery stiffly, as if their necks were made out of paper they were afraid would tear. An old lady in the front row opposite leaned forward to scratch an ankle and next to her an old man in a white anorak slept like a marmot.

The choir's singing soothed him. His pulse became regular and gradually he stopped thinking of the incident outside. He was aware of the secret warmth of these faces. When he looked at them he recognised himself. Unlike his experience of the night before, he felt returned to his gene pool. Everyone his cousin.

Peter went on listening to the choir, and now and then it seemed that a face turned in his direction and stared for a moment and glanced away. Long and thin with watery olive eyes and cheeks like old sails tight-stretched on either side of a straight nose so that the smallest puff might capsize it. Each time the face turned away, he felt breathless.

The choir finished singing and a pastor climbed the pulpit and read from Habakkuk. "'Their horses are swifter than leopards, more menacing than wolves.'" He was descending the black marble steps when the man in the anorak shifted his body to reveal, in the pew behind, a young woman who did not look like anyone else.

Her head moved into the light and fell back. Peter saw her fleetingly, enough for the air to boil around her. He couldn't properly see her face, and leaned forward, eager for another look. Willing her to move forward again.

In the gallery the orchestra began playing again, and now the music reached into him to a level that it hadn't before. He thought of his mother singing in the Bach competition in the year before he was born. Wishing she were seated next to him to whisper the name of the cantata. And it excited him to go on watching the young woman listening to the music, not seeing him.

She opened her eyes and caught him looking at her and their eyes locked. Her mouth fell open a little. She half-turned, gazing back at him through different depths in a slow surfacing. With a shake of her head, she rose to her feet.

His eyes swayed after her. She stepped into the lamplight, a green coat over her arm and at her throat some kind of necklace. Back in Hamburg he would remember Musil's notion that every person has an animal coordinate with which they're connected in some secret inner way. He thought of her then and afterwards as a giraffe. Something fine and pure-bred and delicate with a natural haughtiness that didn't know its own power. When she walked down the aisle, drawing all the light in the church to her face, she led with her nose as if reaching up to chew a leaf.

He watched her cross the nave. He strained to see her breasts and it maddened him that he couldn't.

The congregation filed outside at an excruciating pace. Girls waited on the steps or chatted to parents. He searched for a green coat among the sausage-coloured anoraks, and found it. She stood at the edge of the small crowd listening to a man, about thirty. Round and small with a wide brown beard and a sealskin jacket with pockets for everything.

She put her hands to her eyes. Moved away. And the man with a hangdog expression thrust both hands deep into his jacket.

Peter descended the steps and followed her into the Market Square. There was an intent to her stride, in the way she straightened her back. Slightly gangly, she enlisted the whole of her body when she moved.

She disappeared into a three-storey building on the corner. A banner outside the building read "Leipzig – open to the world" and there was a poster with details of the Book Fair. He paid 7 Marks and hurried to the first floor, a low-ceilinged hall with stalls to the right and left, and began to circle the room.

He tracked her down at the stand of a publisher from Munich. Her back to Peter. Flicking the pages of a book. Scrupulously, she replaced it on the display shelf and when she didn't look up he saw that her gaze was fixed to an attaché case open on a table. She lifted an arm overhead and scratched her back.

"Too bad they can't airbrush my prose!"

At right angles to the same table sat a stout man with a large nose and bulging eyes and hair patted in careful lines over the top of his head. His features only carelessly resembled the handsome physiognomy pictured on posters around the stall. He reminded Peter of the cadaver he had dissected in anatomy.

"Ah!" catching sight of Peter, and Peter recognised the author who had engaged Sepp in conversation on the train and whose name featured alongside Pantomimosa on the invitation to the Astoria.

Peter approached the table heaped with books. "Herr C –," he began, and the author, mistaking his intention, opened the title page. "Who shall I . . .?" His fountain pen hovered.

"I'm with the mime group."

The author hitched up his smile. Closed the cover of *Amazing Scientific Discoveries: Volume 9 – Madame Curie*, and with cold politeness enquired the time of Peter's performance.

"Seven-thirty."

"I regret I have to give a reading tonight," and beckoned Peter closer.

Behind him, a sudden movement. Peter looked up in time to see her snatch a book from the attaché case and tuck it into her black jeans.

She brushed past him.

"See you at the reception," he told the author.

He caught up with her in the square and fell into stride.

"I saw you take it."

She heard him, but didn't turn. "Just keep walking," and grabbed his arm. Now he was happy.

They crossed the square, walking fast. Down a street and through a concealed passage into an alley. Not until they emerged into another square did she give a quick look round and slow her pace.

"You took his book," he repeated.

She chewed the inside of her cheek, breathing hard. One of her teeth was chipped. Strung around her long neck and separated by a hollow bone she wore a pair of marble eyes, acetylene blue, that once might have peered out of a dead animal.

"You have to steal," she said unexpectedly. "Unless you want to read crap. It's the only way to get a good book."

He held her gaze. Her own eyes deep-set and green – the greyish green of chapel glass – and with a slight shadow under them. She's my age, he thought, and reached out his hand. He half expected her to draw back, but she faced him square on, not moving, watching him as he dug down his fingers between her jeans and waist. Feeling for the contour of the stolen book.

She helped him. A novel with a flock of swans on the cover. "You're from North Germany, aren't you?" glancing at his shoes.

"No, England."

"Really? I wouldn't have taken you for English. Why are you here?"

"I'm with a mime group," and described his involvement with Pantomimosa. He sensed her interest fading.

"Why are you following me? I should report you."

"Except you've stolen property on you."

She grabbed back the book and started to put on her coat, at the same time quickening her step.

"I saw you in church."

"I know."

"It's a rare person who doesn't notice someone looking at them," and he hated the inanity he heard in his voice.

She said nothing.

"I love Bach," he went on, making an effort to catch up. Then, as he drew level, he made a stupid remark that wasn't what he meant to say at all: "I forgot Bach spent so much time in Leipzig."

She stopped in her tracks. She didn't believe what she had heard. "This is Bach's city! He spent 27 years of his life here. He *belongs* to Leipzig."

"Yes, I know –"

"What do they teach you over there? Melchior Lotter printed the first music here. Grieg studied here. Clara and Robert Schumann started their life here." She pointed, the East German greyness about her face disappearing as she tried to educate him. "Look. See the Konsum? Richard Wagner was born there."

Even as she spoke his heart sank as it did on occasions with Anita. Something humourless and dutiful had stormed in. An agenda he couldn't locate. Maybe she was a tour guide. Maybe she was a bore.

He apologised: "I don't know much about Leipzig."

"It's a lovely city and it always was." Poised to go on, she changed her mind. "That's OK. Have you a cigarette?"

He offered her a West Light and she inclined her head to his lighter. Long eyelashes and a blackberry undercurrent to her hair and skin that he wanted to touch. He forgot his worries.

"Have you a moment?" squeezing his arm. "Come, I'll show you something."

She walked in long strides ahead of him along a pavement crumpled and broken, as though something under the earth had shifted. She turned into a street and waited for him, smoking his cigarette. "This is the Brühl."

"Named after Count Brühl?" He was pleased with himself.

"No, that's in Dresden. This is the Leipzig Brühl. Our Brühl is Slav for swamp. See those windows? Fifty years ago, this street was the centre of the world fur trade."

She took a deep breath. Closed her eyes. Savoured the air that tasted of coal dust. "This is where I'd come if I wanted a mink coat. Or ocelot. Or moleskin. But I'd make sure to buy my coat in sunlight. Not on a day like today."

He craned his neck at the blackened facades. The sky and topmost storeys dissolving into one another. "Hard to imagine."

"No, it's not," opening her eyes and giving him a heated look. "If all students in the West are like you, they must be a stupid lot. Look, there – below the ledge."

He didn't notice them at first: camouflaged with dirt, the mouldings of three faces. A Chinaman. An African. A Red Indian.

"There's a story of a Canadian trapper. He sent a letter to 'Brühl' – just the one word. It started in February in Montreal. From there it was sent to Bremen and it was here in Leipzig by March."

Without waiting for his reaction, she steered him by the hand to a three-storey building covered in green tiles of which many were cracked or missing.

"All you have to do is raise your eyes and you'll see traces from all over the world, but no-one looks up. They look down and walk along – just like you," and her face was no longer grave but had a mocking smile.

"You should be on commission for the city."

"What do you mean by that?"

"Well, you seem to know a lot."

"Ah, this is what I want to show you," ignoring him.

It was the entrance to a once grand house, its facade now layered with the same coloured filth – the grey of Rodney's anchovy paste – as the buildings on either side. Over the doorway was the ceramic of a man naked save for a fur cape. In different panels the figure had on a fur hat, fur boots, a fur stole, a pair of gloves and a muff.

"You like fur, don't you?"

"Oh, yes. Muffs are my favourite."

She couldn't have been aware of what connotations the word might have for him. Nor did she fear his judgment. A moment before she had seemed regretful, solemn, officious. Now she had the confidence of the old city. He felt drawn to her in a way he never had with Anita.

"My grandfather was a furrier," and gestured at the neglected, begrimed door. "He began here." She stubbed out her cigarette on the wall. "Look!" Under the dull grey paint, a red scratch-mark. She licked a finger and rubbed at the mark, her spittle deepening the colour. "It's the original porphyry. They try to copy this by painting the windows red, but it doesn't work." Even this trivial gesture moved him.

"By the way, my name is Peter Hithersay."

"I am boring you." She began to button her coat.

"And you?"

"I have to go," she decided.

"You mean, I don't get to know your name?"

She smiled her mocking smile. "Why should you want to know, you who go away in a day or two?"

"All right, all right," he said. "Then, what does your mother call you?"

Her mouth hung open and her face had a look of uncertainty. "My mother's dead. My grandmother calls me Snjólaug."

"Snowleg?"

She corrected his pronunciation. "Snjólaug. It's Icelandic."

He uttered the name slowly as if it was an object in his mouth. It still sounded like Snowleg.

"Why does she call you that?" searching for a way to delay her. "You're right. It's not interesting."

He couldn't believe he was asking, but he knew he must. In the same voice that he adopted when urging his grandfather to speak, he said: "No, please. I'd like to hear. Why are you called Snowleg?"

The name, she told Peter, had belonged to a Canadian woman, a friend of her grandfather. She had never met her grandfather – he had died in the Second World War – but her grandmother, with whom she lived during the week, had spoken of him incessantly. As a child she believed she only had to rub the glass eyes of the stuffed muskrat that had been his prized possession and he would materialise before her, soft-voiced and bent and with a cigar roaming under his nut-brown hat.

"I knew him only as a photograph." From the cherry-wood table beside her grandmother's bed, he looked back at her through the veil of tobacco smoke in the way she imagined he examined his pelts, with the gaze of someone not afraid to blow the fur apart and scrutinise the leather and mutter aloud: "Dyed skin!"

As a young man he had worked at 71 Brühl for a Jew from Brody, but he served his most valuable apprenticeship during two years he spent in Canada. In 1925, with the low price of squirrel in Leipzig, a limited quantity of rats were shipped from Rainy Lake on a gas-schooner. "There was a berth vacant on the return journey and he took it."

"The hunter needs to see the wolf," he told her grandmother on the evening he asked her to marry him. He had flung at least a hundred categories of pelt out of his employer's windows to dry on the railings, including cross fox, silver fox, hare flank, opossum, fitch, vicuna, wallaby and Tibetan lamb. "But I haven't seen one in the flesh."

He spent a summer with three trappers at Fort Chipewyan, working at night because of the deer flies. At dawnbreak on the fifth day he wrote to his fiancée: "I've skinned my first animal – a buffalo." He smeared the fleshed skin with fish oil and drummed it in sawdust and that winter used it as a sleigh robe, heading east through the unanimous snowscapes of Manitoba.

Over the following year, he learned that riding in a sleigh wears out a fur more quickly than walking. He wore out the furs of a moose, a lynx and a priceless black fox.

His favourite fur – it became his favourite word – was the muskrat. In Gimli, he lived for a season with an Icelandic Indian and his wife Snjólaug who taught him how to slit the skin at both hind legs from heel to vent, skin out the toes and leave them with the claws on, and pull the skin from the body. From that day on he could never pass a muskrat coat without stroking it, still seeing the animal which had given up its fur, its white bones on the prairie and the coyotes gnawing at the frosted meat. Before he sailed for Germany, he had a muskrat stuffed by a taxidermist in Toronto.

One winter night, three hours down-country from Kenora, his trap caught a wolf. Saliva frothed in the starlight and yellow eyes stared at him, insane and fretful and wild. He saw the bloody knee and heard the rasp of tattered gums on the metal and decided it was time to go home.

He arrived back in Leipzig in time for the first World Fur Congress. He heard Ernst Poland's rousing opening speech and attended a lecture on ear mange in silver foxes and another lecture on the extreme difficulties of bleaching skins. In Gimli, Snjólaug had taught him how to hand-bleach rabbit skin. Within six months he had started his own business in the Brühl, developing her process.

"That's why my grandmother calls me Snjólaug. Because of her, they were able to live."

Peter tore his eyes from the tiled figure above the doorway. Her enthusiasm had infected him. "You can't know, but this might have been my city. Maybe it can be my city. Maybe I can come and study here."

"Why, what do you have to do with us?"

He explained how once upon a time an English girl from Lancashire went to sing in a Bach competition in Leipzig and sheltered a man on the run. "Let me ask: how would *you* go about finding him?"

"Listen," she said, wetting her finger and rubbing at the wall.

"You're here for a weekend. You're not going to be able to reach anyone. The only people who have any idea or who would be able to help are Party or police."

"I've been told I can't go to the police."

"Of course you can. These people are on our side. They're here to provide protection."

"Do you know someone?"

"I know someone in the Party," revealing more porphyry. "He might be able to help."

"Could you speak to him?"

"Gladly. Give me your address. I could write to you."

He hunted without success for a piece of paper.

"Write it here," holding up the novel.

On the inside back cover he wrote down his address and telephone number. "If I ever come and study in Leipzig, will you be here?"

"Come on, we've only just met."

"I think you're lovely."

She looked at him with a grave expression. "You don't have a right to say that."

He wasn't listening. He sensed a thickening in his throat, spreading into his chest. An overpowering desire to kiss her. At that moment the buildings around them exploded into light.

Not until the streetlamps snapped on did Peter realise how dark it had become. She led him into a square and he recognised where they were. "We're back here?" unable to stifle his disappointment.

"The centre of Leipzig is not even one square kilometre," she said lightly. "Anyway, what would you study here?"

"Medicine."

Her smile vanished. "Really? You've chosen a corruptible profession, doctor."

"What do you mean?"

"Forget it. I have to go," and her eyes had the focus of someone with a lot to do all of a sudden.

"Wait. Have you time for a beer?"

She frowned at a clock face on a tower. Five o'clock. "There's someone I must speak to."

"Can't you put them off?"

"No."

"What about another cigarette?" to keep her.

Again she glanced at the clock. Her face saying, We must stop this.

He tapped out two West Lights and lit them.

"Have you been to the Auerbach's Cellar?" she asked.

"No."

"You can't see Leipzig and not see the Auerbach's Cellar! 'Our Leipzig is renowned, A little Paris . . .'" But there was no cheer in her voice.

She took him into a glazed mall where a dense crowd, many in business suits, shuffled beneath a statue and down a stone staircase. They began to follow, but a uniformed attendant prevented them. The Auerbach's Cellar was closed – a special event connected with the Trade Fair.

At the ragged end of the mall was a wine bar. An effeminate waiter led them to a round glass table in a corner. Seated by the window an old lady, her face roofed in with a tight black hat, stared into a flute of white wine. Otherwise, the place was empty.

"You know what I'd like more than anything?" She put down her book on the table, causing the Tiffany-style lamp to flicker. "A vodka."

The lampshade was patterned with red stained glass in the shape of dragonflies. Even after Peter had ordered two vodkas she went on fidgeting with it. When their drinks arrived she retrieved the plastic swizzlestick from her glass and gulped down the vodka in the manner of someone fortifying herself.

He said, "You mentioned I had chosen a corruptible profession. Why?"

She glanced around. The waiter had disappeared into the kitchen and the old lady sat with her eyes closed. "Tell me," she bent forward, speaking in a low voice. "Do you know much about throats?"

He was not sure he had properly heard. "Throats? Why do you ask?"

"I know this sounds strange, but would you look at my epiglottis and tell me what you see?"

78

"You realise," he said deliberately, "that if I'm going to make a full examination of your throat, I will have to charge a fee."

"What kind of fee?"

"Do you mind very much if I kiss you?"

She absorbed his words and smiled. Nor did she pull away.

"Thank you," his voice very quiet. "I very much needed to do that." Able to take in her features for the first time. The height of her cheeks. The green slightly oriental eyes. The dark hair.

Abruptly, she recoiled.

"Why?"

"I'm afraid I may have an infectious condition."

He pulled the lamp close. "Let's see," and tilted the flickering shade towards her.

Again she parted her lips.

He stared down. "I'd say you have beautiful white teeth and rather a long tongue."

"No, no – my vocal cords?"

"To be honest, I can't see in this light."

"Come on. Try," with a smile of encouragement.

"I need proper instruments. Maybe if I had a mirror."

"I'll ask that lady."

A bag was unfastened and out came a tortoiseshell comb inlaid with a mirror. They moved to another table, where he rested back her head against his hand. "Have you had any pain, bleeding, hoarseness of voice?" trying to sound professional.

"No, no, no."

"Open really wide," depressing her tongue with the swizzle-stick and positioning the comb against his forehead until the mirror reflected the light into her throat. Her breath smelled of vodka and he was aware of breathing it in. He wanted to kiss her again. He had never wanted to kiss anyone so much.

"All right, what's the answer?"

Beyond the trachea the light fell on a pale pink tissue of skin in the shape of a miniature spade. "I'm bound to say I see a perfectly healthy, in fact a rather beautiful, epiglottis."

"What! Are you sure? Be honest."

"I swear. It's not much of a line anyway."

"No, really. Is there any sign of something?"

He had her total attention. "Like what?"

"Is this the worst epiglottis you've seen in a woman of my age?"

"What sort of rubbish is that?"

She laughed in a rueful way. "It's a long story. Let's just say not everyone finds my vocal cords healthy." But her voice trembled. Her eyes were filling up. She swallowed her vodka. Once again he had the impression that she was whipping herself up for something she didn't want to do. "Look, I've got to go."

"Excuse me," said the old lady. Come to retrieve her comb. She snatched it and left hurriedly as if she didn't want to be involved.

Snowleg gathered her coat. "Good luck tonight."

"Wait. Maybe you'd like to come and see us?"

"No, I hate theatre."

He laughed. "So do I."

At the door she turned. "Look, we'll meet again. Come to my brother's party tomorrow."

"What time?"

"What time does your play end?"

"About eight-thirty."

"I'll meet you at the corner of the square at nine. By the fountain."

She was out of the door already when he noticed.

"Snowleg!" running into the mall.

She took back the stolen book, thanking him. But her manner had changed. In the wine bar she had seemed moody and distracted. Now her face was determined and set in the way of someone who had reached an unexpected decision. She walked off down the Mädler-Passage and he watched her pause at one of the statues and touch the buckle on its bronze foot in the way that Rosalind used to touch the marble feet of saints for luck.

A few minutes after 7.30 p.m., crippled and hunched and dressed in the garb of a very old man, Sepp inched on stage before a full house at the Rudolph Theatre. Suddenly, his face contorted as if he had seen a beautiful woman. He made a sound like the tap of a heel on a pavement and became erect and young again, building himself up to his full size.

He watched the invisible woman walk by. Shuffled after her in little steps. Panting. Making Japanese-sounding utterances. Until, step by step, he shrank back into the same old person with his face strained into a mask of puffed eyebrows and sealed lips.

The piece, called *Circle of Life*, imitated the strict atmosphere of Kabuki theatre, but the music and sounds were composed by Teo. The aim, as in all twenty short pieces performed that night by Pantomimosa, was to be simple and ironic. There was no language, no political message.

"I'm not a writer," Sepp had told Peter on the train to Leipzig, comparing himself with the dissatisfied author. "I see my job as doing as little as possible. That way, I hope people will feel."

Sepp declared himself unhappy with certain aspects of their opening performance and insisted on their presence at the theatre next morning. Peter practised and practised until he had got things more or less shipshape. It was 1 p.m. by the time Sepp announced that he was prepared to release them.

On stage, Peter overheard Marcus talking in a low tone to Teo about some students with spray-cans who had been marched away from the Moritzbastei. He switched off the stage-light. A moment later Marcus stepped into the cubicle. "By the way, Peter, I had a word with Teo. I know you're looking under every stone, but for Christ's sake take care."

"What are you talking about?"

"I gather you saw a good-looking girl yesterday. You do realise that most of these girls are festival whores? It's no good going about droopy-eyed. Be careful."

"This is different."

Marcus snorted. "They all say that. Wake up, Peter. Just out of interest, did you say to that girl that your father is East German? Did you or didn't you?"

"Yes, I did."

"How simple can you get! You might as well wander stark naked into the nearest police station."

"Why would I be of interest?"

"Why would you be of interest! An Englishman with an East German father . . . Just think about it, Peter. And meanwhile please be careful. Please be aware of how stupid you've already been."

The severity of this admonition startled Peter and when he left the theatre he looked up and down the street. He prided himself on his sharp eyes that could spot a secretive hobby nesting in the depths of a conifer. Confident that no-one was following, he kept walking.

The day was overcast and still. Scarves of thick cumulus lay suspended over the tramlines. He had planned to explore more of Leipzig, but his meeting with Snowleg had wound him up into a feverish state. He felt within a whisker of learning his father's name and whereabouts. At the same time, he caught himself looking out for a second face until his father's abstract features, which he had never been all that clear about, were supplanted by the fresh image of Snowleg. He saw her in the window of the Teehaus in Thomaskirchhof; in the curved back of the nymph mourning Friedrich Schiller, in the white berets and string shopping bags, the posters for jazz, the orange-fringed umbrellas.

For the rest of the afternoon Peter existed in a state of anticipation, an emotion he had always wanted to feel suddenly within his reach. By the time he returned to the theatre for Pantomimosa's second performance his nervousness had dissolved. This wasn't a dangerously foreign country. Any more so than Wiltshire.

They met at the fountain at 9 p.m. He sat on the edge of the basin and watched her walk towards him across the flagstones. Level against his vision the eyes of her necklace winking at him. Breasts up-tilted under a soft wool cardigan and the contour of underwear through her jeans.

"Hello," she smiled.

"Hello."

"What are you laughing at?"

"I was waiting for you."

She zipped up her black parka jacket and raised her head to the sky. "It's going to snow."

He entwined his arm around her neck. He could smell her hair. Her clean skin. "You're beautiful," he said. "Just like your epiglottis."

She rested her chin on his shoulder, letting his remark cool. "I'm not beautiful."

He took her arm and they crossed the square to the tram stop. In the queue she asked about the pantomime. "Did they enjoy it?"

"It's hard to know. The director forbids applause."

"Did you know that Faust began as a pantomime?"

"No, I didn't."

"In Leipzig," she said in a neutral voice, "we see Faust as a forerunner of the socialist mind."

Not until they were aboard the tram did he remember. "By the way, this party for your brother. What's he celebrating?"

She was silent. Then: "He's going away."

"Where to?"

Her forehead creased. She chewed the inside of one cheek and pursed her lips. "The West."

CHAPTER ELEVEN

THE PARTY WAS HELD in a church hall in a dreary part of town where the tramway ended. Parked outside the hall, a white-shuttered Trabi with a white ribbon on the aerial. She untied the ribbon and wrapped it around her hand.

"My brother's," slipping it into the string bag that she carried over her shoulder.

She walked in her springy stride towards the door and knocked. Coming down the cul-de-sac towards them some young people recognised Snowleg. Soon she was surrounded by five or six, all shouting: "Analyse me, analyse me! Tell me why I hate my mother."

A woman appeared at the door. "What's up? What's up?"

"It's her. She's going to be a psychiatrist."

"Shhh," said the woman. "There's a baby in the next room."

One of the group, a flat-chested girl in high boots, burst out laughing.

"You've come to the wrong door." The woman indicated another door and shivered. "That's the one you want."

It opened to the girl's touch. They followed the group along a corridor that smelled of mouse droppings and into a large hall with exposed roofbeams and lamps with metal shades hanging from them. Snowleg's eyes scouted the room. Corollas of tea-coloured light from a rotating sconce. On stage a jazz band playing *Over the Rainbow*. Fifty or sixty people, but she couldn't see her brother.

"They're all here for him?" asked Peter.

"No, no. It's a peace party organised by the church. He's just turning up to say goodbye."

He went to fetch her a glass of red wine. Waiting in line at the long table, he grew aware of a tension in the room. He felt people looking at him. The puritan faces apprehensive that he might report back on them next day. At the same time their eyes betrayed a daring.

She was talking to the short, bearded man he had seen outside the Thomaskirche.

"There'll just be five of us," he was saying. "Bruno, Marta — and maybe Father Konrad and Katharina."

"Where?"

"My place."

"I need to think about it."

"It's your chance to say goodbye. As well as happy birthday to me." He nudged her. "Thirty-three — in case you've forgotten."

She introduced them. "This is Stefan."

Between two long yellow fingers Stefan held a hand-rolled cigarette. He put it in his mouth before shaking Peter's hand.

"I saw you yesterday," said Peter. "At the Thomaskirche."

"He used to be in the choir," she said, distracted.

"Are you her brother?"

"I'm an old friend of the family," Stefan said meaningfully. He had clever brown eyes and a kindly face and would have been good-looking had he been thinner.

"What about tonight?" Snowleg wanted to know. "Did you tell him you'd invited me?"

"No."

"That's a pity, Stefan."

"Look, go and see him. It'll be fine. He's over there with Father Konrad." He took a long pull at his cigarette. Gazed lovingly at Snowleg. "I'm sorry about your grandmother."

"Yes, it's a shock."

"How is she?"

"The doctor says she'll be in hospital for months."

He patted one of his pockets. "Hey, I've got the plug she wanted."

"For what?"

"The cassette recorder. You going to be there tomorrow?"

"I can't say."

"It's only that I wouldn't mind coming by to put it in."

"Well, I'll try to be there."

"Do you promise?"

"For the last time, Stefan, I promise."

He played an air guitar. "Have to go."

She gave him a quick kiss and he raised his hand to Peter and turned and walked into the crowd.

"Who was that?"

"He's a friend of —"

She had seen him. Sitting on a high stool at the table. Long hands spread one above the other on an upturned billiard cue.

"Come and meet Bruno," she said.

Beneath the balding head her brother had the large solemn eyes of a child. They were turned on a young woman with short-cropped orange hair and nibbled fingernails who tossed her eyes to the ceiling. "Ninety per cent don't think further than their nose. That's the honest truth. They don't have the capacity —" She caught sight of Snowleg, her voice dying out.

The man swivelled on his chair and stared before putting on a smile. He was tall and thin like a mosquito. "Little sister!"

"Bruno."

He stood. Crisp crumbs falling from his shirt. "Let me look at you." After a quick embrace, he stepped back. "Should have recognised the necklace. Hey, Renate. This is my sister."

Renate stared at Snowleg glassily. "Hi, sugar."

Bruno rapped the seat of an empty stool. Snowleg sat down, and he lifted his billiard cue and waved it at a heavy-lipped woman arranging bottles on a tray. "Lara, darling! Over here! A drink for my sister. Who has spurned me like a rabid dog. How long is it? Two years could it be? Bloody time goes so quick, doesn't it."

He raised his glass and looked at her over the rim and as he drank he moved from foot to foot.

Snowleg brushed a silver wisp of hair from her brother's ear and studied him.

"And this?" Bruno put down his glass. Investigating Peter with a cunning smile.

"This is Peter. He's English."

He bowed without appearing to bow. "Peter. I'm a bugger for names. Might take a while for it to settle in."

"Think of me as Peter the Great," suggested Peter.

A young cleric glided up. He had a pony-tail and chewed an apple noisily. He placed a hand on Bruno's arm. "If I don't see you again, good luck."

Bruno gave a tipsy nod of recognition. "Love you, Konrad. Don't ever change. Nor your beautiful wife." He turned back to his sister. Solemn eyes not completely candid. Wide pores on his Roman nose and on his blue-black shirt the initial B. "How did you find out about tonight?"

"Stefan," in a flat voice.

"Stefan. Of course. Of course." He removed a matchstick from his mouth and sat down. "Listen, I'm glad you've made it. I meant to invite you . . . I wanted to write." And in a voice that he tried to make softer: "There's just been so much to do. You have no idea. The sheer bureaucracy of it . . ."

She stared at the floor. "When do you go?"

"I have to be out of the country by noon Monday."

Standing before them, the woman with the tray.

"Hello, Lara, darling, how you doing? I'm all right. Seriously, sit down a minute, but not for too long. This is my little sister. We go back 23 years."

The woman sat on Bruno's lap. "Hello."

"To start with, darling, we need another Bohnerwachs. Large glass. And another one of those. Then you come right back here. That's the way – ahuh – I like it." In a strangulated female voice, he added, "Mama, take me away, he sings me disco songs."

The woman slipped to the floor. "One Bohnerwachs. One red wine."

He watched her battle a path to the long table and said in a regretful way, "God makes them faster than I can fuck them."

"Oh, Bruno," said Snowleg. "You couldn't even invite me to your farewell party."

"Hell, one day I'm going to give such a party for you . . . you can't imagine."

The sound of a saxophone throbbed beneath their conversation, mournful and haranguing.

He took a sip from his glass and levelled his eyes at her. "So?"
"So?"

"No, I asked first. Have you got your job – the one you wanted?"

She lowered her head. Hardly able to bring out the words. "Why didn't you tell me?"

The question didn't reach him. He put down his glass on the

table and raised his hand to his head and started scratching a dry scalp.

"Petra will be so pleased if you've got it." He looked around. Waved at a minuscule woman. "Petra, Petra, come here," he gestured impatiently as if ripping paper from a toilet roll. "Come over here."

Out on the dance floor the band struck up a faster tune.

Renate howled with laughter. "It's oompa-pa."

"Count Basie to you," said Bruno. He winked at Peter. "Renate believes that whoever sleeps with you last has you."

A body darted between them – the tiny woman he had waved to. Either she hadn't seen Snowleg or she had chosen not to. She grabbed his hand. "Come on, Bruno."

With exaggerated formality, he balanced his cue against the table. "Excuse me. My wife has invited me to dance."

Snowleg seized her empty glass and peered at it for dirt, but really she was looking through it to see him. Her hands were trembling. She turned to Peter, eyes mutinous. "Dance with me."

It didn't become clear to Peter that Snowleg was a good dancer until the music shifted to a rock-and-roll tune. She was light on her feet and unselfconscious and she danced like someone who had decided to enjoy herself. He could never dance like that without feeling acutely self-conscious. He had always imagined that people must just pretend to enjoy this sort of dancing. Now he saw that it might be possible to yield truly to music.

She withdrew her arm from his back and her hand sought his shoulder and he started to respond and he sensed a number of eyes measuring them as they moved across the floor.

Over her shoulder he caught the despondent glance of Stefan and then of Bruno and suddenly he was looking at himself through their eyes and he felt as if he was gyrating in a dream in which he was naked. He tried to struggle against this feeling, but it won and he didn't know what to do with his arms or his legs or where to put them or how to breathe.

She saw his confusion and quickly came to him. She looped her arms around his neck and he felt his cheek against her skin and she gave him a look that went through his eyes and behind them and she whispered in an altered voice, "Don't slip away. I want you to stay here with me. Just don't go. Don't go. Stay here." Her breath hot and innocent as a baby's.

The music ended and they walked back to the table. She picked up a bottle of wine and filled her glass. Hand at her throat. Brown light licking over her face from the revolving lamp. Her beauty renewing an ache.

He offered her a cigarette.

"No, thanks." She lit one of her own with a Zippo lighter and breathed out. She was aware of her effect and it excited him.

Her brother rejoined them. "I didn't know you liked rock and roll, baby."

"No? Well, I do, so fuck you."

"She's a crazy girl," turning to Peter. "But you know that, don't you?" He sat down on the stool and capsized the rest of his glass into his mouth and licked his lip. He pointed at Peter's glass. "Any more? Simon, wasn't it?"

"Peter. No, I'm all right."

"Hey, Bruno," said Renate. "Asking me?"

"Not especially," said Bruno over his shoulder. He looked at Peter, curious. "So how did you two meet, if that's not a personal question?"

"He's a doctor."

"I'm with a mime group at the Rudolph Theatre."

"Is that so?"

On stage the band struck up *Over the Rainbow*.

Snowleg glared at the musicians. "Don't they play anything else?"

"My request," said Bruno. In his strangulated voice he sang, "Way up high," and he wrapped his fingers around his cue and lifted it in the air. "Hey, little sister, you look like someone who hasn't sung in a while. When was the last time you sang?"

"Can't remember," pouting.

He lowered his cue. There was no billiard table in sight. "You can't remember?"

She tapped out a cigarette.

"What about that one?" said Bruno.

A cigarette was burning in a knee-high metal ashtray. She took it and lit the new one and stubbed the old one out. "Why didn't you tell me?"

He looked at her with a mad grin. "Now, baby, this isn't the place."

"But you told Oma. You told Papa." Her words rang out accusing him. "Didn't you?"

"I did." He scratched the side of his nose. The corner of his dry mouth. "But the reason —"

"What?"

"Don't ask. Just lots of serious bullshit. People's lives. My life!" He reached out, but his glass was empty. He closed his eyes. Concentrating on the path his thought had taken. And Peter had the sense that the fall on either side was steep.

"When did you tell them, Bruno?"

He shook his head. His lips trembled. He seemed collapsed and old sitting there, leaning on his billiard stick that had no table to play on.

"Why didn't you tell *me*?"

"That's the worst of it. I can honestly say that's the worst of it. I couldn't tell you."

"That's too bad," said Snowleg mercilessly.

His tongue appeared pink on his lip and disappeared. "Who told you I was leaving — Stefan again?" he said bitterly.

"Officially? Falk Hirzel."

"Hirzel!"

"I went to see him last night. You know, right up until he told me I never wanted to believe it . . ." Tears glittered in her green eyes. "When did you apply?"

He drew a long breath. "Two years ago." He said this with his eyes closed.

"And you didn't speak to me about it? It's not very brave, Bruno. If you loved me . . . if I mattered at all — even a little — you could still have talked to me and you didn't."

"I always supposed you were on their side."

She laughed and rubbed at her eyes. "Why should a decision you make for your life affect mine, Bruno? Why didn't you say, 'Look, I know this will ruin your life'?"

"I wish you wouldn't say that. Anyway, I'm doing nothing wrong. It's in the '49 constitution. Article Ten. Everyone has the right to leave."

"Shut up! Have you thought about those of us you're leaving?" her fury stressed with sharp tugs on her necklace. "What happens to us?"

"You don't realise! One has no time for feelings. Listen, it's good you're here. I want you to have these." He leaned back and produced from his trouser pocket a ring of keys. "Take them."

She looked at the keys. Flicked them in his face.

Bruno held up a hand, deflecting them to the floor. She started to leave, but he barred her way with his cue.

"Let me go, Bruno." Her eyes overturned rocks. The corollas pulsing across her face.

He leaped off his chair and caught her around the waist. She tried to squirm away, but he pinned her by the arms and rotated her until she was staring straight at Peter.

They stood in a large empty circle on the edge of which people with anxious expressions hovered as if wondering whether it would damage them to be associated with this struggle.

Uneasy at the tone the party was taking, Peter stooped to pick up the key ring. Through the wad of smoke he heard Stefan's amplified voice, kind and calming, over a loudspeaker. "Are you being difficult again?"

Renate stood up. "Seeyuh, Bruno. This time Monday, I'll be thinking of you." She started singing, "Little Johnny went into the great wide world all alone."

Bruno bowed lifelessly. "Love you, Renate. Don't ever change."

A hand on her shoulder. "Seeyuh, little sister."

Snowleg's head on one side and her gaze more intense.

The jazz band left the stage and its place was taken by a group in black jeans and T-shirts. Stefan picked up the microphone again. There was an electric guitar around his neck and he sounded drunk. "I want to play a new song. It's called *Deer in the Woods*. We all know who this goes out to. And it's not to Bruno."

A strained cheer. Bruno raised a hand in acknowledgement, allowing Snowleg to wriggle from his grip.

Stefan played a loud chord, drowning out the cheers. Behind him, a drummer started up a crude, methodical beat. Ten feet from Peter, the girl in the high boots convulsed as if electrocuted.

"Oh, God," said Snowleg, standing beside Peter.

He looked at the faces beginning to quiver on the dance floor and had the impression that he was viewing them through the eyes around her neck.

Hair trailing about his face, Stefan stomped to the edge of the stage and jerked up his guitar and screamed: "Snows are silent on my frozen plain / Why can't I be a snowflake / And fall without aim / Instead I fall in love."

His voice reached a crescendo as the band riffed into the chorus: "We are like deer in the woods / The moon is out / The night is clear / And you can be cruel without trying / You go away / Without knowing the pain / You are hard, you are soft . . ."

Out on the floor, Bruno danced alone. He had taken the tall ashtray, was hitting his head with it, and cigarette butts were flying everywhere as well as sparks from the cigarette in his mouth.

"We've got to go," Snowleg said.

CHAPTER TWELVE

THE SNOW WAS FALLING. She wore thin shoes and had to hold onto his arm. "You're going to ask me what that was about. Don't bother."

Their footsteps squealed in the fresh snow. They walked on, not speaking, into the soft noisy night. At the second tram stop she paused. "We should wait."

He brushed the snow from the collar of her parka. "What does Stefan do?"

She peered down the street. "He works in the Christian bookshop." Easier to talk about him than her brother. "He protested against the blasting of the old University Church and wasn't allowed to study engineering."

"He's in love with you," a shade too emphatically.

"He's not in love. He's in over-valuation."

"Not what I saw."

"Oh, Stefan's always falling in love with someone and writing songs about them. If it goes well, no songs. So he falls for ones who give him trouble and trouble gives him songs."

"And your feelings for him?"

"Stefan's a very old friend. He and my brother go back. But some old friends think they'd like to be new friends," and wriggled her shoulders as if something was crawling there.

A Trabi hissed by. One of its windscreen wipers wasn't working and the metal blade cawed on the glass until the car turned the corner and the street was empty again.

She stamped her feet. Peered once more into the snow-streaked darkness. "We may have missed the tram."

"Let's go somewhere," he said suddenly.

"There's nowhere to go."

"What about this?" holding up the key ring. "Where's this to?"

She touched the keys. "Well done." Her face completely grateful. "Yes. Let's go there."

The larger key unlocked the main gate to a colony of Schreber gardens in the centre of the city. A brick chimney soared into the night, and high up, over manicured fruit trees, lights shone from a huge gymnasium. Otherwise, it was possible to imagine they had arrived before the gateway to a country park and were not in a city at all.

Snowleg fiddled with the lock. Peter started to ask something, but she put a finger to her lips. "Shhsh."

He was desperate to piss. Beside the gate, a streetlamp threw its feeble glow over a glassed-in board. His eyes scanned the notices pinned inside. News of a forthcoming "Children's Day". The date for the water supply to be switched back on. A list of rules. No weeds, bathtubs, clothes lines. And a reminder that it was forbidden for members of the Garden Association to spend the night.

"Come on," seizing his wrist. She led him down a path between lattice fences and he was aware of the sureness of her step compared with his own more hesitant one. She took a right fork and then another, stopping before a chest-high wooden gate. "This is it."

"You go on," he said, and turned away from her, bursting, towards a terracotta gnome. He unzipped his trousers and his piss steamed up from the snow.

Inside the shed, darkness and the smell of broken winter. He heard her scrabbling around in a drawer. "We used to keep them here . . . Ah!"

The sound of a bag being emptied and a flash. In the lighter's flame her throat a blue glow and behind her a bar-fire crackling.

She lit the wick, her eyes staying on the candle stub.

He took off his scarf and draped it across her shoulder. Sparks of snow in her hair. Her breath smoke in the cold. His desire frightening him as the candle flame thinned and thickened.

On the chair were the objects that she had tumbled there. A white ribbon. Two keys. The stolen book.

He picked it up. A card poked from the pages. "You've been reading it?"

"Yes," and taking a half-burnt cone of incense that someone had left on a saucer, she dipped it in the flame. The incense mingled with the scent of squirrels and burning dust.

"Why steal this?" he wanted to know.

"They have everything. We have nothing. What's a book?"

At the way she said "they" he felt another blow of desire. It placed him, for the moment, on her side.

"I mean why steal this book."

"Oh, I recognised his name from school. But I wasn't aware he wrote novels." She mumbled in a rush, addressing herself as much as Peter: "I mean it's insane. It's bad luck to grow up in a place where you have to be courageous just to read a book. There are books which if you don't read them at twenty-three you won't read them at forty, or it's not the same."

Ashamed of his intensity, he tried to transfer it onto the novel. "What's it about?"

The story sounded more like a novel for young adults. A boy breeds swans for a splendid, orderly park that he is never permitted to leave. Restless to escape, he one day hatches a plan to gather thirty swans and lash himself to their feet. He hopes that if he fires a gun to scatter them into the air the swans will carry him over the tall fence to freedom.

"And does he escape?" asked Peter, knowing that he had to yield to the chit-chat and yet grateful to the book for bringing them together like this.

"I haven't found out."

Peter thought of an adolescent boy attached to the legs of thirty white birds. It was impossible, ludicrous. Thirty swans couldn't lift you up. Even if you did manage to scare the swans into the air, they would tangle. This was why he didn't like novels. But he went on with his questions. "Do you think it's possible for swans to carry our weight?"

"I imagine it depends on the swans," she replied, with a child's need for sincerity. "Whether each of them takes off in a different direction. Or whether they decide to swarm in a single flock. And I suppose you don't know what will happen until that moment and neither do they."

"Does Bruno?"

His mention of her brother upset her. "Actually, could I ask a favour? Could you take it off my hands?"

"You don't want to know how the story ends?"

"It's not that."

"What would you like me to do with it?"

"Read it, give it away, send it back to the author. I don't know. It will disappear in the West. Here, it's like having nitroglycerine in my bag."

He pulled out the card that marked her place.

"My medical card! Thank goodness you saw it," and tidied it into her bag.

"So," he said, looking around. "Where are we?"

In the street, she had been infuriated and silent. Now she appeared nervous at her own audacity. As if she had been misbehaving and this was where it was leading to. In a faltering voice she told him that the hut had belonged to her grandmother. "It was a place I used to adore. Whenever we had a weekend free, I wanted to spend it here, helping in the garden, planting bulbs." She gave a quick smile, touching her lip. "My grandmother said my mouth was so big because as a child I'd put it around whole carnations. And I believed her!"

"Why do you say 'used to'?"

It was Bruno's fault. When he married Petra he had wheedled their grandmother into giving him the allotment as his wedding present. He had pleaded and insisted and worn her down until she relented. Not once since then had he invited Snowleg to visit.

"It's a joke – he's never gardened in his life."

"Could he have been trying to protect you? He must have been planning to leave for a while."

She wasn't convinced. Her anger suggested that her brother had betrayed not only her, but their grandmother as well.

"You sound as if you're close to your grandmother?"

"Yes. I like listening to her. A lot of people don't talk, don't want to make judgments, don't want to expose themselves. But she does."

"What does she tell you?"

"If you do things, do them properly, one at a time, with your whole attention. When you eat, eat. When you love, love. When

96

you listen to a person, listen to them, don't let your eye stray across the room and don't think about what you're going to say next."

She rested her hands together between her knees and her eyes darkened and he felt a feathered swish inside him.

He peeled off his hat. She stood to fetch something, but he stopped her. He took her hands and separated them and rubbed one after the other until they were warm and then he raised the heel of her right hand to his chin. The light winked off her cheek and he collected droplets of melted snow from her hair with his tongue.

He led her over to the bed, removed the scarf from her shoulders.

She sat down and lifted her sweater. Underneath, a faded red silk shirt. He moved to unbutton it, but she held his hand and prevented him and as he lowered his hand she kept on grasping it.

He climbed onto the bed. She lay back awkwardly and he steered his head over her stomach, his lips kissing her skin where the book had been, where she had hidden it, slipping his fingers at the same time under the rim of her jeans, pulling down her pants with the jeans.

She pressed her legs together and rolled over. He kissed her bottom, kissing the crease between her closed legs, and slowly turned her on her back.

"I'm a virgin," looking down at him.

"You're what?"

"For this."

She pulled his hair for him to come up. He kissed her and then he lowered his head and she pulled his scarf over her face and he sensed her relax, one hand cupping his neck, pressing his mouth further into her until she fell back on the pillow, long legs up around his neck, and he saw the arch of her throat and the summit of her chin and the blackberry undercurrent to her hair.

In a while she drew herself up and looked down on him with a fleeting expression of regret and then she leaned forward and helped him off with his trousers and feeling his hardness between her breasts she widened her legs and guided him to where his tongue had been, her body warm and liquefying beneath him, his mouth seeking hers, until a long thin sound tore from her throat and for a precarious moment everything in their lives converged.

"What are you looking at?" she asked later.

"Nothing."

She got up from the bed and he thought she was going to wash herself, but she blew out the candle and came back to him. He held her from behind and he held her tight. Tracing the lines of her back under the thin red silk of her shirt until the muscles grew less tense.

He murmured, "I'd love to fold you in my dressing-up box and take you away."

She said, "If you go on doing that, you can."

"Why did you turn out the light?"

She didn't reply and he realised he was inhaling the scent of her sleeping breath and that she had a different smell when she slept.

He woke. A lozenge of sunlight slanted across her face. She was propped on an elbow. Green eyes big and open. Staring down at him with the dawn. The tip of her finger pressed his chin and drew a line up to his ear.

"I had a good feeling about you, but you can have a good feeling about someone and it comes to nothing."

He touched the necklace that still circled her throat. "Big Brother watching me."

She laughed, drawing back. "Who, Bruno?"

"Your secret police," covering the marbles with his palm. "I was warned you can't speak to anyone."

"Bullshit."

"I also read it."

"Bullshit."

"No, it isn't."

"The hell it isn't. I know who to speak to. I know exactly who I can speak to." She came close again. Her fingers crept under his hand and played with the shaft of hollow bone and the glass eyes, separating them.

"Actually," he looked up at her and the tension between them was enjoyable, "what is that?"

It was a bone from her grandfather's muskrat. "Granny had it made into a necklace after he died."

He stroked her breast under the red shirt that she still hadn't taken off.

"This is hers, too," looking down. Covering herself with the shirt.

"It must be very old."

"She said you should only buy the best," and her voice imitated an old lady: "'I am not so rich as to buy cheap things!'"

"Any other words of wisdom?"

She smiled. "I've already told you."

"Tell me some more."

"'It's not necessary to feel guilty, but it's necessary to feel shame.'"

"You're close to your granny?"

"You asked that before. Don't you listen?"

He didn't answer, but started to unbutton her shirt and this time she appeared to make a decision. She waited for his fingers to reach her shoulders, bracing herself for the question, and as his hands mounted her back she didn't breathe out. She felt his fingers discover the first pleated ridges of skin. Watched him inhale. Catch himself. Press his thumbs hard as if testing the skin – "I can feel that" – and continue their journey.

He tickled her and she shook her head out of the spell. "I love that."

And because he never asked the question she told him.

She was playing with Bruno in the kitchen. Her head hit the handle of a pot of coffee on the stove. It spilled over them both. She was 9 years old.

She hoisted the shirt and sat still for Peter to see where the boiling liquid had melted the skin.

He had known what it was straight away and was moved by her loveliness within it. Even so, it surprised him to see the burn-mark. The scar quite waxy and pearly, like hoar frost, and covering her shoulders.

He was aware that she was worried by his response. She was

saying, "I used to wear my hair long to cover it," when he brushed her lips to be quiet and turned her over onto her stomach.

Afterwards, she rubbed the tears from her smiling face. "Once is never enough."

He looked at her quizzically. She rolled over and lay on her back and raised one arm straight in the air. "That's also something my grandmother likes to say. That's her best advice."

It was cold in the room and she snuggled against him.

"What happened to Bruno? Wasn't he burned?"

She shook her head. "Everyone said *that* was the miracle."

"Did you blame him?"

"Oh, no. I idolised him."

He said he wanted to know everything and so she told him. In the cold her words made twice their impression.

As children they had done everything together. Bruno took her to the Natural History Museum in East Berlin to stand before the dinosaurs. He smuggled her into the cinema in Grimmaische Straße, her shoes on his shoes, walking in step under his long coat, to watch a forbidden film. Once in the spring after their mother died they hiked for three days along the Baltic coast.

"And then he fell in love."

Petra came from Dresden, but she had family in the West. She was possessive of Bruno from the first. After their marriage, Snowleg hardly saw him. They last spoke at a party thrown by their grandmother to celebrate the results of her Vorphysikum.

"This was when?"

"Three years ago."

Bruno arrived alone. He had filled his white Trabi with flamingo flowers as high as fenceposts and before leaving in a rage he gave her 200 Ostmarks. They had the briefest conversation. She told him she wanted to be a psychiatrist, do something serious with her life, and he encouraged her.

"You should, little sister. You should do what you want."

Then the celebration turned into a quarrel with her father and grandmother and no-one explained to her what the argument was about. Bruno had stormed off and she hadn't seen him since, not until the party last night.

"I hear nothing from him until a few days ago Stefan tells me, did I know, Bruno's going to the West? I'm astonished, but I'm even more astonished when I discover I'm being punished for it."

"In what way punished?"

The patch of sunlight had shifted from the bed to the floor and was creeping over the red shirt discarded there by the time she finished explaining how stunned she was by the events of the past 24 hours. How her every basis for trust had been shaken to the root.

Until very recently she never had any reason to cross the system. She was considered very bright at school. Had been active in the Freie Deutsche Jugend. Organised concerts and readings. She believed what she was told, that the German Democratic Republic was truly democratic and that her liberty was guaranteed by the constitution. She believed that her country was the "good Germany" and that the Federal Republic, on the other hand, was home to fascists who every day scratched their heads to think of new ways to undermine the GDR. Long before she went to university she knew that she wasn't supposed to watch Western television and that the public telephone in the street was bugged and that there existed people in the regime who might do strange things to those who threatened its achievements. But she thought if she was a good girl things would work out. Things would be different. They wouldn't pick on her. "I never took the regime seriously."

A fortnight before, she expected to hear that she had qualified for a postgraduate place at Karl-Marx-University to specialise in psychiatry. "Everyone told me I'd get it. Even if I still doubted myself, I was fairly confident that I had done well in my exams." The head of faculty had assured her of a place. So had the dean. She had no reason to doubt the future towards which conscientiously she had been working. "You see, it's a crime not to have a job and I had committed no crime. This was what I always wanted to do."

When the rejection came she didn't link it with Bruno. Her

voice shrank as she recalled how, twelve days earlier, she had returned to her grandmother's apartment and found her father waiting in the kitchen.

"They've failed you." The letter in his hand trembled against the stove. "My daughter."

"Have they given a reason?"

"No reason." He was a miner, a Party member, a fervent admirer of Honecker. "There may be a possibility for other employment. But you have to wait a week."

The same evening she overheard him shouting at her grandmother. "This is Bruno's fault!"

Her story brought back to Peter the unendurable loneliness he had felt in his last two years at St Cross. Not knowing who to trust, who he was. He drew her closer and feeling the texture of her back against his chest he caressed the pleated ridges of skin with his lips and fingers, surveying it.

"My grandmother took the lead. She demanded a meeting."

They met at the medical school. Her father and grandmother, the head of her faculty and a man from the university, Sontowski. When they sat down she noticed a sheet of yellow paper in front of Sontowski, with a short written evaluation and then her marks and something else that she couldn't figure out.

Immediately, Sontowski started to pick her to pieces. "If you have marks as bad as these no wonder you can't continue at university."

She was paralysed. "I told myself: He has the wrong piece of paper. He thinks I'm someone else."

But he carried on, becoming more personal. "Someone as stupid as you, they shouldn't want to be a psychiatrist."

"I thought, This isn't me. They must have made a mistake. I haven't done anything against them."

The head of faculty seemed in accordance with Sontowski, staring at her and nodding at what he was saying. Then he spoke, and what he said astonished her. He had always gone out of his way to congratulate Snowleg on her work, but he talked in front of her as if he was being openly critical in a constructive way.

"She is a pleasant girl. That may be her damnation. She has this enormous gift of relating musically to every situation, but she never relates to anything else. Now I've nothing against harmony, but this ability to harmonise very rarely goes with supreme gifts. Certainly not in the line of work she wishes to pursue."

Her father looked ready to explode, but her grandmother erupted first. "Stop this, just stop it!"

"Stop what?" said Sontowski, bewildered.

"You know as well as we do that she's perfectly qualified. Don't do this to her."

At this, her father burst out: "Could you tell me – is it true my daughter is being rejected because of her brother?"

Sontowski didn't answer, talking in empty phrases. "Well, this is not a matter to be discussed here. We're not an inquisition. You should be grateful to the German Democratic Republic because we are able to offer you employment. We've just received the result of the clearing talks. A position has come free." He studied his yellow piece of paper. "The university switchboard requires a telephone operator." He gave her a hideous smile. "You'll still be at the university."

For the second time her grandmother spoke. "No. Never. Never in my life. She's not going to be a telephone operator. She wants to be a psychiatrist."

"Then you're rejecting the only chance she's probably ever going to get to be employed."

Her father was still puzzling it out. "Her brother is leaving for West Germany and you make her responsible?"

Sontowski stared at her. "You'll have to have a voice test. Why not take the chance I'm offering you?" He told them to go outside, think it over.

"You haven't done anything and they treat you like this," said her father bitterly. He resented Bruno for having ruined her career, her future. For causing these strains in their family.

She was too numb to think properly. She was scared. She couldn't sort out what she had just heard. She was starting to believe she really was as stupid as they were saying. And now this information about Bruno!

Sontowski opened the door. What had she decided? Her father and grandmother looked at her. She could see it in their faces. They didn't know what to say.

"Perhaps you're right," she said. "Perhaps I should be a telephone operator."

Her grandmother was unusually quiet on the way home. She shut herself in her room and in the evening put on her coat and gathered her walking stick, muttering that she was going to the "Paulaner". When she didn't come back, Snowleg imagined that she must have stayed out for dinner. The "Paulaner" was her favourite café. She often ate there, tipping the band to play Viennese music.

Next morning Anne-Katrin at the corner shop knocked on the door. The hospital had telephoned: her grandmother had slipped on the ice as she stepped off a tram.

Snowleg went immediately to the hospital in Dösen. A solemn young doctor had examined the shattered knee. It was unlikely that her grandmother would walk again.

For three hours she stayed at her grandmother's bedside before tearing herself away. "I had this voice test to do."

At 2 p.m. she was ushered into a large room at the university medical school. A man, fiftyish with sallow features, pushed a book over his desk. "Read this." The passage was from Goethe's *Faust* and chosen, as Doctor Behrend explained, because it contained a lot of *ss* sounds.

She read aloud while he flicked through a file with her name on it. When she had finished, he looked into her throat.

He withdrew the spatula. Shook his head.

"What's wrong?"

"Your epiglottis."

"Why, what's the matter with it?"

"I've never seen such a decayed glottal passage in a girl of your age."

"But I used to sing in the choir!"

Even as he was peeling off his headband, she knew he was lying. He started to write down something and he had the same expression as Sontowski.

He wanted her to sign. A paper to say why she couldn't work as a telephone operator.

"I can't sign."

"But you have to sign here."

"I'm sorry, I can't. My hand, suddenly it's not able to hold a pen."

She ran outside, down the steps. The bells of the Thomaskirche were ringing.

On those Saturdays when she wasn't in the country with her father, she invariably went to hear the St Thomas boys' choir sing Bach. It was her space for thought. Her freedom within church walls. For half an hour every week she could close her eyes and be herself.

She normally sat with the choir in the seats reserved for their girlfriends and family, but after her experience with Doctor Behrend she couldn't bear to meet anyone she knew. And so rather than climb to her usual seat in the gallery, she joined the congregation in the nave.

"When the singing was over, I opened my eyes and saw you."

On any other day she wouldn't have stopped and talked to a Westerner. But her mood this afternoon was defiant. Such a goody-two-shoes she had been and where had it got her? She couldn't even pass a voice test to become a telephonist. As she sat in the Thomaskirche, she sensed something inside her hardening. "That's why I stole that book. That's why I talked to you. That's why I asked you to look down my throat. And when you told me you could see nothing wrong, I made a decision."

Upon leaving the Book Fair, Snowleg had intended to track down her brother and face it out with him. But she changed her mind after speaking with Peter. Instead of going to see Bruno, she headed directly to the Party HQ in Karl-Liebknecht-Straße.

Because of the Trade Fair, people were still at work. She decided to make an appeal and beg somebody to explain. If she was to live in this system, she had to find out why she couldn't become what she had trained so hard to be. "I still couldn't accept it had anything to do with Bruno."

The door was open to Falk Hirzel's office. Hirzel was the Number Three in the Party. Once at a prize-giving he had asked her to dinner and another time had invited her back to his house where they talked in passionate terms about Fontane.

She walked in and he recognised her. His face beamed until she told him about the ridiculous voice test.

Hirzel closed the door and after a few minutes a secretary came in carrying a folder. Everything was inside the folder. Her application for going to graduate school. The results of her exams — he admitted she had passed them all — and a copy of the letter rejecting her for a place.

He writhed in his chair. His glasses sat uneasily on his nose. He read another document and shook his head. "You have no chance, forget it."

"Why?"

"The reason is your brother."

"Then it's true?"

"Apparently, he has been granted a United Nations visa and will be leaving on Monday."

"Even if that's the case, why should it affect me?"

He was shaken by the question. "You must know that's how it is: anyone in your family wants to leave, you fall into a big hole."

She stared at him. "How could you side with them?"

"Yes, yes, don't tell me."

"Why? Why blame me for something that's not my fault?"

"Unfortunately, that's how it is."

"During the Nazis' time this was called *Sippenhaft*."

He gave her a long look. The statement was simple and yet it cornered him. "You're right," his voice dropping. "Our system shouldn't work like this." He closed the file. "What is it you want?"

"I want to be a psychiatrist."

"A psychiatrist?"

"A psychiatrist."

He wrote it down. "What's today? Give me till Wednesday. On Wednesday I have a meeting with the director of the university. I'm going to see what I can do."

"Next week," she said to Peter, "where will you be?"

"It depends what time of day. But somewhere in Hamburg."

"Please. At eleven on Wednesday morning think of me."

"All right. I will."

"Hirzel is a decent man. He knows a mistake has been made."

"I hope you're right."

She turned over on her stomach. Her lips drew back in a smile, revealing her chipped tooth. "By the way, I asked him about your father."

She had no reason not to ask. "I said to Hirzel, there's this person from Hamburg University. He's here to see if he can find any trace of his father. How can we help him? Who should he talk to, which department?"

"What did he say?" and Peter imagined Hirzel writing down the details meticulously. The thought racing through the man's head: Someone in East Germany has a hitherto undiscovered son who is English. The innocuous question: "You say that he doesn't know that he has a son?"

"He promised to put someone onto it. But he needs dates. Can you let me have dates? He says if you give him dates, he might be able to get the information by tomorrow."

Only the day before it had excited Peter to think that Snowleg might be able to help him in his quest, but now he was appalled that this innocent creature had raised the subject. He knew how perilous it was because he had been told so over and over again. At the same time, it touched him that her grasp was nothing near so full as his. And having been touched it was a short step for Peter to think, What if she's right? What if Hirzel is a decent man? What if this is the only chance I'm going to get? He promised: "I'll ring my mother."

They opened the door to a magical world, the gardens covered in fresh snow and the sun above the tarred roof belling out like blown glass.

"Come on – it's warmer out." She sat on the steps wearing only his shirt, her parka loose around her shoulders.

He put on his jersey and perched beside her. "The first house I lived in," playing with her lighter, "had a communal garden like this."

"Where was that?"

"In London. Near Portobello Road."

She smiled. "London for me is Karl Marx."

"How so?" He had never felt so happy. Snowleg was a tremendous liberation after Anita. This is love, he said to himself. This is absolute love.

"Oh, it's a children's book about Karl Marx taking children from the textile mills to Hampstead Heath. *The Moor and the Ravens of London*. It was my first children's book and I loved it. He has a great black beard and he shows them space, fresh air, food, trees and sun."

"Don't you want to see it for yourself?"

"Of course! I'd ask my father: 'Why aren't we allowed to travel?' I thought it was stupid. I was never going to see London, but I was learning all about the Tower of London. On the other hand, I knew I was not going to change anything. I told myself: 'If you're good at your studies perhaps you'll have a chance to travel.'"

"Maybe you should leave with your brother," he said.

"Do you think it's that simple? What would I do in West Germany? My life is here."

"You call this a life?"

"The Western system doesn't interest me. To get new books, yes – but not to live there."

"What about leaving with me?" and he was conscious of his brows knitting together.

She nudged him with her knee. "What – in your dressing-up box? I don't think so, Peter."

He tried to change the subject. "Then *I'd* like to take something back from here."

"Like what?"

"The eyes around your neck?"

"You may not take the eyes around my neck!"

"Look, I have to take a memento of the happiest day of my life. Can I take the key to your hut?"

"You may not take the key to the hut."

He looked around, willing himself to feel the extravagance of someone about to leave. Able to leave. On the edge of the lawn facing them was the terracotta gnome against which he had pissed.

"What about him?"

"What about him?"

He laughed. "I love kitsch," and he leaped to his feet, planning then and there to extract the gnome from her grandmother's lawn. "I could put him in my study. Although I'll have to clean him off."

He packed up a handful of snow and started wiping the terra-cotta face. Then he picked up the gnome. "What the hell . . .?" A wire led from the feet into the frozen earth. "What is this?"

"Oh, no!" The tendons rose taut in her neck.

"Look, there's something in his mouth." A small device the size of a walnut. "Snowleg . . . they're photographing us."

"They're not photographing us, they're photographing Bruno." She glared at the gnome, the same scalding look she had given her brother. "I'll give you something to photograph," and in blind rage and fear tore it from the ground.

She ran into the hut and started to dress in a hurry. "You've got to leave."

He tried to soothe her, but his words hurtled to the ground in the unpredictable way that he fell in dreams when he thought he could fly. "I don't want to leave."

She pulled up the corner of his shirt and wiped her eye. "You have to leave. Now."

"When am I going to see you?"

"I don't know."

"Will you come to the theatre?"

"I'll come if I can, but it may be impossible."

He walked away, turning his head every few steps, until she melted into the lawns and trees, a white bird so similar in absence of shade to all around her that she seemed created from the same snow.

CHAPTER THIRTEEN

"AND WHERE HAVE YOU been?" Teo sat alone in the dining room, surrounded by empty breakfast plates.

"I spent the night in a Schreber garden," he said evasively.

"You what?"

"OK, you were right. It was a foolish thing to do."

"May I ask what happened?"

"Look, I feel like getting out of Leipzig for a while."

"Do you have anywhere in mind?"

"Yes."

The discovery of the recording device had genuinely alarmed Peter. He knew from studying the map how close Dorna was to Leipzig. On this snowy morning in this grey watchful city it beckoned as the most obvious place in the world for him to visit. He had no expectation of finding anything. He just wanted to smell the village where he had been conceived, to feel he had been there. And to remove himself from Leipzig until he could make sense of the past 24 hours.

"What do you want to see the country for?" asked the landlady. "There's nothing there. Only darkness and animals."

After learning from her that Dorna was no more than an hour away by train, he persuaded Teo to accompany him. They bought tickets and departed shortly before 11 a.m.

The train headed south through the city. Concrete facades rose up, dead-coloured in the snow as though fur had been ripped from them. Soon Leipzig was behind them and the air no longer tasted of coal ash. They passed through a forest. Peter gazed into the white-sheeted trees and battled in vain to picture an East German village, a music professor's house; but instead of a kitchen with a blue-tiled stove where his mother had fed a famished man he saw a young woman stirring awake in a garden hut. He thought of the innocent smile that went through his ribs, the swish in his stomach, her white shiny scar, her breasts pushing against his shirt. And moments later, her expression of horror.

"We're here," said Teo, who had agreed to come, as he said, only to keep an eye on Peter. "By the way, I don't care what you say but we're not stopping to ask questions."

They walked from Dorna station and down an avenue of flowering cherry trees that led up to it. His mother had described a half-timbered house on the corner of Breitscheidstraße. It stood there still, a modest white-painted building with a sagging roof and blue-rimmed windows that looked over a front garden. On one sill a child's decoration, a butterfly cut from cellophane, and beyond the house a riding school with caravans. He had no inclination to knock.

Peter spent an hour in Dorna without learning any additional clues. He walked with Teo up the high street to a cobbled square where a bar was closed. They walked into a churchyard full of the graves of Russian soldiers. They walked to the edge of a frozen and polluted lake. A woman bicycling by glanced in their direction and looked away. Even if Teo had allowed him to stop and speak with her, Peter had nothing to say. He felt no connection. He had not told Snowleg he loved her.

"Seen enough?" said Teo.

"I think so," not feeling even within hailing distance of his father.

"Let's go."

The next train to Leipzig did not leave for two more hours. They got a lift with a truck. The driver was a burly silent man. Stone Age face. Broad nose. Dark leather jacket. He sat gripping the steering wheel, staring ahead, not opening his mouth.

The road ran straight through flat country. There was nothing to distinguish one field from another. There were the fields, there were the hedges, there was the cold white snow.

They reached the forest as darkness was falling. The driver switched on the headlights. The road was in a terrible condition, icy with large holes and rocks, and the headlights bumped up and down. The potholes jolted his spine, rolled him against the door. He was hungry and cold and his bladder was full.

Teo rubbed his hands. He made a noise and Peter saw his lips moving in silhouette, mouthing his made-up music. He had not once asked about the Schreber garden and Peter was grateful for that.

Then something lurched out of the forest and there was a crash.

The driver switched off the engine and joined Peter and Teo by the roadside, crouching to get a better view.

The deer lay panting on the ground in the headlights, the brains viscous and flapping from the caved-in skull and the steam aspiring into the snowflakes. Not knowing what to do the three men continued to kneel. In front of them the animal bled from its mouth, breathing very heavily, eyes open, alive.

"There's blood in its lung," said Peter. He had a desperate impulse to save it. "We could put it in the back of the truck."

"It's illegal," muttered the driver, his eyes fear-coloured against the trees.

A hoof kicked out, scraped a hieroglyph in the snow.

"You could eat it," suggested Teo.

"No! It's illegal," said the driver. "I should report it to the police."

"Why don't we leave it here?" said Teo.

"We can't leave it," said Peter. As though the deer could understand him, an eye swivelled up and caught him in its glare and then a tongue came out and there was blood and gravel on it.

In his youth, saddled on a borrowed horse, Peter had loved the ride through Leadley's woods. The hoofs on the hill above Wardour. The blaze and crackle of fallen autumn. Then he had brushed the twigs from his eye and galloped towards the hounds' cry. But ever since studying medicine he had lost his appetite for the kill.

The tongue roamed over the nostrils as if it had been drinking. One antler smashed and blood forming in droplets on the velvet and quills of ice pulsating. Peter walked a few steps and turned back. All around was dark and everything was focused on the heavy breathing of the animal and the intense black look of its eye, a shimmering half-dome that gazed up at Peter while the blood continued to bubble from the corner of its mouth.

"Do you think it saw us?" asked the driver.

"I don't know," said Peter. "Why?"

He grunted. "If the deer sees you, the meat's not so good." He returned to his cabin and from under his seat grabbed a large jackhammer that curved back on itself like a snake. "Step aside."

Standing with one foot on either side of the animal's head, he lifted the hammer and took aim. The deer lay there. Head at an angle. Not concerned with the driver, but looking at Peter, who plunged his head in his hands to blot out the sound. A little later, he grew conscious of the driver saying: "Hold the back foot."

They seized the animal by the feet and dragged it over the snow and tossed it into the back of the truck.

"I'll take it to the police," said the executioner. He wrestled his hammer into position under the seat and then climbed up and slammed the door and drove away. Peter followed the sweep of the lights and felt the flakes falling thickly on his cheeks and on his nose, not melting but covering him, subtracting him from the world.

He walked back along the road behind Teo. In quite a short time a car pulled up.

"Where are you going?" asked a young man.

"Back into the city," said Teo.

"Fine, I'll take you."

Teo tried to make light of what they had witnessed. "Do you believe that venison is ruined if the deer sees you? A chicken tastes much better if you chase it round the yard!"

Peter sat in silence, his eyes fixed to the back of the driver who had turned on the radio where a voice sang a sad song of nostalgia and regret and love gone missing.

"Tell me," said Teo after a while, his voice more sombre. "Have you ever in your life heard anything like that noise?"

"No."

"Me neither."

The driver turned up the radio until it drowned out Teo and the sound of an animal's deep wheezing and the thud of a hammer against living bone. He hadn't told her that he loved her.

"I love this song!" exclaimed Teo and started singing along.

The driver nodded his head to the music. Trying to participate in their mood of relief.

Teo turned round. "First girl I kissed was to this tune."

Peter had been trying not to react, but the music pitched him into a devouring temper. He thought, I have met the love of my life and I might never see her again. He was aware of his spine pressing into the seat and his thumbs kneading the black vinyl. The song had red eyes and ran furtively back and forth across his mind that was poised between tears and violence and taut with the effort of containing itself. It was a rat dressed up as a promise and he wanted to take it by the teeth and shake it until it stopped. It was a song that made him feel that his heart had been removed and replaced by a cold glass jar inside which he was aware of something frantic and floundering.

He leaned forward. "Can you turn that fucking thing off?"

CHAPTER FOURTEEN

THEY WENT BACK TO their room to wash off the blood and arrived at the theatre with minutes to spare.

Sepp and Marcus had spent the day as guests of the director on a cultural tour of the city.

"What did you get up to?" asked Marcus, suspicious.

"Later," said Peter, grateful to disappear into his cubicle and pull the curtain and concentrate on nothing more than a panel of switches.

In the final act the 5-kilowatt lamp flashed in a confused way and started to pump like a heartbeat. Expecting the bulb to explode, he turned up the light with extreme care.

On stage, Sepp mimicked a luckless fisherman whose predicament the throbbing light emphasised. He sat in an invisible boat holding his rod and gazed for a long time at his line. When no bite came, he plucked a make-believe paper bag from his pocket, took out an imaginary sandwich and tossed the bag into the water. At that very instant, Marcus scrunched up a sheet of paper and attached it to a wire that Peter began to roll in, the paper ball undulating across the stage as if floating.

All at once Sepp saw a duck and moved to chase it away. Teo, blowing into his tubes, made quacking noises and Marcus imitated with his gong the clap-clap-clap of wings beating on water. Sepp swayed in the boat and the sound of waves slapped against the hull until he was still again. Peter faded the light and a second before the blackout Sepp jerked to his feet in great excitement: A FISH!

Peter kept the stage in darkness a moment longer before raising the faulty footlight. The theatre was full as on both previous nights, but tonight, whether because of the presence of a West German diplomat or because this was the last performance or because everyone in the theatre had shared Peter's relief that the light bulb hadn't popped, the audience leaned forward in a mood of intense concentration. They had watched Sepp doing hardly anything – not giving himself away, not speaking a word – and they understood how appropriate it was to their situation. The mime over, they yearned to communicate their appreciation.

The audience started to clap, but Sepp put a finger to his crinkled lips and flattened his hand. Once the theatre had fallen to a concert hush he opened the cubicle curtain and drew Peter out by the hand and crept offstage, followed by Marcus and Teo. A moment later Sepp led them back and the applause again erupted. Sepp held up his finger and repeated his gesture until the audience calmed down. He stood in the centre of the stage, holding the silence in his hands like a polished cup and then he tiptoed into the wings with his finger on his lips and this time the audience sat in absolute quietness expecting him to return, but he did not.

The reception at the Hotel Astoria was not due to start until 9 p.m., and so on their behalf, before departing the theatre and after packing the dressing-up box, Sepp accepted the director's invitation for a farewell drink in the theatre's crush bar.

The room was crowded with young people, hanging around, waiting to offer congratulations, but also to share ideas. "The Book Fair is the only chance for some of these men and women to meet different people," the director had told Peter in the Tagesbar Bodega. "Maybe the only chance in their whole lives." Sepp's refusal to let them applaud had had the effect of frustrating many in the audience, who now wanted to seek him out and thank him personally.

Peter looked over his shoulder and found Snowleg standing behind him. She was dressed in a silver satin shirt, buttoned at the back and with a high collar, and a black leather miniskirt so short that it wrapped her almost like a belt. She wore dark red lipstick and mascara and seemed five years older. On her head was the Masaryk hat which he had left – with the scarf – in the hut.

"Hello, Peter."

"Snowleg! What are you doing here?"

"Well, you invited me."

"I thought you hated theatre."

"I'm here to see you."

He tried to smile. "There was nothing to see. I was hidden behind a curtain."

She tugged on her miniskirt. "I thought you'd be pleased."

"I am." He lifted his eyes to the hat she was wearing, Anita's hat. "I am." But he didn't know what had come over him.

"When do you leave?"

"Tonight. Listen, I didn't have time to telephone my mother."

"Your mother?" She had forgotten.

He went to get her a drink and when he came back she was talking to the young woman with marmalade hair.

"I saw you last night," the woman said to Peter. "I have a photographic memory for faces. I'm Renate, by the way."

At that moment Teo came up. Soon Teo and Renate were absorbed in conversation.

Snowleg sipped at her beer. Nervous sips, like at the wine bar. Steeling herself to do something. "I thought you'd think I wasn't interested if I couldn't cancel my plans." She spoke in broken pleasantries as if someone might be listening. "What I had to do tonight – I got out of it easily enough."

"What did you have to do?"

"It doesn't matter." Then: "It's Stefan's birthday."

"Shouldn't you be celebrating with him?"

"I'd rather be here." She looked at him in a strange way. "Maybe if you really want something you can make it happen."

"Your grandmother?" But he knew that what he said, the awkwardness of his expression, wasn't reflected in his heart.

She resumed, colouring. "I was thinking of Bruno." Then in a move so unexpected that it punched away his breath she put her arms around him. She spoke urgently into his ear: "Look, I'm coming back with you. I want to go in your dressing-up box. I will fold myself so small you won't notice me. I can't spend one more night in this country." Her embrace relaxing. "Ah, Renate . . ."

"Wait here," said Peter, taking her empty glass. He pushed his way to the bar, trying to master his confusion, the dispute in his head. That morning she had left him feeling frightened and short of confidence, but dwelling on her as if she had planted in him some question vital to his well-being. All day, he had tried to put himself in a state of not wanting. Now he heard his heart hammering in his ear, *She wants to come home with me, she wants to come home with me.*

He paid for the beer and threaded his way back to Snowleg. Renate had vanished and she stood facing him and he thought, *She's so attractive.* Her greenish voluptuous eyes filled the room and she was staring at him as she had at Bruno's party, aware of his desire.

He didn't understand his emotions. A minute before he had felt panicky. Now he felt bold, noble, until it wasn't Peter who stood before her, but Sir Bedevere. He handed Snowleg her glass and his look kindled something in her eyes. *Why not take her home? She's in distress. Of course, I must help her.*

He led her to the little back room and opened the wickerwork trunk. He chucked the contents onto the floor. Marcus's gong. Sepp's clothes. The faulty footlight. He was hatching the plan as he went along. "Listen, they're about to take this to the station. Our train leaves at one in the morning." He kept back the green curtain and wrapped it around her shoulder, hugging her passionately. *They hadn't searched the trunk when he crossed the border. Why would they search it on the way out?* "Get in."

Snowleg was about to step inside when a voice stopped her.

"Aha!" Teo's eyes lingered on her. "*Here* you are. There's a very delightful reason for your delay, Peter. But we're late. We must go." He said to Snowleg, "Sorry to take this man away, but he has to be somewhere else."

"Where are the others?" asked Peter.

"Already left. Come on."

Just then Renate appeared. A beer bottle in each hand. "Hey, trying on clothes?"

"I was packing up," said Peter, taking the curtain from Snowleg and throwing it into the basket.

"Where you going?" Renate said.

"Only to some party," Teo said.

118

"We could come with you."

"You don't really want to come," Teo said. "It's just an official reception. It's actually going to be fucking dull."

Snowleg touched Peter's arm. "I'll go with you."

"Yes, why don't we all go?" Renate said.

There was an awkward pause. Peter looked at Teo. "What do you think? Would they be allowed?"

Teo said in a much sobered voice, "Can I take you to one side?" And when they had moved into the corridor: "This is not on, Peter. We can't do this. Do we or do we not wish to spend our lives in an institution in this godforsaken country?"

"You're not going without us?" Snowleg said, coming into the corridor.

"Listen, you two girls," Teo said. "Peter and I are going to this party because, like it or lump it, we're official guests."

Peter looked at Snowleg. "I'd love you to come."

It was snowing hard. The four of them piled into a taxi and rubbed hands and shivered.

"Watch out!" called Renate as they nearly ran into a van with a fish painted on it.

On the radio a woman's voice sang, "Komm, gib mir dein Herz." Renate giggled and Teo listened in a morose way as she talked some more and Snowleg, sitting next to him, gazed at Peter with the expression of someone who had woken up in an enormous hurry to the reality of life. If she looked expectant, wasn't it because he had given her reason to be? "I'll put you in after the reception," he had whispered as they left the theatre. "It'll be there on the platform. You'll have to move like lightning."

"What's that smell?" Teo lifted Renate's arm and sniffed her wrist. "No." He gave Snowleg a hysterical look. "Nice perfume."

"It's French," she blushed.

Peter hadn't noticed her scent before. Suddenly it clung to everything in the car.

Teo leaned forward. He whispered: "Were you going to smuggle that girl in the basket?"

"Yes."

"Don't do it, Peter. This isn't part of the game."

"Fuck off," said Peter.

But Teo ignored him. "This is unbelievably stupid. You really don't want to spend the next 14 years mixing cement and chopping it up and mixing it again."

Teo sat back and Snowleg smiled at them, wanting to explain something. "My grandmother made me buy it. The only scent I had was Polish. 'You can't wear that!' she told me. 'It really is awful.' So she gave me 100 Marks to buy a French perfume."

But the smell made Peter queasy. Everything that had been proof of Snowleg's naturalness and lack of affectation suddenly seemed indicative of a sophistication that didn't sit well with her. That reminded Peter suffocatingly of his mother.

You can make a life in a night. He took his tie from his pocket and started tying it, struggling to lose the voice of his mother in his head.

How in God's name had he got himself into this position? In a heated moment he had made an impossibly romantic promise and Snowleg had called him on it. He lifted his chin and noosed St Cross's mauve and green diagonals around his neck. He noticed her chipped tooth and heard the slushiness on her words, the rough Saxon accent, and experienced a flicker of revulsion. She's no different from Renate. He tried to stop himself, but couldn't. He pulled out one black thought and there was another one clinging to it. Why has she dressed like that? Why did I invite her to this reception? Why did I tell her to meet us afterwards at the station? And he spattered her with his black thoughts until she was no longer visible.

Hungry for Teo's attention, Renate took his hand and pressed it against her cheek. Snowleg turned to Peter and said in a lowered voice, "I didn't know which one to buy so I went to this café in Neumarkt. It's a place where artists go for lunch. A teacher from the graphics college was there. I asked him to come with me to Exquisit and pick a perfume. He chose this."

She kept her eyes on Peter's face for some sign that he liked it. That he did mean to fold her away in his dressing-up box. But she saw in his face that she had read it wrong. And then she must have caught sight of herself as she leaned over. She tapped his knee and instead of saying something she burst into song and he suspected she had just observed a flash of Stefan in the mirror and had seen that she looked exactly like Stefan at her brother's party and that it was the look of a sad and hungry animal. "You can be cruel without trying . . ."

He didn't hear the rest of the words. Only the roar of his own panic. *She's upset, she's needy, and I've agreed to take her out of the country.*

The Astoria was cordoned off, but a policeman waved through the taxi. It set them down beneath a long brown metal canopy that extended from the hotel entrance into the freezing night.

A doorman stood in front of a sliding glass door and with keen eyes followed their progress towards him. He was slimly built, in a highwayman's jacket filthy with gold braid.

Peter stepped ahead, already separating himself from Snowleg. "We're with the Hansen party."

The doorman pressed a white glove against the peak of his cap. "Sorry, sir, they can't come in."

Snowleg caught up. Took his arm.

"You can't go in." The doorman addressed her, speaking in a strong way. Like a security guard.

"But she's my guest," said Peter.

"I'm sorry, sir. It's invitation only."

"Leave this to me," said Renate, in a voice that made the doorman turn his head.

Peter felt Teo's hand on his shoulder and they were through.

Once inside the lobby, Teo exploded. "You're mad! You're off your trolley. You really thought you could smuggle her out? Can't you see what would have happened? We'd have been torn to shreds at the frontier. She'd have been hauled out onto a freezing platform at two in the morning and we'd all have been locked up. We've only got about three hours left in this country. For God's sake, don't spoil it, Peter."

"*There* you are!"

Sepp gesticulated from the end of a corridor hung with jellyfish lights. He was standing beside a nervous-looking man who was dressed in a well-cut suit. He still had make-up on.

"Where have you *been*, for Christ's sake? Poor Herr Wettiner here is starting to lose his rag." Sepp steered Peter away before he could explain. "Someone's about to give not the first but the third toast. Get into that blasted room in a hurry."

Peter gave a last look round. Outside, Renate was talking to the doorman and the doorman was listening. He couldn't see Snowleg.

The banqueting room lay at the rear of the building. Czech chandeliers and gilt-framed oil paintings and at intervals, positioned along the middle of it, square white pillars edged in gold. Against the far wall and separated from the rest of the room by a worn curtain patterned with tropical flowers stretched a long oval table.

Sepp had failed to impress on Peter that the reception was not in fact a cocktail party but a formal dinner. About thirty people sat around the table. Peter was introduced too quickly to remember who they were. He recognised the author from the Book Fair and a children's publisher who had paid for their train tickets. The remainder were diplomats and businessmen visiting the Trade Fair. They shook his hand and half rose from their seats before resuming their conversations.

Peter was seated next to the Permanent Representative's wife, a bulbous white-haired woman in a sturdy jade dress with leg-of-mutton sleeves. She opened her mouth as soon as she learned who he was and filled it quickly with polite conversation, from time to time rearranging crumbs on the white cloth.

"What a marvellous performance," she began. "You're so clever."

He had been concerned about Snowleg when he sat down, but the praise of this smartly dressed woman much older than himself overtook him. She asked about his plans after university and whether he intended to go on working with actors, and when he told her that he was hoping to specialise in paediatrics she confessed that she too despised the theatre and how wonderful that he was going to be a paediatrician because people who helped children, in her experience, led the most rewarding lives. He let her words flow over him, allowing himself to be impressed by her house in the wine-growing region of Bavaria, a library he was welcome to visit any time, a river – did he like fishing? – and even their official residence in Hannoversche Straße where she and her husband – "that's right, the lugubrious gentleman at the end" – entertained visitors to East Berlin.

The waiters had started to clear away the soup plates and the white-haired lady was talking about her husband's last post, in Africa, when he became aware of a scuffle behind him.

He turned in his chair. In the corner, by the door, the doorman struggled with a young woman. Snowleg. He felt a contraction in his gut.

Everyone stared. In the bright chandelier light, her leather skirt looked cheap, her make-up garish, her top like a fake Japanese blouse. Peter saw the shadow of her necklace through the silver satin and he shrank back in his seat, clenching against the lipstick, the clothes, the new effect. In that moment, everything changed.

"Oh dear me, how very awkward," murmured the Permanent Representative's wife. It was apparent to her and to everyone in the room: this was a girl of the Leipzig streets.

Gripped from behind by the doorman, Snowleg looked up. Her frightened eyes located Peter and she pointed. "That's him."

The doorman, still holding her arm, thrust her forward and thirty faces – intrigued, shocked, amused – exchanged rapid glances. Together the couple walked towards the table as the guests sawed at their pork with their Potsdam cutlery and cast their eyes at the tablecloth, the wineglasses, the peculiar flowers on the curtain, the carpet.

The doorman moved her step by step down the length of the table until she stood opposite Peter. "Sir, this young lady says you invited her to dinner. Is she with you?"

His tone outside had been trenchant, but now he asked his question in a more reticent voice. Almost, in fact, as though he hoped that Peter would say "Yes".

Peter heard the rustling quiet of the room. The people faded away and Snowleg looked directly at him, her large eyes imploring. Now she would be vindicated. Now he would rise to his feet.

Now he would take one of the inlaid chairs from the wall behind and say: "Yes, I invited her. How wonderful to see you. Please, sit down."

She waited for the answering gleam, but he stared back at her with a terrified glaze in his eye.

"No."

A single syllable and yet as soon as he uttered it he had a terrible clairvoyance that he had become someone else.

Snowleg received the news with a look he would never forget. And then all expression fled from her face and disappeared, leaving her eyes dead, as if they had fallen into a hole.

"Thank you, sir," said the doorman in a quiet, disappointed voice.

She stood for a moment, cradling her silence, and he was reminded of Sepp on stage at the end of the mime. It was the silence of someone betrayed and as the doorman began to pull her away it resonated in the room.

He regretted his answer immediately. With horrible detachment, he was released into seeing her beauty again. Something in the line of her back seemed straighter than before and the word "dignity" came to his mind and stayed there. What tortured him was that he could see himself getting up and running after her and it was a surprise to discover that he was still sitting there as though immersed in water. He couldn't feel himself, nor the air on his skin. He was seeing Snowleg as he saw her at the beginning, in church, at varying levels of depth.

"I think there must be some mistake, some mistake . . ." He broke through the surface and she was gone and the woman's hand on his was not hers, but that of the Permanent Representative's wife.

"Don't worry yourself. In Africa, we always had these people."

Around him everyone started talking at once, but nothing was the same. His lips felt seared. The air was misshapen, unbreathable. He had flunked. And you can't do that if you're a perfect, gentle English/German knight. You simply can't. Someone at the table winked at him, another gave him a ruthless look. Teo leaned over and patted his shoulder and said something, but all he could hear was the shouting in his blood, the receding gallop of hoofs, of the visored figure he had once dreamed of being, in clinking armour, who tilted through a forest clearing to pluck maidens from the scaly clutch of dragons. He scraped back his chair and made to rise, but remained anchored to the spot.

CHAPTER FIFTEEN

"HOW WAS LEIPZIG?" IN Hamburg the following night, Anita sat beside him on his sofa. "Did you find out about your father?"

"No."

"What happened to the hat and scarf I gave you?"

"I lost them."

"Both?" staring down at her lap. Stricken, she began to separate the Polaroids. Grinning in a crowded church. Holding a dense bouquet of tiny white flowers. Trying on the veil.

Peter moved to embrace her. To assure her that his affections had in no way altered. But he had left behind more than a woollen hat and scarf. He had come back from Leipzig smitten in all directions. So in love, so muddled, so guilty that when Anita arched her back for him to unzip her dress, he felt like a creature asleep in formaldehyde. His features frozen in the reflex of his cowardice.

"Peter, I'm waiting."

But he was still dreaming, dreaming of Snowleg. The thought of what he had done to her ripped into him. It had been there when he ran onto the platform at Leipzig's Main Station, and it didn't abandon him when the guard, noting the trickle from his eyes, said: "Yes, it's very hard to leave this beautiful country."

At the end of the platform had stood three policemen in jodhpurs and jackboots and a furious-looking man with an Alsatian. Peter recognised him from outside the Thomaskirche. His dog was sniffing in an excited way at the corner of the wickerwork trunk. The man unholstered his pistol, his antagonism fuming up with his dog's breath. He pressed the barrel to the lid.

"Do you want me to open it?" said Peter.

The man looked at him with a smile that was almost pleased. "No need. I'll just put three shots through the middle. Just to be sure."

Peter was surprised that the trunk should be quite so heavy, but all was explained in Hamburg.

"What the fuck is that?" cried Marcus. Into the space where should have been Snowleg was coiled a thick black painted rope.

It horrified Peter to think that the rope had been put there by people to whom Snowleg had talked about him. More unbearable was the idea that because of his cowardice she could have fallen into their hands. How differently his mother had behaved. She had stuck by his flesh-and-blood father and shown an unhesitating courage. Against her gallantry and prodigality, her reckless openness to adventure, what had been Peter's reaction when fate took him by the arm and asked to know the sort of person he was?

His denial of Snowleg in the Hotel Astoria was the moment that defined Peter to himself. He knew now who he was. A *Duckmäuser*. Someone who kept their head down. Someone who said: "I know thee not."

At 11 a.m. the following Wednesday he wrote Snowleg a note on a postcard he had bought in Hamburg zoo. "How will you ever forgive me?" In a PS he added that the giraffe on the back reminded him of her. He addressed it to "Snjólaug" at the faculty of psychiatry at Karl-Marx-University. On Friday, he telephoned the faculty to find out if she had been awarded her place. He telephoned the following day and the day after that. Nobody picked up.

He was still writing letters six weeks later. In May he sent four of his favourite novels as well as an edition of Malory. He had no way of knowing if she had received the parcel, or whether she was choosing to ignore him.

One night Anita said: "Why do you do that?"

"What?"

"Shut your eyes."

"Do I?" opening them at once. "I didn't realise."

"Maybe it's English," with a buckled-up look. The women shaved under their arms while the men made love with their eyes closed. "It's just that you've never done it before."

A fortnight later he telephoned Karl-Marx-University and this time someone answered.

He spelled out the letters.

"Snjólaug?" repeated a bureaucratic voice.

"It's her nickname," said Peter. "Somebody in the department might recognise it."

"We require a surname," acidly.

Her silence reproached him. He waited in vain for a letter from Leipzig, a call. He hardly dared to leave his building. Fearful that the payphone in the hall would start ringing, Snowleg at the other end.

Sleep was his only refuge from her silence. He couldn't bear to wake because that was to be him again. He longed for the morning when he opened his eyes and didn't think, immediately, of Snowleg.

Each time he thought of her, currents of fear shot through him. In his obscure distress, he kept asking himself: Did she get into trouble that night? Would she forgive him? Had the university accepted her?

On good days he was able to persuade himself that his denial was unimportant. No-one had overheard her speak to him in the Rudolph Theatre. No-one knew of her intention to escape. She would be safe.

To get the guilt out of his head, his shocking behaviour, he tried to console himself. He wasn't the first person to have acted like this. He had done what any young man might have done in similar circumstances. Snowleg would have known the score. She might have been angry for a moment, but then she would have forgotten the incident. It was nugatory, the sin he had committed. Chances were she had folded him away and didn't think of him, not at all. Sometimes it's like that, he told himself. Those who are offended against forget everything while those who offend remember for the rest of their lives.

On bad days, he thought of himself as the boy on the bicycle who had reported his father in Dorna. In his mind he had murdered her. And in a way he did murder her by offering up a flawed version of that night.

In June, without telling Anita or warning his family, he returned to England for a school reunion. It was the first time he had been home since going to live in Germany. At the end of the meal – in a downstairs room of the Garrick – the old boys sat around and paraded their most embarrassing moments in the six years since they had met, before becoming bankers, lawyers, journalists.

Leadley told an unlikely story of how he had appeared in his underpants on a balcony of the British Residence in Paris and had been mistaken by a crowd below for President Nixon.

Tweed revealed that he had caught the clap off the sister of a friend at Cambridge who was an earl.

"What about you, Hithers?" said someone. "Fucked any strippers on the Reeperbahn?"

"Actually, I did meet a girl," Peter replied, fuelled by calvados and laughter and an unanticipated desire to belong. "But not in Hamburg."

They turned their heads to hear.

Sometimes you retell a story in order to reshape it morally and digest it. That night, as anyone does to quell something dreadful, Peter tried to refine and smooth his experience with Snowleg into a version he could live with. Even as he shaped it for himself, he wondered if he need include every detail. Much as his mother might have done, he started to offer up a drained account. One that thereafter became his account. In which Snowleg was converted into a girl whom he had met for the first time at the crush bar following the final performance. A person he barely knew. Who just wanted to come to his party.

Peter finished speaking and to his ears the silence was like the silence in a room where a hornet has settled and no-one knows where.

"Oh, that's not so bad," said someone.

"No, I know, but it was pretty bad at the time."

"So was she or wasn't she a prostitute?" asked Tweed.

Peter smiled enigmatically.

It was Leadley who rescued him, a bully's sad look in his small brown eyes. "Aren't they all?"

He flew back to Hamburg and retreated behind his door.

Anita left notes. She knocked and he heard her sighing on the other side. The more he ignored her, the more frequently she called at Feldstraße until one afternoon, returning from a lecture, he found her sitting in a heap on the landing.

"Teo let me in." She scanned his face like a dog who has seen its master's suitcase. "Why don't you answer my messages?"

"I haven't been here."

"What's the problem? Tell me." She wanted it spelled out. A reason. Was it something she had said or done? "I didn't grow an extra head while you were in Leipzig. What happened? Did you meet someone? Be honest."

He struggled with the urge to blurt it out, but it was too late to tell. "OK, you want me to be honest. Right." He plunged his hand through his hair. "I need space."

"I thought you loved me." Not wanting to be excluded by them, she couldn't bear to look into his eyes.

"I do, but I'm not in love with you."

She looked at him and burst into tears. "That's so awful! Listen, please don't make any decisions about us. I can give you space if that's what you want."

"I don't want . . . That's not what I mean," in the soughing voice of a man no longer in love.

She bumped into him two days later. He was sitting in a bar with a student nurse from UKE. He pretended not to see Anita. Her vulnerable, pale face. Her swollen eyes. They exchanged glances, but when he looked for her again she was gone. He continued his small talk, deep down hating Anita for her obvious suffering, and in the morning wrote her a letter. "I can't make any promises to you and it would be wrong of me to lead you on. But I don't see a future."

When his door was taken off its hinges, he assumed it was Anita's brothers.

In August, he moved into digs in Haynstraße. He stopped playing in Teo's football team and strenuously avoided the two other members of Pantomimosa. All his chivalrous intentions having failed, he swore fealty to medicine and threw himself into his clinical studies. Trying to work so hard that it didn't hurt any more.

One term passed like this. Then another. Until, in his final year as an undergraduate, his sister came to stay.

———

Rosalind had finished catering college that summer. To celebrate, he invited her to Germany.

"I'll meet you in Berlin," she said. She had a hankering to peer over the Wall.

On a cold July morning he examined the passengers emerging into Tegel airport. He hadn't seen her for six years, not since she had waved him off on his way to Hamburg.

"Bedevere!"

The voice he recognised, but not the face. Puffier, with her father's deep-set eyes, and framed by thick crinkly hair that reunited in the cleavage of a yellowish Laura Ashley dress. He was surprised at how small she was. The whiteness of her skin. How very English she looked as she took stock of him.

"Rosalind," he said with formality.

On their first morning together they went to a Turkish restaurant in Charlottenburg. She asked him to explain the menu, and after he had done so said with a stern expression: "Everyone sends their love."

"How are they?"

"Mum wants to know if you got her last care package?"

"Of course I did." A CD of Beethoven's *Missa Solemnis* with another of her letters: "Ros gave it to me for Christmas, but I've already got it. I'm sure you'll love it. Do write from time to time. I don't mind your being gone five months, but you've been gone six years. Is there any prospect of my becoming a grandmother? Because as far as we can tell Rosalind is not going to help us out. Perhaps you have some friends she can come and meet . . ."

"You might drop her a line," said Ros. "She might not take it from me that you're still alive."

"And Dad?"

"Dad's not so good, you know. Mum's driving him mad with her music. Although he sends her bonkers in other ways."

"Oh?"

"He's had this friend staying from Morocco."

"Not Silkleigh?"

She laughed. Her father's sad little laugh. "He comes and goes, promising to repair Daddy's finances with his schemes, but so far not a sausage."

"I thought he was writing a book."

"Oh, that's firmly on the back burner until, so he says, he gets the right title. He went clean off the last one! No, his great ambition at the moment is to open a restaurant in Abyla – that's in Morocco. I have a suspicion he wants yours truly to advise him, but so far he's only invited me snorkelling. I have to say, he's a pretty good riot. You should see him trying to get Mum to do a duet. He took me aside after the last row they had and whispered: 'Your mother wasn't born, darling, she was *quarried*.'"

But Peter didn't want to hear about Silkleigh. "What about you, Ros?"

"Oh, I'm doing fine."

"No boyfriend?"

"No boyfriend," and asked quickly: "How long are you planning to stay in Germany?"

"I've no idea."

"Surely you want to come home?" She didn't conceal her irritation that as far as she was concerned her brother had gone chasing after Germany, or rather his misconceived idea of it, in the same embarrassing manner as once he had pursued her girlfriends. "Mummy hasn't said anything, but now Grandpa's died I'm sure she's hoping, well, you know, that you'll come to your senses."

"Which means?"

"Be a doctor in England, for God's sake."

"No, I can't, not yet. I'm stuck. I can't go on living this life indefinitely, but I am going to qualify first."

"Peter, do you know what you're doing to our parents by not being there, not visiting? Grandpa was so proud of you and you didn't even come for his funeral."

"I'm sorry, Ros. I didn't have the money. But I have promised to visit when I finish my exams."

She wasn't to be parried. "You don't have to apologise to me. All I want to understand is, why are you here and why are you so unhappy? There has to be a reason. You're my brother. What are you running away from? Was it something at school I don't know about? I saw Tristram the other day and he said that after your birthday you were never the same again." She gave him a merry look. "By the way, Tristram's fallen head over heels for Camilla."

"Ros, I'm not running away from England."

"So if you're not running away, what else is keeping you? It's perfectly ghastly here. Humourless and ghastly. As for the food . . ."

"I'm not here for the food."

"Listen. Something clearly isn't working in your life. Is being here making any difference?" Then: "Don't tell me you're still looking for your father?"

"If you like." He hadn't talked to anyone about it, and with that extra level of loneliness which her being there had emphasised, he revealed to his sister the story of his frustrated visit to Dorna two years before. "I managed to get to see the village where Mummy met him. But it wasn't enough. I couldn't find his name. Incidentally, you can say to your mother that if there's anything she can do to find a name or date . . ." But even as he asked, he knew that his mother had told him everything she was going to tell him, and was even more stung into regret.

He went on: "You can't imagine how fantastically difficult it is. In England, you just go to the local council and ask. Not over there. Even if I did come across him or his relatives, there was no way I would have recognised them. I couldn't go wandering around saying, 'Excuse me, do I remind you of anyone?' Anyway, the village was completely demolished in my memory by the journey back. I can still hear the deer being killed. It was terrible, Ros."

But she knew him too well. She wasn't satisfied that his unhappiness could be laid all at the feet of his German father. "There's something else, isn't there?"

"Maybe you're right."

Beaming like a midwife, Rosalind said: "Is it a woman?"

He went quiet.

"Peter, I know that expression. I almost wish we were in Hamburg because I'd like to see who you're sleeping with. What happened to Anita? Still seeing her?"

"No, we had a slight falling out. In fact, I'm completely off girls, partly because I'm working so hard and partly because, since you ask, I did lose my heart."

"Where was this?"

"In Leipzig."

"Come on, we're all grown up."

"We spent the night together. We only had one night, but I haven't been able to get over it. I did this appalling thing. I panicked in a way . . . a way I can hardly bring myself to describe."

"Tell me."

He needed a fresh packet of West Lights to do so.

Afterwards she said, "Have you heard from her?"

"Not a word. I've written letter after letter. But she's a young woman," he said brokenly. "She probably does it with all sorts of people, all sorts of stage managers."

"Steady on. She must have been pretty taken with you to barge into the hotel like that."

"I dare say it was a mixture of love and fear, but the truth is it can't possibly be explained by love."

"And why the fuck not, my liege?"

"Because if you boil it down all we had was two cigarettes and a glass of vodka. She saw me as a ticket out of the country."

"Peter," her cheeks bulging with bread, "you understand absolutely nothing about attraction. Can I know her name?"

"Snowleg."

"Snowleg! Doesn't even sound German."

"No, it's not a name. It's her grandmother's pet name for her."

Rosalind could not believe that he had fallen for a young woman without a name. "That's frankly a little bit dim. Even by my big brother's standards."

Next morning he took her to the Wall. She stood at Checkpoint Charlie and stared in horror across the border. "My God, Peter, how can they do this to each other? The same people!"

"I know," and went on looking at the Wall. Picturing a blackened rope. Caught between worry and hope and his utter relief that the Wall was there.

Over a beer, he found himself returning to the subject of Snowleg. "Why did I say I didn't know her, Ros? Why?" Abject, he had no answer.

His sister put her cigarette out in the empty bottle. "You're acting as though there was a reason. And perhaps there isn't an explanation. People do inexplicable things." And tried to suppress the irritation that was entering her voice. "Look, we all mess up. It's human. It's hard work being anyone. You've got to let go of this fantasy that you've made a terrific impact on this person's life. Maybe for you it was a moment of extreme significance and you've been stuck in it. But maybe for her it was just one milli-moment in a myriad stream of moments. Maybe if she were sitting where I'm sitting she'd say to you: 'Yes, I was betrayed and the course of my life shifted, but it was much more altered by things that happened later.' Maybe she'd tell you that she's forgiven you long ago. That you didn't do to her anything that her country hasn't done to her all along and without apology. Think of the Wall, for God's sake. I still can't get it out of my head."

Not that the Wall could eliminate Snowleg. He had tried to stamp out the memory of her like a plant between the pages of a heavy book he had returned to the shelf, but she lay in him dormant and unexploded. Ever since he had got back from Leipzig, he felt stuck in a perpetual dusk at the hour of his denial, snow falling and a cold dread in his heart. He wanted nothing more than to love someone. It never happened. He couldn't admit to his sister that he had completely lost the appetite for loving anyone.

Once or twice in the months following Rosalind's visit Snowleg stole into his mind when he wasn't paying attention. On one occa-sion he saw her on the platform at Blankenese, her trim waist in a cherry dress and her breasts up-tilted. But the woman he startled was Italian. Another time she sat in bright clothes on a bench overlooking the Alster, face absorbed in a gardening magazine. She only looked back in a painting. The Easter before his final exams, he visited the Kunsthistorische Museum in Vienna and was taken aback to see Snowleg in a portrait of a young woman by Bellini. Looking back and feeling sorry for him.

Sometimes he felt a moment of calm as if someone a long way off was thinking kindly of him. Sometimes he felt a moment of terror as if the opposite were true. But these moments came less and less until, by the time he entered the examination room at the end of six years of medical school, he had managed to persuade himself that he had, as his mother would have wanted, put the past behind him.

One week after he completed his Staatsexamen, Peter flew back to England to honour the promise he had made to his parents. By the time he boarded the train at Waterloo, he had made a decision to draw a line under Snowleg. He was not going to spend the rest of his life whimpering "If only". He was not going to die aged ninety-five like his grandfather without having engaged himself. His sexual antennae were telling him to take a break, get on with it. Expecting shortly to qualify as a doctor, he determined henceforth to avoid thinking about Snowleg, about East Germany. Whatever had happened there had had the effect of depoliticising him. His action had tainted that place and he wanted nothing more than to turn his back on it. Not wanting to be reminded of what he had done, he would try to forget it like a sin.

PART III

England, Hamburg, Berlin
1986–96

CHAPTER SIXTEEN

"PETER!"

His mother sat on the piano stool, caught by surprise. Meringues of uncombed white hair and a blue tracksuit dusted to the knees with pollen. And an animal that sprang across the carpet, barking. His dog.

"Honey!" She leaped up and grabbed Honey by the collar and he remembered his grandfather's words. *With dogs, dear boy, you get what you put in.*

"Mum."

They kissed. His mother all face-cream and blushes. "I heard the door slam and I thought, That's Peter."

"And it was."

"Why didn't you telephone? We were expecting you tomorrow." But she wanted to look at him more than she wanted to know the answer. "How long can you stay?"

"A week," giving Honey a cursory scratch under the chin. "If that's all right?"

"Stupid boy." And she meant it.

He found Rodney seated on a scroll-back chair among his photographic chemicals and open bottles of black ink.

"Peter!" and threw down the card he was sketching. *Captain and Mrs Rickards request the pleasure of your company at the marriage of their daughter Camilla to the Hon. Tristram Leadley.*

"Dad," wondering why he felt nothing and thinking they'll name their children Annabelle, Horace and Lavinia. "How are you?"

"Well, well." But the lump on his neck had grown and his skin had taken on the brownish tint of his developing fluid.

"I hope you're seeing someone about that?"

"Don't worry." Rodney had always treated his infirmity with jovial tolerance. "I'm in good hands."

"Where's Ros?"

"She's living in Grandpa's flat. Until she finds her legs."

Seven years Peter had been in Germany and for a split second he took Rodney's words literally. "Her legs? Something's happened to her?"

Rodney smiled. "She's using the flat for her catering business. Your mother didn't think you'd mind."

"Mind? Why should I mind?"

"Well, it's yours as much as it is hers."

Twenty minutes later a red Mini braked in a bow-wave of white gravel, his sister waving through the open window.

"Why didn't you tell us, you horror? I'd have cooked something special," running to embrace him. Still frizzy-haired, still puffy-faced. Still wanting to play Scrabble after dinner.

That night, with a professional air, Rosalind drew out seven tiles from the bag, originally a felt pouch for Rodney's watercolours.

"You start." But it was her only concession. After a particularly long interval, she warned: "We'll have to set a time limit."

Peter studied the board. There was an open G. He rearranged his letters. Then stared, chest thumping. Using his blank, he could spell SNOWLEG.

"One minute more," warned Rosalind.

"What about this?" And lined up three tiles on the board.

"SLOG." Rosalind enunciated the word with the seasoned Scrabble-player's look of avarice. "What a waste of an S." Then: "Daddy says you're forgetting your English. Is it true?"

On Sunday it was hot enough to sit outside. He lay on the lawn reading the *Observer*. The news seemed parochial, the pages full of people he didn't know. He thought, I've come back to what I knew as my childhood home and I feel like a spy. He reflected on what would have happened if he had never walked up Revelation Hill. By now he would be a journalist or a publisher.

"Darling?" His mother walked towards him holding a cardboard box. "Can I tempt you with this?"

What was she up to now? Despite his long absence, he still felt her neediness. The massive biological engine of her claim on him. Ever since his sixteenth birthday, since, in fact, she gave him Honey (on the advice of her doctor who said a pet might be good for him), he had shrunk from her presents.

She knelt on the sun-warmed grass. Curled inside the box was an ill-looking puppy, the runt of Honey's litter.

"It looks like conjunctivitis. I've washed the eyes in cold tea, but not a lot's happening." So much dried mucus – greeny-grey and growing yellow – had leaked into their corners that the eyes had cemented together.

He had already rejected Honey. Not once on this visit had he taken his dog for a walk. "I don't think so, Mummy." But went on studying the puppy asleep in her arms, wheezing in small noises, its eyes flickering under the gummed lids. He reached out a finger and peeled off the sealing crust. "I really don't think so."

In the morning, a call from UKE. "You've passed Go," said his registrar. "Eleventh on the roll!"

He ran to find his mother, who was busy hanging out what Rosalind joked was seven years of washing on the clothes line. "I've qualified."

"Oh, Peter."

She hugged him. Eyes watering. "I just wish . . ." And shook her head. "Grandpa would have been so proud."

"About the puppy," he went on.

His change of heart gave his mother a flash of hope that he would decide to stay after all. Become a country doctor like her father. But the dog, intended to keep him in England, became his excuse to keep away.

CHAPTER SEVENTEEN

IN THE SUMMER OF 1986, at the age of twenty-five, Peter returned to Hamburg to specialise in paediatrics, his daily renewed determination to become what his German father had wanted to be.

He lived in Eppendorf, in a second-floor apartment sublet from a stammering obstetrician at UKE. A bedroom, a small kitchen unchanged since the 1950s, and four steps up to a living room with a low ceiling, two windows and a bar-fire. "My old p-p-p-layroom," said his landlord, who blamed his impediment on the fact that his parents had quarrelled in front of him as a child.

In the evenings he boiled water in a frying pan, splashed in a little white vinegar and watched as the egg poached into a perfect rubbery planet. As Rosalind had taught him.

And in the morning trod the goat path between his front door and the department of paediatrics. His mind on his work. Burying Snowleg beneath a procession of sick children and fluorescent corridors and long hours. Bolstered by his English talent for appearing to sweep anything very serious under the carpet. And Gus, whom he walked twice a day in the botanical gardens where he met other dog-owners and talked to them about their children's snotty noses and the cold weather they were having. So extreme that he could hear the bark cracking in the arboretum.

The great scare of paediatrics was that children fell sick very quickly. The great attraction: most recovered just as fast.

The bread and butter of his work was asthmas, rashes, fevers of unknown origin. He learned that dealing with children was all about distraction, getting down to their level and not frightening them. It relieved him not to have to wear a white coat like residents in other specialities. He went on his ward round with a teddy bear tied to his stethoscope and his pockets full of sugar-free lollipops and stickers to put on plaster casts with mottos like "I had an X-ray and survived."

One on one with a child, Peter loved it, but paediatrics was also about treating the parents. In many cases they were the most difficult part of the equation. As a neophyte physician he did not always understand how traumatic it was for them, especially when they sensed his tentativeness.

His strongest memory of his first year's residency was of a patient in the urology ward. The boy was in urinary retention and his bladder was full and his urethra too traumatised to accept a catheter.

"You look rather junior to be doing this," said the boy's mother. "Are you a qualified paediatrician?"

"No."

"Which year are you?"

"First."

"How many times have you done this?"

"Oh, I've done many."

"How many have you missed?"

"That depends."

"I'm sorry. I want the most senior person touching my child."

"Listen," he said gently, "I will use my judgment and if I'm not confident I will get someone more senior."

This time he came up over the pubic bone, put the needle through the stomach wall and anchored the catheter to the bladder.

Later his registrar congratulated him, adding: "You may make a professional judgment that this is beyond your limit, but you must never panic."

It was work like this that led him to Bettina Grau.

A few months before he met Bettina, Peter had a conversation in the canteen with a second-year resident called Draxler.

"You seem a bit worn out, Peter."

"I'm absolutely wiped out."

Draxler looked up. Like all people in paediatrics, he was a short person, and Peter towered over him. "Well, we're all worn out practically the whole time. Did you ever try fentanyl?"

"No, I never did."

"Try it," said Draxler.

One January afternoon, a 3-year-old boy came in for a hernia operation. Peter asked the ward sister for an ampoule of fentanyl and signed it out. But upon examining the boy after the operation, he decided that he would better benefit from a simple pain reliever, and inserted a suppository of Panadol. He slipped the unused ampoule into his lab coat and forgot about it until 2 a.m. when he was looking for a Biro. He rolled the capsule in his palm. By now – his seventh month of residency – he was barely sleeping four hours a night. Working so late that he was unable to sleep, unable to keep awake. As if he had lost his punctuation.

He locked himself in the toilet, snapped the curved top, filled a syringe and injected himself between the toes. The effect was rapid and lasted an hour.

Fentanyl became the string that led him out of the labyrinth – the wilderness of hospital passageways, the heart-sagging physical and emotional exhaustion of paediatrics – and up into the jazz clubs and theatres of Hamburg. The insomniac who dreaded socialising, who, after he stopped seeing Anita, didn't bother with bars and movies and cappuccinos, discovered in a startlingly short time his aptitude for serial self-abuse. Each time was the last, he promised himself. But quite soon he was injecting himself regularly whenever he wanted to unwind.

And fentanyl had a further side effect on his febrile intelligence, at least in the first days. On fentanyl, Snowleg was razed from his consciousness as if the experience had happened not to him but to someone else, like an older brother or parent before he was born or a boy he didn't recognise in a photograph. As if it was a history that didn't belong to him and he was not a participant.

In June, after a cold snap, the weather refound its heat. In the same week an invitation arrived for a mime that Pantomimosa was performing in Uhlenhorst, a neglected area of the city where the underground didn't reach. On a stifling evening Peter reeled up late at the Kampnagel Theatre. He hadn't seen Sepp and Teo for five years.

He was heading for the bar when he tripped over a turquoise dog-lead, causing a piercing yelp.

"Pericles!" A straight-backed woman darted out. Late thirties, medium height and expensively dressed in a blue polka-dotted dress and straw boater. Despite the intense heat she wore black suede mittens, like motorcycle gloves, that left her fingers exposed. She kneeled to soothe a long-haired Dachshund.

Peter apologised. He offered to buy its owner a drink.

"No."

But he insisted.

"A malt whisky, then," she said.

He brought over her glass and raised his to Pericles. The dog looked ready to take a mouthful of his trousers.

"I'm Bettina Grau," she said, removing her boater to reveal a hewn white face and a fringe of blonde hair parted in the middle and smelling of coconut shampoo.

Dark brown eyes scrutinised him, alert for his reaction. Then, realising with a small thrill that her name meant nothing, that he didn't have a clue who she was: "Do you always go around with your shirt on inside out?"

Installed on a bar-stool she talked easily about herself. "You're a doctor? My father's a doctor. Most of my art is inspired by medicine," and described an exhibition she was preparing, "The Body and its Transgressions", for which she had taken transparencies from Freud's early works and superimposed them on Ojibway tribal medical charts.

Peter nodded. He had never heard of a medical installation artist. But it dawned on him that he was familiar with one of her sculptures, a tree-house constructed in his wing at UKE using children's prosthetic limbs. She wanted to hear his criticism of it and when he withheld this – he considered the sculpture ridiculous – she bent closer. "No, say exactly what you think. It's important to me."

At that moment Sepp came up and, without noticing Peter, whispered in her ear. He pulled away and Peter could tell by his expression that he expected Bettina to follow.

145

She took several steps. The floorspace had almost swallowed her when she stopped. A gloved hand reached back to Peter and the once-sharp eyes filled with a sort of longing. She was probably ten years older, but the expression on her face at that moment was that of a child. Under the dominion of her stare, Peter was filled with a tenderness that he hadn't felt in a long time towards an adult.

"Peter!" exclaimed Sepp, recognising him at last. "Join us for dinner, why don't you? If Bettina agrees."

Their fingertips brushed.

"Bettina agrees." Her eyes shining brown like a Vietnamese doll. Cut from a stone he had never seen. Taking in every tall, thin inch of him.

"It's the Syracuse," Sepp was saying. "Teo will give you a lift."

In the car, Teo turned to him: "You know, I'm rather cross with you, Peter. I've sent you at least ten invitations. Concerts, dinners – even an invitation to my wedding. Concerts are one thing, but a wedding . . . When you didn't reply to that I figured you were lost to me."

"Your wedding?"

"Exactly." Teasing, but with a hurt edge, Teo said: "My wife tells me I'm humiliating myself if I make the next move."

"What can I say? I've been working."

They talked about foolish things and laughed and after a while they arrived at the restaurant.

Teo parked the car. He was locking it when he said, "You don't seem yourself."

"I'm all right."

"What's the matter, Peter?"

It had upset Peter more than he could have predicted to see Teo again. Ten years later he might have told Teo that he hadn't been in touch because he didn't like to think about that period in his life, their four days in Leipzig; moreover that he blamed Teo in some obscure way for not allowing him to demonstrate his courage and for ruining his adventure. On this warm evening in Hamburg, he searched for an explanation that would clear the

146

air, but when he reached for it he felt weighed by a fatigue – a nagging unpleasantness – where language disappeared.

Not knowing how to begin, he said: "Bettina. Tell me about her."

At the mention of Bettina, Teo issued a strange warning call like a cockatoo.

"And what," said Peter, "is that supposed to mean?"

"In her own words? Instinct like a sewer, heart like a fridge. She's intelligent. Rich. And fucked up."

"How so?"

Teo chose his words with care. "Bettina has a lot of scar tissue."

"Explain."

"You won't tell Sepp?"

"I promise."

"Just bits and pieces I picked up from him. An uncle who abused her. A best friend who was an accomplice in the killing of Jürgen Ponto. Sepp thought he could sort her out. She practically destroyed him."

"How?"

"Oh, I think Bettina mistakes having a dog for having a heart. She's convinced she has a massive dose of love to give, but she's kidding herself. She has much more to take and she uses it to staunch a wound that has nothing to do with love."

"What, then?"

"Everything is subsumed to her artistic ambition. Stay away, Peter, that's my advice. I lived with an artist once. It was hell. No, worse than hell."

Even as Teo delivered his verdict Peter clenched himself against it. By the time he was in the restaurant he had unheard it. The Syracuse was a Greek restaurant in Barmbecker Straße. Twelve people sat around a table. Bettina had saved Peter a place directly opposite her with her suede gloves. "Sepp's filled me in. I know who you are." Her father was a close colleague of Peter's registrar. Over dinner she questioned Peter about his work. Precocious about medicine, she wanted evidence that he was on his way. He sensed that her interest in him might fade if he didn't make his ambition glamorous.

147

Because of a flood in her studio, she had taken a room in a hotel off Barmbecker Straße. He offered to walk her back. In the hot night she shivered as if tormented and welcomed it when he put his jacket across her bare shoulders. She invited him to her room and they sat on the sofa drinking Lagavulin out of bathroom glasses. She talked of her previous career as a medical illustrator and told him in hair-raising detail how she was molested by her uncle and how she stabbed him and spent a year in a reform school near Muntz, a watered-down prison for girls. Again, he felt a flux of tenderness.

She uncorked a second bottle: "How do you know Sepp?"

"I don't know him well." Instead of Leipzig he told her about England and the books he read repeatedly. In a sentimental, drink-slurred voice he quoted a verse from a favourite poem.

"I love Tennyson," she said, approvingly. He was surprised and impressed.

It was past 2 a.m. when he left. He was kissing her goodbye when for the second time that evening he lost his balance. He felt his spread fingers on her shoulders, fingernails scratching the skin. Their mouths met and they fell back into the room.

Afterwards, she lay on the bed with a small red smile. He heard a rhythmic slurp and her smile broadened as he propped himself up, trying to locate the noise. Their laughter was intimate when he realised that it was her dog licking itself.

"Why did you come so quickly?" she said, lifting her hips and pulling her black pantyhose up over her rump.

She described the second time they made love as "exponentially better". He discovered over time that she was indeed a little bit frigid. She was articulate about sex, but not particularly sensual. She couldn't have sex – even oral sex, which she preferred – without first taking some barbiturate or other. Otherwise, she wasn't that interested.

The second time, in her sixth-floor studio in Sierichstraße, he was on fentanyl and she was on ecstasy. A sound woke him in the early hours. At first he thought it was Gus – he had had to lock his dog in the bathroom after Pericles became aggressive. Then he saw Bettina's silhouette on the window ledge. The curtains were open. She was wearing his jacket, her long thin legs drawn up under it, and she was looking down at the Alster. Smoking a cigarette and weeping.

"Thank you."

"For what?"

"You've freed me . . ."

He put his arm around her.

"From the social body."

He had no idea what she was talking about. Tenderly he stroked her arm through his jacket. "What social body?"

"The public self."

He guided her back to bed. Extinguished her cigarette. Held her to his chest. She was quiescent as he pulled off the jacket and extracted her arms. Before she would allow him to touch her she had to tell him something. "You don't have to say anything." Her words smelled of hand-rolled tobacco, a strand of which he had tasted in their first kiss. "I've never said this before. But I have to say it." And declared herself.

He savoured the silence. Not yet feeling what he was about to say, but thinking, I will feel this. He lay beside her in the dark and said after a pause: "I love you too." He could hear Gus whining.

In the dawn the sky was red, like a torch held up to a hand. When the sun peeped over the Alster and into the two front windows, he recognised the studio. The place where he had first met Sepp.

Lying on top of him, Bettina asked about his other relationships. He told her about Anita.

"Why did you break up?" she said, animated, and he wondered if this was her domain.

"It had run its course."

"Oh, come on. Which one of you was unfaithful? Someone's dumped or someone dumps."

"We inflicted on each other our growing pains," he said awkwardly.

"One can tell by a man's chin whether he's been unfaithful," stroking the phrase like a dog she had just fed.

"What does my chin tell you?"

She laughed annoyingly and sat up, folding her arms on his chest. "Who was she?"

"Nobody."

"An affair?"

"No, it wasn't an affair. I was very young. I was impetuous. She wasn't anyone important."

"Don't you dare say that about me one day."

"I'll never have to." Then: "Hug me." Then: "Please don't let me let you go."

Later that morning he bumped into Teo in Gänsemarkt. "How easy it seems. It *is* like falling."

They went to exhibitions and to restaurants, where he paid, and to clothes shops in Gänsemarkt, where she paid. She wanted him to be wearing Thomas-I-Punkt. "Sweet, I'm so tired of seeing you in those sophomoric garments of yours that I'm going to take you to a proper store."

She became his first serious companion since Anita. He could tell that her artist friends thought they were tremendously unsuited, but he felt happier than in a long while. She was twelve years older and much more experienced. It was the first time in his professional heart that he had been leaned on. That summer he shallowed himself in a procession of opening nights, champagne dinners, camera flashbulbs.

He had known her six weeks when a photograph appeared in a gossip column above the caption "Wedding bells for Artist Bettina Grau?" The text referred to Peter as a paediatrician, anticipating his appointment by two years.

"You look like you're posing in a mortuary," he said.

She quite liked that. "Then you know what that makes you, sweet?"

It was at the end of a warm day, bright but not radiant, when she asked him to marry her. He had taken her to dinner in a new Italian restaurant off Gansemacht. They were walking along the Alster to her studio when she said, "Do you want to get married?"

He was taken aback and in a strange way relieved. "Yes," he

said. Then, concerned that she hadn't heard: "Yes."

"But no children," she said, stopping to untangle Pericles's lead. "You can't be a serious artist and have children."

He, who specialised in children, felt ambushed. Even if he didn't want children at the moment, it was an enormous thing to have to digest and dissolve. Not wishing to betray her, he swallowed his alarm. "Of course," quickly looking at the lake, the sky inflamed as if stung by a bee. "Maybe the best paediatricians don't either."

They went upstairs, where they kissed. She touched his lips with the tips of her fingers and he smelled the dark nail varnish and felt her full breasts against his chest, the almost purplish nipples pressing through her shirt like Pericles's nose.

"I want to come in your mouth," she whispered.

No date was fixed for the wedding. She didn't tell anyone else and nor did he. They had exchanged promise rings, but chose not to wear them.

What they had in common, he would come to realise, was the complicity of pathology. Bettina had an eczema on her hands, behind her knees, and a lot of different complaints he could walk her through. She quite frequently took ecstasy and sometimes cocaine. And under formal clothes liked to wear bras and panties in the neon colours of her dog leads.

For a while, Bettina's outrageous behaviour amused Peter. He was keeping this artist tensely, slightly nervously happy, and it seemed not to matter that she didn't seek to supply a commensurate need in him. He was adding to his life, he thought. There was no reason it couldn't last. His chin on her blonde pubic hair, he told her: "I want to be able to talk and endure with you."

In August, a fortnight after their engagement, she introduced a new fragrance at the Ascan Krone gallery in Isestraße. She handed around home-made perfume bottles and dared her stylish guests to spray themselves. The response was exclamatory. It was the new green-tea fragrance, but better than green-tea. A mixture of bergamot and peach kernel. She was lauded in *Tagesspiegel* as the new Annick Goutal. Then it was revealed: the fragrance consisted largely of chilled dog urine. Even Gus had pissed in the bottles. The debate was taken up in Berlin by *Lettre Internationale*. That autumn Bettina was hailed as the new Damien Hirst.

She never slept a night in Peter's apartment. She talked of couples who kept separate establishments as a model. Once he finished his time as a locum maybe they would move in together. Meanwhile, he spent the weekdays in Eppendorf and the weekends in her studio, twelve minutes by bicycle, where she cleared a desk for him, an angle-topped davenport at which he liked to sit and watch her sculpt in the gallery above. She still fascinated him. He wanted to be near her, even though he knew she was a fantasist. While she, even though she was contemptuous of his bourgeois aesthetics, had grown covetous of his tough admiration.

Six months passed like this and then as the days lengthened it all went wrong.

When lovers first meet they expose their tenderest nerves to the shock of an intimate breath. But as they get to know each other there is a tightening of armour.

What he remembered most about the summer of their unwinding was not the situation in East Germany – the rigged elections in May, the Monday prayer demonstrations – but the sculpture Bettina was working on in her gallery: a railed-off area reached by a green spiral staircase and where she never allowed him to trespass.

The sculpture became her excuse. Her alibi. She was always having to see someone about it. Work on it. Haunt the medical supply stores and hospital dustbins for the esoteric materials that she insisted were needed for its creation.

She didn't say so then, but the sculpture was of Peter. Years later he would be coming down a corridor in a Berlin hospital when he would gasp for breath. Less at the sight of the statue than its title: *Saint Peter*.

The demands of his residency made him unpredictable in his routine. At first he blamed the tightening between them on UKE's Department of Paediatrics and a work schedule that physically and mentally drained him.

"You of all people should understand," he told her on one occasion, arriving late at an opening. "You're the daughter of a medical man." He got into her brown Mercedes-Benz two-seater and she drove very fast to Blankenese and they watched the ships disappear into the night until all they could see were the flashes of phosphorescence in the churned water. They had dinner in a restaurant beside the Elbe where a couple recognised her and she drank too much and talked too much. With difficulty he persuaded Bettina to calm down. He paid the bill and supported his fiancée on her high heels up the steep steps to where she had parked her car and she became less hysterical and tiresome.

But it was obvious that she had never been involved with someone she couldn't control or whose schedule couldn't be readjusted. She began to retaliate.

In the spring, to celebrate their emergence from four months of fur wraps and legs reflected in puddles and wind that groped like a hand under his coat and flipped Gus's ears inside out, he planned a holiday.

"Listen, why don't we go camping on Helgoland?" By now, the beginning of April, the leaves were back in the trees.

"All right," said Bettina.

Then, at the last moment, she cancelled. The sculpture. She had promised it for an exhibition. It still wasn't finished.

"Look, I'm sorry about the opening," he said.

"Don't be ridiculous. Medicine calls you – and 'the business' calls me."

He absorbed this, but it happened again.

"Where were you?" he would ask. Not once, but once or twice a month. "I waited an hour." He knew it wasn't unreasonable to ask. He knew he wasn't as tedious as he sounded. Sometimes it was two or three hours before she turned up with Pericles at the end of a blazing lead.

"Oh, I had to see a dealer from Berlin." Or an agent. Or a journalist.

She had claimed that she wanted to marry Peter, but he couldn't ignore the possibility that he was discardable. Little by little, with each act of carelessness the fact of their engagement subsided into an embarrassment not to be mentioned until it grew clear to him that marriage was out of the question and yet to discuss it risked bringing down the card-house.

And in this stew he met someone.

"It's not me you're fucking," she said one morning, looking daggers at Peter as if he were her uncle. From somewhere under the bed he heard a slurping. "It's someone else. Who?"

One Sunday in early January he had been working in her studio when he switched on the radio and experienced a strong déjà vu. It was a cold winter's day and he was hungover and something about the cast of light outside her window made him shiver. Here am I, he thought, sitting at another desk. And was reminded of his desk at school. Of the cubicle where he had stood in this very room. That he was not in control of his life. Still behind the curtain. Evading himself.

On the radio Bach was playing. Bettina was saying, "I'm sorry, sweet, I have to work tonight. I have to get this thing finished," when he recalled a cantata that he had heard in the Thomaskirche at the age of twenty-three.

He bought five CDs of Bach cantatas and spent the evening in Eppendorf listening to them with Gus. None contained the music he was after.

The idea of tracking it down devoured him, and when Teo sent free tickets to the Musikhalle where a friend was performing in a Bach string quartet he went along.

Teo searched over his shoulder. "Bettina?"

"Sends her apologies."

After the concert, Teo introduced him to a tall violinist, seven years his senior, with prominent eyes. Peter told her that he came from England, the land without music. "There are worse things," she said. "Perhaps you were busy doing something else." On the following evening he waited for her by the players' exit.

Their first time in bed, he asked for her assistance. "I want to find this piece of music. A Bach cantata." And started humming it, but not in such a way that she was able to identify the original.

It became a habit. Every time they made love, she had to play a different CD, to see if he would recognise the cantata. Her long face seemed to become more angular each time he shook his head until the moment arrived when she told him that the impossible had happened. The music of Bach had begun to depress her.

On their last night together, she put on a cantata composed by Bach in 1727 of which only this recording existed. She had bought it at considerable effort and expense from a collector in Wedding. She was convinced that this was the piece he was looking for. He shook his head.

In the morning she unhooked her duffel coat for the short walk to the rehearsal room. She did up the fake bone buttons and picked her violin case off the floor. Then she turned off the light and waited for him in the doorway. "I'm tired of this. Time to go. Now."

He had been on his trip. Now he had to unpack his bags.

"There's no-one," he told Bettina. Which had the virtue, by then, of being true. But after his experience with the musician he had sobered up. He needed to be accountable. His final exams were in a few months and he was scared.

He got out of bed and walked over to the window and looked down at Sierichstraße. It was midday and the traffic was thinning, about to change direction.

"Peter?" said Bettina, chewing on the word as if her head were still in his groin. Pericles, hearing her tone, cocked his head. "Please answer me this. It's all I want to know." She took a pillbox from her pocket, her face hardening, her Omen jacket the colour of the car seat where Kirsten had spread her long and Lycra'd legs for him. "Why have you drifted away? You weren't like that at the start, when I asked you back to my room for a whisky and you recited that poem about the Death of Arthur. I'd have followed you to the end of the earth. The last cliff. And then you became distracted. Why?"

She wanted to know. Genuinely.

"I don't know," he said, very tired. His chin pointing down to the street.

She arranged the pills for her attention-deficit syndrome and swallowed one. "Down, Pericles." Then, because he stood at the window and stared at a girl in a samphire-green coat with a fur trim, "Are you sure you'd rather not be with someone else?"

"Yes."

"Here, come with me."

She put on her man's paisley dressing gown and led the way up the spiral staircase.

At last the sculpture was ready. She needed his opinion.

He said nothing, not wishing to hurt her feelings. Initially, he had been amused by her work because of its novelty. On fentanyl he could play the role and provide a suitable reaction. Sober, he found to his dismay that he had nothing to say.

"It's absolutely wonderful."

She looked at him sharp-eyed. He had seen her give critics the same expression. "That is the most vacuous reaction I've ever heard. That's just English rubbish."

"Let me get you a coffee."

But she was on to him. "'It's wonderful, it's riveting.' Come on, what do you really think?"

With great reluctance, his eyes settled on the naked figure sculpted from used bandages and already sold to a medical institution in Berlin for a substantial sum. "Listen, I can't do art criticism to order. It's hard enough to transplant a liver."

"What did you say to me? 'I want to be able to talk and endure with you.'"

"I can't handle this now."

"What does that mean? Will you be able to handle it tomorrow? I thought you'd signed on for a lifetime of handling it."

"Stop this, Bettina. I have to walk Gus."

Her hand slipped into his pocket. But she wasn't after his penis. "You're not walking anywhere," grabbing his key ring, "until you tell me what you really think of it."

More than the traffic had changed. Suddenly, she was no longer confrontational. "I need to know, Peter," in a surprising soft voice.

He told her and her eyes reddened. She smiled wanly as if crushed and then looked away to her sculpture. But it was a wound that passed. He saw before his eyes the blood dry, the clot form, the white skin unblemished. From the moment of impact to the healing, no more than a few seconds.

"Here," giving back his keys.

"Let me make that coffee," he said.

She accepted the cup and stared down at the Alster.

"You're like my uncle," she blurted suddenly, between hot sips, "who would weep tears of love and then hit me."

CHAPTER EIGHTEEN

HE WAS SOBER FOR another two weeks and then a 10-year-old girl died on him.

It was a sweltering afternoon in June. All day he was booked to see children in the clinic. "For Christ's sake, you're a medical student," the registrar would say afterwards in his defence. "You were being pulled in twenty different directions. You were busy, busy. And you were interrupted. That's why most people hate paeds. Ninety-nine per cent of the time it's clear coasting. But that 1 per cent when they do get sick, it's panic-button terror."

In the lunch interval, he went to pour himself a cup of water and a woman bustled in with her daughter.

"She's having difficulty swallowing," said the mother, who wore a silver trouser suit with lavender cuffs and a matching lavender scarf. "I just brought her in because she's prone to strep and I wanted to get a prescription now."

The girl's name was Hannelore. He sat her down. She had a pale round face and thin braids of dark hair hanging to her waist. There was a hesitancy about her when he looked into her throat. An anxious expression in her eyes.

The mother sat observing. She was flustered and distracted and fanned herself in the heat. She was throwing a dinner party and was impatient to take the prescription and leave. She still had to buy ice and flowers and was running late for a hair appointment.

He couldn't see much. "I think it's just a viral pharyngitis. But we'll take a throat swab."

He had examined hundreds of sore throats and yet this little girl touched him. Was it something she said? The way she opened her mouth? The vaguely worried look on her face?

"I'll give you a prescription for antibiotics anyway," he told the mother. "Don't fill it in till we get a call from the lab. If she gets worse, please bring her back."

He wrote out the prescription and looked again at Hannelore.

There was an undercurrent to her hair. Something about it familiar.

The nurse interrupted. "The ward sister's trying to reach you. She's doing a dressing and wants you to look at it."

"I'll be there directly."

As Peter walked out of the room he heard Hannelore make a croupy cough like a barking dog and the thought flickered through his head, God, could it be haemophilus influenza? But already the ward sister was dragging him away and his mind was filling with the next task.

Hannelore's image pursued him through the afternoon. He remembered the chokey cough when he left at night. He was aware that he shouldn't have sent her home. Her colour wasn't good, he thought, she was a bit too silent. I didn't follow up in the way I meant to. Uneasy, he stopped the car and from a telephone kiosk contacted the hospital for her address and telephone number.

He rang Hannelore's home. No answer. He knew the address – he sometimes bought fish in the same street – and drove there. "Doctors don't usually do that. And a medical student never," the registrar would say. "Really, you have nothing to blame yourself for. As I always say, we're more lucky than good."

In the leopard light of a summer dusk he turned into a smart drive in Eimsbüttel. Cars on the gravel. The evening humid. The curtains still drawn. He loosened his tie and crunched towards the house. The mother, in a green organdy dress and holding a plate, flitted between tall open windows. The guests stood around. A bald man in a dark blue suit accepted one of her cocktail dainties.

He thought, pressing the brass buzzer: This is why she had to hurry Hannelore away.

After a while the door opened. She didn't recognise him at first.

"How's Hannelore doing?" he asked.

"She's in her room. Why?"

He rushed upstairs.

She was sitting forward on her bed, drooling, scared, trying to breathe. She couldn't swallow her saliva. Couldn't call for help. Hungry for air, she fixed him with round widened eyes. Her hair tangled. The colour wiped from her face. From her mouth a fluttering moan.

159

Right away he could picture it. A swollen red ball like a large cherry blocking her trachea. But he couldn't take out his spatula and look down her throat – it might kill her instantly. There was a Biro on the bedside table and it raced through his head to slit her throat and stick the Biro through to allow in air. But he was too junior. Too scared. This wasn't the moment to perform his first trach.

He carried her, lamblike, downstairs and into the drawing room.

He heard the intake of breath. Was aware of the mother running towards him. His sharp voice warning: "Don't touch her!" He ordered the mother to open the front door and then the door of his car. "I want you to put this child carefully on your lap and hold her."

He drove to the hospital, the girl sucking the air beside him in deep stridorous gasps.

They paged Anaesthesia as soon as they saw her. They called Ear, Nose and Throat and senior people took over. He followed her into the resuscitation room. He was allowed to watch because he had to learn.

The nurse calmed her and speedily and gingerly attached a heart monitor. The doctor tried to intubate her, but the swelling of her larynx obstructed the airway and he couldn't get the tube past. He yanked back her pigtails and palpated her neck and made an incision. Jelly-like clots of blood welled up as he stuck in the tube. The nurse noted that the girl's lips had gone purple. "I can't find a pulse."

Afterwards, the doctor cursed the heat. A colder night would have constricted the blood vessels, he said. Her epiglottis would have shrunk just enough so she could breathe. Peter, half-listening, looked at Hannelore and thought, Why didn't I do the trach in the bedroom?

The doctor had another call. He started to tell the nurse to go and inform the mother.

"That's your job, I'm afraid," said the nurse.

"I'll go," said Peter.

He tightened his tie and washed his face and walked down the grey speckled floor to face the woman in her green party dress. Seeing Hannelore on the table, the blackberry undercurrent to her hair, the innocent face, he realised of whom she reminded him.

Remorse. The bird that never settles.

CHAPTER NINETEEN

HANNELORE'S DEATH AFFECTED HIM like no other patient's.

He told Bettina: "I keep thinking of what the doctor said. 'Had it been cold outside, she'd be alive.'"

"Want some of this? It will help." Bettina nodded at her hand-held mirror. A gunpowder trail of white.

"No, no, no."

In the following weeks he existed as a sleepwalker. He couldn't have accounted for his chronology. All he knew was that he attended her funeral in Nienstedtener Friedhof and several times visited her grave. On the bell-shaped headstone her mother had had inscribed a verse from the Book of Kings. "Is it well with the child? And she answered, It is well with the child."

In his sleep he convulsed with the spasms of the dying girl, waking from dreams in which she stood by his bed. Dark braids to her waist. Accusing eyes on his naked physique as if he were a drawing Rodney had rejected.

"Why didn't you do a trach at home?" she asked, raising a braid to expose her neck. "Or were you again too embarrassed to spoil a dinner party?" She had Snowleg's face.

"I could have made the error myself," said his registrar, going out of his way to reassure Peter. "Concentrate on your exams. That's the best way. I expect you to pass with the highest distinction."

For the next three weeks, as he had learned to do at St Cross, Peter submerged himself in routine. He spent his evenings, Monday to Friday, in the library. On Saturday mornings after their walk he would lock Gus in his room and bicycle to Bettina's studio.

She was working hard to complete the catalogue for her forth-coming exhibition. While she wrote, he studied. But his music that had filled her studio since January was forbidden. She was anxious to hear the news from East Germany, not his Bach CDs.

"It's incredible," letting him in one day.

"What is?"

"What's happening in Leipzig."

On her radio, reports spoke of protesters filling the streets of East Germany's second city and bursting into song, any song that came into their heads – before troops and trucks arrived to arrest them.

"Apparently, the Trade Fair was the incentive," she said. "They wanted the television cameras to see them."

In the second week of September Hungary opened its borders and Bettina summoned Peter to dinner.

It was a Thursday and he was reluctant to drag himself from his books. In a fortnight, if all went well, he would have achieved his father's ambition. But there was another reason he didn't want to accept her invitation. Bettina's demands had become so persistent of late that she sucked the air out of him. He could no longer provide her with what she most needed, which was why, he had no doubt, she turned to whatever it was she swallowed or inhaled.

"I don't think I can risk it. I have exams in four days."

"Sweet, I insist," said Bettina. "I really do insist."

They got drunk and when he woke up he couldn't recall whether they had made love or not.

At 8 a.m., he put on his jersey and went to close the window. Outside, a discoloured sky, the air colder and the traffic louder. She was running late for something and he heard her rummaging through the bathroom for a contact lens. "Christ, Peter, your stuff is everywhere."

She came out of the bathroom and flung his boxer shorts at him. "You're wearing the same underpants you were wearing last week. Surely your patients can smell this? Surely the children comment on your smell?" She said with contempt: "Don't you look at yourself in the mirror ever? Don't you have any pride at all?"

He retrieved the boxers from the floor and sat on the edge of the bed.

She was still looking at him in a concentrated way. "Your jersey's on the wrong way around. What do you think it means to wear a jersey back to front?"

"That I'm not vain?"

Up flared the sharp brown eyes, two claymores darting right between his ribs. "Wrong! It's designed to draw attention to yourself. In fact, it's a form of extreme vanity and selfishness."

Bettina marched back into the bathroom and picked up her eau de toilette. He watched her face in the mirror. She was spraying her throat with the fastidiousness of someone who might have slept with him, but was going off to meet another lover.

She wiped her arm and his shaving bag went flying. "Oh, fuck." Then silence. He sat up on the bed, heart thudding. She clipped out of the bathroom, back straight, and held up the needle triumphantly. She knew what it was. She had even injected herself on occasions. It was the easy way out.

"Not only a pig." Her voice had a note of cold finality, as if he wasn't there. "But a fucking junkie."

His head on his knees. Not looking at her. So she bowled him the needle along the floor. "I'm sorry, sweet, I don't think I can marry you." She went on: "I'm sad to have to say this but I no longer love you," and stared at the Alster, the lake like a spread of Rosalind's silver foil. "In fact, I feel betrayed. I came towards you and you let me down. I feel bitterly let down."

He wanted to say "I love you", but the words remained in his throat. He found it physically impossible to utter them.

Still her voice ploughed on. "I tried to fight against it and it's a lesson – you can't," her face at the window tight and bunched like a bulb that refuses to flower. "I've never felt so lonely as I've felt since I met you. I hope I never feel that in death. You were never there for me. I've been trying to end it since the summer, but you wouldn't let me. I don't mean it that I don't love you. I do. But you're not the person to make me happy."

Slowly, he dressed.

"You know what I blame as much as anything?" the cocaine she had taken in the bathroom making her voluble. "Your English education. There are so many layers of artifice ironed into you that you find it hard to be real. Oh, there's a sweetness to you, but you leave no taste."

He put on the designer jacket that she had bought him, the trousers made out of sailing material.

163

"Why didn't I see the signs? Of course, you were going to tread on me. You trod on Pericles," checking her fringe in the mirror. "I admit, at first I was taken in by your schmaltz. I don't suppose you remember what you said as we walked from the Syracuse? 'People have lied to you, I can tell. But I won't be that man.' So plausible you sounded, and then you recited Tennyson. It took a while to realise you were addressing your poetry to my panties, not to me."

He stood up.

"But do you know what *really* did it for me?" applying a rhubarb lipstick the same colour as her hatband. "It was the most trivial thing, but it struck at my soul. *It was the way you constantly took off my music and put on Bach.* Why, all of a sudden, were you so interested in Bach? You never paid any attention to classical music before."

He waited at the door while she hunted for a leash and then filled Pericles's bowl with mineral water. "The trouble with you medical men is you consider yourselves Renaissance figures. You think you know about art, you think you know about music, you consider yourself a healer. But me, I was raised in a medical family, I have two secondary degrees. Sometimes I get up in the morning and I start to write and time passes and I don't know where I am, but I have gone so deep into myself that I find it difficult to come out. That's a form of automatic writing you wouldn't have access to. There's a Berlin Wall between your psyche and your intellect. But it's not a strength. It's because you don't know what to feel. Or how."

By the door she pulled down his head and kissed him full on the mouth as if she needed this last taste of him. "Goodbye, sweet."

The weight of her rhubarb lips, the ache in his chest like a dry socket.

Instead of bicycling to the faculty, Peter walked to a bar on the Alster and smoked his way through a packet of West Lights, drinking one glass of Weißen after another. Shortly after 2 p.m. – these details he learned later – he stripped off his Omen jacket and trousers and tossed them in the lake. He had no recollection of seeing a dog hurl itself into the water or of walking into the Thomas-I-Punkt store in Gänsemarkt where a diminutive roly-poly woman in a bob-cut was folding a jersey. She looked up and started to ask how might she help. It was then she noticed that Peter had nothing on. Not a stitch. Not even a pair of Birkenstocks.

"I thought he was German," she told a local reporter, whose story was spiked at the last moment because of the momentous events taking place in East Germany. "But he kept speaking in this refined English voice. As if – how can I put it? – he was trying to sing."

To everyone's astonishment but his own, Peter flunked his membership exams. Days short of completing his training as a senior houseman he was found collapsed on the toilet while a child with a blocked carotid artery waited in the operating theatre. A search uncovered two needles in his locker. Confronted by his registrar, he confessed.

CHAPTER TWENTY

ON THE LAST MONDAY of October, Leipzig's city centre – the
length and breadth of its streets – filled with men, women and
children holding candles and walking along Dittrichring in one
of the processions that would earn for Leipzig its sobriquet "City
of Heroes". The same evening Peter entered the psychiatric clinic
of Ochsenzoll in the north of Hamburg. His registrar had given
him an extended leave of absence to pull himself together. Peter
Hithersay, he wrote in his report, was the best student of his year.
It would be a tragic waste not to grant him a second chance.

"Fentanyl!" sneered the heroin addict in the Narco-Anonymous
class Peter was compelled to attend. He looked at Peter in the
way a hippy might regard a yuppie. "That's the lowest rung. I
thought coke was the lowest. But fentanyl!"

In the evenings the patients watched television or dozed. Late
one November evening Peter saw a stream of gleeful faces pouring
through the Bornholmer crossing point.

The heroin addict, who came from Berlin, was upset. "Look
at this cesspool being tipped into our streets. I want the Wall. I
need the Wall. I don't want these bastards loose in my city. Get
it back up!"

"That's right, get it back up!" said a voice from behind him,
a woman's.

In the corner a man with a deviated septum sang, "There's no
getting over that rainbow."

"What do you think, Herr Doktor Peter?" The heroin addict
nudged him. "Should we let them in?"

"That's my home," he said, his vision coloured by his crazed
muddled head. "That's where I'm from."

"Well, ducky, there's no-one there. Are you going to Berlin to
squeeze through the Wall? Because the tide coming this way is so

massive that before we know where we are we'll have dealers from Moscow all over our streets."

Ten days later Peter was again in the television room. On screen a vast crowd stood shoulder to shoulder outside a building with a curved facade, gazing intently up at the windows.

"Where's this?"

"Stasi headquarters in Leipzig," piped the bandaged nose.

The heroin addict glowered at Peter. "Do you know what they're doing over there? The cunts are burning everything. I mean, everything. In fact, it's time we sent some of you fentanyl fuckers back so they can burn you."

The refrain was taken up. "That's right! Burn you!" Soon everyone was chanting, "Burn you, burn you, burn you."

Peter made a vow. I am going to get better. I'm going to go to Leipzig however long it takes me. At some stage in my life I'm by God going to find that girl and atone.

CHAPTER TWENTY-ONE

DAY AFTER DAY THEY had stood in their thousands in Dittrichring. Not moving on. Staring up at the building. Chanting. But today, for the first time, the ginger-haired man was nervous. Another file was missing. Someone had been here before him.

"How will you ever forgive me?" he hummed and slammed shut the cabinet. He knew who it was. He knew fucking well.

Early December and behind a shuttered window on the second floor of the Runde Ecke, Kresse was destroying everything his gloved hands could seize. In continual use for three weeks, the shredder had given up on him. All afternoon he had been ripping up documents, but there seemed no limit to the files that crammed the shelves and cabinets.

From the street came the sound of singing. Kresse recognised the hymn from his childhood. They had been singing it every night. "Wake up, wake up, O German land. You have slumbered long enough."

He strode through the sacks bulging with shredded paper, parted the slats of the orange blind and peered sullenly out. The night was ablaze with what looked like Halloween pumpkins. The faces of numberless ghouls who held candles beneath their chins and placards bearing the same message: "We're staying here," and "We are one people". The ghouls had been peaceful so far, but he sensed that this was the last evening on which they might be prepared to see smoke billowing from this building.

Unseen by them, Kresse surveyed their exaggerated features and remembered the night three weeks before when he had mingled with such a crowd. He remembered how the radio warned of people being crushed because the platforms couldn't cope with the numbers. It was like a zoo, all the animals leaving. Why go into their cage? he thought. But on that November day he couldn't very well remain in his country – there was no-one left.

He remembered the young mother with two small children in

the queue, and recognising this was Marla – he stood so close he could smell her hair – and his relief when she looked around and smiled at him, not knowing who he was, saying to her daughter, "Come here, Katya. Stay together." He remembered being propelled through the gate and into the West. People everywhere. One moment he was walking among them, enjoying the pressure of his feet on the pavement. The next, he was flowing half a metre above the ground. He had the strange impression that he was still and his surroundings were moving. That he was a rock in a river and the people were swimming by. "Boss, it was like a fucking drug trip," he told Uwe.

The crowd carried him to a branch of the Dresdner Bank where the West Germans had promised them each 100 Marks. He remembered Turks passing by and spitting as he queued for his welcome money, and thinking: If the Turks in West Germany are spitting at us, then they must think of us as an inferior race.

Kresse had always imagined West Berlin as looking like Leipzig done up. But it seemed to him like any bombed-out city from the 1950s. Not showy at all. Around him families were running like lost people, children hanging onto their parents' arms, looking at shops with huge eyes. It was winter, but in the supermarkets there were cucumbers, strawberries, everything.

He bought a yucca plant for 15 Marks, and a kilo of oranges. In East Germany he was used to green Cuban oranges, fibrous and bitter on the tongue. He remembered how he said to the woman, "Are these oranges sweet or will they clench the pores of your skin?" She looked at him bluntly and then a large Turk came out from behind a curtain holding a knife. He thought, He's going to kill me. But the Turk took the orange, cut it in half and offered it. "Try."

He sucked at the rest of the orange in the queue for the Pornokino. The audience consisted of old grannies and children, all choosing, like him, to spend their first evening in the Golden West watching *Texas Chainsaw Massacre II*. The orange tasted sweet.

But now he was back in the Runde Ecke where some fucker, whether to protect the individuals concerned or to create more trouble or simply as a matter of personal insurance, had removed certain files that he, Kresse, had been ordered to get rid of.

He let go the blinds and unlocked another cabinet. Yet again there was a yawning space. He checked the index for the name of the missing file. "How will you ever forgive me?" he hummed through the gap in his teeth. The cabinet contained records of political prisoners arrested in the central Leipzig district between 1958 and 1961. He twisted his head, but the telephone was ringing.

At the other end, Morneweg's voice. "Kresse. How are you getting on?" He sounded old, a man with a rusted inside.

"As well as I can, sir." In fact, he itched to tell Morneweg that it was a fucking miracle what he had done. Since November 10 he had incinerated more or less the entire Information Research System as well as records for operational payments, not to mention files belonging to those whose freedom the West German authorities had purchased, together with details of the bank accounts.

"Where have you got to?"

"Nineteen sixty, sir. That's going back – what you wanted."

"Look, I've some stuff in my office that I've kept. I really need you to sweep it away."

"More files, are they, sir?"

"No, Kresse, glass jars."

And Kresse, whom Morneweg had promoted from dog-handler two years before, immediately understood: Morneweg wanted help to smash up Uwe's smell pantry.

"Sir?"

"Yes?"

"Have you sent anyone else to take files?"

"What do you mean by that?"

"Well, sir, an awful lot of files are missing."

"This is not a help at a time like this, Kresse. You've probably seen the news."

"Yes, sir." Kresse had watched the reports with fury and alarm: the authorities crumbling, the weak-kneed liberals jostling to replace them, the talk of tribunals.

"What are we talking about, Kresse?"

"I've counted so far – it's a biggish number, about six hundred."

"Whose files are they?"

"Since you ask, sir, since you ask, the case officer responsible for the majority of these files is Lieutenant Uwe Wechsel."

"All of them?"

"Yes, sir, nearly all of them, apart from yours, sir, the ones that are signed out to you, sir."

"OK, get onto Lieutenant Wechsel."

"He's dealing with the university records, sir. His office is locked. Do you want me to take the door down?"

"No, be careful. I want you to be careful, Kresse. Lieutenant Wechsel knows where the bodies are buried. Your bodies and mine. I want you up here as soon as possible."

"Very good, sir."

He put down the phone. Something had altered in the room and he didn't know what. Then it came to him. The crowd had stopped singing. A sound rose from downstairs, the drumming of fists on steel. He picked up his night-stick.

CHAPTER TWENTY-TWO

Six years after Hannelore's death a journalist from the Berlin *Tagesspiegel* would watch Peter bandage a child's wrist in a kindergarten overlooking Lake Wannsee and observe a touching affinity that was wholly different from the bedside manner he adopted with the elderly. With children, she would tell him, it was as if he became a child.

"God, you were so good with that kid. I'm surprised you didn't go into paediatrics."

"I almost did."

"What happened?"

He looked at the serious, straw-haired woman with the mauve shawl that she kept adjusting on her shoulder, and a tiny tape recorder that she pointed at his face like a policeman trying to catch him speeding. And said: "A girl died when I was about to qualify. I got it wrong. I missed something."

"Missed what?"

She appeared to be in her early forties and had a wide mouth. He couldn't help noticing how determined it became when she urged the tape recorder closer and asked her questions. How defensive his answers.

"It was a long time ago and I really don't want to talk about it."

The journalist's name was Frieda. She had contacted Peter after reading a case report submitted by him to the *Lancet*, on a case of insomnia associated with delayed sleep phase syndrome. She recognised her own father's symptoms and was moved to write an article on his work for her newspaper's Saturday supplement. "Ideally, I would like to spend a day with you, accompany you on your rounds . . ."

About to throw away the letter, he noticed that she had stapled to it samples of her journalism, including a piece on the post-Wall fate of East German guard dogs and another on Daniel Schreber, the founder of Schreber gardens. He read it twice. Every word. Then telephoned Frieda. "Yes, why not spend a day with me?" and joked – but in an English way: "As long as I'm not the subject. As long as I make that perfectly clear."

Afterwards, she liked to complain, "I came to interview you, and rather than reveal a single detail about your life you seduced me. In an old people's home!"

On this particular Tuesday afternoon, Peter had driven Frieda from the Hilfrich Klinik, where she had spent the morning observing him at work, to a nursing home called the Lion's Manor in the south-west of Berlin. He was on the point of guiding her around the home when Sister Corinna ran out to say that a boy had fallen badly in the playground of the kindergarten next door.

"Do you mind?" he turned to Frieda.

"Go ahead."

The boy, it turned out, had fainted after being made to laugh by the other children. They had learned that if they made him laugh really hard he would fall down, and so they had surrounded him in a group and told jokes until his legs gave way.

"It's only a graze," Peter reassured the boy. And to the teacher: "He seems very sleepy."

"Yes, he used to be so attentive, but now he falls asleep all the time."

"This isn't any of my business, but tell his mother I would be happy to talk to her."

All this while Frieda stood under the new basketball hoop, taking notes. He apologised for keeping her waiting.

"What do you think is wrong with him?"

"Well, it's not a vasovagal attack. Nor a cardiac arrhythmia. I wouldn't be surprised if he's suffering from narcolepsy."

Musing, she let him shepherd her from the playground. "I can't stop thinking of that line you wrote: 'The eye never closes. It's the lid that closes over it.'"

He smiled. "We're a lot like trout."

But she wanted to be serious. "Gerontology's an up-and-coming speciality. But it's not – and I hope you won't take this in the wrong spirit – very sexy."

Peter laughed. "It's one of the lowest paid sub-specialities!"

"Then, why choose it?"

His registrar at UKE had asked the same question. "But, Peter, it will be humiliating to go back." The faces so much younger. The nights not his own. A different city to negotiate. The loss of income. "A lot more people die on you in geriatrics! Are there not simpler ways to atone?"

But at that moment in April 1990, after Hannelore's death, after the implosion of his relationship with Bettina, after his descent into the fentanyl pit, Peter sought regression. Instead of returning to UKE, he decided to rebuild his career in a place that wasn't Hamburg. When he considered all the things he might do to purify himself, he could think of nothing to cleanse his mind so thoroughly as to repeat medical school. At seventeen, in disobedience to his daemon, he had abandoned history and embarked on nine years of preparing to be a doctor. Second time around, the volume of work offered a blessed escape. In Berlin, he yielded to his studies and eventually, after four further years in which he immersed himself in circadian rhythms and cataplexy and the effect of exercise on bone density, he pulled himself up again.

"Why gerontology? Possibly because of my grandfather," he told Frieda as they strolled back through the gate of the adjacent building. "I feel guilty about how he spent the end of his life. You see, I owe him a lot."

That much was true. Peter had learned his gift to be gentle and caring with the elderly from his dealings with his grandfather. In Berlin, he rediscovered his talent and the transformative effect of being listened to. Old age, which brought with it so many indignities, he found he was able to suspend. Past achievements were not distant achievements, but right there in the room with the patient. He refused to allow anyone to identify too closely with their bodily functions. Old age, said his eyes, was an unfortunate inevitability, but it wasn't personal, and with his sigh he participated in the dismay of those who wet themselves or needed help to put in their teeth, while acknowledging that it wouldn't be long before he would be crapping in his bed too.

"But why Berlin?" she persisted. Looking sideways at him, her eyes watchful, poking about in his darkness.

Another good question, but harder to answer. It was an unfailing source of regret to Peter that if his German father hadn't been so keen to avoid Berlin, he might have escaped to the West. The borders were still open. He could have taken the S-Bahn, rather than attempting to cross the border through Russian patrols. But Peter didn't reveal this to the journalist. Nor did he speak of all that he himself hoped to escape by moving to Berlin.

"Because it has the largest concentration of elderly people in the country," he waffled.

Or was it one step closer to Snowleg?

Despite the vow he made at Ochsenzoll, he had not visited East Germany. He shrank from it as from a black hole. When he went to define it, it had gone; when he went to meet it, it had gone. The idea that a whole country could disappear overnight, and so thoroughly, encouraged in him the hope that he might – in the same way – wipe out his guilt, his regrets, the memory of what he had done there. Once he qualified as a gerontologist – in 1994, at the age of thirty-three, with the third highest marks of his year – he turned down a number of invitations to lecture in the former GDR as well as several prestigious job offers. After the Wall came down, he avoided articles, television and radio programmes. Anything that discussed "die Wende" or served to remind him that Leipzig was a historical fact of life that predated the GDR. The thought of it had preoccupied him since he was sixteen, but now if he chanced to see a map of united Germany he made certain to avert his eyes from a chunk of it in the way that as a child he had hopped over the pavement on Tisbury High Street, warning Rosalind: "If you step on a crack, you break your mother's back."

"I still think it's weird," persisted the journalist. "I mean, to go from children to old people. That's one heck of a leap."

"I know what people say," as they walked into the grandish hallway, past the hat-stand and up the chunky mahogany stair-case smelling of beeswax. "'They're going to die anyway, they've had a life.' But I can help them. I can listen to their snores in the ward and believe it the most comforting sound in the world. As I keep telling my students, they're not bed-blockers, they're your mother and father."

"Tell me more about yourself," and she re-angled the tape recorder.

Well, he worked Monday to Friday, and weekends when on call, 8 a.m. to 6 p.m., with a break at lunch to exercise his dog in the park outside the Hilfrich Klinik, his teaching hospital in the west of the city. Then Tuesday afternoons he came here, to the Lion's Manor.

But the journalist wasn't interested in the Lion's Manor. She had visited enough old people's homes. "Where do you live?"

"I have an apartment in Charlottenburg."

"Tell me, are you single?"

"Am I what?"

"Are you married?"

"Is this relevant?" He stopped on the staircase. "No."

"Why not? You're an attractive man. Everyone seems to worship you. Or," blushing, "are you not interested in women?"

Her words hung in the air. He held his breath. Then turned and smiled at her, this determined woman with the wide mouth that didn't stop asking questions. A wide mouth and wanting to know all about him.

"Oh, I'm interested." But how to explain that no sooner did he reach out than something froze in him? That ever since coming to Berlin, like a knight waiting for a sign, he had trotted from one unsatisfactory selfish sexual liaison to another? How to explain that he might be alive and vibrant in the eyes of others, but for himself emotion had abandoned him? He had floated away from himself, not in a violent way, but gently, and now when he looked back he was no longer there.

She devoured his troubled face with candid green eyes. "Don't you want to have children?"

"All these questions," and took her gently by the arm. "They must be making you thirsty. Here, let's go into the kitchen." Opening the door on another affair.

PART IV

Berlin, 1996

CHAPTER TWENTY-THREE

ANOTHER SIX YEARS WOULD go by after Peter's interview with Frieda. A child born. A thousand and one deaths. If he looked back at this time he saw the tips of his fingers shushing a wide mouth and lips parting and small-boned hands tugging at his belt. He saw a sailing holiday in Hiddensee not long after Frieda told him, trying to see what could fly; the pearly heave of the sea, windmills rotating frantically on a flat grassy bank and his tiredness like the insects that appeared after the thunderstorm and crawled on his thumb and over his brow and flopped exhausted into her plate of herring and curry sauce. He saw himself looking at the rugby ball of pinkish grey tissue and realising what it meant to be a father. He saw in a procession of staccato images, like cage flies pestering a bird: the evening when he offered to marry Frieda; the letter appointing him consultant gerontologist; the moment when he went into the room in Otto-Braun-Straße hoping at last to discover his father's identity. In all of those years, with the exception of one visit home, he did not see his mother and his stepfather and his sister. Most of all he did not see Snowleg.

PART V

Berlin, England, 1996–2002

CHAPTER TWENTY-FOUR

MILO WAS BORN AT 9.02 a.m. at the Hilfrich Klinik on a beautiful Sunday morning with the sun still burning off the mist in the park. He weighed 5.5 kilos and measured 59 cm and was the biggest baby the midwife had ever delivered. He came out with a head elongated, rather like a crumpled bullet, his cone covered lightly in dark hair, and cried immediately.

"That's not a baby, that's a giant," the doctor said.

Frieda held him. She had looked radiant throughout. After a while, she offered Peter the baby. He lay quietly sucking his thumb with soft slurping noises, his squashed ears like oysters and his nose speckled with milk spots. Then he opened his narrow right eye and a fierce blue disc measured his father with a hypnotic gaze. Neither hot nor cold, neither focusing nor focused, neither old nor new, but a film of coloured life poised between the extremely ancient and the just-begun.

The heartbeat came regular and strong, like cavalry, on the monitor. Peter smiled at Frieda. "You realise he's just completed the longest, most treacherous 6-centimetre journey of his life."

"Now we've got to find a name," she said.

Peter hadn't given a thought to names. But the birth of his son had altered him. Going to wash his hands, he caught sight of his reflection and it was as if a hand had passed over his face.

"Milo?" repeated Frieda on his next visit. "Not very German."

"I was very close to my grandfather."

"What about your other grandfather?"

"I don't know his name."

So Milo it was. Frieda's last concession.

Until Milo was born, Peter's instinct had been to deny him, but this vanished at the first touch of purplish skin, and the spectacle of his son looking so serious and vulnerable (and so remarkably like his grandfather), prompted a visit to a building in Otto-Braun-Straße in former East Berlin. To settle once and for all the identity and fate of his father, he applied to see the Stasi file of Henrietta Potter.

He queued for two hours, at the end of which a harassed-looking woman told him flatly that the file was restricted to the file-holder.

"But my mother lives in England. Could she not give permission?"

A form was produced. Yes, the authorities might agree, there was a slender chance. But the process could take four years. And first Peter would have to return to England.

CHAPTER TWENTY-FIVE

"I. DON'T. WANT. TO."

His mother stamped her foot and looked furiously out of the window. The rain had been pelting onto the lawn for three days. No prospect of a picnic.

A morning in early June, 1997. Yet again he had come back unexpectedly. His mission this time: to persuade his mother herself to apply for her Stasi records.

"Well, I would like to read them," reaching into his jacket.

"Then, read them, why don't you?"

He hadn't brought Milo with him and she was taking it out on him. In one of her letters she had written: "Ros heard from someone that I was a grandmother. And you never told me."

"I've already explained it to you, Mummy. Only you can read your file."

"How ridiculous."

"That's the law."

He produced the documents that he wanted her to sign. The first gave him power of attorney. The second attested to the fact that she was too ill to travel to Berlin.

"But I'm not ill at all."

His mother, if anything, had become more herself. More eccentric. Still batting whatever she didn't wish to discuss into the attic in her head. He had always hoped that old age would deliver her to him, but she had contracted away to a territory more or less defined by her piano stool. "The sheer density of Beethoven", Rosalind had joked in her most recent letter, "has caused Daddy to threaten to go and live in North Africa."

"I take Honey for a walk every day. If it wasn't raining cats and dogs I'd be outside right now. Rodney's the one who's ill."

Rodney was in the dining room, uncorking a bottle of Moroccan red. Peter had been shocked at the change in him. His Derbyshire neck had become Derbyshire throat. Derbyshire lungs.

"I don't want to bring Dad into this."

"Well, don't, then."

Beyond the noise of rain, Peter could hear Rosalind preparing Sunday lunch. Her catering business was blooming – as was her waistline – and although she had use of their grandfather's flat she preferred to sleep in Peter's old room, at the rear, overlooking the fields. His sister struck Peter as depressed. She was unmarried, with no plausible husband on the horizon – unless one counted Silkleigh – and the thought crossed his mind and left it that she might be a lesbian.

"Ros, do you think it's healthy to live at home at thirty-three?"

"Probably not – why do you ask?"

"You can't have much of a nightlife here." And glanced around at the renovated kitchen and the blue French pots that dangled from the ceiling, easy for her to reach and for Rodney to pass under, but which Peter bumped his head into. So too, he suspected, did their mother, who, happy to hand over the cooking reins, seemed to deal with the new situation by never coming into the kitchen at all.

"Nightlife! That's a good one. The best I can hope for most nights is not to smell of onion."

Secretly, it relieved him that Rosalind was living at home. Their parents would never go hungry. She would keep an eye on them. But his sister wasn't concerned by their parents. "You criticise my life, Peter, yet you're the one who seems miserable. Did you ever find that girl?"

"No."

"I'm not sure any more if it would be remotely kind of you to walk into her life. Because I've seen you walk out of Daddy's life. As soon as you knew you had a father somewhere else, you were gone. What are you going to say to your father if you find him? I haven't seen you, Peter, for more than about a week since you were eighteen and a quarter, and I'm your sister, remember?"

All weekend he had had to endure her chastisement. "You know, Mummy brags about you horribly. The longer you stay away, the more illegitimate children you have, the more passionately they adore you. It is outrageous." And she poured another glass of Harvey's Bristol Cream. "It really is outrageous."

"I won't." He flattened his hand, refusing her offer of a top-up.

"What I want to know is, why are you never here?" she went on. "Remember when Mummy broke her hip and I rang and asked: 'What are we going to do?' You replied: 'Take her to Odstock.' But that wasn't what I meant. Oh, why are the ones who go away always let off the hook?"

It annoyed her, too, the way that Peter tried to make these visits his own by not announcing when he was coming. On this occasion, he had arrived home to a cold empty house. Rosalind out working and his parents at a drinks party. Notwithstanding the rain, his mother had turned off the central heating so that he couldn't even take a bath. He had crawled into bed under a dodgy electric blanket which at the last moment he decided not to turn on. He thought, How do these people live like this? Say what you like about the Germans, they had sorted out central heating.

"Well, what do you expect?" Rosalind said. "You never give us any warning. You show up and everyone's supposed to drop everything. It's always about you – *your* timing."

In the living room he put his arm around his mother's once-firm shoulder. "I'm a doctor, Mummy. I'll write that your husband's too ill to allow you to travel."

"Is that ethical? I mean, when I'm perfectly all right?"

"Mummy, please!"

"What good will it do, Peter?"

"It's my last chance to find out."

"Find out what, for God's sake?" stamping again.

"Drinks, everyone," announced Rodney, nudging open the door with the tray.

"If he's alive. His surname." And went to help her stepfather.

It was still raining in the morning. Everywhere in the garden puddles, and overhead summer thunder like a heavy bed being dragged across the sky. Rodney had left his yellow scarf on the kitchen table and Peter went to take it to him. He was surprised to find Rodney in the doorway of his studio, not sheltering but exposing his goitre to the flinch of wind and rain.

"Ah, that's where it is," and looped the scarf in a delicate knot around his neck.

"Dad, tell me what they're telling you," Peter said.

"Don't worry yourself, I'm in good hands," Rodney assured him with his light laugh. The steroids had given him a moon face. "They say it's manageable. That's what they say."

"Then, tell me what they're asking you to take."

"Perhaps you should tell me what they're asking you to take? We hear so much about young people on drugs. I sometimes ask myself whether my friend Silkleigh isn't on some narcotic. Extraordinary chap. Knows a few things, as your sister will tell you. He's become thick as thieves with Rosalind. He has this interest in a restaurant in the casbah. Said it would be marvellous if she came out to Abyla and taught the staff how to cook. Even offered to put her up in his spare room. She's been there several times and loves it. In fact, I have a mind to go myself."

Peter let him finish, then followed him into the darkroom, where he had some prints to make. Last Saturday, Camilla Leadley's third baby had been baptised in Sutton Mandeville.

In silence Rodney mixed the chemicals. Soon the room was filled with the acid scent of the fixer and the sweeter fragrance of the developing fluid.

"So," said Rodney, drying his hands. He looked at Peter, at the ropy hair and the dark skin, as if wanting to see himself in his stepson and not able to. "I have to think hard to calculate how long you've been away."

"Ten years."

"Is Odysseus coming home?" gently.

"Sorry, Dad. Not yet."

Rodney turned off the lights. Leaving just the yellow safe-light on. Peter watched him slide the negatives into the enlarger.

"You must know it breaks your mother's heart that you won't come home. She doesn't understand why you can't at least call. OK, you're building your career, but there are six-month periods when we don't hear a thing. I don't mind very much, but your mother does."

The enlarged image appeared on the sheet of white paper. Peter recognised the freckled features in the black face. All Rodney's stalwart artistic ambitions come to this. Camilla Leadley née Rickards. Holding Leadley's daughter over the Saxon font.

Rodney went over to collect the paper, a soft light bouncing back into his face that had taken on a look of stranded consternation.

He tried again. "Your mother would love to see your son. Even a photograph . . . You know your mother – heck, Peter, can't you see how much we miss you?"

It was another two days before his mother capitulated, and only after she had extracted a promise that next time he would bring Milo. On the day before Peter flew back to Berlin she allowed him to drive her to Salisbury, where he had made an appointment with Rodney's solicitor.

"Where do you want it – here?" and rapidly, as if signing a warrant, she wrote her signature.

She had always tried to leave it as a fairy story, but as they returned to the car, she said: "You know, it's not what I wanted" – and instinctively reached out to touch his cheek as if to acknowledge there had been compensations, but that these would be greater if her son stopped playing at being a German and came home. To this end she had left beside his bed, along with an article on "Passports for Pets", an advertisement scissored from the *Blackmore Vale*. Placed by the Salisbury District Hospital, for a senior gerontologist.

"What stops you from applying? Odstock's a very good hospital. Rodney swears by it. *This* is your home, darling, not Berlin."

But there she was wrong, and he felt himself fleeing the undertow of her maternal affection. He thought, I wonder if I can ever be English again. Berlin is home because it's little Milo's home. Germany is home. Even the East would have been home in the sense that I was once in love in East Germany.

"It's Gus," he replied. "I can't come back till they change the rabies laws."

"Oh, nonsense," she said, doubly irritated. With herself for giving him the dog in the first place. With Peter for using Gus as a reason to justify these brief surprise visits.

"Mummy, are you not interested in what happened to my father?"

"Of course I am, but there comes a moment, as you will one day find out, when for your own sanity you have to say *Genug*! At the moment I'm far more interested in my little grandson. You won't forget to send photographs."

"I won't forget to send photographs."

"What about his mother? Will you marry her?"

"I offered to, but she said No."

Frieda had wanted his child but not Peter. He didn't blame her. He had treated others no differently, taking only the crumbs he needed.

"This isn't the way, darling."

"All these lanes look the same to me."

His mother stared out of the windscreen. "You know, I don't think I've ever been down here before." Then: "Look at that blue comfrey. It seems nice, but don't ever let it in your garden. It's a complete thug."

After they had finished the lumpy gazpacho that Rosalind had left for them – a leftover from a wedding reception at Wardour – Peter borrowed his mother's car and drove to the post office in Tisbury. He wanted the application out of his hands.

"Can this go Special Delivery?"

Laboriously, with one or two crossings out and spilling across several lines of the space for the address, the postmaster copied the words into his ledger: "Der Bundesbeauftragte für die Unterlagen des Staatssicherheitsdienstes der ehemaligen Deutschen Demokratischen Republik".

"And how are you finding Berlin?" sniffed Mr Hesmond at last. His counter still gave off the comforting aroma of a polish that Peter had never smelled beyond this room. "A few more Germans than you'll find in Tisbury, I'll wager."

June 12, 1997, said the calendar showing Old Wardour Castle on the wall behind: 14 slow years and more since his denial of Snowleg.

CHAPTER TWENTY-SIX

IN HER ARTICLE ON the guard dogs, Frieda had written this:

A person who walks down a street or up a flight of steps or into a room emits a register of different scents. They vary from desire to shame to fear and they enter the air, clothes, furniture, to be picked up by the nose of an alert animal.

In his pioneering study of dog psychology, first published in 1910 and consulted by East German police until 1989, Colonel Conrad Most describes how, in addition to his own scent, the track of a human being comprises various smells. Shoe leather. Trodden grass or plants or insects. Dung.

Colonel Most makes several recommendations. Above all, urging the handler to treat his dog as an animal beyond good and evil, living in a world without moral values. A dog's ability to grasp an idea is akin to that of an infant who hasn't learned to speak. And like a child, the dog will learn not by logical thinking, but through the faculty of memory.

Early or late in the day provide the best chance of finding indentations in the soil. Leaves slashed by a walking stick. Twigs dislodged by a shoulder. In the dawn as in the dusk the earth is damp and where the foot falls the smell is stronger. Noon is not an ideal time to be looking. A sun high in the sky flattens shadows and footprints and the task of following someone through the undergrowth is that much harder.

Much later it came to Peter that a man of forty – stuck midway between his birth and his death – would be, from Most's perspective, in just about the worst position to read the track and to find what he was looking for.

On a snowy March afternoon in his twenty-third year of self-exile, Peter left the Hilfrich Klinik and drove to the Lion's Manor, the breath of an old golden retriever on his neck.

He parked in a lane below Wannsee station and walked up Am Sandwerder, the bland pad of his footsteps in the snow and the wind whipping large particles into his face. Growing up in England, he had never acquired the habit of gloves and when he reached the gates he put down his Gladstone bag and puffed on his hands, waiting for Gus to catch up.

Aloof from the street, the Lion's Manor stood at the top of a steep slope leading to the Wannsee. Bold facade of wine-dark brick. Chrome-painted stone pediments. Polygonal tower. So pompous and busy and squat, in unconscious mimicry of its first owner, a Viennese shoe-manufacturer, that tourists mistook it for the House of the Wannsee Conference on the bank opposite.

Peter's first sight of the building had been on a postcard that arrived at the Hilfrich Klinik, in which Sister Corinna congratulated him on his appointment as consultant and hoped that he would continue the tradition of Tuesday afternoon visits established by his predecessor. The photograph, coloured in the over-blushed technichromes of the 1950s, made the lakeside residence appear pinker and architecturally more pleasing than it was in life. A casino for American officers after the war, the Lion's Manor had served as an artists' retreat before its conversion to a nursing home, the local authorities believing that proximity to water would benefit the patients.

In the photograph, cherry blossom grew in a garish pink line against black-painted railings and oval leaded windows. This afternoon patches of snow piled beneath the trees glared at Peter with the dazzle of accusing eyes.

"Gus!"

He scanned the street for Gus's pale coat and a feeling of disquiet gripped him, a foreboding he didn't comprehend.

The snow had turned the landscape into a spectre of itself. On the frozen lake it fell in big, shining crumbs. The rim of the Wannsee was indistinct, but emerging onto the centre of it were a pair of skaters. Watching them, Peter had the familiar sense of floating beneath a rink of thick ice. His legs were horribly tired.

"Gus!"

He gaped into the spongy whiteness and felt himself blurring, an emotion so intense that he had to reach to a railing for support, in the next instant pulling back his hand as if he had touched a hot stove. The snow emphasised his feeling of incompleteness, a sensation of being jammed and branchless as though he was impersonating the person he used to be. He had loved snow as a child, its reindeer promise, but this afternoon something about it terrified him.

"Gus!" His cry whipped the white air.

Then his dog came panting up the pavement, through the open gate, onto the long front lawn. No longer deaf and overweight and half-blind, but behaving like a city dog released into a field, veering this way and that, with no care or purpose save to run.

Peter looked at Gus making mad figure-of-eights in the snow until he wasn't seeing a grey muzzle chasing flakes that fell from the sky like pieces of wet bread, but a puppy on an English lawn, eyes gummed shut.

At the thought of England he picked up his bag, the cold getting in under his clothes and snatching his breath. It was something solid he passed through and before he walked on he glanced over his shoulder in the way of someone looking to see whether he might have left his shape behind, an earlier self who watched him through the gate in ghostly surveillance.

Two nurses came out of the tower-room. The older closed the door behind them.

"She is a handful," said the younger one. And stood recovering on the landing.

Sister Corinna took from her the clip-board that contained Frau Weschke's notes. "The Herr Doktor will be here soon. He'll have her eating out of his hand."

The young student nurse looked up. It was the second day of her six-week rotation at the Lion's Manor. She had high cheek-bones and a prominent forehead. A slight laziness in one of her eyes gave them an attractive cast. "Does he have a way with them all?"

Sister Corinna was taken aback by the directness of the question. "You could say that."

The young nurse began to speak, but seeing something in the other's eye stopped herself.

Downstairs the door slammed and Sister Corinna felt her heart lift a little. Peter Hithersay never simply closed a door.

From along the corridor her newest patient continued to unleash her brimstone, but already Sister Corinna had tucked Frau Weschke's file under her arm.

"Nadine, come and meet Herr Doktor Hithersay."

Sister Corinna had worked at the Lion's Manor eleven years, the last six with Doctor Hithersay. She had an intelligent face and thick chestnut hair tightly knotted in a green bow. She was widowed with two teenage daughters and at forty-seven was seven years older than Peter.

She slowed as his familiar figure came into view. He had on his blue wool Masaryk hat and under his coat the usual uniform. Black turtleneck. Black trousers. Dirty white trainers. She liked the way he violated the dress code. The sight of him inevitably produced a sense of life beyond the Lion's Manor. He might be forty, but he had the shabbiness of someone still taking pleasure in being out of a school uniform. She understood why the nurses fell for him.

Sister Corinna watched Peter unbutton his coat, the only man she had let into her bed since her husband died. She remembered the moment in her office when she became aware of him standing behind her and seconds later his hands on her shoulder. Smelling of Pears soap, kebabs, strong English tea, his leather watch-strap. There was nothing of the dormant widow in her response. He touched her in places Thomas, her late husband, had always avoided and when he scurried his fingertips over the small of her back and between her buttocks, it excited her in a way she had not been excited since as a 9-year-old in Bremen she pretended to smoke one of her mother's cigarettes. He had known exactly what to touch and how, and she recalled telling him that he had intelligent hands and then realising from his reaction that he had heard it before.

In fact, it took a remarkably short time for Sister Corinna to realise that Doctor Hithersay was not a one-woman man. Over a toasted cheese sandwich at the Hilfrich Klinik's canteen, she had had to listen to a former student of hers – Sarah, another girl with cheekbones – crow about her nights with him. The girl was blissfully unaware that he juggled many women, but Sister Corinna had seen it for herself. Oh, yes.

One afternoon, coming silently through the swing door to fetch a glass of milk for a patient, she found Peter standing against a table in a corner of the kitchen. Kneeling before him was a woman in a plum-coloured shawl. Her head in his groin.

His eyes fell on Sister Corinna and there was something cut-off and grieving about them. He said nothing. She said nothing. His mouth was tight. And on the woman went, her lips against him in greasy ecstasy. The way a young girl might imitate a porn video.

He closed his eyes as if to say "Please go", and hugged the woman to him, not happy, not really there at all, but taking stock from a distant place like someone temporarily staying an execution. And so she retreated. Creating the dimension that would make possible their own odd relationship.

Oh, men with sad, slanted, olive eyes, you should all have been drowned in a bucket at birth.

Half an hour later, the couple came into her office.

"Corinna, this is Frieda. She's writing a profile of me for *Tagesspiegel*," he said dismally, and Sister Corinna saw what had happened.

"How very nice to meet you," and sweetly smiled at this slightly flushed woman with her shawl still hardly disturbed, who seemed to have no inkling that she had been observed. "I look forward to learning all about him."

But later Sister Corinna would want to know, levering out a slice of cheesecake and transferring it to his white plate stamped with a lion rampant: "If you're going to go after these girls, why not show more discretion? It's as though you want to be caught. There are plenty of places in the Lion's Manor to have a blow-job where you're not going to be surprised. Why do I catch you every time? Oh, my God, maybe I'm not catching you every time. The mind boggles."

He rubbed his face, his dented cheeks, and was contrite. It was terrible what Sister Corinna had had to witness. He had only consented to the interview on the understanding he talked about his research into the elderly. "But she started to get personal."

Sister Corinna regretfully forgave him his seduction of the brooding young journalist. He always clammed up when people asked about his past. But even she could see that Frieda's prying wasn't entirely to blame. He was lonely and she flattered him. She knew about his life. He didn't have anyone to have dinner with. In this desultory way they began their affair. He liked Frieda staying overnight every now and then, and she enjoyed being there. Until she found out she was pregnant and then she just went away, having already made up her mind that he would be a perfectly hopeless husband.

Sister Corinna had learned all this at first hand some months later, but she had backed off when Frieda became pregnant, and Peter had had the discretion not to call her. Although this was not a courtesy he extended to Sarah, who had wheeled Frieda in for an epidural not knowing that the journalist was having Peter's baby, or indeed anything about his involvement with the woman shrieking on the trolley, and still ludicrously imagining that she and Peter might one day marry.

"Why didn't *I* get pregnant?" Sarah despaired to Sister Corinna.

"Come on, Sarah, then you'd be shackled to him for life."

Once was a time when Sister Corinna might have wished this fate for herself, but no longer. She had long ago recognised that he would never be her solution nor she his. There was something barren about Peter's heart, something missing, something punitive about his unwillingness to give it all up – the 40-year-olds, the 30-year-olds, but mostly the 25-year-olds – in favour of settling down.

Sometimes when she caught his face in repose he looked like a man under the spell of a terrible passion that had torn up his life. She would have liked to ask him what was the source of his misery, but her will to improve Peter was not so powerful as her wish to preserve him as a colleague and a friend. She knew that if you went too close, or to where he had no wish to go, he simply glided away, as had threatened to happen some weeks before when she approached him with an invitation from the head of the medical council in Saxony. "Peter, I want you seriously to consider this. In the interest of reunification, I've been asked to persuade you to give a talk in Leipzig. It's terribly important. They would love it and they'll pay expenses. Here are the particulars. I'm willing to make all the arrangements. You'll only be gone two days. "

"No, I won't. I don't want to go to Leipzig."

"You didn't even give that two minutes' consideration."

"I'm not going to discuss it, I'm afraid."

"Don't be silly."

"No, Corinna, I won't change my mind."

"Peter —"

"Schwester Corinna!"

It was their most difficult moment. She had gone away disappointed, but with their relationship intact.

Her passage from lover to friend had been smoothed to an extent she couldn't have foreseen by the arrival of Milo. Soon after his son was born, she sent Peter a postcard: "Fifteen free hours of baby sitting." It only happened two or three times a year and he didn't take advantage of her kindness, but if something came up at the Hilfrich Klinik that threatened to chip away at his already limited day they had an agreement she would take care of Milo, whom he looked after every third weekend and whom Sister Corinna had first seen throwing his smiles from a pram, face just like his father's.

Peter was always grateful for her help, not least because he didn't want to prove himself unreliable to Milo's mother, still less provide her with an opportunity to reduce his visiting rights. Frieda, as a result, was furious any time Corinna's name was mentioned.

And stealthily he had crept back. He brought Milo over to watch videos and play with her two daughters, who loved the boy. Her family were convenient for him and the arrangement suited her precisely because she had two children and hardly any spare time. But she wasn't deluding herself. She wasn't a young thing vying for marriage or children, and when one night he asked "Shall I stay over?" she said, to his relief, "No, I'd rather we didn't. We've had all that. I love Milo and I love you, but I'm not going to put my heart on the line. In fact, it's marked in my diary. February 12. The day on which I promised myself I would stop dreaming about you."

At the sound of the curses flailing down the stairs, Sister Corinna removed Frau Weschke's file from under her arm.

"Coming," she called in her soothing voice, the one that told a patient to sit up and eat or they wouldn't sleep a wink. And went on down the stairs.

Peter looked up and his mouth cracked into a grin that made his face longer and, she thought, sadder. "Corinna!"

He finished tying Gus's lead to the base of the hat-stand, and peeled off his hat and hung it over his coat. A fishbone of white scalp showed through his black hair.

"And who is this ravishing creature?" catching sight of the young nurse on the staircase, and crossing the hall with a bounce in his step.

After she had introduced Nadine and Nadine with a troubled look and a blush gathering on her cheek had walked away, he warmed his hands on Corinna's chest. "So. Who do I start with today?"

The new patient's name was Frau Weschke. She had arrived in an ambulance the previous Wednesday with her granddaughter from the Anderson-Nexö in Leipzig.

He brushed the snow from his collar and from behind his neck. "Why on earth send her here?"

"The home's been closed for refurbishment. The superintendent persuaded Frau Metzel – her granddaughter – that in this particular case West was best."

They climbed the staircase.

"Any children?"

"One daughter, who died some years ago. Frau Metzel is appointed next of kin. I think she was frankly just relieved to have found somewhere for her grandmother."

They reached the landing and Peter took the file from her and flicked through it. "How old is she?"

"She's 103."

The only confirmation of Frau Weschke's advanced age seemed to be a letter of congratulation from President Ulbricht on her seventieth birthday. In his letter, Ulbricht noted she had been a member of the Socialist Party since 1910 and paid tribute to her work as Secretary of the Socialist Women's Union in Leipzig, and after the war – her husband had died in Theresienstadt – for her contributions to the Association of the Victims of the Nazi-terror. The letter was dated August 17, 1969, and had been forwarded from the Anderson-Nexö, a retirement home for "distinguished socialists" which she had entered in 1983.

"Frau Metzel apologises for the lack of paperwork. That's all there is. The government's been pressing her grandmother to exchange her GDR passport, but she refuses. She complains that she's carried the passports of Austria, the Czech Republic, Germany and East Germany. She's too old for another change of identity."

"Don't you sympathise?" groaned Peter.

"The last two years have been bad for her." Sister Corinna pressed on ahead of him. "Her eyesight's failing. She refuses her food. She lives on bread and wine."

Sister Corinna tapped the door and went in. "Hello, Frau Weschke," in a jocular tone.

On the bed lay a petite old lady with pink thin cheeks and, behind a pair of rimless glasses, eyes of a very light grey-blue. She had on a blue short-sleeve shirt and was sipping noisily from a porcelain spa-mug.

"Here is Herr Doktor Hithersay to see you."

The old woman twisted her head and ignoring Peter gave Sister Corinna a vinegary stare. "Schwester Corinna, this fish is off."

"What about the cake? Didn't you like the cake?" Sister Corinna had bought it with her own money from the bakery beside the railway station.

Frau Weschke dismissed the cake with a wave of her tiny thin arm. "No."

She opened one hand and counted off what she liked. Leek

soup with marjoram. River crabs with carrots. Sweet and sour lentils, and a slice of Leipziger Lerche pie.

"But I thought you liked cake."

Frau Weschke looked down at the slice on her plate as if she wished it would start eating itself. "I hate cake. I would rather be crushed into pulp a hundred million times than eat this cheesecake."

"It's not a cheesecake."

At that Frau Weschke suddenly asked, "Have you been to Leipzig?"

"No."

She glared at the nurse. "Isn't it exquisite that I who have eaten river crabs should be served cheesecake by a woman who has never been to Leipzig!"

Peter squeezed Sister Corinna's elbow. "Leave us together."

Frau Weschke scrutinised him after the door closed. She angled a hand over her brow and after a little grunt said, "I bet all the women in your life, Herr Doktor, have enabled you to do exactly what you wanted."

He thought about what she said.

She laughed. "To be on good terms with that one you have to tell her to go right straight to hell. I shout to her: 'Hedgehog! Cherry-picker! Berliner!'"

Her stern expression cracked. She glanced at something on her arm, slapped it. "Do you know the loveliest German word? It's not Prussian. It's Saxon." Her voice had become round and soft. "Moodschegiebchen. Ladybird."

Peter sat in the metal-framed chair beside her bed and experienced the sensation, as whenever he visited the tower-room, of being abnormally high up. It was a tall-walled, brightly lit and warm-smelling place, on the faded ceiling of which a fresco of two hunters in a forest looked down from another century. Dominating the room was a large window with a view through a corridor of lime trees to the Wannsee. Visible on one side was the kindergarten playground, with its rusted basketball hoop; on the other, an abandoned house with an overgrown garden and two ancient Citroëns without their tyres. All sheeted with snow.

He picked up Frau Weschke's file. Typical multiple illness. Bad knee. Cancer. Heart. Oedema.

He took the stethoscope from his bag and placed it against her chest and listened to the blood-chatter.

She coughed.

"Lean forward."

She moved her hips and lay on her side while he ran the stethoscope up and down her back.

"Any chest pains?"

"No," she said.

"What happened to your knee?"

"I fell on the ice once."

"You're not short of breath?"

"No."

He removed the tubes from each ear.

She turned and said: "Do you know what I would love? A sip of apple juice. You get so dry." She held up the mug – the name Karlovy Vary glazed in azure florals on the side – and pointed to a plastic bottle on the sideboard.

He rose from the chair and unscrewed the top of the bottle and felt a pang when he smelled the contents.

"Give me the mug," she called.

"Where did you get this wine?"

"None of your business. Give me the mug."

She looked at him in a pinched, terrifying way that made Milo's mother a Madonna by comparison.

He filled her mug to the brim. "You're going to the bathroom on your own?"

She gestured at the end of the bed. Her furniture had shrunk to a lacquered black cane with a silver horse-head handle. "I have that," taking the mug from him and fastening her lips to the porcelain straw.

"Do you have any questions?"

"No."

"For your low spirits, there's a new drug. In theory –"

"I don't believe in theory. I've had to be a Monarchist, a National Socialist, a Marxist, a Capitalist. And now I'm a very old lady." Her left hand went up to the film of white hair and she touched the scalp beneath, brown with age-spots. "No, young man, you can't fool me with anything revolutionary. The greatest privilege I know is to be stupid, especially very stupid," and her eyes flicked over the room as though every object that didn't emanate from Leipzig affected her with disgust.

He followed her gaze. There was an old fur coat with a torn lining on the back of the door and on the dresser beside the door half a dozen books.

"Do you read?"

"I don't want to, for some reason. I just want to be quiet."

"What about photographs?"

"Photographs?"

"Of you younger. I bet you were good-looking."

There was a loud colicky gurgle and silence. She watched him over the rim of the mug.

"I bet you were. Or what about a photograph of your daughter? Or granddaughter?" So that those who worked in the Lion's Manor didn't see Frau Weschke as a body in a bed. "You have to find the character of that person and make sure it never gets squashed." That's what he taught his students. What he had told Sister Corinna at their first meeting.

"No," she said dourly. "No photographs."

"What's this?" He hadn't noticed it at first. A board about 6 inches square. Lodged between the books. Flecked with strange beak or claw – or even paw – marks.

"My granddaughter. She made it."

He looked at the painting for a while as though he could hear a sound coming out of it. "It's good. I like it."

"I don't understand it," she shrugged. "I prefer things I can understand."

He propped it back and glanced at the newspaper discarded on her bed. "Would you rather be in Leipzig?"

She stared out of the window. Her face had become gaunt and he knew she was not looking at the skaters on the Wannsee. Her vision of the frozen lake was dissociated from what images raced before her glassed-over eyes.

"I would." And he heard her thinking. In Leipzig the girls were prettier, the men taller. And you could taste the food. "Leipzig is a great city, doctor."

"I know," he said gravely.

She turned her eyes on him and he saw himself in them like a cell divided. "You have been there?"

"Once, when I was a student."

"Once!" she said. "Once is for dilettantes. What do you do *once* that's worth anything? You can't see Leipzig once. Once is never!"

He closed his bag and prepared to stand up.

"Wait." She looked at him with renewed curiosity. She elevated her chin, her gaze nimble all of a sudden. "You're not German?"

"I was brought up in England. My mother's English."

Again she scrutinised him, her mouth open, her teeth shiny. The gaze of someone who had woken up. "And your father?"

"He came from East Germany. Before it was East Germany." He felt himself serve up the information.

"Ah." She nodded.

"My mother knew him for a day. I never met him."

They regarded each other and he forgot the depression that had overtaken him just now in the snow.

After he told her the story Frau Weschke stared at him in a way that suggested that what he had said affected her too. "Dorna! I know Dorna. A lovely village. It has a medieval forest and a lake like this one. You should go."

"I did, but I have to say the whole visit was coloured for me by an accident. We ran into a deer."

"You ran into a deer!" She put down her mug and gave him an incendiary glance that declared never in her life had she heard an excuse so pitiful.

"It must have escaped from the forest –"

Frau Weschke did not want to hear about the deer. "Did you ever find out about your father? How do you know he's not alive?"

She lay very still, her eyes focusing on his ears, and her question revived in his mind a campaign almost forgotten.

"I don't," he said.

In Berlin, the application to read his mother's file had got lost in the system for four years. Then last April a letter. Summoning Peter at a certain hour to the building in Otto-Braun-Straße.

He registers himself at the desk. Shows his passport. Receives a pass.

Presently, a skinny square-faced woman appears wearing a pleated fawn-coloured dress. She signs him in. "Please – this way."

He fixes his eyes on her dress, tined like a saxophone reed, and follows it along a balconied atrium – down below he glimpses his silver Golf and a grey muzzle poking from the window – to a silent reading room and a cubicle that cannot be overseen. It puts him in mind of a dream that often plagues him in which he has suddenly returned to St Cross to sit an exam that is crucial in some way and yet for which he is utterly unprepared and which furthermore he knows in advance he cannot pass. A dream in which his medical qualifications count for nothing.

"You may take notes with a pencil," she whispers and disappears to fetch the file. Then a man comes out, there is some muttered commentary and Peter is ushered into an office. Open on a desk is his application. Nervously, the man checks the documents. Item: a letter, signed by Peter, to the effect that his father is too invalid to allow his mother Mrs Henrietta Hithersay to travel from England. Item: a letter, signed by his mother and witnessed by a notary, giving her son power of attorney. Item: a letter permitting Doktor Peter Hithersay to read her file and take notes on her behalf.

"I'm sorry. There was a file on your mother, but in this region a very large number appear to have been destroyed. I can't say why."

"What about mine?"

For some reason it depressed Peter almost as much to learn that no file on him existed. It hadn't been removed or destroyed; it hadn't been compiled in the first place.

From downstairs, a stamping of feet and the babble of young voices.

Frau Weschke cried out, "What on earth is that?"

It was Peter's project on Tuesday afternoons to invite children from the next-door kindergarten to play for an hour with the elderly. "Society celebrates the beginning of life," he had told a dubious Sister Corinna when he proposed his "adopt a grand-parent" scheme. "We're not so much interested in the end. But we have to find a way to meet our end. Not shrink from it."

One of the first things to strike Peter about Germany was how the generations didn't speak to each other. Unlike in England, the grandfathers and fathers and sons of Hamburg all drank in different pubs. At the Lion's Manor he hoped, bit by bit, piece by piece, to dismantle this barrier. Shortly after he started to visit the nursing home, he contacted the kindergarten next door and encouraged the children to select a grandparent and bring them home-made cakes.

He started to enthuse to Frau Weschke about his project for integrating the old with the very young and his hope of what both generations could offer each other, when the door to her room burst open, slamming against the wall.

A grinning boy stood on the threshold. About 5 years old, with long dark lashes and a cartoon face emphasised by red spots on his forehead and cheek, the last vestiges of chicken pox. He looked from Peter to Frau Weschke and when he saw the old woman's expression he raised a tasselled tube to his lips and blew.

"This is Milo," said Peter, removing the tube from his mouth and leading him to her bed. "My son."

CHAPTER TWENTY-SEVEN

WHEN PETER VISITED FRAU Weschke the following Tuesday afternoon, he found her books littered about the floor and her mug upturned over a month-old copy of the *Leipziger Volkszeitung*. The room smelled damply of white wine.

"It's not me!" she wanted him to know. "It's him." Milo lay under her bed, a brown crayon in his hand. "He came in here and he knocked my cup over."

"I'll take him away." Peter always tried to get to the Lion's Manor before the children, but as he was leaving the Hilfrich Klinik his longest-surviving patient had had a stroke.

"No," she said. "He'll learn." She looked from father to son. "I tell you what. You won't go missing yourself while he's alive."

He stood over Milo. "What are you drawing?"

"River crabs," said Milo without looking up.

She had been describing for him how, as a young girl Milo's age, she used to catch brown crabs on the Pleiße. How they clung to the willows, very intelligent, very fast, and you had to creep up behind them.

"Maybe, Milo, you ought to go –"

"No." Frau Weschke looked at Peter sharply. "Let him stay. I had a child too, but no more."

Milo scrambled to his feet. "Look!"

Frau Weschke inspected his drawing and the smile warmed her face like a sable pelt. "Now *that* is what I call a river crab," in an altered voice. "Put it there so I can look at it. That's right, above the other one. And to think, Milo, you haven't seen a river crab! I tell you, it's not easy to catch them even if you do see one. And now I'm told they don't exist," she went on with a sigh. "But perhaps you know the taste, Herr Doktor? Didn't you eat them that time you went to Leipzig?"

"No."

She picked up her mug. The afternoon sun in her bone-white

hair. "Well, if you didn't eat river crabs what on earth did you do in Leipzig?"

She waited for his reply. Even Milo seemed interested to know his answer.

"I was part of a theatre group," he said carefully.

"You used to be an actor?"

"Only in the operating theatre," he tried to joke.

"No, I'm serious. Were you ever an actor?" her question bowed with implication.

"It was a mime. I was in charge of the lights."

"A mime?" She received the news with a strange look. She opened her mouth and with a scrawny finger traced the empty runnel between her eyes and down her cheek as if her face was not a face but an old right of way grown over with grass and wire and rusted cars. She went on looking at him and was on the verge of saying something when they heard the sound of children shouting.

A knock. A head poked round the door. "Come on, Milo," said a formidable lady with a whistle.

"See you on Friday," said Peter. Kissing the top of his head and breathing in the smell of crayon.

"Goodbye, Milo!" Frau Weschke called after him, her voice sounding faint. Distracted, she turned her head to the window.

They were alone in the room.

"Why don't I take you outside?" he said on an impulse.

She went on staring out of the window. Educating her eyes to sit still. Outside, the trees in white fur and two skaters curving backwards.

"Did you –" she began with great effort, but he interrupted.

"We can walk down to the lake."

She sipped from her mug. "Tell me about Milo's mother."

"I knew her for a month before she got pregnant."

"Do you live together?"

"No."

"Tell me I'm speaking out of turn, but have you ever married?"

"No."

"You have loved nobody?"

"No, that's not true. There was someone."

She turned. "Herr Doktor Hithersay, you know who is the unhealthy person in this room, don't you?"

"Come on," before she could speak again, "it's a beautiful day."

She embedded her stare in the door, still piecing something together. "All right," she said, as if she didn't want to reach a conclusion. "If you bring me my coat."

Frau Weschke insisted on putting on her coat herself. Her arm slipped through the torn lining and got lost in the sleeve and the coat settled on her bowed shoulders like an awkward cape. He tried to rearrange it, but she turned out of his reach. "This way my fingers will stay warm." Her annoyance seemed a continuation of a life-long argument with someone. "Fetch me that," she said brusquely.

He unhooked from the end of the bed the black cane. She gripped its silver horse-handle and with her other hand held onto his arm and they descended the staircase.

"What's that dog doing there?"

He introduced them. "Hello, Gus," she said, and to Peter, "Something's wrong with his eyes."

She shuffled forward and stopped. "You know the difference between a man and a dog? If you rescue a derelict dog and take it in and feed it and nurture it, it doesn't bite you." She looked down at the floor, avoiding Peter's eyes. "Can Gus come too?"

He untethered the dog from the hat-stand and the three of them passed into a dark loggia with its ceiling of carved teak and out onto a glassed-in veranda where two children from the kindergarten played Skat with an old man in a blue dressing gown.

"Twenty," said the boy.

"Twenty-one," said the girl.

"I'm passing," said the old man.

"Uli, Katarina, Petra."

The old man raised a waxen hand. Deafness cocked his head at the angle of a vintage car. "Afternoon, Herr Doktor."

"How are things going?"

"What was that?"

"I said how are things going?

Uli waved his hand as if chasing a fly.

It was one of the pleasures of being with old people. The ice above him – encasing him – melted. He felt light.

At their first meeting, he had grown unusually alert, almost happy, when Frau Weschke asked him to relate the story of his father. Conscious of her critical regard for him, he had looked forward all week to another afternoon in her company. Her abrupt change of attitude mystified him.

On the lip of the slope she paused and lifted her cane. A dense flock of swallows dipped out of the clear sky and flew between the lime trees, settling on the tower's lead dome. "That's early for swallows," she grunted.

"Everything's out of joint," he agreed and mentioned how at the hospital there were swallows already outside his window. They had arrived out of a gore-stained sky two days before and begun to build a nest under the roof.

She stared around vacantly. "I like swallows. But the way we live is destroying our planet."

The pale sunlight fell on her coat. A cormorant with a broken wing.

"Isn't that coat a weight on you?"

"No. Just my age. Come on, Gus."

The path descended under the trees to a concrete balustrade beside the lake. Down they went, right to the water's edge. Green lichen speckled the concrete and the sunlight flared in a trembling web over the pillars.

Frau Weschke had to stop to lean against the balustrade. He waited while she caught her breath. "In Leipzig, I had a garden," she said, looking back up the lawn.

Wriggling past them, Gus thrust a grey muzzle through a gap in the pillars and barked.

"Look, look!" Peter pointed. Two swans curled against the sky. Wings creaking, searching for a hole in the ice.

In a gruff, muddled voice she said, "You like swans? I think of them as large white pigs with feathers."

The swans flew on towards the opposite bank. On the lake a skater waved and Frau Weschke gave a tiny regal salute with her sleeve.

"Now," smiling, "I think we might go up."

He offered his arm, but she was determined to return on her own. Halfway up the bank she stumbled. When he went to take her hand all he touched was a cuff.

"Let me help you put this on properly."

"No, no. I like it the way it is."

He ignored her. He disentangled her arm and guided it back through its proper sleeve. "You should get that sewn."

She smoothed the thick fur with the hand he had liberated. "You only get a good fur if you treat animals right. My husband gave me this on the day of our marriage. When he put it on I was the Queen of Sheba —" She glanced around to see what on earth he was doing, but already he had scooped her up and was carrying her in his arms towards the veranda. He swivelled her through the door and her expression, which had started out as one of implacable hostility, changed as she met Uli's startled eyes.

Whatever it was that bothered her about the Herr Doktor, she had to admit that she had loved her ride up the bank.

CHAPTER TWENTY-EIGHT

FRIEDA INSISTED THAT PETER, on the weekends when he had Milo, would collect his son on Friday evenings and return him on Sunday nights. But this weekend she had an interview to do for *Tagesspiegel*. "You can have Milo for four days because I'm going to Leipzig."

"What are you doing in Leipzig?"

"Can't say. Read about it in the paper."

That was unlikely. He found her journalistic morality more unappetising than he would tell her, built on stilts of gossip and envy and allowing Frieda to peer from an affected height into the mess of people's lives, as if her subjects were in reality beneath her – and her own time, by contrast, more exciting and valuable. Her profile on him had drawn complimentary remarks from colleagues at the Hilfrich Klinik, but after reading the opening paragraph he had never got round to finishing it. Another thing that enraged Frieda.

"Well, next time I go to Leipzig," he said, "can you look after Milo for four days?"

"I'll bring him on Friday afternoon to your place," ignoring his tone. "Two o'clock. Sharp."

After her call, Peter found himself tidying up. The chaos in his apartment seemed to exaggerate the absence of someone who could, as Corinna would have put it, "look after" him. The living room was no bigger than his bedroom, low-ceilinged with two small windows that faced the railway line. One shelf of English books mixed with medical journals and CDs, a leather easy chair with a rip in the arm, a television and video (Frieda had insisted on this) and a faded orange sofa-bed – that was all his furniture, apart from the seventeenth-century oak refectory table from the vicarage in Tansley on which he piled his dirty plates.

Milo slept in the largest room, the walls decorated with his drawings of animals and with skeletons that glowed in the dark.

At the end of a narrow corridor, behind a door on which Peter hung a dark blue suit and tie – the only tie he possessed and which he kept for official occasions – was his bedroom. Two pairs of trousers, their underpants and socks still in them, vied for carpet space with abandoned shirts and trainers.

Even if Frieda didn't come in, it gave Peter satisfaction to know that his fifth-floor apartment in one of Charlottenburg's dingier streets was not in the state she would expect. But he was tidying up for Milo's sake as well. It had upset Peter when Frieda seized on Milo's chicken pox as a pretext to keep him home. As a result, he and Milo hadn't spent proper time together for a month. The only glimpses he had had of his son were at the Lion's Manor. Encounters which felled him.

An emergency kept him at the Klinik in the early afternoon. He got home just as Frieda was driving away and he had to follow her for some distance, flashing lights. They argued in the road, Milo observing everything from the back of her car.

"I've been waiting half an hour," she shouted, so angry that her shawl slipped from her shoulder. "Why didn't you ring, you bastard? Don't say you don't have my mobile number . . ."

He rescued the pashmina from the tarmac and in his most rational tone explained about Albert, his long-standing patient from Linz who had suffered another stroke. It was something that he knew annoyed Frieda, the way his voice went very quiet and polite when upset. She considered it overly English and hoped that her son wasn't going to inherit this trait.

"You have Milo once every three weeks, for fuck's sake," snatching back the shawl. "Can't you give up something to be with him?"

He peered into the car at their only point of contact. Scrunched his eyes at the serious face in the window, wanting to make it laugh. "Then please, Frieda, next time he's ill, I'd like to look after him."

"You would, would you? You mean you wouldn't dump him on Schwester Corinna?" letting rip at the top of her voice. "Does that mean next time he's ill you'll give him a revolting kebab from your normal street-stall and keep him up all night and not bathe him properly so that he comes back sunburnt and dirty? Why is it that the clean clothes I dress him in never come back? How many toothbrushes do I need to buy? Do you think I'm made of toothbrushes? For God's sake, this time *you* buy a fucking toothbrush. Prepare. Have things there. Absorb the fact you have a child."

"All I'm saying, Frieda, is that I'm perfectly capable of looking after him."

"Then why didn't you notice when Milo broke his ankle?" almost screaming now. "You kept saying: 'I'm sure it's fine – if not I'll take him in tomorrow.' And what happens when you take him in? He has to be given intravenous Valium! I tell you, next time Milo gets ill, I'm not letting him within 20 kilometres of his so-called father. I'd rather he go to the emergency ward."

"Stop it! Stop it! Stop it!" Milo was standing between them. Refusing to go with either parent unless they were quiet.

"Can't you see how gutting it is for me to leave him with you?" she spluttered, adjusting the shawl over her shoulders. "It's not as if we're splitting it and having an equal share in looking after him. What was it you said when I first met you? 'The shoemaker's son always goes barefoot and doctors' wives die young.'"

"I said I would marry you. I give you all the child support you ask for. If you don't –"

"Oh, shut up," though if she hadn't interrupted he didn't know what he was going to say.

"How is he?" he asked.

She glanced over at her son. His hands flat against his ears. "Better," edgily.

Along with Milo's overnight bag, she threw Peter a bottle of calamine for the spots. "Remember. I like him to be in bed by eight. Otherwise he comes home cranky. And to wear glasses when he watches television. And not to eat sweets, right? The last thing I need is an oversugared, overtired child who calls me 'Daddy' for the first day he's home."

She drove off and he took Milo to the Anti-War Museum in Brüsseler Straße (on Sister Corinna's urging) where Milo admired a pale butter dish in the shape of an Iron Cross, and then to a funfair in Mitte where for an obstinate hour they shot at wooden ducks and missed.

Next day they walked through a park near his apartment building where the snow lay grey and rough. They scraped together snowballs and lobbed them and afterwards he bought his son a lollipop and a video.

Back in the car, Milo studied Peter as though his father were something he had seen in a picture book. "I like snow," he said with emphasis.

Peter held his sticky hand and drove home to Charlottenburg where he had promised they would spend the evening watching *Star Wars*. "Once you've had your bath."

It was in the tub that Peter noticed the Biro marks on Milo's chest. Fascinated, he traced them with his finger and thought of his first incision and the dotted line his registrar in UKE had made with a marker pen. In the days when he was able to cut through a patient's mattressy skin.

"What's this?"

Milo looked down. "A man."

"Who is he?"

"Dunno." The day before, Milo's best friend at the kinder-garten had drawn the lines between his chicken-pox spots.

Peter scrubbed the flannel over Milo's face, but was reluctant to wash off the figure on his chest. All at once he had the sensation that his son was more joined up than he. He saw what Milo would look like as an old man. And while he couldn't discern Frieda's features in the arch of the brows, the wisps of uncombed hair, the glistening lips, he did perceive his own and this comforted him and at the same time gave him a wild brief stab of longing for the father he never had.

Pitter-patter and Milo came into the room with the video. Peter started the tape and they sat beside each other on the sofa-bed, Milo every now and then flashing him a sideward glance to make sure that he was enjoying it too.

"Good, isn't it?"

"Yes." A word he had spent a lot of time teaching Milo to say.

Milo returned his face to the screen, but Peter went on looking at him. Remembering the moment when he uttered his first word. As if Gus had suddenly started to speak.

He couldn't keep his eyes from his son's rapt profile. The boy sat there like an exclamation mark and Peter was overcome by gratitude that through Milo he had learned to see things again in primary colours. He thought, You wouldn't be here if your mother hadn't asked to interview me, and the arbitrariness of that fact, and of his own conception, seized him with a kind of solemn horror.

"Daddy, look at the film."

He tried to watch it, but couldn't concentrate. Who could Frieda be interviewing in Leipzig? And his mind drifted back to the letter she had written six years before and her article on Daniel Schreber.

Doktor Daniel Schreber was a Leipzig paediatrician with perverse and possibly dangerous ideas of education. His first son shot himself; his second went mad in a way that intrigued Freud into developing his theory of paranoia. He never lived to see the project for which his name became most widely known. Months before his death in 1861, Schreber came up with a plan that would overnight transform our nation's attitudes to gardens much as Father Kneipp had altered its conception of water: he proposed that the Leipzig authorities set aside the city's waste ground as an area for children to play in.

An anarchistic bureaucrat and an admirer of Dickens, the progressive more than the novelist, Schreber had observed at first hand the debilitating effects of industrial life on Leipzig's young population. He believed the only sane person was the farmer and envisaged a network of "pauper's gardens" in which the infant proletariat might exercise in the open air under adult supervision and learn to plant flowers, fruit-trees and vegetables.

After he died, Schreber Garden Associations sprang up all over Germany and even attracted the endorsement of Nietzsche. The gardens followed the model established in Leipzig. Land was cleared, mainly in the city centre but also on the outskirts bordering the railway tracks, and divided into allotments. Each allotment was the same size and each contained a small hut.

Intended as a domain for children, the garden colonies

were swiftly hijacked by adults – within two years in the case of Leipzig. Strict rules came to govern the number and variety of trees, the hygiene of plants, the height of the grass and hedges. In March, usually during the Leipzig Trade Fair, the water was turned on and in autumn it was turned off. A rule in force throughout the year banned anyone from spending the night in their hut under penalty of expulsion.

In times of fascism, many people hid in the Schreber gardens. Jews. Communists. Social Democrats. Lovers. Times change and yet in these allotments it is still possible to come across the hardy patterns of old East Germany.

On screen Luke Skywalker and Princess Leia prepared to swing across the abyss. As the music swelled, they kissed.

Milo squirmed: "Eeew, girl germs!" Then looked at Peter and in a matter-of-fact voice that confounded him: "You and mummy don't love each other."

"Well, we both love you."

CHAPTER TWENTY-NINE

ON TUESDAY MORNING, AS though Milo had invoked it, the snow fell again.

Sister Corinna had wanted to take him shopping. "I'm going to insist. I've never insisted before, but I'm going to now. You look like nothing on earth. You're frightening the staff. You might get a haircut at the same time."

"Corinna, I'm not – on your one morning off – going to let you shop for me."

He was relieved to be inside. An icy wind thrashed through the hospital grounds and lifted the pigeons from the trees, slamming them into a stone-coloured sky. The turn in the weather had confused the swallows. Black and white birdshit spread over the balcony outside his window, flecked with small feathers as if the wind had smeared one of the newborn birds on the ice.

"What a ghastly, ghastly day," commented Angelika, his secretary. She might have been pronouncing a death sentence on the sky. Everyone in the office looked pale and miserable.

At 2 p.m. Peter drove with Gus to Wannsee. He was about to go into the chemist to buy Milo a toothbrush, when his attention was caught by a young woman in a lemon-yellow jacket opening up the charity shop next door. She scraped the snow-sealed entrance to reveal a window piled with bric-a-brac. Without thinking, he followed her inside and noticed through his breath, balanced on a radiator beside a bunch of artificial leather flowers, a small pen-and-ink sketch of a giraffe.

He tilted the sketch to the light. A scene from a zoo. The giraffe accented in a quick blue wash and the figure of a man leaning against the railing. No signature, but the artist had written: "Leipzig – 1899."

"It's just a sketch but I like it," said the woman, who was older than her little suede jacket suggested. "It has energy."

"Look what I got for Frau Weschke," showing the giraffe to Sister Corinna. "Can we wrap it?"

"I thought you didn't have time to go shopping."

"What about that?" He nodded at a white bag.

Sister Corinna removed the boots she had bought and replaced them with the picture.

"See," he said. "It fits!"

"It doesn't look very festive, Peter."

"What if we put a ribbon on it?" He put his hand on the back of her neck and rolled away the bow bunching her hair.

"She's been quizzing me about you," watching him tie her bow to the strings of the bag.

"What did you say?"

"What else but the truth?"

"Which is?" to tease her. But he heard her thoughts. I've stopped fighting you for being a self-centred prick. I know what you give to your patients. It's admirable. I don't know when I met a doctor who has given so much, and if you weren't a doctor I'd probably loathe and despise you for how little you've given to anyone else.

She reached out and touched his ear as if she had scent on her fingers and wanted to perfume it. "To keep out of your way at all times."

He grinned sadly back.

"How do you know I didn't tell her that?" removing two dog hairs from his turtleneck. "I could have done. How do you know that I didn't?"

"Corinna, enough. How is she?"

"Not a good night," shaking her head and tidying up his knot. "I had to give her morphine this morning."

He kissed her on the cheek. "Thanks for this." And bounded up the stairs.

"Frau Weschke? Hello? Hello?"

She lay quite still. Her face at an angle towards the Wannsee. Her pillows propped up so she could enjoy a view of the frozen lake. Discarded on her bed was a copy of the *Leipziger Volkszeitung*.

"I've got something for you," he said before he had accustomed himself to the quiet of the room. Ordinarily when he approached the tower-room he would hear her squalling against one of the nurses.

She turned her head. At their first meeting two weeks ago, she had had the baby face of an old woman. Now her skin was taut with a carved-out look.

He put the bag on the dresser. "How are you?"

"I'm all right," she said roughly. "I'm full of beans."

"You look thinner."

"That would be some help if I was 80 years younger."

He read her chart. "The nurse says she's noticed some black stool. Maybe it's related to the aspirin."

"Could be," and reached up to her throat in the way of someone wishing to touch a necklace they have taken off.

"We don't want you to catch a cold."

Frau Weschke grunted as he took her pulse. It was no higher than normal. Her wrist gave off a scent of soap and it moved him. He heard the beat through his stethoscope and suddenly had the sensation of feeling closer to Frau Weschke than to anyone. Even though he knew little about her.

"Where's Milo?" she asked.

"He'll be here soon."

After a moment she said, "I think the time is coming for me to stitch that coat."

Her feet were cold, her nails the blue-grey of her eyes.

"Has your granddaughter been to see you?"

She shook her head.

"Try to drink."

He held her mug and she brought it to her mouth and then pushed it aside, sending her newspaper to the floor. Peter picked it up. The pages were open at a photograph of a snow-covered garden. "That's a very pretty picture."

"She sent it to me," in a voice that didn't seem to come from her but from another place.

The caption read: "Schreber gardens in winter."

"I was there once."

She twisted her head and looked at him with a different intensity. "Tell me about it."

He could see she was dying. "I spent the night in one of these gardens with a woman I loved."

She studied him. The muscles tightening around the eyes.

"Everyone thinks you're such a fine man, Herr Doktor." A pillow had slipped and he tucked it back under her shoulder. "I'm just an old lady. Why do I feel sorry for you?"

"Because I work so hard."

She darkened. "Always these games."

He fetched the bag and put it on her bed. "Look what I brought you."

He untied the bow and pulled out the sketch and held it up. "Just imagine. You might have seen that very giraffe."

She gazed at the animal and then at Peter. There was an opacity in her look and yet she seemed to be taking him in.

"Didn't you go to the zoo?" he said.

"I went once."

"Once?" But she wasn't in a mood to be teased. He continued in a gentler tone, "Weren't you born in 1899?"

"In 1899, I was 2 years old." She coughed and closed her eyes.

He did his rounds and a little after 3 p.m. slipped into the kitchen. A dark room of chequered oilcloths and long oak tables and institutional fridges that hummed. A bold shadow detached itself from a wall in the corner.

"Hello," said Nadine.

He unbuttoned her shirt and he felt her heart beat fast and her skin hot on his lips. He ran his hands under her skirt and between her legs and she raised herself on the table.

One eye sagged lazily. "Tell me this is a one-off."

"This is a one-off."

"Liar."

"Is that what you think?" with a lopsided smile.

"Is this where you break in all the student nurses?"

"Shh."

He started to kiss her into silence, but she twisted away.

"How long did it take to bring Schwester Corinna in here?"

At 3.45 p.m. he returned to the tower-room. Sister Corinna was standing at the head of the bed. He tried to catch her eye, but she wouldn't let him. All her professional focus on Frau Weschke.

The old lady's eyes were fixed on the ceiling. They moved back and forth over the fresco and she started to smile and then her face lost its expression and she looked frightened and frowned.

He leaned over her. What she was seeing showed in her face. She was acquiring lines of youth and joy and fear. "Frau Weschke?"

She began to mutter. "I left it out for you. I hoped you'd see it. I'm glad you saw it."

"What are you saying?" asked Sister Corinna.

He leaned closer. "I can't hear you, Frau Weschke. Speak up." He reached for her hand and she gripped him.

She moved her gaze from the ceiling. "I know what you got up to in Leipzig."

He squeezed her hand as if there was no need to say anything more, but she wanted to speak. She raised her head and the large pale eyes in which Peter saw himself divided stared right through him. "It's all right," and the thick nail of her thumb was pressing into his pulse. "None of us are very chivalrous or very brave."

He went downstairs and poured himself a glass of milk from the fridge and pretty soon his heart felt steadier. He turned out the light in the kitchen and passed through the swing door into the lobby, and flung on his hat and coat.

"I'm going now," he called to Sister Corinna and walked out, Gus at his heel, the door slamming behind them.

Outside, the snow piled up in dunes. He scraped it from his windscreen and climbed in and drove back to the Hilfrich Klinik. The car felt no warmer inside than out and his breath began to fog the windscreen. He wiped his hat over the glass, leaving streaks on it through which he dimly saw the street and the gobs of snow falling and below him the frozen lake and the lights pulsing on the far bank orange against the snow.

I know what you got up to in Leipzig. Frau Weschke's words kept coming at him. He tried to drive them away, dispatch them over some boundary from where they couldn't pursue him, but like a batsman setting off for a run that wasn't there he was conscious of the words hurtling back. His eyes flickered over the road. The snow rendered everything it touched so uniform that he missed the turning and ended up in a flow of traffic that carried him towards the dual carriageway. He manoeuvred into the right-hand lane and turned off at the next exit, realising too late that he was on a slip road leading into a parking lot.

Behind him a car hooted. He retrieved the ticket from the automatic barrier and the pole jerked up and he drove over the ramp, looking for a space to park. At every level the long line of cars followed. He drove until he came out onto the roof.

He parked in a polar landscape, ran one hand over his face and stared ahead at the city.

After a while, he opened his Gladstone bag and took out his mobile and dialled. The number was busy. Ten minutes later he called again. "I'm sorry I left like that. How do you think she is?"

"She's dying."

"Could I ask you to call when you think it's time? I'd like to be there."

"Of course."

"You promise?"

"Peter, I promise."

"And we should contact her granddaughter."

"I've been trying all day, but there's simply no answer."

"Keep on trying." Then: "Have the children arrived?"

"Don't worry. We've put Milo in with Uli."

"What did you tell him?"

"I said that Frau Weschke had gone to Leipzig to get some river crabs."

"That's kind, Corinna."

He remembered nothing of his drive to the hospital.

In the ward Albert's eyes were closed and his toes no longer moved. A junior doctor mopped his cheeks. He was 101 and his family in Linz had a street named after them.

"How is he?" Peter had looked after him for the past four years.

"Calmer," said Frau Doktor Ekberg, relieved he had come back. Peter picked up Albert's hand and felt the weight of his once-green fingers. According to Albert's daughter, he had been the best gardener in Linz. Grown the biggest apples. "They couldn't grow bigger!" And then one day something fused in Albert's head to make him dig up all his smallest apple trees and replant them upside down.

"Is that his X-ray?"

"We were unable to hold him still so it's rather blurred." She talked quickly. Oval face. Long nose. Hair cut short on jet earrings. "I thought the feeding tube would benefit him, because he's still not eating."

He looked to where her finger indicated. "That's his pacemaker, not his feeding tube."

"Then where –"

"There."

She stared at the X-ray and her face drained of colour. "Oh shit. That explains everything." She spoke urgently into her pager.

He said in a solicitous way, after she had finished speaking, "If his respiration rate drops below eleven breaths per minute contact the anaesthesiologist. I'll ring you in a couple of hours."

Peter entered the lift to go down, but it was going up. It stopped on the fourth floor and instead of pressing the button he stepped out. Swing doors led to the canteen. He chose a sandwich and joined the queue at the till. Two nurses were laughing over a date one of them had had with a real-estate agent from Wicpersdorf. "He gave me a way out so of course I stepped in."

He had not eaten since breakfast. He took a bite of the sandwich and chewed slowly and didn't take another bite. After a few minutes he rose and flicked the rest of the sandwich into a bin and when he left the canteen no-one looked at him.

On his ward round the patients came to Peter as through a gauze. He stood and listened to the low groans and snores and the men whispering in the mixed ward, like boys at school after lights-out. One of the doctors, a Bavarian with a pockmarked nose, walked up close and waved his hands, "Yoo-hoo, are you there?"

His second surgery was from 5 p.m. till 6 p.m. A patient was talking to him when Peter gasped.

"What's the matter?"

"Nothing, nothing," he told the patient. "Go on." But whatever

223

was being said, he couldn't take in. Frau Weschke's words buzzed at him and the memory of a young woman rose up like boiled milk.

When he was done he went through the day's charts. He checked the lab results. He dictated a letter to a referring physician. At 8 p.m., he telephoned Frau Doktor Ekberg. "How's Albert?"

"Asking for a newspaper."

"Eating?"

"They're feeding him now."

"That's good."

She said nervously, "Thanks for saving my bacon."

"I'm sure you'll find ways to do the same for me."

Before he left for the night, he dialled the Lion's Manor. Against every professional instinct, he hoped to hear that Frau Weschke had broken back into consciousness.

"Her throat's inflamed," said Sister Corinna.

"How much time left?"

"Her breathing is steady. I'd say you can go home."

In Charlottenburg, a message on his machine. "What time can I expect you?" He had made a vague promise to have dinner with Nadine at her apartment on Friday.

He crawled into bed without turning on the light and was up early to find a letter from Rosalind.

Dear Bedevere,

How are you? You never write back so how can I know? Here it's raining as usual. Daddy is asleep. He sleeps a lot these days. He has decided to hang up his camera (good) and is on a new course of pills (good) which make him very tired (bad). Mummy has driven to Tesco's. She's crankier than ever. She refuses to use the microwave, but is always asking me to heat up her tea/porridge/shepherd's pie.

I won't bore you with details of my business (good) or love life (chequered) or my last week's snorkelling in Abyla (a bit of a disaster). My love to Milo, whom I'd like to see not just in a photograph. And to you. Although, my liege, I fear I have forgotten what you look like.

XXXXX Ros.

PS. I did a shooting party for Camilla the other day. Tristram (rather sexy!) kept asking after you – in rather a vindictive way, I thought. "When I think of your brother, I do think: one of those people who should have done better." I showed him a photo I took of you in Berlin and all he said was: "If I hadn't known him at school it would be easy to mistake him for a Kurdish refugee." Blah blah blah. Camilla puts it down to the fact that he's lost his job at Morgan Grenfell (taken over by the Germans?).

PPS Do you still play football?

She enclosed a tongue-in-cheek column from the *Independent*, inspired by an England–Germany soccer match. "They haven't got a sense of humour. They are fat imbibers of beer, gobblers of sausages. Their country is boring. They are still Nazis. They are addicted to giving and receiving orders. And they are incredibly smug. We hate them all."

To which she had added in her looping schoolgirl hand: "Except MY BROTHER!"

He folded the letter away – he would write to her, he would write to her – and telephoned the Lion's Manor.

"Still unconscious," said Sister Corinna.

Tiredness gnawed in his head. At 2 p.m. he shut the door to his office and closed the blinds and tried to sleep on the couch. He had been asleep for 20 minutes when he heard a rap on the window. He rose and walked to the blinds, prised back the slats and looked out.

The balcony might have been a hot skillet and the swallow a pat of butter melting away. Then the rolling stopped and the bird hung its head and shivered once. One eye stared at where its snapped beak left a reddening trail, and a few seconds passed and then the bird lifted its wings to arrange them more comfortably and was still. There was a tiny arc of bird breath on the glass. He watched it fade until it disappeared.

At 2.35 p.m. Angelika opened the door and looked in. "Schwester Corinna on the line, Herr Doktor."

"Peter, you ought to come. Her feet are cold. She's shutting down."

He walked up the drive, feet slicing the snow and the soft flakes blowing into his eyes and gouts of breath pluming.

No-one in the lobby. On the first floor the sound of voices speaking in a hush. He climbed the staircase in long strides as if someone were following him. The words burst out when he saw the nurses in her room: "Dead? But I wanted to ask her something."

Sister Corinna calmed him down. "She slipped off very suddenly – quietly . . ."

They parted for him. Frau Weschke lay shrunken in her bed-jacket. Her face composed, almost beautiful. The skin as delicate and white as sunbleached shell. She was quite wasted even from the person of a week ago, her cheeks smoothed of pain and concern and time, her body loose and separated from her, careless like a coat she had hurriedly put on to greet an interruption to a long siesta.

Peter rested his hand on Sister Corinna's shoulder, but she moved away. He walked out of the room and down the stairs, thinking that now he was never going to have an answer.

CHAPTER THIRTY

ALONG AM SANDWERDER, IT was a day like the day he had suppressed. The trees seemed frozen to death and when he looked through their branches at the lake his chest tightened and he felt his consanguinity with the snow.

He crossed the street. Next to the station was Meyer's bakery, the haunt of single old ladies from Babelsberg. To knit himself to Frau Weschke, he ordered a beige Torte and attacked it miserably with a spoon. But he couldn't summon Frau Weschke. All he saw were the images stirred up by her last words and the tailfin of a 19-year passion.

I know what you got up to in Leipzig. It's all right. None of us are very chivalrous or very brave.

He nursed the words. Her death had snapped him. All at once he felt himself fully emptied on this freezing Berlin afternoon, the white tonalities of the sky and the snow falling.

From her stool in the corner a lady with a face of burl walnut watched him push away his plate. She raised a violet-papered cigarette to her lips and what she breathed out was wispy and grey like riflesmoke.

Of course, she knew about Snowleg, he thought. Because I told her.

He rocked back in his chair. Until the dying old lady seized his wrist, he had almost succeeded in forgetting. But Frau Weschke had penetrated the permafrost in which he had existed since March 1983 and the memory of Snowleg standing at the table in the Hotel Astoria returned with extraordinary violence, the memory fresher to him than when he had lived it.

He closed his eyes in order not to see her. He reminded himself: All over Berlin at this moment people are dying. And yet when he opened his eyes it wasn't Frau Weschke or Albert who stood, unageing, before him. He had battened down her memory for 19 years, but all the time she had been there. A white bird flying through the snow. Tracking him.

On Thursday morning, 9 a.m., he delivered a paper on geriatric recreation and after the seminar telephoned Frieda at her office. She answered, but he couldn't speak. After he had hung up, she rang back: "Don't ever do that again."

"I was going to say that I've got to go to a service at the Lion's Manor. I could collect Milo early if you like and drop him off later."

Silence. Then: "All right," unaccustomed to such gestures.

His tray spilled over with paperwork, but he made time to compose a letter to Frau Weschke's granddaughter on his own stationery. He wrote in his assured hand: "My son had come to think of her as his own grandmother." He signed his name and when he looked at the signature was overcome by an impression that he didn't belong to himself, that a counterfeit Peter Hithersay was sitting at his desk. He folded the letter into an envelope and copied out the address that Sister Corinna had put on a telephone sticker.

His mother had written, enclosing an appeal from the St Cross Development Programme. She always wrote to him at the Klinik, perhaps in the hope that he would treat what she had to say more seriously. She was worried about Rosalind. "I think it would be brotherly if you invited her out again. She's getting into a frightful rut and unless I'm much mistaken, Tristram Leadley has developed an unhealthy interest in her. Could you put her up in Berlin for a bit?" A PS from Rodney, which his mother would have been hopping mad to see, added: "Unless you would rather have Camilla? PPS A rather startling dividend has arrived from Silkleigh, so we'd pay for R's fare." He had included a photograph, a view from the ridge down to the house. Taken last summer.

At 11 a.m., Peter looked at the gift that his mother had presented to him on his sixteenth birthday (and which he had had repaired at tremendous expense in Bond Street). He changed his trainers for a pair of black shoes, put on his suit and tie and made his way to the chapel at the Lion's Manor.

Sister Corinna sat in the front row. She had spent much of the past two days distraught, trying to contact Frau Weschke's grand-daughter. According to neighbours, Frau Metzel's children, who might know where she was, had gone to stay with their father. In the end, there was nothing Sister Corinna could do. Frau Weschke's cremation had, according to her explicit instructions, taken place yesterday. Today, likewise, was to be the simplest possible funeral service. The family were not to be put to any bother.

Everyone Frau Weschke had insulted was assembled in the chapel. A dozen nurses and old people sang two hymns in weak, rattling voices. The only outsider was the kindergarten teacher.

"Milo will be upset," she said afterwards.

"I don't know why she had this service," interrupted Uli, grip-ping the pew in front for support. He wore dark lenses and the collar of his nightshirt poked up outside his dressing gown. "God is a fairy tale, that's what she told me."

Nadine looked round, gave Peter a wide-eyed look. He knew this look. It said: "Call me."

Not until after the service did Peter learn that contact had been established with the granddaughter. The previous evening Frau Metzel had telephoned from London where she was organising an exhibition.

"She went all quiet when I told her Frau Weschke had died." Sister Corinna was on her knees, packing the old lady's belong-ings into a white cake-box that she had picked up from the bakery. "The poor dear was dreadfully flustered. She's an artist and her exhibition opens tonight, you see. And I had the impression it was taking place in some village hall, not The White Chapel in London!"

"The Whitechapel?" Peter's ears pricked up. He squatted down to help. "By the way, you never told me what she was like."

"Just your type. Tall, blonde . . . booby."

"I didn't mean that . . .!"

"With glasses. Possibly bi-focals."

"Corinna! Stop it. I meant, is she a chip off the old block?"

229

"Anyway, I'm pleased she rang," said Sister Corinna, ignoring him. "Frau Weschke made me promise to take the ashes to her and to take this letter with them. Well, actually she asked you to deliver it, but I told her that was out of the question. You said you would never go to Leipzig." She pointed with her finger at the envelope on the dresser. In a wavy line across the width of it, Frau Weschke's handwriting like a bird-track read "Marla Metzel". Also on the dresser was the small board painted with beak marks. Peter stood up and handed it to her, then the books underneath: Dreiser, Dumas and a copy of *Gone with the Wind*.

He pulled open both drawers. The empty wine bottles rattled with Frau Weschke's inside-out laugh. Less than a week after arriving at the nursing home she had inveigled the kindergarten teacher, a teetotaller, into acting as her chief supplier. Usually, she made do with a Bulgarian white, Goldener Herbst, but her favourite was Saale-Unstrut, a rather dry white wine from Saxony.

One bottle of Saale-Unstrut remained. Peter put it in the cake-box, recognising with a twinge the page from the *Leipziger Volkszeitung* with the photograph of the Schreber garden. Sister Corinna had used the newspaper to wrap something. "What's that?"

"Her ashes. They came half an hour ago," and tucked the Karlovy Vary mug into a sleeve of the muskrat coat. "Everything? What about that?"

On the floor beneath the dresser was the shoe-bag. He took out the sketch of Leipzig zoo. "The cleaner must have tidied it away. Why don't you have it?"

"Oh, Peter," shaking her head. "If I hadn't noticed, it would have stayed right there."

"Please, I'd like you to keep it."

She poked around inside the bag and retrieved her green bow. Four days she had worn her hair down – had he noticed? She flicked back her head, twisted up the thick chestnut hair into a formal knot. "I tell you what, I'll put it on that wall."

Peter held down the flaps of the box while she taped them together and in her efficient way wrote out Frau Metzel's address with a felt marker. "There's just one thing won't fit," and she nodded at the end of the bed.

He unhooked the cane. The black lacquer had flaked off in chunks, leaving a mottled look. The silver horse-head was tarnished, but fitted comfortably into his palm. He waved it at Sister Corinna in the way that he used to brandish his grandfather's walking stick at Rosalind, and there shot through him – even as he raised the ferrule – the old, jubilant sensation that he wielded not an old lady's cane, but an ancestral sword. "Couldn't we send it with a tag on?"

"The post office won't insure it. Not unless it's properly wrapped."

He looked at her uncomprehendingly. He had no patience for this sort of thing. "Leave it to me. I'll take it to the post office."

"I promise you, you need to wrap it first – and they won't have a box for that size."

"For God's sake, woman, of course they will!" Before she could argue, he had seized the envelope from the dresser, tucked the cake-box under his arm and gathered up the cane. "I do love you every second of your blessed existence and you've been more than your usual brick-like wonder with dear Frau Weschke, but sometimes . . ."

A moment later the door slammed and she thought for the umpteenth time: This kind of impulsive behaviour really must annoy Milo's mother. And yet Peter's behaviour this afternoon was bizarre even by his standards. Before, whenever a patient died, his habit was to melt away and allow Sister Corinna to do his difficult work for him, like a child held at a railway-carriage window to say goodbye. He had never responded in this way to a patient's death.

Peter drove with Milo to the post office in Gartenstraße where the queue snaked as far as the stationery shelves. He selected two sheets of brown paper and a spool of tape and started to wrap the walking stick as the line hobbled forward. People in the queue watched with frank amusement as he struggled to copy Frau Metzel's address onto the crumpled paper. He had nearly achieved the wrapping of the silver handle when he reached the counter. "I want to insure this."

"No," said the woman. "Not unless it's in a box."

"Where do I get a box?" he asked, irritated.

"Go out, turn left and when you reach Wallstraße there's a store on the right, Krüger's."

He was marching Milo through the door when she summoned him back to pay for the paper and tape.

"I need a box," he told the man in the store.

"Well, you've come to the right place!" On his doughy face the hint of a moustache. "What kind of box? We've got boxes for books, boxes for clothes, boxes for china. We've even got wardrobe boxes."

"I want a box for this."

The man cast an estimating glance at Frau Weschke's cane and drew a long breath. "Not sure about a box for that."

Peter declined his eventual recommendation of a wardrobe box. "Look, it's just a walking stick."

"What you need is a speciality box," said the man. "A place that sells canes, maybe they can give you a box."

"Can you recommend somewhere?"

"No."

"Who might know?"

"Look in the business pages."

"Have you a phone book?"

The man laid a directory on the counter. "Excuse me, sir, but could you be quick, please," and went to attend another customer.

Peter telephoned an address in Theodor-Körner-Straße and with mounting annoyance listened to the phone ring. Milo had all this while kept silent, but his expression said: This is a lot of trouble to go to, Dad, for a walking stick.

"And the size of the cane?" asked an elderly male voice with a sniffle.

"What is it – about a metre?"

But the old man insisted on knowing a precise dimension.

"Look, I don't have a ruler."

"Then it's better you bring it in," giving an address at the other end of town.

Peter shouted: "It's easier for me to walk this stick to Leipzig than to mail it!" He banged down the receiver, grabbed the cane and was ushering Milo from the store when a voice raucously demanded that he pay 50 Pfennigs for the telephone call.

It was cascading snow in the street and the traffic had come to a halt. Peter opened the passenger door for his son and suddenly all the things that drove him insane about Germany rose up to torment him, crowned by the prospect of dinner with Nadine.

He stared at the bit of sticky tape dangling, the shred of brown paper, and boiled with so much fury that he wondered for a moment if Frau Weschke's spirit had invaded him. Her smouldering voice continued to address him from inside the cake-box. *I know what you got up to in Leipzig.*

He telephoned Sister Corinna on his mobile. "I've been halfway round this fucking city. It turns out you were right, which is no comfort. I'll deliver the goddamn things myself. If she's not there, I'll find the children or a neighbour. I feel I owe it to the old lady."

"You are going to Leipzig?" she said.

"Leave this to me. I've always been impatient to see Leipzig again."

"Peter Hithersay, you tell more lies –"

"You don't have to believe me. Just because for once in my life I'm doing the decent thing. Give me the telephone number."

"Well, it was her last specific wish. 'As soon as I'm dead, I want this letter sealed and to go with my ashes to my family.'"

"I'll do it for both of us," he said heroically. "Come with me, why not?" and for one terrible moment he thought she was going to say yes.

"Anyway, she doesn't live in Leipzig. Milsen's on the Czech border."

"The number, Corinna."

"Here it is. But she's not back before the weekend."

At last Milo spoke. "What are you up to, Dad?"

"You heard. I'm going to Leipzig."

"Can I hang on to Gus?"

"What would your mother say?"

"You know what she'll say. She'll be stark raving mad."

233

"OK, if she's going to be stark raving mad, I'll drop you on the corner."

Alone in his apartment, Peter poured himself a brandy. He packed a suitcase and made two telephone calls.

"Nadine?" But it was her answerphone. "Listen. You're not going to believe this. Someone's fallen ill. I'm afraid I've got to stand in."

And to Angelika at the Klinik to say that he would be – unexpectedly, but unavoidably – gone for the next three days.

"I'm taking compassionate leave."

"Who's died?"

"My grandmother."

Frau Doktor Ekburg could return the favour, he thought. But he didn't understand himself.

Not until he poured a second brandy did Peter begin to realise the extent to which he was completely unfree of his past. The alcohol that made him sentimental also made glow brighter the light dawning in his feverish head. Perhaps the fact that he couldn't claim to be free told him he was not such a shit after all. Maybe if he could scratch around at the bottom of his soul he would find a Rip Van Winkle of a knight who, if he behaved impeccably for a while, could rescue him with his soul exhibiting not one particle of decay.

The horse was saddled, his foot in the stirrup. Half an hour later he was in Bahnhof Zoo station, waiting for the Leipzig train to leave. Not pausing to examine his impulse, just following it. His instinct not so much that of a 40-year-old doctor with a wealth of commitments as that of a bird responding to the tug of the return flight.

It's all right. None of us are very chivalrous or very brave.

A very old lady had issued him with what he took to be absolution and he was going with a light heart.

PART VI

Leipzig, March 2002

CHAPTER THIRTY-ONE

PETER LAID HIS *HERALD Tribune* as a deterrent on the seat beside him and watched Berlin recede.

He found it hard to connect the city in which he had spent twelve years with the country the train was now speeding through. The snow, thinner on the ground, had in many places melted altogether, yielding to dark turfless soil. Fields without hedges prostrate between the villages, and houses the colour of bone boiled away.

When he arrived in Berlin, it consoled Peter to discover how few colleagues at the Hilfrich Klinik were curious to visit the former GDR or to renew contact with relatives there. They shared the attitude of Milo's mother, who, in one of her pieces, compared travelling through East Germany to watching television without the colour.

It surprised Peter to see that nothing had changed since 1983. This was the landscape that had once been dearer to him than anything in West Germany. Plain though it was, the countryside seemed to have more depth and texture.

At 2.35 p.m., the train stopped in Wolfen. Visible through a web of overhead wires were the stacks of a factory. The sky had the muddy wash of one of Rodney's watercolours. Grey chemical dust on the rooftops and a foul steam in the air.

A country itself has an odour too. The first time Peter had smelled East Germany was on a train. In his third year at UKE, he spent Christmas with Anita's family in Nuremberg – as he couldn't help calling it, still in the habit of thinking of German towns by their English names. They changed at Crailsheim where every second train came from Prague on its way to Berlin and Paris. And while East German passengers had to get off at the border, the trains went on. The brown plastic seat left all his clothes impregnated with an odour much like the industrial-strength turpentine with which his stepfather oiled his press. Anita had to explain that it emanated not from the fabric, but from the detergent used to clean the seats.

"Wofasept", he had heard or read somewhere, was still made in Wolfen.

Beyond the platform was a row of pylons with paint flaking from them. Graffiti on a boarded-up house read: "Foreigners out." Twelve years had passed since a disgraced Chancellor's promise that all this would soon be a flowering landscape.

Beyond Wolfen, the fields flew into dark forest. The trunks straight as nails into the sky, as if hammered up through the earth. Peter peered through his reflection into the trees rushing by his window and a trick of the eye made them roll back towards him.

He leaned his head against the window as when a child in his stepfather's Rover and the vibrations of the glass revived a journey through an unchanging landscape of chalk downs and blackberry bushes.

At Buchholz Zauch, the train rocked into a siding. He looked back along the line at a station straight out of his childhood. Salisbury, Tisbury, Gillingham, Yeovil. Apple trees. An unpainted bench. Geese in a yard. A dog ran between the disused tracks where tiny Christmas trees sprouted and men with guns advanced in a line across a vast field.

"What do you think they're hunting?" he asked a woman opposite, likewise watching.

"I hope it is the Minister of Transport," she muttered and went back to her crossword.

The field was ringed by a wood of silver birch. A deer ran out of the trees and froze on the horizon. The train began to move, the dog running and barking alongside. The smooth chortle of the wheels on the track had the tempo of a video rewinding. Far off the cough of a gunshot and through the sound of wheels and the dog's bark and a tunnel of 19 years, Teo's voice: "I think we've hit a deer."

As they came into Leipzig, the woman tutted: "Four thirty-eight."

Peter stepped down from the train and, tucking Frau Weschke's cane under his arm, he wheeled his suitcase behind him up the platform.

From beneath the station clock, he dialled Frau Metzel's number on his mobile. A boy answered. "Could I speak to Frau Metzel?" Peter said, wondering how close Milsen was to Leipzig.

"She's not here."

He gazed around the enormous station. The fluorescent lights. The escalators leading down to food halls. "When do you expect her back?"

He heard the boy ask someone in the room: "Katya, when's Mutti back?"

"Monday," said a man and a young woman together.

"Monday."

"May I speak to your father?"

A man came on the line. "Hello, how can I help?" His voice sounded awry. He might have been drinking.

"I'm Frau Weschke's doctor. Well, I used to be. Look, I have something for your wife."

The voice grew less guarded. "She's in London. And she's my ex-wife," and explained that he had come to collect his son for the weekend.

Regretting a little his impetuosity in setting off before Frau Metzel had returned home, Peter revealed that he had with him her grandmother's ashes and a few possessions.

"What kind of possessions?"

Peter struggled to recall the belongings wrapped in scraps of *Leipziger Volkszeitung*. "Some books, her coat, a spa-mug –"

An announcement came over the intercom.

"Where are you speaking from?"

"I'm at Leipzig Main Station."

"Then drop the box off at the left-luggage office, why don't you? I'll collect it some time next week?"

The man's tone made Peter uneasy. Offended by the casual reaction, he felt a spasm of anger that made it all the more important that he give the cake-box in person to Frau Weschke's granddaughter. Plus the letter. "I would prefer to deliver it in person."

"Then you must wait till Monday," the man said.

239

He unsheathed the walking stick from its ramshackle scabbard. His hand fitted comfortably enough over the handle, but the cane was far too short and it forced him to stoop in a way that reminded him of its old owner.

It was clear when he stepped into the street that winter was breaking up. He stood on the kerb and breathed in the cold scent of mud, redolent of the snow's underside and full of life. A cyclist rode by, plotting a path through patches of gravel, and on the news-stand, sharing the front page with the story of a murdered Turkish student, the *Leipziger Volkszeitung* forecast an end to the freak variations of weather.

The newspaper brought back to him the photograph on Frau Weschke's bed and a vision of snow-draped gardens. He had formulated no plan, but now he reached a decision. On Monday when her granddaughter came home he would take her Frau Weschke's ashes and then go back to Berlin. Meanwhile, he would explore Leipzig. He told himself: There's a sporting chance the gardens will be open. I'm going to walk around the city in the snow.

As he headed in purposeful steps towards a line of gleaming cream-coloured Mercedes, he was distracted by a word in the sky. On the parapet of the dilapidated building opposite, and spelled out in gigantic letters the colour of a ripe fig, he read -STORIA.

Peter threw the walking stick into the air and, catching it halfway up like a marching girl, he crossed the tramlines. He had no doubt about his destination. He would spend the night at the scene of his crime.

Graffiti splotched the curving limestone facade. "Ole has something against the Nazis". "Reality trashes brains". "Venom". Something flapped in the wind and he raised his head. Strung across two windows, like a holiday flag, a large banner advertised a renovation firm. Cautiously, he advanced beneath the canopy and pressed his face against the heavy glass door.

Stranded behind the glass, his shadow fell across a broken radio and objects heaped in the dust. A doorman's cap. A scroll of citrus brocade wallpaper. Calico overalls splattered with yellow paint. He wouldn't be staying at the Astoria.

It amazed Peter how the building had deteriorated. The gust of freedom seemed to have blown everything away. Of the gilt-framed oils, the counter where he had removed his coat, the Czech chandeliers, there was no sign. Mounds of rubble obstructed the corridor down which Sepp and Teo had shoved him. The floor was raw where carpets had been torn up and everywhere, as if something had exploded, were fragments of wood and metal and glass.

He reeled back and a shape moved in the dust. He looked straight into his face and was disgusted. He had the powerful impression that he had taken an ageing potion. That he was the memory of someone who had been caught in that explosion and died a long while ago.

The dapper young man in the tourist agency, establishing that Peter would prefer private accommodation, telephoned an address in Kantstraße.

"Anna, darling," smoothing his satiny double-breasted jacket, "I've a friend who needs a room, best discount." He glanced up at Peter. "What's your name?"

"Hithersay."

"Hithersay," he said for the benefit of the person he was speaking to and afterwards wrote down the address of the Pension Neptune, indicating the location on a tourist map and the numbers of two trams that would take him there. "You pay me 10 Marks and 37 to the landlady. Anything else?"

"Yes. The Astoria, when did it close?"

The young man knew a little about the Astoria. It was state-owned, then rented to Maritim – "who got out". Talks to sell the hotel to an American group had collapsed and the decision was taken not to refurbish it. The building had lain empty for a decade, one of, oh, so many monuments to the mishandling of state property post-reunification. "There's been talk of a new bidder. Although myself, I'd buy the Kempinski-Fürstenhof."

The Pension Neptune, which Peter reached in less than 20 minutes, was a modest brown-brick house with its own garage. He unhitched the freezing latch and walked down a narrow path at the same time as a fastidiously dressed woman came out to put up a "No Vacancy" sign.

Frau Hase, the landlady, was a snobbish but helpful spinster in her mid-forties. Bavarian, jug ears, cravat fastened at her throat with a plaited leather ring – and a yellow duster in her hand that she dabbed in a lunging, discontented fashion at all surfaces within reach. She had just finished redecorating his room which was why, she explained, it smelled of paint. She had difficulty opening the window and he helped her.

"I think the paint's made it stick," he remarked.

The room was simply furnished. Pink-washed walls, pine beams and six hooks along the door, from one of which dangled a white towelling dressing gown.

By the stubborn window was a round pedestal table and a pair of cane-bottomed chairs to which she had added identical covers, tapestried each with the outline of a sleeping cat.

The trousers of the previous occupant were still on the back of a chair and she gathered them up. They belonged, it seemed, to one of her regular guests. "Herr Mehring," she said, meaning to impress, "is a gentleman of experience in the manufacture of security doors."

"Is that so?" said Peter.

"He comes from Munich. Like me." She opened a cupboard, releasing a pent-up gust of lavender, then strode to the bed and switched the bedside lamp on and off. "The rooms have no telephones, but there's a payphone downstairs."

At the door she hesitated. Looked at the walking stick. "Are you ill?"

"No."

"I thought you might be ill."

He told her he was a doctor who had decided to spend a holiday weekend in Leipzig.

"Have you family here?"

"I'm looking for an old friend from the theatre, but I haven't seen her for some time and I don't know where she lives."

She smiled a broad smile. "Leipzig is a mere village with only half a million people. That is what they told me when I first came here – and it's true. Meet someone and it will take you half an hour to find someone you both know."

"Can I hold you to that?" opening his suitcase.

"You can." She seemed eager to prolong their conversation. Perhaps he would become a regular guest himself, like Herr Mehring. "And when you have found your friend perhaps you will have time to relax? Kurt Masur is conducting the Seventh at the Gewandhaus. I have the details below."

"Thank you."

She watched him lift out the cake-box and put it on the table. Would he be dining in? Tonight was seared haunch of venison with jus de juniper berries and cabernet sauvignon from Chile.

CHAPTER THIRTY-TWO

PETER WOKE TO A clear day and the chatter of birds. A sparrow vibrated its cry against his window and the sun glinted on the pine knots above his head. He sprang out of bed with more optimism that he had felt in years and after a breakfast of cheese, pickled onions and black bread he set out for the city centre dressed in a clean white shirt, a sports jacket, the trousers of his suit and the midnight-blue tie he had worn for Frau Weschke's service.

The sky was clear. It was the end of March, the beginning of spring. Maybe he would go to that concert, browse in bookshops certainly, and on Sunday make an excursion to Dorna. But first he was going to visit the Schreber garden where he had spent the night with Snowleg. There was probably a coffee shop there by now. He would drink coffee and dream a little.

At the end of Kantstraße, he hailed a taxi. "Yes, I know the gardens," said the driver, who had long hair and a squint and came from Croatia, where he was a famous poet. He was happier to be in Leipzig, though. "This car," he told Peter, "is two months old."

The traffic was thick and slow. Streets that Peter recalled as empty were bumper to bumper with new Mercedes-Benzes. They crawled past buildings concealed beneath scaffolding and house-sized advertisements for Pilsner.

Recognising nothing, Peter settled back into the corner of the taxi, the better to avoid its tart smell that reminded him of the innards of the fridge he had bought in a Christmas sale.

Two proper meals and a good night's sleep had calmed him. He felt able to concentrate on his quest, even if he hadn't defined to himself the nature of this quest beyond an impulse to retrace his footsteps.

As they still had some way to go before arriving at the centre, Peter repeated to the taxi-driver what the landlady had said. "How long do you think it will take to find her, driver? Half an hour?"

"What's the name of your friend?"

"Snowleg." Inside the car the name sounded cabbalistic. It thrilled him that it had stayed fresh, unmelted. His invention.

"Shit, what kind of name is that?"

"It's Icelandic," said Peter fondly.

The driver chuckled. "Less than half an hour. Man, there can't be many Vikings with that name in Leipzig."

"The problem is she's not Icelandic – and it's not her surname."

"What's her surname?"

"I don't know." He hadn't known his father's surname either – and was shocked at the coincidence, which hadn't crossed his mind until now. His single lead was his nickname for her. Based on a mispronunciation.

"You're looking for a woman with no surname? What are you, man, a crazee guy?" and his good eye checked Peter in the mirror. "What she do? A singer, is she?"

"When I knew her she was a student."

"What school she go?"

"I don't know."

A woman turned to look at him through a rear window and he saw a round face.

"When you last see her?"

"Nineteen years ago."

"How you know she still lives in Leipzig?"

"I don't."

"You haven't made it easy for yourself, man."

"No," and regretted that he hadn't returned to Leipzig sooner.

"You realise she could be anywhere?" said the taxi-driver, parking outside an iron gate. "America, Peru, Poland, Australia, Canada, Croatia – no, probably not Croatia . . ." His atlas petering out, he gave Peter his card and urged him, if he needed a reliable driver any time, to ring the number, any time. "Man, you realise she could be dead?"

Peter walked impatiently through the gate, looking to the right and left of him for a hut with a lime-green door. Gardeners stood greeting one another over their fences and privet hedges. From a boiler-suited man sanding a gatepost, he learned that the water had only recently been switched on after a six-month break. On this early day of spring, everyone wanted to savour the sunshine and their faces turned to collect its promise of heat.

He walked back on himself. Set off along another cinder track. Each time he stopped to look up a path he pictured, lounging on the steps at the end, his then self. Self-deceiving. Unkind. Cowardly. Not noble like Bedevere, but one of Leadley's barbarous Huns.

Was that the hut? He peered with an ache in his heart at the newly tarred roof and the pole from which a white and green Saxon flag stirred in the morning breeze. Beside a plastic pond a messy grey coil of hose had the appearance of guts.

Or that? In the next garden they were trying to light a bonfire. A smell of kerosene-soaked branches mingled with thick smoke. Children chased each other through a collapsible marquee and to one of the guy-ropes someone had tied the Ferrari flag.

Or that?

But none of it was familiar. He had come here at night when the gardens were covered in snow. Now the snow shrank into the earth, the big soft snowbanks turning into hard cones in the sun, and he didn't recognise the place. It was a lot smarter, a lot trimmer, a lot more *spießig* than the colony of his memory. And look where he would, no lime-green door.

Around another corner was a noticeboard. He marched up to it and began reading as though he would find Snowleg's name there. *Morilia frutigena*. A warning to "garden friends" about apple blight. A circular from a company intending to take earth samples. A reminder that dogs were to be kept on the leash.

Something smelled rotten. Under a hedge, revealed by the retreating snow, a scrap of grey fur with ants running around each other. Ants in March? He heard Frau Weschke's disparaging voice. *The way we live is destroying our planet.*

At the centre of the maze stood a white two-storey building. The upper floor was a museum devoted to the achievements of Doctor Schreber, and downstairs there was a bar. Peter ordered a coffee and sat at a table, listening to the chat of three men playing cards in the corner.

The lukewarm coffee stimulated in him the thought that the last moment he was conscious of being happy was in one of the allotments he could see through the window. He said to himself: At the very least, I can find out where she is. I could buy her a lovely scarf and a nice postcard. Maybe I could walk past her house before I post it? He composed the postcard in his head. "I have come back to Leipzig. You've been on my conscience all this time. I want you to know I haven't forgotten you and I'm bitterly sorry for the way I let you down. But I hope you've had a good life." That was what he wanted to say. It sounded to him like something Frieda might have written. And too much left out.

He put down his cup and went to the table in the corner. The smack of cards ceased as he approached. "Excuse me," he said, "but there used to be a hut here . . . with a green door."

One of the Skat players lifted his head. Fiftyish. Strong. Fat. "A green door?" looking at him with suspicion. "Sacha, do you know a hut with a green door?"

His companion had a pigeon-breeder's badge and a bald cranium. "Young man, I have known literally dozens of huts with green doors."

"It belonged to an old woman who passed it on to her grandson."

"The woman's name?"

"I don't know."

"You don't know?"

"No."

"And her grandson?"

"He was called Bruno but I don't know his surname."

They looked at him with pity, not bothering to shrug.

"Does the name Snowleg mean anything to you?" he said clumsily.

"How do you spell that?" asked the pigeon-breeder.

He spelled it.

The third player rose to his feet and called out of a window. "Willi!"

A moment later, a man shuffled in with guarded grey eyes and dark bushy eyebrows like kindling wood.

"Willi has been a member of the Garden Association since 1957," explained the bald man.

"Willi, do you know anyone called Snjólaug?" said the fat man.

"No."

Peter thanked them and plunged back into the pruned labyrinth, seeking an exit to the street. He consoled himself that the garden most likely belonged to a West German who knew nothing of the previous owner. He turned right at a fork and walked until he came to a dead end.

He retraced his steps. The hedges passed under his hand and from a branch a blackbird looked at him. By day the garden colony was a lot bigger than he could have imagined. Everything the same as if the disciplined hedges had been cultivated deliberately to confuse him. A conspiracy of trees and hedges.

Nineteen years before, he had had Snowleg to guide him. Without her, exactly as on his first night in Leipzig, he was lost.

Pouched in wrinkles of nut-brown skin, two eyes glittered at him with the sad fervour of his grandfather on the last occasion they met. Then the old man turned away and continued digging and Peter remembered other faces. Frau Weschke. Rodney. Alfred, his patient from Linz. All at once appreciating the impulse that had driven an expert gardener to dig up his apple trees and replant them upside down.

I know what you got up to in Leipzig.

"Please," he called over the fence. "Can you tell me how I get out of here?"

He burst into Aachener Straße. With each step that took him further from the Schreber gardens he felt his optimism fading as well as the prospect of attending a Beethoven concert at the Gewandhaus. The message he had framed in his head kept drumming at him, impelling him irresistibly into the search.

Peter's questions drew blank looks among staff at the Rudolph Theatre. No-one recalled a tall, dark-haired young woman with a name like Snowleg. Still less a 23-year-old student in a leather miniskirt, blue lambswool hat – "like this" – and wearing a strange bone necklace. The person who might best have remembered the theatre in 1983 was the director, currently in the United States on a scholarship to explain the former East Germany to the citizens of Bloomington, Indiana.

At 10.30 a.m., he visited the school of the St Thomas's choir. The door was opened by a man with a large moustache.

"Could I look up someone?"

"Who do you want?"

"She's called Snowleg."

"I don't know any Snowleg."

"Who do you know who could have studied here about 20 years ago?"

"I don't know any Snowleg."

He tried the Dmitrij Language School with the same result.

At Leipzig University, a helpful archivist, lately from Baden-Baden, she was anxious to point out, searched through records of students matriculating in psychiatry for that period, when it had been Karl-Marx University. She could trace no student who fitted Snowleg's description nor even a list of graduates. After 1989, she lamented, many papers had disappeared. "The bastards *I'd* like to track down don't even have nicknames!"

"But why would somebody sack a university records office?"

"The people at the Runde Ecke, that is to say the Stasi headquarters, went through the records of every university, every hospital, like locusts, scooping up all they needed."

"For what?"

"Ask them at the Runde Ecke – and when you've found out, please tell me."

Tugging at the back of Peter's farewell was a small surge of relief. Right up until the moment when he entered the Runde Ecke, he did not think he was going to mind if he drew a blank. This had been a dream. Rosalind was right. He couldn't just expect to walk in on Snowleg's life and say he was sorry. She was bound to have married, bound to have children. On innumerable occasions at St Cross he had willingly gone to chapel and not expected to discover God. This experience was little different. And while something was driving him to look for her, he didn't admit to himself that anything was at stake. Here on his first morning in Leipzig, he was conducting his pursuit in a carefree spirit that suited him. Lightly. In a manner almost cat-like. Terrified to be too earnest, or too hopeful, he was going through the motions of looking for Snowleg without inhabiting them. Conscious that at any moment he could turn on his heels and catch the next train home.

Four different architectural styles had merged in the former Stasi headquarters in Kleine Fleischergasse, the building capped by a black watchtower that sprouted from the pantiled roof in the shape of Darth Vader's helmet.

Peter reached the entrance down a lane that slunk behind a drab six-storey building erected in the 1950s. Panels above and beneath the windows were composed of an in-between colour like dirty carrot. To demonstrate a spirit of openness, not a single blind was drawn. And yet it made no difference. Another security service might be in place, but daylight continued to shun the windows and even the trees looked dead around the building. Their branches quite still in the afternoon air. Too frightened to move.

He arrived before a grandiose nineteenth-century doorway carved with putti that he could picture Rodney itching to sketch, and climbed the steps.

Inside the Runde Ecke, a former fire insurance office, Peter ran up against the impossibility of his quest. A man behind a Plexiglas screen confirmed what he had suspected all along and what his experience of investigating his mother's past had taught him. He might apply to read his own file, no-one else's. Applications were taking six years to process.

He received the three-page application form in the spirit of someone accepting a flyer outside a theatre and looked in a daze at the familiar list of queries, the blank spaces to fill in. Already, Snowleg's absence from the university register alarmed him. Had he read her name on a list, he might have stopped this search there and then. She would have achieved her ambition. But the omission was ominous. Why had her university file disappeared? Had she been harassed by the Stasi? Had he in some way contributed?

Peter had started out that morning hoping to cleanse his spirit, but now on all sides questions assailed him. Was she alive? Where was she? What had happened to her after she was taken away? How was he to find her? Questions he had once asked of his father.

He sat down to tie his laces. It wasn't until he stood that he made the connection. His mother's file would have been compiled in this building. Beneath the black watchtower the state police would have supplied details of Henrietta Potter's height, the colour of her eyes, the shape of her nose – even the book she had with her when she met his father.

About to leave the Runde Ecke, he noticed a flight of steps leading to a doorway opposite. The Stasi museum was open.

CHAPTER THIRTY-THREE

Peter went into the museum with the apprehension of someone walking into an examination hall. Since 1983, he had deliberately turned his back on the GDR. Over the next hour he absorbed himself in the regime that had separated his mother from his father and had nurtured Snowleg.

The boy in the turquoise tracksuit was eighteen. He lay on the asphalt in obvious agony. In another photograph crouched the Stasi officer who had shot him. Cigarette in mouth. Hands clasped around a pistol. The teenager was jailed for 20 months. His crime: Republikflucht. One of 63,949 arrested for attempting to leave.

An extract from the confiscated diary of Angela, a punk: "We have no freedom, we live in a mousetrap, I want to see other countries."

A cartoon of the British Bulldog as Death.

Images tacked to the walls of a cramped corridor assisted Peter through a history of the East German security police. He had overheard the statistics too often to be shocked. They had drifted over him like a Lesson in chapel: 174,000 unofficial collaborators, 132 kilometres of files, 360,000 photographs, 99,600 audio cassettes, 250,000 political prisoners, 25,000 dead, 33,755 bought free. His eyes skimmed over the case histories and he read without concentrating how twelve of the 19 committee members of the Writers Association were Stasi. He read how the novelist Christa Wolf suppressed all knowledge of her contact with the Stasi until a file prompted her memories. "I never told them anything that could not be heard anyway at any public gathering." He read how Knud Wollenberg had reported on his wife Vera under the name Donald. "I was reporting on myself as much as anyone . . ."

Peter served the elderly and it sickened him to think of how a gang of insane geriatrics had presided over this breakdown in trust. The permanent exhibition – it went under the name of "Power and Banality" – didn't evoke a country so much as his boarding school. A pressurised place where people behaved worse than in the natural world.

Half a dozen smallish rooms led off the corridor. The first had been a Stasi office. A map of Leipzig. Pipes on the ceiling. The rust-edged leaves of a dying pot plant. He noted the files clustered like fruit-bats in a cabinet and on the desk a manual typewriter in a corn-coloured plastic cover. The office was nondescript. What jolted him was the odour coming off the scratched lino.

Peter had remained sanguine while looking at the photographs, but the turpentine-smell of "Wofasept" pricked him. Oddly awakened, he passed into another room and found himself face to face with a selection of instruments used by the East German regime to watch over its people.

Once when a student in Hamburg, he had been moved by Canetti's description to make an expedition to Grünewald's altarpiece in Colmar. Neither Canetti nor any reproduction prepared him for the painting of the crucified Christ. So with these horrific works of art, salvaged from the Runde Ecke in December 1989 following a three-week frenzy during which staff had fed into the flames and shredder the evidence of a regime that had lasted 40 years. His age.

He stood engrossed. Recalling the disbelief, the impotence, the pornographic thrill that had shot through him at the sight of his first dead body.

A shelf of Leica cameras and radio bugs concealed inside watering cans, bird-houses, tree-trunks. An assortment of fake rubber stamps from Brussels, Tokyo, Buenos Aires, to make it look as if letters had in fact reached their destination and the Leipzig Post Office was simply returning them to sender, "Name unknown". An enormous gherkin-green shredding machine to convert personal files into pyramids of adobe.

The exhibits reached back to his science lessons at St Cross. Only, instead of creating earthquakes and volcanoes from papier mâché, this gerontocracy reduced the world to ant-heaps where everything that did not lie in its place was hostile.

He came to a wardrobe of disguises. "Supracolour" make-up

powder. A rubber patch to transform a full head of hair into a bald pate. A false belly with a camera-hole for navel. He looked into the cheating navel and all at once the stomach yielded to the image of the gnome in the Schreber garden.

His words returned to haunt him: *I love kitsch.* And he remembered a line of Canetti: "With kitsch he thinks he can protect himself against his future."

It both unnerved and aroused Peter, this material proof of how one fifth of the population had spied on itself. So much so that when he came to an ordinary-looking display case he was on the verge of walking past. The exhibit struck Peter as unremarkable compared to what he had seen. And yet for a long time after he left the Runde Ecke the contents of this particular cabinet took on a cardinal significance.

The two glass jars contained strips of yellow material about 4 inches square which might have been scissored from Frau Hase's duster. Something about the cloth strips – they resembled nothing so much as foetuses – took Peter back to his first medical experiment. Beside the jars a xeroxed page with typed instructions had turned grey. He paused to read and the heat rose in his bones.

How to preserve traces of smell

Every protagonist who comes into contact with the environment leaves behind, without noticing it, their own individual smell. Clothes or a chair can carry this smell. It's always a place where there has been direct physical contact.

To preserve this smell you need a sterile cloth and a pair of sterile tongs (which must be sterilised after each use). With the tongs, take the sterile cloth out of the jar and lay it on the trace material. Cover the cloth with aluminium foil and place something heavy on it. Keep the empty jar closed. After a minimum of 30 minutes – when the temperature is extremely cold or hot you will require at least two hours; or if you have trace material that is burnt or wet at least four hours; or if the trace material is made of paper or cardboard at least 24 hours – process the cloth and place it in the jar. Close the lid and stick a label on it and write whatever is necessary on the label. If you have collected tiny pieces of evidence which carry the scent, put these with the cloth inside the jar.

Certain things you should be aware of:

- These smells can be damaged by other people, animals, car exhaust fumes. That's why you must be quick and careful when getting the trace material. Before you start, think of where you will be most likely to find the individual scent of the protagonist. Think of how he/she might have acted so that you find the right place.
- Beware of getting your own scent on the aluminium foil. Please make sure you know exactly which person's scent you have taken. The best trace materials are: a chair, a bed, a pencil – or whatever they are writing with. If possible, place the cloth under the protagonist's belt between the T-shirt and underwear.
- Don't forget to close the jars and write on the label the date, the time, the place.

A friendly seeming woman he hadn't noticed sat at the reception desk and fanned her mouth as if she had eaten something hot. Mid-fifties, with short hennaed hair and the youthful complexion of the overweight, she glanced up at his approach and with a fine instinct for his mood enquired if he would like to know more about anything he had seen.

"Tell me about the jars," hoarsely.

She put down her hamburger and jumped up. Somewhere – if she could lay her hands on it – there was a photograph. She unlocked a cabinet and tugged out a black folder.

Addressing him in the garrulous manner of someone who had waited a long time to be asked this information, she told him that the Stasi had conceived the idea relatively late, at the beginning of the 1980s. In their mania to control everything, and in every way, they assembled a voice collection, a fingerprint collection, a saliva collection and finally they decided on a collection of smells. One of their intentions was to establish a direct link between

255

forbidden written material – underground literature, subversive leaflets, even graffiti on walls – and the person responsible for writing or distributing it. In 1982, a specially trained dog was bought from the police and kennelled in a villa in Leutzsch in the north-west of Leipzig. She had one word to describe the system: "Perverse".

"How many smells were collected?"

"Thousands. Now we know why there was a shortage of jam jars!"

"Where were the jars stored?"

A plump index finger pointed at the ceiling.

"What happened to them?"

For the second time that morning he heard the phrase. "Please tell me if you find out."

One winter night police had arrived at the Runde Ecke in a hired Volkswagen lorry and driven away the entire collection. On December 4, 1989, a large number of jars were discovered in police headquarters, including a complete collection of the Leipzig opposition. These jars had since disappeared, either smashed or confiscated. "No-one knows who took them, where they went."

She produced a page-sized black and white photograph. "Here's your dog."

The Alsatian sat on a bare planked floor as though at the centre of a clock face. Arranged in a circle were a number of glass jars identical to those in the museum's cabinet. Each contained a folded cloth impregnated with a suspect's smell. To judge from the pose – eyes glittering at the photographer, front paws thrust forward – the dog had identified one of them.

Peter was surprised to feel a kinship with the animal, even a quiet envy. The dog was innocent. Moreover, it had found what it was looking for.

He returned the photograph. "Tell me, how would I track down someone from that time?"

"Someone whose scent the Stasi –"

"Maybe," he said.

She stared at the dog. "I don't know – unless you can speak to someone who was Stasi." But as Peter doubtless was aware, the government had granted an amnesty to anyone working for the security service. "They keep themselves entirely to themselves."

"If I wanted to talk to such a person, how would I find them?"

She shrugged and her voice was despairingly downbeat with none of his landlady's polished cheeriness. "Luck? Coincidence? Serendipity?"

He headed along Dittrichring, head spinning. Exhilarated that a moment so transient might be preserved until now. At the same time fearful that he had pitched Snowleg into this evil, manic world.

His alertness spread into the street and set off the car alarm he heard. He liked the idea of a jar filled with Snowleg's smell, then argued the thought away. Not everyone was investigated. Wasn't he proof of that? It was naive and foolish – part of his romantic Western mythology – to suppose that because Snowleg had made an exhibition of herself in the Astoria her life would be endangered. The Croatian taxi-driver was right. Maybe she was dead or lived in the United States, Peru, Winnipeg. Maybe she had married a millionaire, like a depressed poet he had known. Maybe she lived in Charlottenburg!

He felt tender with hopelessness. He had found out nothing. He had no idea what to do next and coming to a little park he stopped to look at his tourist map to see if it might jog his memory. But the streets of Leipzig, like its university, operated under a new identity. Probably Snowleg had also changed her name, whatever it was. Anyway, she was bound to have a new name if she was married. And there was no point in looking for Bruno because Peter didn't know his surname either.

He kept on walking, feeling his frustration and impotence, not knowing where he was going. The street ranged ahead of him and he pictured 132 kilometres made up of files. But how could Snowleg have disappeared? Someone must remember her. She was too lively to be forgotten. And in the same way that as a 17-year-old in Hamburg he sought his father, he caught himself peeping into the eyes of people squeezing by. He yearned to communicate what he felt to those going about their business. He wanted to rush up, seize their lapels and ask: "Have you seen Snowleg?" For the first time since his arrival in the city, it was imperative he find her and make amends. And if he couldn't find her then at the very least to use this journey, which was going to be his last journey to Leipzig, to lay her ghost, cost what it may, suffer as he might. But where to begin, at least begin?

The railway station came back into sight and he recognised the word that jutted into the skyline, each purple letter the size of a man. The Astoria, at least, had remained faithful to itself. The day before, he had felt combative towards the hotel. But this feeling fizzled out and he looked with emotion at its entrance. Beyond that rusting brown canopy lay the room in which he had last spoken to Snowleg. Someone who had been in the Astoria that night, wouldn't they be able to tell him what had happened to her?

He returned to the tourist agency. Bursting into the office as if someone was grabbing him by the arm and pulling him back to a long oval table.

The young man recognised him. He had on a different suit. "Is Frau Hase treating you well?"

"Tell me, how could I get to speak with someone who worked at the Astoria in 1983?"

"With difficulty. Unless you find an old telephone directory in a jumble sale!"

Peter opened his wallet. "I can offer 100 Marks."

"What about Leni?" said a girl at the next desk.

"Leni. I forgot about Leni."

"Leni worked in the Intershop," the girl said. With the other's approval, she looked up a directory and dialled a number.

The voice that answered sounded reluctant. Leni was too busy. She had to go to the dentist.

"But surely you know *someone*?" said the girl. "What about Wilhelm's mother?"

Peter understood from their conversation that if Leni could help without being traced, she might be more open. "Tell her . . ."

The girl covered the mouthpiece. "What?"

"Tell her I'm trying to get in touch with old relatives."

Soon the girl was writing down the number of a woman who had been in charge of the hotel's kitchen. The young man took his money and passed him the piece of paper.

CHAPTER THIRTY-FOUR

"I SUPPOSE YOU WANT to sell me a second-hand Golf?" the voice said with something almost like fury.

"No, no. It's personal."

"I already have a nice satellite dish, thank you."

"I'm looking for a relative, a young woman you might have known."

"Who gave you my number?"

"The tourist office."

"What's your relative's name?"

"Her name is Snowleg."

"You mean Snjólaug? No, I don't know any Snjólaug. Where could I have known her? How could I have known her?"

"No?" unable to hide his disappointment. "Then I'm sorry to have disturbed you."

Frau Lube would tell Peter in due course that he had telephoned in the middle of prayers for World Peace. She was watching the afternoon service on television and had just completed a prayer for her late husband when she heard Peter's foreign-accented voice ask if it could come and speak with her. And immediately she felt the old and irrational dread that she had done something wrong. She thought of the overdue telephone bills. She identified with the child-snatcher whose photofit was in the newspaper. All the crimes committed in Saxony over the past year lurched through her head.

"Goodbye, then." On screen, the liturgy summoned her.

"Goodbye." But still he hung on, like someone wanting to order another coffee after the bill is settled. "No, wait! Were you at the Astoria in 1983?"

"Let me see. Yes, I was in charge of kitchen staff."

"Then I'd still like very much to talk to you."

Peter was to discover that nothing upset Frau Lube's enjoyment of her day so much as an interruption to the religious services she participated in from the comfort of her chair and which a satellite beamed to her from as far away as Wisconsin and the Philippines. And yet having decided the previous moment not to see him, she changed her mind. Her bad leg making it difficult to leave her apartment, her craving for company had deepened since her son had emigrated to Adelaide. As she would acknowledge early on in their first meeting, it was an awful thing to lose touch with a relative. Even if she couldn't help the Herr Doktor, he would be someone to chat with for a while.

"OK, I will speak to you. But don't come before four. And only for half an hour." Her grandson – Wilhelm's son – was coming to tea.

On the dot of 4 p.m. Peter climbed to the eighth floor of a pre-fabricated tower block in Zingster Straße. The landing smelled of fresh concrete and through a gap he saw the grey rim of a satellite dish and a skyline dominated by a metal flock of aerials and receivers and cranes.

He pressed the bellpush and waited. From behind the door came the tape-recorded barking of a dog.

The door opened and an old woman stood looking at him, lumpy but smartly groomed with curly, blue-tinted hair. A bottle-green dress fell over her large bosom and in one hand she held a Bible.

"You're younger than your voice," removing the pair of sandals from her doormat and fussing him in. "What is your accent? Are you from Berlin? You don't sound like a Berliner."

He smiled. Her face was powdered for God, or for Peter, like one of Rosalind's floury scones. "How do Berlin people sound?"

"A Berlin accent is short and snappy and bites you."

"I'm English."

"English indeed?"

With eyes raised, she accepted the rather wilted hot-house lilies and hobbled before him into her living room.

On television the German Chancellor was delivering a speech. She turned down the volume and tugged a sleeve over the handkerchief wedged there. All at once her face looked anxious. She gave the impression that she didn't know quite what to do with Peter or his flowers.

"Is that yours?" he said to start a conversation.

She followed his gaze to the poster of Che Guevara.

"No. It's my son's," and waved with the lilies at a photograph on the television set of a young man in his twenties with ropy black hair. "That's Wilhelm. Just before his accident."

She told him the story. The boy who always wanted a Volkswagen. The unscrupulous dealer from the West. The gear that jammed in fourth. The silver birch on the bend outside Luckenwalde.

"He was in the burns unit for a month."

With her free hand she picked up the photograph. Looked at it. Put it back. "Now he's in Australia. See."

On the wall a postcard of Ayers Rock, tucked into the frame of an old riverscape.

"Can it really be that colour?" She contemplated the rock, patting her hair. "That's what Wilhelm says."

"Why not?"

"Do you have children?"

"A son, 5 years old."

"And how old are you, may I ask?"

"Forty."

"Ah yes. Wilhelm's forty-two. Men in their forties, that's when things happen."

Peter waited for her to explain, but already she was sliding open a door onto a glassed-in terrace. She looked upset. Something about his face troubled her. A strange Englishman was in her home. What did he want? Really?

On the terrace were two low and uncomfortable-looking chairs and a beach umbrella.

"Sit down, sit down," she said, and went to hunt for a vase to put his bruised lilies in.

Peter walked to the edge and looked over. Below was a small lake which, Frau Lube explained through the sliding door, had once been an opencast lignite mine. Around 6 a.m. she liked to sit in her chair and watch the swimmers dip themselves in the freezing water. Just as she always slept well in rainstorms, so she felt warmed by the sight of those swimmers. Glad not to be in Rosentalgasse again.

She chattered on from inside the apartment and he was happy to listen. It was what he did well. His currency.

Frau Lube had abandoned her house in the old quarter with no regret. "Linoleum goes very cold in the Leipzig winter." The cold floor had pressed up through her bones and played havoc with her feet. The roof had leaked. Bricks poked out of the plaster. Whenever she stepped into the entrance she was assaulted by a smell of decay and damp and old mops.

In a spirit of optimism five years ago she had come to this housing estate in Grünau. "I thought life would be cheaper, and so to begin with it was." The only aspect she found distasteful was the dirty street leading through the estate. There was mud on her shoes whenever she walked up the steps, but it was a good new flat.

Slowly, her hopes had disintegrated. Wide cracks appeared in the concrete. If she turned off the radiator, the walls shook. The rent went up from 79 Marks to 710 – "with no improvements!" Her new neighbours were not so warm. "I liked the first ones, but they went to the West with their children."

Frau Lube limped from the kitchen and after setting down a vase of water on the television set she made a face. On screen Chancellor Schröder continued his silent speech.

Peter cleared his throat. "You know, I hope that –"

She cut him off. "There's something wrong with him. They say he dyes his hair!" and addressed the politician. "As long as people like you are in the Party, why would I want to be a member? First clear your Party! After what I've been through, don't I have a right to have good people in charge?" She turned to Peter and rested a hand on each haunch, her eyes radiant. "I'm going to tell you something you may not believe. We were happy when we had the Wall! There, I've said it. We had no criminals. Or heroin. No fascism. No graffiti. And these are just a few examples! Then come the Wessis and Ossis are worth nothing. The Wessis know everything better, the Wessis can do everything better, the Wessis can speak better. In Saxony, we're told that people don't work, are stupid, don't know enough." Again, she spoke to Schröder, supplying the words. "But would a puppet like you have withstood 40 years of communism and problems and done as much as a Saxon?"

"It's been a difficult time here, hasn't it?"

"We are the bad conscience of a great people, Herr Doktor," she said with melancholy, as if this was an expression she had acquired from her television screen. "I want to be German again." And switched Schröder off. "Coffee?"

"Yes, please."

Her words continued to reach him over the sound of the kettle filling. "The Wall was a part of me. I knew how far to go. Now I can't handle what's happening. It's too fast. What people say is true. I feel like an emigrant in my own country. If you behave badly no-one cares. Then at least someone cared and came after you. Now you have to take care of yourself." Like Schröder, she rattled away without being present. "I'm angry today, I'll tell you why. Everything I found important in my life and fought for has been lost and devalued by dye-haired people like him. They behave as if 66 years has no more value than this mud on my shoes. And yet who is going to say of their life that it has been a history of mud? No-one!"

Peter felt despair rising at the torrent his visit had undammed. He wasn't here on a geriatric round. Unusually, he found it hard to concentrate. He considered standing up. Taking command of the situation. But her monologue had a muting effect and he wondered if she wasn't silencing him in the way she had silenced the Chancellor. He began to shadow Frau Lube's words like an exterminating knight. Looking for a chink, an opening. Somewhere to land his thrust in this claustrophobic apartment. For that was now the shape his quest had taken.

Eventually, she appeared on the terrace with a tray. "Do you like sugar or milk?"

"Milk," he said.

She sat down. "Of course, we did things differently. But we did things. Men like Schröder, they have turned our world upside down. You know what's wrong today? They have created a world in which you can't afford essentials."

"Frau Lube —" and he tried to massage a question into this outpouring, but she was chinkless.

"Bread, transport, heating, rent — they're too expensive. You can only afford luxuries. Here, have one of these."

The box was labelled "Cologne Specialities". Since the Wall had come down, she was able to indulge in two luxuries only imaginable in her previous life. She had, via satellite, discovered a universal God. And she had discovered West German chocolates. Infinitely superior they were to the Russian mints that were left on the Astoria's pillows and which she had regularly pinched.

Nearly every chocolate in the box had tooth marks.

"Or don't you like chocolates?" she said cheerfully.

"I was thinking of my grandfather. He used to keep them in the freezer."

"I hate the creams," oblivious to Milo Potter.

He selected a strawberry cream with a corner missing and placed it on the saucer of his milkless coffee.

Frau Lube scratched her leg. "I'm not saying —"

But he was looking down. "What have you got there?" Without reflecting, he seized her leg and without resisting Frau Lube offered it up to him.

"That's quite a bad eczema."

"Is that what it's called? These doctors, I never understand what they tell me."

"What are you doing for it?"

"Doing for it? I'm scratching it."

"There's something you can use which would be quite straightforward."

"It's easier to scratch."

"I'll get you some cream."

A suspicious expression entered her face. Was he being showy? She gathered her leg. Leaned back. Picked up the box.

"These are my balm. Herr Doktor Peter, have another one. But you still haven't eaten the first. I tell you what, store this in your pocket. You never know when you might need a toffee-whirl," and passed him the only chocolate to survive intact the investigation of her teeth and thumbs.

He put it on his saucer, next to the other one.

She smoothed out her dress. "I warned that you were wasting your time," abruptly tucking her leg under her. "Who is this girl Snjólaug? A relative, you say?"

He prodded tentatively at the strawberry cream, rearranging it. "Let me come clean with you, Frau Lube."

One tells it best to strangers. And yet even as Peter described his meeting with Snowleg, he told the version that he had told his schoolfriends at the Garrick. The one he could live with.

Frau Lube sat very still. Only her mouth moving. No longer looking at him, but between two window boxes of black-eyed Susans.

"I will never forget her eyes as she stepped backwards," he said. "It's how I never wanted to treat someone – how I never wanted to be treated."

When he had finished he couldn't decide if what he had said meant anything to her or not. All the powers of her expression were in her mouth, eating a chocolate.

"Frau Lube, do you have any recollection of this young woman?"

She gave him a satisfied smile. "Oh, there are always girls like this. But they blur in my mind. Herr Doktor, this was a long time ago. Do you realise how many girls must have passed through the hotel?"

He opened his wallet and took out some banknotes. "What about this girl? Someone would have noticed her – surely?"

Frau Lube looked at the money. "All this for a simple drink at a crush bar?"

"That's not the point," he said quickly. Feeling the guilt and hunger of 19 years.

Frau Lube, who in her life had experienced hunger, folded away the banknotes and selected a hazelnut whip.

"And why do you want to see her?"

"I want to see her . . . To ask her – to see that she's all right," and he tried to make it less serious by laughing.

Slowly, she rolled her hazelnut. Sucking it clean. Her nervousness melting with the thin layer of chocolate. "Snjólaug, you say," pronouncing it correctly. "No, I don't know that name. And you do realise it may not even be her name?"

"What do you mean?"

"Many of the girls had special names. This name sounds very special, wouldn't you say? Maybe she was a whore. Maybe her name wasn't Snjólaug at all. Maybe the one thing you seem to know about her might be wrong."

"You're right, you're right." And the futility of it dejected him, sitting here on this chill terrace under a Bulgarian beach umbrella while a woman dressed for afternoon service ate chocolates. "But all I can do is ask and maybe someone will remember something, a detail, which will lead me to her."

Her face softened. "OK, you want details. Let me think. Details." She stored the nut in her cheek. Her hand touched a thick neck and then reached down to scratch her ankle. "There was a girl."

He looked up.

"If this was the incident you're talking about, which I don't say it is, it was much discussed in the kitchen. And while we don't agree on who she is, this girl, we all ask ourselves the same question. Why did the doorman allow her back in and not just get rid of her? I remember the cook saying, 'It's obvious who she is, otherwise why would he have taken such a risk? That's a Konsum girl' – what you would call a Stasi girl. There are many such girls in this time, you understand. The hotel is full of them. And there were others, students who prostituted themselves for money during the Book Fair. You know, for pantyhose or dollars. For very little anyway. And that's what one of the staff believes. He is vehement on the subject.

"So we don't all agree. This is sometimes the nature of our work, to amuse ourselves in the kitchen. And let me see what I say. Um, I say, this is a girl who may be very naive. She may be full of vodka. Or she may . . . no, to me, it's obvious, she's absolutely in love. And such a girl in such a state is capable of many things. She's capable of courage she doesn't normally have. This is a girl drowning, she has ten times her normal strength. The strength of a mother who can throw a car off her child. Do I need to go on? Yes, this girl knows what she wants."

"So you remember her!"

"A very short skirt, could she have had?"

"That's right!" his heart beating as if it was taking off.

"She was standing with the doorman in the staff corridor. To start with, I think it's one of the festival girls from the way she's dressed. She's young and I can see she's upset by something. For the first time in a situation, Anton – he's the doorman – doesn't know what to say or do. He's trying to calm her down. It's strange, but I feel an immediate pity for her. I ask her what's wrong. She's been done over by a Westerner, basically," and Frau Lube gazed down at her cup. The reflection of the coffee made a halo on her face. "I next recall seeing her in the bathroom. She's in front of the mirror and scrubbing off all her make-up as if it's terrible to her. And when she finishes the job she looks in the mirror for a long time. She didn't know I was watching –"

"Where she is now? Do you know?"

"This is many years ago. How can I know this?"

Now it was his turn not to believe her. He flung back his head. "Because you seem to know everything."

"Ah, Herr Doktor Peter, this is what young women want to hear. I'm too old. Now drink your coffee or it will get cold."

This was her only power left. To deflect him. And it seemed to Peter as though Frau Lube, pulling out all the defences of old age, had found to her surprise that she was less charmed by the man sitting beside her on the terrace than she was by herself.

The doorbell sounded, setting off a mechanical yapping. "That will be my grandson."

"Frau Lube, if I wanted to find young people, theatre people, anyone who might conceivably have been involved in the Astoria years ago . . ."

"Slightly younger than me?"

"Yes, where would they go? Where would they be drinking?"

She pondered the question. In the hallway, the dog continued barking. "You have to go to the Mädler-Passage. Down the steps. I can't go down there any more. The Auerbach's Cellar, it's called."

He licked his lips. "Look, I still need to talk to you. Can I come back tomorrow?"

A strong breeze had blown up, flapping her umbrella. "That's a rotten wind. Listen to it," she said happily, and struggled to her feet. "Maybe tomorrow you will come with another box of chocolates and I will remember something else. I prefer liqueurs to creams. My grandchildren don't get into them."

CHAPTER THIRTY-FIVE

PETER HAD NOT FORESEEN the relief he would feel, talking about Snowleg. When he mumbled her name to Frau Lube it became a solid wafer-like thing that drew the moisture from his tongue. Once he had told her story – even if it wasn't the whole story – she was there. Like a declaration.

He walked along Zingster Straße growing lighter with each step and with the sense of having seen a small bubble rise. Like a bubble on the Itchen that told him where a trout was feeding. By the time he reached the S-Bahn he was whistling to himself.

A train took him back to the centre. It was good not to be at the Hilfrich Klinik. In his new mood of liberation, he hunted out the building where Snowleg's grandfather had worked as a furrier.

A mania for restoration had swept through the Brühl. All around he heard hammering and banging and yelling. Suspended on platforms, figures in orange helmets sandblasted the blackened limestone and out of the grime and grease and soot of the old city the face of a younger Leipzig was emerging.

At last he found the building. A Red Indian in a red feathered headdress grinned down from the cleansed facade of the Dresdner Bank. From another doorway two eyes looked out at him, gummed and shiny. "Haven't heard that song in years."

Still whistling, he walked into the Market Square and registered the changes. The air in the back of his throat tasted of hamburgers, not coal. Couples sat eating under Peter Stuyvesant umbrellas and water splashed into the fountain where he had waited for her.

It was a bitter blow, therefore, to discover the Thomaskirche sheeted in tarpaulins. A "Bronto Skylife" crane blocking the entrance and an electric saw shrieking from inside. In his unbalance, Peter walked to the rear of the church where a notice declared the Thomaskirche closed for renovations. One glance at the double doors and he was coming out of them again. He saw the slimmer figure of his youth run down the steps and a green raincoat bobbing between grey faces, across the flagstones, into the brick building on the corner. There were seagulls on the roof and her image hovered before him like a bird.

What was she looking at now, at this moment? If only he could stand there and interrupt it.

It was striking six o'clock when he walked into the Mädler-Passage. The chimes vibrated into him, and catching sight of himself in the boutique windows, his dark blue tie like a pennant, he had a sense of time leaking away. He quickened his step as though he was trying to keep up with someone. Wishing her back into this mall so he might change what had happened.

Halfway along the Mädler-Passage he saw two statues, one on each side of the mall. This vision of Faust and Mephistopheles sharpened his recollection. He rested a hand on Faust's square-capped bronze toe as he once had seen Snowleg do, and cast his eyes over the shop windows for the wine bar. Nothing. Where his memory situated an art deco lamp were glass shelves stacked with Belgian chocolates.

And then he saw: the statue guarded the entrance to the Auerbach's Cellar.

Down, down, down he went. Through a warm hallway. Into a low spacious room with a vaulted brick ceiling. The place where Snowleg had wanted to take him. "You can't see Leipzig and not see the Auerbach's Cellar!"

His thirst increased at the sight of so many people drinking. He ordered a Weißen and drew back a chair and sat down, browsing the room.

Overvarnished paintings on the walls depicted scenes from Goethe's play. They had been restored so often that the original characters were somehow lost, but one in particular drew Peter's eyes – a panel of Faust mounted on a barrel as if it was a horse – and there rose, suggested by the cape and ruff, the image of himself as a medical student dressed up for the mime. The painting reminded Peter that Faust was a doctor too. Out of a sense of superstition he tried to make a connection between their two situations, but he couldn't.

He had been observing the drinkers at the bar as they assembled in tailor-made suits and sleek broad ties and as he watched them nudge one another – the way they clapped each other's shoulders, grinned, their cartoon welcomes and departures – he became aware of a woman with garnet-coloured lipstick taking him in. She sat at the bar and from time to time glanced round. Dressed in electric colours like a tropical fish, the bulk in her shoulders suggested someone aspiring to a corporate image.

At last she picked up her glass of wine and handbag and gravitated over toward him. "Are you an actor?"

"No," he said.

"Singer?"

"No."

"Schoolmaster?" enjoying the game.

"Why schoolmaster?"

"You look unhappy." She drew up a chair and sat down. "It's a true proverb," in a glib, seductive tone. "In Leipzig we say when there's room enough for one, there's room enough for two."

She took from her handbag a catalogue with a mannequin on the cover and dropped it on the table between them. She might have been trying to sell roses for a sweetheart. "Sure you wouldn't like something special for the lady in your life? Sometimes women are too shy."

He looked at the model and thought of a woman on a beach advertising Lamb's Navy Rum. "No, thanks."

She flipped open the catalogue. "Now, wouldn't it be fun to get up to a little cheekiness in that?" Amused, she repeated the description underneath. "The colour of morning's first light on the horizon . . . The ladies' styles are trimmed with feather-soft fluff and are perfect to tickle your man's fancy."

"No, thanks, really."

Her eyes delved into his. Her pitted complexion grouted with face-cream and her forehead scattered with bumps like a tablecloth with crumbs on it. "I never forget a face," and licked her lips. She may have been a little drunk. "I have a photographic memory for faces. I've seen you before. Where are you from? You're from England, aren't you?"

"That's right."

He saw her trying to place him as if he had been a client. And then she sat back nodding to herself. "OK, I've got it. If you buy me a drink, I'll tell you who I am."

He thought, God, have I slept with her somewhere?

"Have we . . .?"

"No, sugar, it wasn't me you fucked."

"Listen, I think you're mistaken."

"It was Snjólaug."

Peter gave a little gasp as though she had hit him.

"Hotel Astoria. You stood her up in, let me think, eighty –," and paused. "Nineteen eighty-three. The year the canal froze over. That was the year I broke my ankle and had to leave the profession."

The time stretched over her face and in vain he tried to read it. She sucked in her cheeks to help him. Put a hand to her head. "My hair, it used to be red. What if I said Renate?"

He battled to picture a slim woman with short marmalade hair, dark eyes and nibbled fingernails. In the line of her back, only, was there a vestige of the girl who had held Teo's hand in the taxi.

"Renate!" pulling forward his chair. "Of course. Renate!"

"I'm not Renate now. I have a different name – I'm Christiane." Changed it because she'd got married and had a daughter and hadn't wanted her daughter to know about her old life.

"What are you doing in Leipzig?"

Today, she sold lingerie in people's houses. "Direct sales, you'd call it. It seemed an obvious choice. I was used to dealing with the public," and winked. "It's sexy, but it's not raunchy, if you know what I mean. Grey singlets, stretch lace – satin's really popular. I've got a good eye for women's sizes. I can look at someone and see what size cup they are, what will look nice on them, what won't. Is this boring?"

"Oh, no. Fascinating. Do continue." And focused on her all his powers of attention as though what she had to say was bound up with his continued existence.

"In the old days," she went on, enjoying his concentration, "I'd

273

go up to town and have my bras fitted and there'd be a lady who went into the dressing room with me. It would take three hours and I'd come home in tears. I'd come back with nothing! It's particularly bad for women with children. If you live in a village, you can't just go into a shop and buy something. You have to go to town and there's fifty million other things to do and shopping for a convertible bra ends up bottom of your list."

She raised a plump orange arm to attract the waiter. "It's done by referral, pretty much."

"Tell me —"

"We sit over coffee, wine, whatever. Look at the clothes. Try them on. In no time, they're all running to the dressing room and saying: 'Well, what do you think?' Women like to have other people's opinions. You can't trust the shop assistant, but you can trust your friend to say: 'That makes you look like a whale.'"

Her eyes measured him and her voice sweetened. "You also get quite modest women who undress with their backs to their friends. Snjólaug was probably like that."

"Snowleg — have you seen her?" He tried to say it lightly.

She pointed out a pair of Petra trousers. "Now what about something like that? Wouldn't that add a little summer sunshine to her life?"

He read: "Get retro in these funky 70s-inspired hipster, bell-bottom pants with side splits."

She wasn't going to talk until he bought.

"All right."

"Colour?" Businesslike, in the way that Rosalind totted up the Scrabble score, she produced a notebook and a pink felt-tip pen. "They come in moondance, black magic and aurora."

"What do you advise?"

"Moondance is a lucky colour for a Pisces. Is she a Pisces?"

"I don't know."

"Don't know much, do you? We'll go for moondance. Size?"

"I've no idea. Let's say tall and slim."

She wrote it down. "Too slim, actually. Probably anorexic, if you ask me."

He fought to suppress his desire to ask, but it was like an erection he was powerless to hide. "Are you in touch?"

"The Spring range highlights the slightly sallow complexion," she said in a sonorous voice and waited.

"Then I'd like one of those."

"We don't have that in stock right now." She plucked at her sleeve. "Something like this would look lovely on a dark-haired lady." She pointed it out in the catalogue. Double the price.

"I'd like to –"

"What about a 'J'adore Capri' shirt for you?" She found the page. "'Your heart is mine in any language in our fun J'adore range.'"

"One of those too."

"Watermelon, forest mist or peach blossom?"

"You choose," exasperated.

Her eyes catalogued him. "Forest mist. Where are you staying? I actually have these articles at home. I can bring them round tomorrow and you can pay me then."

He gave the address of the Pension Neptune and she put it in her notebook.

"You want to talk to me about something? So, let's talk."

"I'm looking for Snowleg."

"Snjólaug," in a flirtatious way as if the name had come up for the first time. "Now that is one oddball."

The church hall. That was where they had met. "That's right, the party." She laughed. "You might have thought, Bruno being married to my cousin, we'd have bumped into each other before. But all the time I was fucking him, he never talked about his sister."

"Her brother was married to your cousin?"

"That's right. Petra."

"Then you must know his surname."

She looked at him with a lip-swallowing smile.

"Well?"

"Berking. Bruno Berking."

"Berking." He repeated the name. Trying to see Snowleg in it. "What was her first name?"

"That I didn't know, and I still don't. I knew her as Snjólaug because I heard you call her that in the theatre. As I said, Bruno never talked of her."

"Go on." He was sitting on the edge of his chair.

"Well, the night after the party there she was at the Rudolph Theatre – with you again. And your friend, the musician. Anyway, I'm thinking since you and Snjólaug are together, I'll go with your friend – I can't remember his name."

"Teo."

"OK. You see, they liked us to go with Westerners. Even artistic ones! They gave us special rooms, sometimes paid us. So we get in the taxi and as I recall Snjólaug confused me. This wasn't some tart who'd waxed her pubes into a Mercedes-Benz sign. I mean to say, it was possible to look at her and think completely the opposite. It was possible to think: This is a pussy who isn't going to catch one SINGLE mouse. But it did cross my mind she might be a student whore. You know, extra money at Fair time. And why not? And I suppose that's what I thought when I saw her with you in the crush bar and I didn't change my mind until I saw her fling herself around your neck. Something about her expression, the way she was dressed, I don't know, but it made me want to come closer. And when I heard her asking you to take her out of the country, I thought, This one, I'll get. I'll have her. But there was no time to warn anybody. I saw Teo leaving the bar and I followed – and there she was, about to curl up into that basket. Well, if I hadn't believed it before, I believed it now. She wanted to leave with you! And if that was the case, I was going to make sure I earned some credit with one or two people."

She studied her shoe. "I knew the doorman at the hotel, Anton. When he didn't let us through, I said to him, 'Can I have a word?' and told him it was important, I had to speak to Uwe – Anton knew who I meant. 'When Uwe hears what I have to say you'll be certain to let us through!' But Anton has his orders and he won't listen to me. 'You're not coming in and that's that.' Meanwhile, Snjólaug behaves as if she doesn't know anything. She behaves like an Olympic gold medal cuckoo, if you know what I mean."

"No, I don't. How do you mean?"

She drank her wine and licked her lips in a way that made them appear redder. "Well, all the time I'm speaking to Anton she's looking through the door to see if you are going to come out. Then I see her walking over. She's upset, I can tell. Hookers are full of pride. I don't know the experience you have with hookers. You can say something and they won't touch you again for a million dollars. But not this girl. I take her into the car park and I start to lay into you. I mean," shooting him a look, "it was pretty fucking tacky to ditch us without a word of goodbye, especially after you had agreed to take her to the Golden West! I even felt sorry for her, and when I feel sorry for someone there's not much hope. I told her: 'Forget it.' And gave her a whole heap of cheek about what cunts you and Teo were. But the stupid little bitch keeps looking at the entrance as if you're going to run out and save her from me.

"Next moment, she starts walking back to the hotel and this time it works. She gives Anton something. He takes her inside and I realise what's going on."

He watched her with intensity. He felt he was walking towards a woman with a gun. "What *was* going on?"

She flexed back her toes, testing the leather. "She was Stasi."

Into that gaping dreadful stillness cut the peal of complacent male laughter. A face at the bar took a quick look round and went back to a jollier conversation.

"She wanted you to smuggle her out so she could blow the whistle at the border."

"No." He didn't believe it. That wasn't his Snowleg. Because if it was . . .

She touched his arm. "Let me finish. Otherwise, she couldn't have got into the Astoria. No German girl would start to talk to the doorman as she did with Anton. In Warsaw, Kiev, Minsk, maybe. But in East Germany, we're all well educated. We know the rules. Really, it's impossible that she wasn't working for the State. It's really impossible."

"You don't mean —" But the rest of the sentence was already stiff in his mouth.

"I don't know how much you know about the Stasi, but even if you worked for it you'd never be aware of who the others

277

are. Two or three at most. And I thought, This has all been arranged. Anton doesn't know who she is and she's telling him. It's a long time ago, but I remember thinking something else." Eyes conspiratorial, she said: "Supposing she were to overhear me, she wouldn't like what I'm about to say, but even though she was about to play a trick I think the stupid little bitch had a real feeling for you. She was so aware of you in the taxi, presenting the nape of her neck to your gaze, that she almost broke *my* fucking heart. You probably don't know this, but she spent all her money on a perfume she hoped you'd like. And then you treat her like a window-smasher. Like a 10 D-Mark whore."

"Did you see her again?" still astounded, still fighting to digest this. Still not able to believe it.

She looked away, opening the catalogue as if to find the words. "Sure, I saw her again. I saw her come out of the Astoria and get into a Wartburg, didn't I? The two men with her are Stasi, I can tell by their clothes. And I'm nodding to myself: That's right, she's with her own."

The waiter had left a tin tray on the table. Peter stared down into his elongated reflection. "Stasi . . ." The thought had never occurred to him. Was it possible? Was he, not Snowleg, the victim? Did Renate's revelation make some sort of awful sense? Was that why Snowleg never gave him her name? All those improbable sob-stories. Her dashed hopes for a university appointment, her epiglottis, her brother. Concoctions to elicit the sympathy of a naive student from the West.

"Look, so what if she was Stasi?" Renate said this quite charitably and lightly stroked his arm to lessen the blow. "She had to have liked you."

He snatched away his arm. Repudiating her version. Clinging with a frantic strength to the precarious image conjured by Frau Lube. He had loved the girl he invoked to Frau Lube. Loved her.

"God, I need to see her," he said after a while.

Renate sat back and shook her head. Eyes merciless all of a sudden. "Honey, grow fucking up."

He stared at the tray.

"Aren't you a little late?" Her plucked brows quivered and in her eyes there flashed a complicated hostility. She sipped her wine. Her laugh resentful. "Sure you're looking for her? Sure you're not looking for someone else?"

"Who?" he bristled.

"You tell me. Someone in a smart white shirt and dark blue tie, for instance?" She toyed with her glass. "You know, when I heard what you did to her, I was jubilant in my horrible female heart that someone could be so mean to another woman."

"Where would I find her?" barely controlling his impulse to skim the tray into her chest.

"Let me ask you something," and she might have been examining a dubious garment that she wished to return to the rail. "What would you do if you did find her?"

"I'd tell her how sorry I have been all these years."

"Oh, really? Still in love?"

"Maybe."

"Honestly?"

He wanted to say: *Fuck you*. "Sure."

"Hah!" she said, stiffening and hostile. "Hasn't it crossed your mind that maybe you wouldn't even *recognise* her if she came down those stairs?"

"Don't be ridiculous. Of course I'd recognise her."

Her head moved back as if his breath were bad. "People like you, you're so educated, but you don't even know where the heart is."

"Renate . . ."

"Christiane."

"Christiane, do you know where I'd find her?"

She shrugged. "I'd try and find someone who was in the Stasi. Either someone who worked with her. Or someone who interrogated her." She measured him with a syrupy expression. "Depending on who you still think she is."

He tried to turn on his charm. Not a drop came out. "These people in the Stasi, how do I speak to them?"

"Money, of course!"

"So you're saying it's impossible!"

In the bluntness of her words he heard Renate telling a client that the garment they had chosen really didn't flatter them at all.

"It's impossible to find the people who were directly involved. You find them only by chance. You walk into a lift and you remember a pair of eyes, a face. You sit in the Auerbach's Cellar at the end of the working day and order a drink and talk to someone and it resurfaces. Or maybe the person at the next table is the person you're looking for. Otherwise, forget it."

He swallowed hard. "What would you do in my position?" He had never heard this voice he had. This note of irritated, chastened desperation.

"What would I do?" For the first time, she seemed to feel some of his emotion. And catching his expression she altered her tone. "I would put an ad in the paper. The Stasi are scared of us. As we used to be of them. They won't tell you anything. But for money, yes. People will do anything for money."

He reached for his wallet, but she stopped him. She wrote down something in her notebook and ripped off the page and tucked it under his glass. "Take this. It's a formula. A code they'll understand. Put it in the personal columns. Another way, you'll search until death." She finished her wine. "As for me, I've talked quite enough for one night."

She was preparing to sweep the catalogue into her bag, when she paused and her hard eyes liquefied at the sight of the model. "Forest mist. It suits us both – in different ways. Know why?"

"Why?" in a recovered voice.

"You couldn't care less, but I'll tell you." With lipsticked sententiousness, she said: "Ossis are watchful, like animals in a forest. But Wessis are lost. You don't know where you are. The forest is inside." She pushed the catalogue towards him. "Keep it. You may want to order something tomorrow. Seeyuh, honey."

CHAPTER THIRTY-SIX

IT WAS PAST 8 p.m. when Peter left the Mädler-Passage and crossed the square to the tram stop. He walked through the slush, a salty grey soup that seeped over his ankles and made his socks wet. He had set out from the Pension Neptune that morning in a spirit of optimism, buoyant at the thought of Snowleg and of the possibilities the day held. A tram rattled to a halt and he climbed aboard with his head forward and his arms away from his side as if carrying two heavy suitcases.

People looked up. Friday evening faces going home. A fat girl eating a sandwich and in the back three pimply boys throwing something bright between them, back and forth. They seemed to be teasing each other. He took them for American students.

He punched in his ticket and sat with his back to the driver. His thoughts were extreme and he couldn't co-ordinate them. They kept swooping back to Renate, modifying the idea he had of Snowleg. One moment she appeared at Renate's shoulder as a spy and seductress, like a girl from the catalogue in his pocket. The next on Frau Lube's arm as a victim of his cowardice. And he recalled his conflicting impressions during their first walk together through the Brühl. The book-stealer in the black jeans with the cigarette had been sexy, but the righteous tour guide from the Leipzig information centre had not.

The tram stopped. Behind him doors hissed open, bringing into the carriage a gust of chill air.

"Fucking tourists."

An old couple hurried past his seat, faces tense.

Figure after figure emerged from the collage of speculation and memory. He couldn't help thinking of the overvarnished portrait in the Auerbach Cellar, the versions superimposed and proliferating so that they blurred. Faust on a barrel blurring into the image of himself on a barrel and then into Snowleg.

"Hey, you! Fat pig!"

In the back of the tram the cries had grown louder. A whistle blew and one of the boys jeered at the girl. She ate without registering their taunts. There was something sad about her hugeness. Short-haired with glasses, her cheeks expanding as she chewed. Perhaps she was retarded.

"Fucking elephant!"

The tram picked up speed and the girl straightened her back. He felt his mouth on Snowleg's scar. The texture of pearl. Why had he said "No"? Shocking and strange, but compelling his tongue to taste it. How did the same lips arrange themselves to permit that word? The skin softer than kid glove leather. Pale. A young honey. His teeth on the scar. Biting it. Smooth as the velvet wax of an artichoke heart. The surprising hardness under tongue and tooth that he can't draw into his mouth. The white of a child's eye refusing. The white of her eye at the table, refused.

"No wonder you're alone," came a depraved, unstable cry.

And he had said, "No."

The tram stopped. Three sets of eyes staring at him in his dark blue tie and his gloom.

"What you looking at? She a friend of yours? Know her, do you?"

"Yes!"

The girl didn't take on board that he had defended her. She hauled herself up and moved hastily to the exit. Seconds later, she passed beneath his window and he saw her looking back, fear on her face as she lumbered off. Other passengers followed and in a marshy corner of his mind he was aware of the tram draining, doors closing.

He raised his eyes. Only the three boys left. Their heads close-cropped in a uniform haircut as if with the same shaver.

The driver, enveloped by glass, concentrated on the tramlines.

Galvanised by Peter's answer, one of the boys ambled down the aisle and took up position a few inches in front of his face. Belt buckle. Black leather trousers. Maroon jacket of boiled wool.

Crudely sewn into the sleeve, the insignia Peter had mistaken for a college crest read: "The Run-Over Babies".

The boy held out a brown paper bag in parody of a busker's

hat. He had a referee's silver whistle in his mouth and blew it softly. A low glottal vibration.

Peter dug into his trousers and tossed two Marks into the paper bag.

The boy peered into the bag, then at Peter's clothes. His free hand, the one not holding the bag, reached out and rubbed Peter's tie between his fingers. With one of the fingers he tapped a turned-up nose of which the pores were collected with dark bits of night.

"I think you can do better than that," he twinkled. "Don't you?"

Peter hesitated. "But I haven't —"

The boy drowned his reply with a louder whistle in which the glottal disappeared.

Peter looked around to see if the driver had taken notice.

The boy lowered his face to Peter's ear. Close to, he reminded Peter of no-one so much as Leadley. Sinuous and conniving with a mouth constructed from another part of his body. He blasted a third time. A piercing shriek that knifed through Peter's skull and skewered him against his seat.

He took out his wallet. The boy grabbed it, removed all the cash. Threw it back into his lap.

The tram stopped. Peter clutched at his wallet, his ears ringing, his mouth dry. He stood up to say something to the driver, but the three boys were behind him all at once.

He stumbled out. As soon as he stepped onto the road he realised it wasn't his stop. The door hissed shut and he heard a snigger. They had followed him off.

Peter tried to walk away as if he knew where he was. He slipped his wallet into his jacket and headed briskly down a road that soon tapered into a housing estate. The thought crossed his mind that this was probably where they lived. Suddenly, there was nobody around.

The walls on either side rose in a steep cliff of tower blocks and grey facades. Pocked, filthy with coal dust, the stucco peeled to the brickwork.

He was very frightened now.

And then he was being tackled below the knees. He had a tendency to fall easily on the soccer pitch and he buckled onto the gravel. But his hand in his pocket held onto his wallet and he wasn't able to protect his fall. The side of his head hit the ground and someone was grabbing his legs and another was clamping his head in the vice-like grip with which he used to hold down children when stitching their foreheads.

"Fucking foreigner."

Hands were exploring his jacket, his pockets. "Look, Hans, look!" and held up his mobile like the captain of a winning team holding up a sports trophy.

Then a frightened voice said: "What's this?"

They had found his bleeper. From their reaction they must have thought he was a policeman. They stamped it to death and tossed it back to him. "Give that to your fucking pig friends."

He clawed at the mangle of plastic and wire. Beyond his reach he saw a boy's thigh, fingers undoing a belt buckle, a knife. And heard the rumbling of his fear. A face loomed, a succulent malice in the eye, and a tongue wagged in a lewd way and there flashed on it, near the tip, a silver stud.

"Fucking, fucking foreigner, with fucking pig friends."

The boy stepped back and unzipped his trousers.

He's going to rape me, he thought. He started to whimper. I'm going to die. Then something descended over his face and hovered there, obliterating his vision.

"Oh, Snowleg, where are you?" in sudden command of his voice. And something in his tone alarmed them.

He felt the grip on him loosening. He managed to sit up, but all that his desperation achieved was to bring himself closer to the curly black hair and the moist fold of skin and the cheeks parting an inch above him.

"Hurry! Hurry!" urged the frightened one who held down his head.

"Fuck off, I'm trying. Wait. It's coming, it's coming."

The mouth puckered open, pink as a young tongue, and a fart blasted into his face.

"Here we go!"

Peter threw away his tie and staggered into a street, stopping an apprehensive jogger to ask the way to Kantstraße.

"But this is it."

He bolted upstairs before Frau Hase had a chance to see or to smell him, retching as soon as he entered his room. Worried that he might be concussed, he started to run a bath and then realised that he didn't want to sit in the boy's excrement. He took a shower and afterwards sat on his bed and towelled himself dry. He yielded to sleep just as he was preparing to drag himself downstairs to telephone a doctor.

He woke with a headache and a full bladder, labouring to breathe, round about midnight. He winced to the bathroom. Pains shot through his back and shoulder joints where they had kicked him and there was a large tender swelling under his hair at the side of his head. But no concussion.

He walked back to bed and when he trod on Frau Weschke's walking stick he cursed aloud.

In the next room, reflected against the dark window of the house opposite, a light switched on. He propped the cane against the table and lay back rigid on the bed, conscious of someone listening. A minute later the light switched off.

He tried to sleep, but sleep scorned him. He smelled morbid, of carrion. To get rid of the foul smell, he got up to open the window, but the window remained stuck. A shadow created by the street-light fell over his bruised stomach like a hand trying to discover a heart. He listened to his breathing. He heard nothing. A vast emptiness was taking root in him and he felt he had stumbled beyond the scope of anyone's forgiveness or care.

A group of berserkers passed below the window yelling the name of a football team. He turned and the streetlight followed him back into the room, casting wolf ears on the ceiling and picking out a few surfaces. The catalogue on the table. The cake-box. The silver horse-handle. He breathed in the stuffy air, the asphyxiating aroma of undried paint. This was the person he was.

Not yet ready to go back to bed, he unhooked the dressing gown from the back of the door and finding some coins in his trouser pocket went downstairs.

In his moment of need, a call to Sister Corinna was no longer an option. He had come up against a memory of his life that had blown her away.

Longing to tell the intimate details, he dialled his parents' home in England. He hoped that Snowleg had found someone to tell. He let the telephone ring and ring.

"I'm sorry. We're not here at the moment. But if you'd like to leave a message . . ." Rodney, speaking on a cheap machine. His voice warbling and uncertain, not confident he had been recorded.

Anyway, what was he going to tell Rodney – that he'd been crapped on by a Neo-Nazi thug? Or if his mother answered was he going to tell her, finally, about Snowleg? She had produced a life from one night. He had nothing to show. Nothing.

Despite the hour, he telephoned directory enquiries. "Berking," he whispered, fearful of waking Frau Hase. Did she have an extension in her bedroom?

"Did you say Bernhard?"

"Berking," louder.

"Business or personal?"

"Personal."

"Initial?"

"I'm afraid I don't know."

"Address?"

"I don't know that either."

"Please wait."

Despair is not despair until you admit it, and then like your reflection in a tin tray, it has a face that goes on for ever. Before, when he read the words "despair" or "desire" or "shame" he believed he knew what these words meant, but his definitions were shallow compared to the emotions he was experiencing in the zealously polished hallway of the Pension Neptune. He thought that if he were to understand deeply he would go mad a second time.

"I'm sorry. We have no-one listed under Berking in the Leipzig area."

He started sobbing.

CHAPTER THIRTY-SEVEN

IT DUMBFOUNDED PETER NEXT morning to look into the mirror and see no evidence of the assault. A stench rose from the bathtub, a smear of shit, piss, vomit and mud. Before he left his room he washed and washed the shirt and hung it in the bathroom.

In the hall, Frau Hase investigated with a mystified expression the payphone's mouthpiece.

"Herr Doktor! I was thinking of you. Have you found your old friend from the theatre?"

"No."

"I'm sure you will find her today," in the optimistic tone, tinged with urgency, of someone who had made a casual promise and was now concerned that her reputation, as well as that of the Pension Neptune, might be linked in an obscure way to its fulfilment. Peering closer: "Are you all right?"

"I'm quite all right, thank you, Frau Hase."

"It's just that yesterday I don't remember you using a stick."

At the Dresdner Bank in the Brühl he tried to draw out 1,000 Euros with his credit card. The machine refused, and he remembered that payments to Frieda were deducted at source at the end of every month. He tried again for 500 Euros and this time was accepted.

At 10.30 a.m. he limped into the offices of the *Leipziger Volkszeitung*. Twenty minutes later a copy-taker read back to him the words Renate had written with her pink felt-tip. Her formula. *On the evening of March 27, 1983, I was at the Astoria and the Rudolph Theatre. Were you there too?* The notice would run the following day.

A painful 15-minute walk to the Mädler-Passage, where he bought postcards of the Thomaskirche for Milo, Corinna, his family in England; and a special cream for Frau Lube. Along with his credit card, the thugs had left untouched a spare prescription form he always carried.

"Who is it for?" enquired the pharmacist.

"One of my patients. She's too ill to walk here."

"You are prescribing it?"

"Not only am I prescribing it, I am paying for it and I am going to administer it." He was on the point of asking whether he could in fact borrow the pharmacist's telephone to ring Frau Lube, and while he was about it to cancel his mobile, when he noticed, just across the mall, the window of the confectioner's. Damn it, he thought. I'll just turn up. She's at home anyway. She won't mind so long as I bring her chocolates.

The girl behind the counter was humming.

"My legs were too thin
You didn't like my scent
You were rude to my friends
You never brought me presents
You cancelled every plan I made for yoo-oo-ou"

He ordered 500 grammes of liqueur chocolates. Fixing his stare on the mound of dark lumps the colour of fish blood rising in the bronze weighing bowl.

"You never washed up
You read my diaries, my letters . . ."

The gauge trembled at 600.

"Actually, that will be fine."

The doorbell barked. Presently, a shuffling in the hall and the drawing of a bolt. Two eyes examined him over the chain.

"Herr Doktor Peter!" a smile climbing the web of her cheeks.

"Please. I have to see you."

Frau Lube pulled back a cuff the colour of an old hymnbook and looked at her watch. "I didn't expect you so soon. Are you all right? Something's happened."

"There were some young thugs in a tram."

"Did they rob you?" closing the door after him.

"They didn't take much money, but they held me down" – he laughed nervously – "and made a filthy mess of my shirt." A relief to say it. And then, immediately, the involuntary tug of English reins. "Nothing that couldn't be showered away."

"Did they hurt you?"

"My back's a little painful, but I got off lightly. I should have seen it coming. I was so distracted, I wasn't paying enough attention."

"This is what I mean. It's not safe to go out at night. Imagine how it is for old people! We live with this fear."

"These things happen everywhere. In England, too."

"Yes, but they didn't happen here. This is what twelve years of reunification brings!"

"Look, I've brought you something."

Frau Lube was pleased with the cream. With greater circumspection, she accepted his Belgian chocolates. She lifted the brown packet. Scrutinised the name. Squeezed it a bit and frowned. Then put it away into a drawer that seemed to spill over with other such packets.

"No chocolates before church. Today you only get coffee. Unless it's something stronger you want?"

"Coffee would be fine."

She took it to him in the main room where he stood beside Che Guevara.

To be in her good graces, Peter began to admire the photograph of her son. A tall young man in his early twenties with dark eyebrows and a boyish grin. Several years before his accident.

"I almost told you yesterday how much you look like Wilhelm," she said. "But seeing you again, it is rather remarkable. I'm sure you'll agree."

He stared at the face until he no longer saw it. "Similar colouring," he said politely. *Men in their forties, that's when things happen*. "What happened to Wilhelm?"

"A girl at the tourist office – although he didn't tell me. It was something I discovered much later. Sometimes not even your children tell you their secrets. He said they'd just kissed in his car in the parking lot. But why else would his marriage have broken

289

down so soon after? For a kiss? Not in my experience, Herr Doktor Peter. You don't leave your wife for a kiss." She gave him a look. "Any more than you go seeking someone you met once in a theatre. Not unless your heart is as soft as watermelon."

"You're right. What I told you yesterday, it wasn't the whole story."

"Is that so? No, wait. Before you go on, I'm going to set the alarm."

She had hardly stepped back into the room when he confessed. "I did know her, Frau Lube. In fact, I had met her two days before. I had a girlfriend in Hamburg, but I'd fallen in love with Snowleg."

She examined him sympathetically as if he were a beggar in the S-Bahn whom she might pity, but not trust.

"She wanted to leave the country and I was going to help her."

With a little frown, she picked up the ointment and then her cup and led the way onto the terrace. Peter was determined to restrain himself, but he had to ask. "Frau Lube, what happened to her?"

"Look. The sun's come out for you." In her unhurried eyes a warning to proceed slowly. He hadn't told his whole story. Why should she? He took 200 Marks from his wallet and tucked the notes on the low table, under a plastic bag with many coloured wools tumbling out.

"No," she said. "You keep that. You've been robbed."

"Give it to your charity, please."

She left the notes where they were. "It will go to the church."

He tried another tack. "Last night," as they sat down, "I bumped into one of the festival girls. It turns out her cousin is married to Snowleg's brother."

"Who is that?"

"Renate."

"Oh, yes? Renate was often at the Astoria. And did she help you?"

"I have to say that our encounter left a sour taste."

"I suppose she tried to sell you her tarty clothes?" She opened the cap and began to rub in the cream.

"She did."

"That shameless woman came here, to my door. I took one

look. 'Not for me, dear.' Well, I mean to say, it was obvious she hadn't anything for my kind. She told me about her new life. Her new name. Can you imagine? Changing your Christian name! To what, I can't remember."

"Christiane."

"That's it! She really wanted me to use it. So embarrassing."

He put down his cup on the table. "She says Snowleg worked for the Stasi."

Frau Lube pulled a face. "Well, she'd know about that."

"What do you think?"

"You could tell me anything about those days, I'd believe it."

"If you'd asked me yesterday, I'd have said No, impossible." She turned to him. "And today?"

"Tell me, where did she go that night? Did she have trouble?"

"Of course she had trouble. This was the system. But in the end she was all right."

"In the end? What does that mean?"

"She might have had some problems."

"What kind of problems?"

"The kind of problems that happen after you burst into a Minister's banquet and a guest of honour rejects you," she said smoothly, leaning forward, rubbing in the cream. "There'd have been no Stasi for her if you'd been more of an English gentleman, Herr Doktor." She sat back and gave him a good-natured smile. "You know what I thought yesterday, after you left? How you reacted in a way typical for an East German of 20 years ago — while she behaved like someone from the West."

Again, the question escaped before he could stop it: "Where is she now?"

"How could I know? I'm not her keeper."

"But you know something about Snowleg — more than you've been telling me."

"To know and to tell are two different gifts. You should understand that. You of all people, Herr Doktor."

"Frau Lube, please," he said huskily.

"Herr Doktor Peter," she replied with exaggerated patience, "you ask me how it was, but to go back through one's life is not so simple as crossing a city." She squeezed out more cream, sniffed it and rubbed it into the other ankle. "Besides, we have met once – and on that occasion you were not, as you admit, entirely candid. Yes, you bring me money and fine chocolates and ointment. But maybe this ointment of yours won't work. Maybe it will be just like your promise to help this girl. Or maybe it will be miraculous. We shall see."

She stretched out. Exposing her sore legs to the sun. Enjoying herself. For many years she had eaten chocolates in the belief that they would cure her eczema.

Peter picked at his watch-strap. He was used to listening to patients for their sakes, but not to having to listen for his own sake. Frau Lube's pace was agonising and there seemed no way to speed it up.

"Is there anyone else I could talk to?"

"Oh, I doubt many of them noticed Snjólaug. Most of us were professional non-observers."

"You have a good memory."

"I was just freer than most."

"In what way free, Frau Lube?"

"My husband died young." By which Frau Lube implied that widowhood had left her lonely, but it had carried certain privileges that were not available to her married or single friends. And she had her secret partner in God. "Let's say there was less at stake for me to remember things."

"Then, help me –" His gesture had snapped the stitches on the buckle and the watch face was dangling from its black leather strap. He hunted in his lap for the buckle and slipped the watch and useless strap into his pocket. "It's just that I have no idea how I can find her . . ." He heard the crack in his voice and was aware of her looking at him as though she had glimpsed someone else through it. And having been resistant to his suave overtures, his Belgian liqueurs and his fancy lotions, she succumbed to this raw note.

"OK, Herr Doktor Peter, ask me something," she said. "It's a long time ago. I don't promise that I have the answers. But ask your questions because I still don't know what it is you want to hear."

"Was she Stasi?"

She thrust her hand into the plastic bag and pulled at a ball of pink thread. "I've heard the stories. I don't know how true they are."

"That night," he pressed on, "after the Stasi took her from the Astoria – what happened to her?"

"Herr Doktor Peter, let me tell you what I saw and you make up your mind."

She was knitting a quilt for a church raffle as she talked. "The night you're speaking of. Whatever this girl did, we in Leipzig were not accustomed to it. Leipzig is a small place, everyone will have told you. I heard many rumours. All I can tell you is what she told me."

No pause for breath, like Gus bolting his food, he said: "Did she talk about me?"

"Of course she talked about you, Herr Doktor Peter! You were the cause of all this trouble. But I am not prepared to say one more word until you answer me this. Did Renate mention Morneweg?"

"Morneweg?"

"It was the name he used. He only came at Fair times."

"Who was he?"

"Oh, he's not interesting in himself, but he's important for your story. He listened to what was going on in the rooms and we were meant to report to him."

"Go on."

She touched her leg. "Morneweg. Morneweg. How to explain Morneweg? To look at, an anonymous old man. Pot belly, hair on his fingers, like one of those men you see in business pages. But in fairness, pleasant to me. Sometimes too pleasant, Herr Doktor Peter. He hears I'm a widow and this becomes embarrassing. He was always coming up and putting his clammy hand on my waist and asking how was I? He even sent a photograph of himself and me taken in the Galerie! It got to a point when I had to say to him – over coffee just like this – 'Herr Morneweg, this is not how it should be.'"

"Morneweg was the doorman's boss?"

"He was the Leipzig ringmaster! Very senior. No-one knew how much so until the end. He had a small cubby-hole downstairs and for three or four days at Fair time you'd see him writing notes with his headphones on. Eyes shut like this. Just listening to his tape machine.

"Now why does he do it? In his position? The fact is, he doesn't trust anyone to hear what he hears. He makes it his business to know all the voices. Businessmen. Ambassadors. Even the sound of me praying, Herr Doktor!

"One day I'm in the pantry and who is standing behind the plates, watching me intently? He'd heard this strange noise on his machine and he's come to investigate." She chuckled. "I see the disturbance in his eye and I can smell him. The girls used to complain that he smelled like something he'd shot on one of those hunts he liked so much. Like something dead.

"I warn him that I don't like his look: 'Don't underestimate the power of prayer, Herr Morneweg.'

"Later, I go by his cubby-hole and he stops me." She made a throat-cutting gesture with her needle. "I'm expecting a reprimand. But he wants to know if I have children. I tell him about Wilhelm. Turns out he has a son the same age. This surprises me because Morneweg – well, even in those days he must have been over seventy. He shows me a photo of his son and I suggest that the boys get together. He says that's impossible. Suddenly I'm angry. Does he think his son too good for my Wilhelm? Then out it comes. His wife has taken their child to the West. Morneweg is so busy listening to Leipzig that he hadn't heard the warnings in his own house.

"Anyway, everyone knows Morneweg is the informer-in-chief. Everyone has to sit around playing cards with him, smelling his rank smell. And what can you do? Nobody in the hotel is pleased to see him, but it's like a ship at sea. You can't move out." She put down her cup and tugged out another ball of wool. "You're sure Renate didn't tell you any of this?"

"No."

"Well, that surprises me. Because it was Renate, as I understand, who was responsible for getting Morneweg so worked up about your Snjólaug. Now, I don't know what Renate tells him, but Morneweg has fixed ideas about what kind of a girl it is who bursts into a room with a West German diplomat present. He sends her to be interrogated."

"But she was released, wasn't she?"

Frau Lube went on knitting. She might have been sitting at an execution. "To speak the truth, I forget all about her. And then one Saturday, about three or four months later, I see your girl again. She's crossing Kochstraße with someone – a man.

"I was pleased to see her. So I stop and say, 'Remember me?' She's not startled at all. 'Of course I do.' And this is the strange thing, Herr Doktor Peter. I'm certain her name isn't Snjólaug. I am certain she's called something else, but I can't remember what.

"She introduced me to her fiancé and it's no good, I can't remember his name either, but I see her effect on him. She wasn't beautiful, and yet she could be." Frau Lube crossed and uncrossed her ankles, luxuriating in the sunlight.

"And that was the last time you saw her?"

"Did I say that?"

"Frau Lube!" cried Peter, just like his mother, a horse stamping its foot.

"As it happens," she said quietly, "I did see her one more time. Ten or eleven years ago, not long after the Change. I'm walking along Nordstraße when all of a sudden someone stops and touches my arm: 'Remember me?'

"'Of course I do.' We have a good laugh over that. We're right outside the Bei Mutti and like a wicked girl she asks me in for a beer. She's left home after an argument with her husband and she's all upset, but happy too – and suddenly so am I! Anyway, we have a beer and I'm sure she tells me other things, I can't recall, but I show her photos of Wilhelm. You see, he's had his accident a few weeks before. He was a good-looking boy, but after the crash his eyes became dead. He hadn't had his ear done, although he could cover it with his hair. Well, I tell you, she was sweet. She insisted the day would come when he'd forget he ever had a scar. At first I didn't believe her, but she kept promising. She sounded so sure of herself, I wanted to know why – and then she tugged down her shirt. I knew what it was straight away. This one was light, not purplish at all.

"Forgive me for going on about this, but it was a link she

understood. The fact is, she had taken an interest in my son. She was curious about him, what was he like as a child, did I have more photos? I showed her others, from when we lived in Rosentalgasse, and she went on staring at Wilhelm's face and her own face had such a tender expression, I can picture it now. As if my son was someone she loved as much as I did! I'm not saying that I didn't get along with my daughter-in-law, but it did cross my mind that if Wilhelm had met your Snjólaug at the right time maybe he wouldn't have had to go to Australia.

"Anyway, we drank another beer and she told me a little about what happened when the Stasi took her. It wasn't pretty. It never is. And reliving those difficult times made us sad. Two single women, ordering another drink."

"What about her husband? I thought you said she was married."

"Oh, she was – to a childhood sweetheart. But it was as good as over. He wasn't the right man. The point is, she had been in a bad way and he was there for her. Maybe not someone she loved, but someone she could trust. You see, from what she was saying, she'd reached a stage when she couldn't trust anyone. While she was in prison someone – I think she said he was from the Kulturbund organisation – went around to her apartment building, asking questions. Was she with someone, who were her friends, had she a job, a car? – all the questions someone might ask if they wanted to marry you!

"And that's not the whole of it. The neighbours started telling stories. Dreadful stories that had been planted, Herr Doktor Peter. She tried her best to ignore them, but then something happened that she couldn't ignore. No, don't ask what, she didn't say, but I can tell you whatever the Stasi did, it revolted her. She wouldn't talk about it, not even after two beers in the Bei Mutti. On top of everything, she had just discovered that she was pregnant.

"We have another drink. This time she orders a vodka. It reminds her of life before marriage. Once she gets married, everything happens so fast. She has two children and no money and in the exhaustion of getting by she hasn't had a moment to think about what she's done. I tell you, regrets for that sort of thing only happen when your children leave home. Or when you meet someone who reminds you of how life might have been.

"She picks up Wilhelm's photo again and her eyes shine and it's obvious to me that she hasn't been living, she's been surviving. Maybe it's because of the vodka, she starts to talk more freely. It seems to me she doesn't feel understood. I have the impression that she feels inadequate to her husband's love – because how can you blame the lover? Her husband is blameless. He's good with the children, adores her. And though she doesn't love him she does feel sorry for him. As a woman it's easy to have pity for the things that depend on you. The things sucking the life out of you. Even if you want to, you can't pluck them off your arm because you can't bear the sight of that broken face as you chuck them away. That's how it was with her. She told me he'd implored so much that there behind the fence, in the hut with her hands on the sill, her clothes still on, looking at the pear tree . . . She told me these details! And that's why, when she found out she was going to have a baby, she agreed to marry him – because she thought he would make a certain aspect of her life so much easier. Until the Wall came down, she lost herself in that.

"But now she doesn't know which way to turn. He's drinking his life away. If she challenges him, he tells her that he drinks because he feels she doesn't love him. What do you say to that? What do you do when your husband wets your bed? Or halfway through dinner there's a clunk and his head's in the plate? If someone's going to pass out in their soup night after night some damage has been done. When he promises to kill himself if you leave him, you start to resent. And that's what's happened. He's sent her a long and suicidal song on a cassette saying that unless she goes back he will kill himself. I ask what she's going to do and she says with a sense of doom: 'Go back.' She's decided that she wants to blow on the embers and save her marriage.

"Poor girl, all I can do is put my arm around her. She finishes her drink and looks at her watch and mutters that she has to catch a train. We say goodbye in the street and that's the last time I saw her. As I say, I can't tell you where she's living, whether she's still married or even what her name is. But I'll always remember the look in her eyes when I showed her my photos of Wilhelm."

———

The oven bell shrilled from inside. "My only alarm," and Frau Lube hastily tucked away the pink woolly rectangle and stood up. Time to get ready for the midday service. Time to do her face. She checked her legs. "No change yet," wrinkling her nose.

"It'll be a few days before you notice the difference."

She hobbled before him into the hallway. "Whoever she now is . . ." She was talking over her shoulder with a crescendo of purpose, coming to the end of a hymn. "Trust me. Everything will turn out the way God intends it."

CHAPTER THIRTY-EIGHT

PETER LIMPED TO THE S-Bahn, shaken by the force of his longing. The need to find, even to set eyes on Snowleg, even if she was today happily married, tore away at him. How Snowleg came to be married to a man she didn't love was not something he could bear to dwell on.

He walked through Grünau uncertain of his destination: red and green painted buildings, a children's playground with a capsized slide, a boy extracting a chip of gravel from the wheel of his skateboard. He couldn't recall, not since he became a consultant, when an afternoon stretched empty ahead of him like this. No Milo to entertain. No dog. No mobile or bleeper to reel him in. And as he made his way between tower-blocks coloured like Frau Lube's balls of wool, he tried to relish the idea of being out of touch. He didn't want to be at Corinna's beck and call, though he loved her. Or stalked by Angelika, Nadine, Frieda. But Frau Lube's words had stranded him. Take away his medical context, his lab coat, Milo, Gus – and what remained? A 40-year-old man picking his bruised path through a never-ending housing estate on a too-short cane.

As he reached the S-Bahn, he thought of a dream told him by the violinist in Hamburg. Of Brahms walking through a landscape and all his used notes trailing behind him like acolytes. Pursued by his own Eumenides, Peter was relieved to have left Berlin and his scorching other life. In Leipzig, maybe he could untie the little black notes of his nightmare and pick up his parallel dream.

He noticed that his injuries had adapted him more neatly to Frau Weschke's cane, which tapped the steps down into the station with a spirit of its own. Under the impulse of his longing, he decided to search for the boarding house where Pantomimosa had stayed. It was an absurd idea, one he would have smiled at in a patient, but by the simple procedure of stepping again into that house – its flavour of Toast Hawaii, its lignite bricks, its message in a bottled aubergine from God – he hoped to rediscover his sense of proportion, of what was sacred.

Erich-Ferl-Straße, when he managed to locate it, was now Dresdener Straße. The street named after a person had had character. This one did not. He spent 20 minutes wandering stiffly up the pavement and back on himself. Past the sides and backsides of old buildings. Boarded-up windows. Stained brown bricks. He couldn't find the house.

His turmoil dragged him to the park where he had walked on his first night in Leipzig. An elderly couple sat on a bench – the man in a flat cap, the woman in a baggy dark sweater – feeding in silence from a packet of crisps. On the edge of the park, in mist that the sun had failed to burn off, a few black trees stood out as if splashed there by the same artist who had sprayed "Venom" across the Astoria's facade.

The river, swollen by snowmelt, stampeded past him and hurried into a reed-filled gully. He watched a trout flick between chutes of white foam and then tail back into the fast current and lie there, a shadow again.

On the bank was a willow tree and its branches reaching into the stream reminded him of hair over a girl's shoulder. He pictured the young Frau Weschke creeping up on her river crabs and heard a murmur from the water: "Leipzig is a great city, Herr Doktor."

Acceptance comes in stages. That's what he told his patients. You can only face up to what you can absorb. At 6 p.m. he returned to his lodgings holding a bottle of whisky.

Frau Hase met him in the corridor. She came towards him desperate, holding her nose up like a river rat above the water. "You have a guest. I put her in the front room. I think it's her!"

A woman sat on the sofa reading an old magazine. Long after her face had become a blank, he would remember the green cocktail dress. Spaghetti-straps. Knee length. A virulent insect colour.

Her gaze wandered down the cane. "What happened to you?"

"A run-in with the *jeunesse dorée* of Leipzig."

"I wonder if it's the same gang who murdered the Turk?"

"I don't think these ones had murder on their mind. Just robbery and humiliation."

"Sounds sexy," in a lipsticked voice.

"Not really. They offered me a vision of the city I won't forget in a hurry."

"A vision of what?"

At that moment the landlady poked her head into the room and looked eagerly at Peter. "I forgot to ask. Will you be dining in?"

"No, thank you, Frau Hase."

Her eyes shifted to the sofa. Draped over the leather arm were the garments he had ordered. That Renate had in mind for Snowleg. "Oh, and I've put your shirt through the wash, Herr Doktor."

"That's most kind of you," and he suggested to Renate that they go to his room.

Peter hung the clothes in the lavender-scented wardrobe while Renate sat at the table and flicked through the catalogue he had left on it. "If I sell a thousand Marks worth, I qualify to win a cruise abroad." The condition was unspoken. She would talk once he had spent this amount.

He put down the whisky on the table and drew up the other chair. Gamefully, he ordered a Parisienne Nights dress in stretch lace ("perfect for any after 5 event"). Two pairs of black Rip-Off shorts. Moo trousers in "trendy rawhide cowprint" . . . His eyes flew more and more rapidly across the pages and he stopped reading the descriptions. He had always been indifferent to clothes.

She calculated what he owed. "Eleven hundred and twenty Marks!"

"I don't have that, at least not in cash."

"Herr Doktor – did I hear her call you Herr Doktor? – I will take a cheque."

He limped over to his suitcase and took out his chequebook. Thank goodness he hadn't unpacked it.

Her dress gave a cellophane rustle as he wrote out the amount. He wondered who he could possibly give these clothes to. Nadine?

Angelika? Frieda? Corinna? If she could fit into them, it might improve Rosalind's chances beyond recognition.

She folded his cheque into her bag. "My job keeps this active," tapping her head, "that's the main thing. When I first started, you Wessis tried to stop me. 'Go ahead, offer them new jeans. You'll find they have no ass to put in them.' But what do Wessis know about ass?" She leaned forward. Her face had a glossy brightness. "Can I tell you something, Herr Doktor? Leipzig was a passionate town."

He nodded.

She smiled and pinched off her earring and touched her ear lobe as if it was sore. "There was great understanding between people. And, yes, sometimes this understanding created passions which were extremely dangerous."

"Yes, yes, I understand." Had she been drinking?

The cane creaked as she rotated in her chair, the light falling on her full and freckled cleavage. "Of course, today we're not supposed to remember how it was. There are those – I hope you're not one of them! – who would prefer us to remember nothing."

He endured her stare. She was enjoying her teasing. The effect and sound of her words. She knew what he wanted and she was going to make him wait.

"I may have been one of those," with a doctor's sage nod. "But no longer."

"With Wessis, it was different," she went on. "I just told them nonsense. I hated them because they were in a different situation. They believed everything, and when I told them fairy tales I enjoyed how stupid they were. I knew problems would follow if I spoke the truth. I didn't want problems. I wanted to sit in a beautiful bar and drink whisky. And afterwards – eyes closed, a few minutes, it passes – you forget. But you don't forget whisky." She looked at the bottle. "Before we blow away in dust, are you going to offer me some?"

He fetched two glasses from the sink and poured them out and pushed her one.

"The sort of thing I told them was –"

"Let's get to the point. How do I discover where Snowleg lives or her married name?"

She dipped her finger in the glass, licked it. "Still thinking about that time you were such a prick?"

"Yes, Renate, I am."

"So you haven't found her?"

"Not yet."

"Did you advertise like I said?"

"It comes out tomorrow."

"What else did you do?"

"I saw Frau Lube."

She gave a corrosive laugh and below the table kicked off one of her shoes. "Frau Lube! She's still alive?"

"She lives in Grünau – on chocolates, as far as I can tell."

"Prost!" She clinked his glass and drank and a pleasant shudder passed across her face. "I suppose she's going to pray for you? It was a joke among us, Frau Lube's prayers. She was banging on about God last time I saw her – that's right, in Grünau. 'Renate, trust me, the Almighty knows someone out there who will honour you.' Almighty intuition, almighty bullshit! Her religion just allows her to see things that are not there. Like the fact I'm not Renate, for one thing."

"Perhaps it's her way of coping," said Peter.

"Coping?"

"Her son. His accident."

"Her son!" rolling back her eyes. "Ever since his near fatal car crash he's become a bore who spouts nothing but clichés. 'Live each day, to your own self be true, treat others . . .' I tell you, if he hadn't left his wife and run off to Australia I'd have murdered him for being so boring."

"He looked cheerful enough," said Peter, feeling a curious need to defend Frau Lube's son, this person who was supposed to look like him.

"It's a lie. Wilhelm was a moody man and I never liked moody men, but I always end up with them. You're not moody, are you? Actually, you remind me of him."

He looked up sharply. "Frau Lube doubts that Snowleg was Stasi."

"Oh, fuck Frau Lube. What does she know? She's just a time-server. A housekeeper. With a military rank, I wouldn't be surprised." She stared back with a haughty expression. "You think I don't know Snjólaug? Maybe she was Stasi before that night, maybe after it. But she *was* Stasi – I would even be tempted to say she worked in Section 9 recruiting unofficial employees to defend the integrity of the state." She levelled her eyes at him, loaded with antipathy. "They had people like that, to target Westerners – especially at Fair time. Finding ways to exploit the meetings, the friendships formed. Hidden cameras, microphones, I'm sure you can imagine . . ." In the crude blue of her eyes something almost sparkled. "You ask me, Snjólaug was sent to hook you."

"Why do you say this?" a streak of flame in his voice. "What other evidence do you have?"

She fell silent and rubbed the chapped ear between her fingers. Then: "OK, did she take you to her Schreber garden?"

"Yes." He folded his arms.

"Well, then. The place was bugged – and she knew it was. Bugged her own brother, I wouldn't be surprised."

"How do you know?"

"What colour's this?"

The dress grinned at him.

"Green," he said.

"Just green?" tapping his leg with her toe, playing with him.

"Forest mist?"

"Exactly." And again: "Exactly. Certain things you know for a fact, Herr Doktor." She raised her glass. "Could I get one more of that?"

He poured the whisky. "Frau Lube says you spoke to Morneweg about her. What did you say?"

Again she dipped her finger, licked it. "She's wrong. I didn't speak to Morneweg."

"Who did you speak to?"

"Sure you want to hear this, sugar?"

"Yes."

She gave a meaningful sigh. "It was one of Morneweg's people, someone I knew well."

"Tell me."

"Well, since you ask, it wasn't long after she gave the doorman whatever it was she gave him – you know, that persuaded him to

304

take her into the hotel. I have to say it surprised me so much that I walked back to the entrance and when Anton came out I used Morneweg's name like I should have done all along, and of course this time he let me in. You see, even though I was beginning to think she was Stasi, it didn't matter. Uwe still would have expected me to pass on information like this. I needed to be sure it was something he knew about."

"Was it?"

"Oh, yes, I could tell by his excitement. You see, as soon as I got into the Astoria I telephoned him from the reception. He listened to what I had to say, how I'd heard her whisper that she was coming with you in your dressing-up box, and immediately he said, as if it was all planned: 'It's important Anton lets her in.' When I told him that Anton already had let her in, he said: 'Leave this to me. In fact, leave the Astoria altogether. I'll speak to Morneweg.' And he must have spoken to him because, as I say, a few minutes later I saw Uwe and Morneweg getting into the Wartburg with her."

Peter refilled his glass. It rattled him, what she was saying. There was so much he wanted to ask, but he noticed how Renate started to become surly if questioned directly. She had to make it slow, difficult. Come back and spring it on him.

"All right," he said with distaste. "Let's suppose she was Stasi."

"It's what she was, sugar."

"Frau Lube told me she got married not long afterwards."

"So I believe."

"She implied that Snowleg – even if she was Stasi before – had fallen out with them."

"That's right."

"Do you have any idea what the Stasi did to her?"

"Of course."

Peter watched her bring out a pack of cigarettes from a shiny black bag. He was getting somewhere.

She offered him a cigarette and he declined. "I thought all doctors smoked," she said.

"I was on sixty a day."

"All or nothing, eh? How did you give up?"

"I went to a hypnotist."

Suddenly Renate chuckled. She knocked back the whisky and lit her cigarette and stared merrily at him. "They put it about she had gonorrhoea."

"It's the summer of 1983.

"I'm sitting one evening at the Bodega – about three months after you ditch us. There's a tug at my arm and it's your Snjólaug and she's in a hell of a state.

"She unfolds this letter from the Ministry of Health. It refers to some epidemic law from the 1950s and she is specifically named. It orders her to take her medical card and go at noon next day to the venereologist for a skin check and do this every other day for 14 days. There's a list of everything she must not do. No travel. No alcohol. No sex. And she's warned about the danger of infertility if she's not treated immediately.

"'It's probably nothing,' I told her, and asked if she had any reason to be concerned. She said there was one man. But she hasn't had sex with him for three months. They've known each other for ever. To him, she's God's gift. Thing is, she honestly doesn't know if she's got gonorrhoea. I like the way she asks *me*. I tell her a man would be screaming the roof down every time he pissed. Obviously, this man is not screaming at her. 'Sure there's not someone else, sugar?' I ask. At which she goes all silent. Turns out, five days before she fucked her childhood sweetheart she fucked an English medical student." Renate smiled. "That's you, sugar. In fact, I go so far as to suggest that perhaps it's you who has named her. She won't have any of that. Oh, no. It's the Stasi.

"'Do you really think so?' I say acidly. You see, what I'm beginning to suspect is that she's setting me up. They do that sometimes. Pretend to be so naive that in sheer exasperation you tell them more than you dream of telling anyone, even your own daughter. 'And why do you think that is?'

"She was full of mistrust, she told me. Didn't realise she was being watched. Basically, Bambi's finally woken up and found Stasi paw prints all over her pretty little life.

"You see, what's upsetting her as much as the VD notice is that she can't find her medical card. She has to present it to the doctor. It was there in her drawer and now it's not. She suspects me in some way. And maybe she had reason to. But I never stole her fucking card."

"Then what reason?" said Peter with a nip of anger.

She blew out a trail of smoke and gave him a long look through it. "Her brother, probably. Snjólaug's boss paid me to fuck him."

"Morneweg?"

"That was one of his names," and ground out her cigarette.

"Even though Bruno was married to your cousin?"

"So what? He'd applied to go to the West, hadn't he? It was well known. Anyone who wanted to go West was put under full –"

"Let me get this straight. Morneweg bugged you and Bruno?"

"And if he liked what he heard, he paid."

"Where was this?"

"Sometimes in the garden, sometimes the Astoria." She laughed involuntarily as though someone was tickling her feet. "Strange. I went upstairs with so many men, all sorts and conditions of men. But at the Astoria the only face I ever saw in my head was Morneweg's. Eyes looking at me like this," and she made an expression. "Lips like a trout. This smell he had . . . I'd pass him in his cubicle – headphones on, hands over his ears and a damp patch under his arms. Sometimes when I was with someone I wanted to scream at the light or the wardrobe or wherever it was he'd put his microphone: 'What do you do with all the fucking you hear?'"

She ran a hand over her face, touching her make-up. "But you had to tread softly with that one. You could never talk about him out of his hearing – he'd walk through the wall. When he wasn't sitting in his cubicle he was quite close to Mr Party. I don't know how close, but it was Morneweg who decided that so-and-so would be arrested or get gonorrhoea. That's why everyone kept out of his way. Me too, except I'm an impulsive person. I sometimes do foolish things. Like the afternoon I'm walking past his cubicle and see no-one sitting inside and the place like a coffin, tapes up to the ceiling. When I see the tape machine, I'm curious to know how I sound. Quickly, I squeeze inside, put on the headphone, press play. And what do you think I hear?"

She wiped her eye. "The tape is of a young boy talking. I

couldn't believe my ears. I don't know what I was expecting, but not that.

"Now, just think of it. Mr Party's right-hand man listening to a boy go 'Papa, papa!' My feelings about Morneweg changed in that moment. It was around this time I heard how his wife had gone to pieces and left him, taking his son to the West. It was Frau Lube who told me that."

She shook her head. "This sounds curious, but it's true. The one key to his tongue was Frau Lube. He had this bizarre thing for her. Happy as a harness bell, he was, whenever he saw her in the kitchen. Always looking for little ways of making himself known. 'Renate, would you give this cup back to Frau Lube – and by the way tell her the coffee was excellent?' And when you reported the message to Frau Lube she'd give you this petrified look as if she'd been overheard saying whatever it was she used to mutter on her knees in the crockery cupboard. Poor creep. All those listening devices and he never found out that the woman couldn't abide him. A Christian she might have been, but she couldn't be left in the same room as him! And it wasn't just her, I tell you.

"Well, fuck all that. One summer evening – this is, oh, about eight months before Snjólaug comes to me with her letter – I'm at the Bodega and out of the blue it's Morneweg. He's pressed for time, because he orders me a Grauer Mönch but not one for himself. He's heard I have a good memory, he says. Then gives me a square of paper. He'd like it if I gently enquired about this person. Get some dirt on him, his family, friends. I look at the name and I say, 'I know this man! He's married to my cousin.'

"'That is correct.'

"'I'm sorry, Herr Morneweg, I don't know much about snooping. On the other hand I know something about fucking. I'll sleep with him and you can listen all you like, but don't ask me to write down a word because I won't.' Well, Morneweg wants me to sleep with Bruno so bad that he's prepared to offer 100 Marks. It's only a few times and I tell you it's not very pleasant either. As you probably found out, it's freezing in that Schreber garden. Not a drop of cream – I had to take off my make-up with butter."

"Please. I don't know if I want to know so much."

"What? Do you want me to stop?"

"No."

"I'm not doing this for free. Once you get me started . . ."

"Go on, go on."

She rose to open the window. "Is it me or is hot in here?"

"You won't be able to do that. It's stuck."

She opened it and sat down.

"How —"

She plucked her strap higher, shrugged.

He tilted the bottle. "More?"

"I'm doing very well. Although," she said, indicating the box on the table, "I wouldn't mind some of your cake. All this talking, it's made me famished."

"It's not a cake," he said. "And it belongs to someone else."

"That's a pity. I could eat a nice piece of cheesecake."

He refilled his glass. Breathed in the fresh air. The air stirring up a question he had put to one side. "So you were Stasi too?"

"Yoo-hoo birds, yoo-hoo bees. Just a working girl trying to make a living. You asked me for details. I'll cross my legs now if you want me to."

"I'm just floored by all the double dealing. Morneweg – where is he today?"

"No idea, and that's the truth. In government, most likely. Hidden behind a moustache like everyone else. They were wise to him, but no-one was game to print it. Bump into him in town and he'd be on his way to church, smooth as this silk."

Softly, she raked her fingers over her cleavage and looked at him provocatively. Her dress gleamed unnaturally. *Renate believes that whoever sleeps with you last has you.*

"So what happened to Snowleg?"

"OK, back to Snjólaug. I assure her that I didn't name her or steal her medical card. I explain that she needs to bark up another tree, but she refuses to listen. Suddenly the letter represents for her the whole system. There's a terrible scene. She goes cuckoo – and rips up the letter in front of me.

"She's sick of explanations. There are no explanations, only betrayals. And she storms out of the Bodega and that's the last time I see her."

He toyed with the earring she had left on the table. "Where is she now?"

In the care with which she chose her words she might have been picking bones from a fish. "I heard she was living in the country somewhere."

Reluctantly, he moved closer. But he had trespassed into her space. She drew away and having been familiar she became extremely prim. She picked up her earring and secured it, her eyes staying on him as she positioned it back to the centre of her ear lobe. Then her expression changed. Very tenderly she reached across and he, mistaking the gesture, recoiled.

"No, no, no, you don't have to worry. It's just that your ear lobes – let me touch them. They're so slender."

He followed the line of her arm and stared at the round nose. The plucked eyebrows. The buffeted skin. Her face had a look like a page after water splashed on it has dried. And yet, like a habit, she mesmerised him, this woman who couldn't take foreigners seriously. For whom Leipzig held no secrets.

"Look, I have to go," and she rustled to her feet. "I'll get someone to deliver the clothes. How long are you staying?"

"Till Monday."

"If I win the cruise, you'll come with me, yes?"

Peter listened to the hard tap of her steps down the staircase, along the corridor, onto the pavement. Then he replaced the top on the whisky and got to his feet and carefully closed the window. He stood in the dark looking out, touching his ear. A hot moon climbed over the rooftops. Its reflection on the glass had attracted a hatch of greenfly and a moth fluttered up against the window eating one fly after another.

CHAPTER THIRTY-NINE

SNOWLEG. SNOWLEG. SNOWLEG. THE tinnitus drilling of her name rose to a pitch that interrupted his sleep. A moment later there was a knock on his door. "Herr Doktor Hithersay? Telephone for you." It was 8.10 a.m.

Frau Hase waited downstairs, excitement on her face. "She's read it."

"Read what?"

"Your notice in the paper. She says she knows you."

It amazed him that someone should have responded so quickly. He had had no faith in Renate's plan. He took the receiver from her, afraid.

"Hello?"

"Who am I speaking to, please?" Her voice was quiet. Late thirties.

He gave his first name. The air burning. Along the corridor Frau Hase rubbed her duster up and down the banisters.

"Peter? Is that you, Peter?" exploding with great enthusiasm and asking could it be true, she had thought of him often, sometimes in the bath as she washed, always knowing he would try to make contact, such an experience, she had never forgotten, it had happened only once before, an Irishman, but it wasn't the same . . .

He battled to picture Snowleg in the voice. "This was at the Astoria?"

"Don't you remember? We had dinner and went upstairs and I asked: 'Why did you choose me when you could have had any one of them, why me?'"

"This was after the mime?"

"Mime? What are you saying, Peter? I don't remember any mime."

By 10 a.m., three other callers had rung. A nasal voice had requested 500 Marks before he would speak further, ringing off when asked to describe Pantomimosa. Another caller was apparently on a ceaseless quest for a wife he had last seen during the interval in the Rudolph Theatre. In the middle of a performance of Heiner Müller's *Quartett* in 1982, he said.

The third one was obviously calling from a public booth.

"Is it a particular woman you're after?" The voice was local. Rolling r's. Petulant. High-pitched.

"Yes."

"I worked for some people who might have known her."

"What was her name?"

"I knew her by her working name. She was called Marla."

Peter asked for a description. The man couldn't remember her face too well, not after this time. But something about her he hadn't forgotten. "She wore this thing round her neck, not exactly a necklace —"

"Where is she?"

Silence. The sound of people talking echoed down a corridor.

"You want information? It will cost you. I'll have to dig about. Give me an idea of what it's worth to you."

"What about three thousand Marks?"

The snort was almost vicious. "That won't get far. We're talking about unlocking an archive. I happen to know the file isn't where it ought to be — just as well, or it would have been burned to ashes. But under certain circumstances I know how to reach it."

"Four thousand Marks, then — if you produce information that gets to her."

"You don't sound like a gentleman from Leipzig. You wouldn't be familiar with the procedures. This is going to be so dangerous, so tricky . . . I would say it's the equivalent of five thousand Marks."

"All right, all right." Then: "Where do I meet you?"

"You free this afternoon?"

"Yes."

A pause. "I will ring back."

Peter waited 40 minutes. Shortly before 11 a.m., the landlady

312

appeared at his shoulder. Another guest was anxious to use the telephone.

"Remind me, Frau Hase, how does one redial the number of the last caller?"

She told him.

After a long time, a hesitant voice said: "Hello?"

"Please can you tell me," Peter asked, "where you're answering from?"

"I'm in a ward. I don't know where I am. I was waiting outside and I heard the phone go."

"A ward where?"

"Dösen Hospital."

Frau Hase brought him a cup of coffee. "No, no, it's on the house. Tell me, how is it going?"

"Not very well."

"I'll be here if anyone rings," she said.

He left the house and walked to a park. There was a pale blue sky and the thaw was deepening. In the space of two days wintry March seemed to have turned into early summer.

He slumped down on a bench and was left to reflect on the man who had telephoned from the hospital. Why a hospital? Another red herring perhaps – or had the necklace belonged to Snowleg? He rested Frau Weschke's cane against the arm-rest and the past, drifting up in bubbles, absorbed him completely. He dozed in the weak sun.

A bell tinkled like a chemist's door. He pulled his legs back from the path and three girls bicycled by, yellow hair frothing in the wind.

He stood up. Balancing on the cane, he dug a hand into his pocket where his fingers encountered something sticky. Frau Lube's toffee-whirl had leaked all over his watch-strap.

To get change for the payphone, he bought a copy of the *Leipziger Volkszeitung* carrying his advertisement and returned to the Pension Neptune.

"Did he ring back?" he asked Frau Hase.

"Oh dear, no."

"Any other calls?"

She shook her head, more disappointed than he.

He telephoned Frieda. "It's me."

"Milo!" she called. "Your daddy."

"Wait, it's you I want to speak to."

"Me?" suspicious.

He looked around nervously, but he couldn't see Frau Hase. "I want to apologise for the crappy things I've done."

"What, all of them? I don't have that much time, Peter."

"I mean it."

"What the hell are you talking about? If you're talking about the dog, that would be one place to begin. I tell you, I've had your dog up to my ears. Last night it vomited over my favourite shawl."

"I actually wanted to apologise for making the situation worse than it is. I want it to work better from now on. I mean . . . we're parents."

"Peter," she said penetratingly, "this is not the time and wherever you are this is not the place for you to be having this conversation with me. If you were sitting on the other side of a table maybe I'd give you five minutes. Hey, Gus, stop that!"

"I just want to be involved with Milo and I've been neglectful and I'm sorry for that."

"Here's Milo," she said eventually, upset.

"Daddy, Daddy, have you seen Frau Weschke? She promised to catch me a river crab."

"I haven't seen her," heartened to hear his little familiar voice. "But that probably means she's catching it right this minute." He rehearsed the pain he would feel if Frieda took Milo to another country. "Darling, it would be a very great help to me if you brushed your teeth tonight."

"Actually, Gus has eaten my toothbrush."

"Oh, no."

"But that's not all," said Milo heavily.

"I'm not sure I can take much more," said Peter.

"Well, I'll tell you what he did. He pulled the computer off Mummy's desk."

Peter's last call was to his telephone company to cancel his mobile. Then he climbed to his room and lay down and shivered. He wiped the perspiration from his face. Exhausted by this remembering.

He thought, What have I got out of this? Here am I chasing dead people when I'm not taking enough care of those closest to me.

It had cost him a fortune to find out exactly what? That Snowleg had been interrogated by the Stasi. That she was Stasi. That she was married with two children. That her name might be Marla Berking. He couldn't think of her as Marla Berking, any more than he could see her as older than twenty-three, or without the doorman holding her shoulders. All I can think of, he told himself, is this butterfly pinned down, this crucifixion. It's too sickening. I have to assume that she died in that moment and rose again into another life and is perfectly all right. In any case, I can't find her. Despite his best efforts she remained a prospective fantasy like the model in Renate's catalogue. If ever he did track her down she would probably have become a Renate, selling satin underwear to make a living. It was time to stop looking. Time to be a father to Milo. Time to be the father he had never had. Anyway, where on a Sunday would he find 5,000 Marks? He would go downstairs and tell Frau Hase that he was calling off his search. He was terribly happy he had put an ad in the paper, but the answers he had got were more than heartbreaking. They were a freak show. A sad old buffer, an off-the-wall woman and what sounded like a very unpleasant person who had not rung back. No, he would close the case, pretend that Snowleg was a patient who had died.

A rapping at the door. Frau Hase. "Telephone!"

No background noise this time. The man spoke urgently. "I'll meet you at four o'clock."

"Wait. I think I've changed my mind."

"I reckon you must be the Englishman from the Schreber garden."

Without a pause, Peter asked: "Where can we meet?"

"At the zoo. The giraffe compound."

"How will I recognise you?"

"I have reddish hair, but anyway I'll recognise you."

"About the money —" But he had rung off.

Below on a rock in its moat, a polar bear watched with impatience as the keeper gave Peter directions. Then opened its jaws to field the next tossed fish.

The giraffe compound was the other side of the bird cages. Peter came up the cinder path, hot and perspiring. So impatient to be here that he had come without his coat and the cane. He looked to the left and right for a figure he had come to associate in his mind with the Black Knight – one of those responsible for daily, hourly suffering. But there was no-one there.

He leaned on the rail, one foot up, breathing deeply. The last of the snow lay in patches along a bank, grey and melted from within as if a straw were sucking it away through the soil. Half asleep, a male giraffe eyed him from across a pond. The water threw back the reflection of its neck. The chestnut hair broken into blotches the shape of stars.

The female stood alert over her newborn, scanning the rail. Her eyes in contrast were dark wells, the rippled pattern on her coat as though a stone had been hurled into a pool. When she registered the way Peter stared, she gave a raucous cough. She snapped her head back and her hoofs stamped into the grass.

Unhurried, the calf left her side and moved in an elegant-awkward amble towards the pond. She splayed her forelegs and quickly bobbed down her head and started to drink.

Snowleg had reminded him of a giraffe. Such sweet animals.

The mother's turn to drink. She looked at Peter with a reproachful gaze. Large eyes behind long lashes shying from a flame. And giving him the sense that he had stood at this rail before. But when? Seconds passed. Not him – rather, a quickly sketched figure in the watercolour he had bought for Frau Weschke.

"The head is lower than the heart – a phenomenon that fascinates psychologists."

The man spoke in English. He had the look of one of Peter's biology masters who was good at cricket. Tall, a year or two older than Peter, with a worn friendly face beneath the cloth cap. He rested his crossed arms on a large padded envelope, and sticking from his ankle-length black coat was a sailing magazine.

"You or me, we'd be giddy by now, we'd black out," and a hand slid under his cap and scratched his head.

It wasn't the person who had telephoned. This man talked in an educated, measured voice. His thinning hair was grey.

He didn't turn to look at Peter. "Another thing: they never scream. Not even when a lion attacks."

A panic seized Peter. It's no good, he thought. It's not him. He twisted from the rail, shards of cinder crackling under his heel – and was about to walk away when the man said: "You advertised."

"That's right," stopping.

"You were expecting to meet my colleague. My colleague is a tiny bit indisposed." The words had a sorrowful quality. His eyes, red-rimmed and narrow, were tired. He could have been the last survivor of his race. "Anyway, I've brought the files. And I want to make this very clear from the beginning: I'm not here for money."

CHAPTER FORTY

HE SAID HE WAS called Uwe. He knew who Peter was. He hadn't seen Peter's advertisement because this morning he had been otherwise engaged: his mother had passed away in front of him.

For five months, her spinal cancer had eaten his life into large holes of which Sundays formed the largest. On Friday, he had come to realise that he wouldn't be taking her home and asked for the machine to be switched off. Ever since, he had wanted to give away her things, but he couldn't really do this, not until she died. This morning had been the third day of her coma. He had been sitting beside her bed at a loss to know what to do, watching her hand roam over her cheeks where an oxygen tube used to be and thinking dully that he might take advantage of the thaw and go sailing, when an orderly came in and said: "You have a visitor."

Uwe recognised the voice humming to itself and then around the curtain came that sullen face with its bulging eyes. Kresse. He had grown an uneven moustache, one side half an inch longer than the other.

"Boss! So glad to run into you. I need your help. Look." Across the bed with his mother's wheezing body Kresse told him about the notice in the *Leipziger Volkszeitung*. "The Englishman's come back. Finally, the man's come back – and I've spoken to him. I'm seeing him this afternoon. But I need the stuff."

"Explain yourself, Kresse," fighting an urge to laugh. The moustache looked like something stuck on in a hurry and in slightly the wrong place.

"You remember that Marla Berking?" Kresse drew up a chair and sat down. "Remember that girl who didn't go away in the dressing-up trunk? Did you hang on to her file?"

"You know perfectly well what happened."

"I know perfectly well what was supposed to have happened,

but this is the position, boss. I've got to have the whereabouts of this girl, and I have some idea that her file is not destroyed."

"Blackmail, is that it?"

"Yes, of course, what do you expect? But I can't recall what became of her."

"This isn't the time, you cunt," and his eyes flew back to the pillow where life was throbbing away.

Kresse, indifferent to the dying mother, moved closer until his elbows were resting on the blanket. A stranger coming in might have thought they were from the same family, praying.

"What's the name of her husband?" The breath reached Uwe over the still legs, gaseous and smelling of the past. His nostrils picked out mechanically the yeasty bread, the hard-boiled egg, the instant coffee with the long-life milk.

"I don't know. Maybe if you hadn't got rid of the bottles . . ." It still had the power to rankle, even after all this time, even at this moment. While Uwe was burning files, Kresse was going down to the lake and tipping Uwe's bottles into the water. All his years of smell-hunting, his samples − he had emptied the whole laboratory.

Kresse opened his mouth, and it vaguely interested Uwe to see that there was no longer a gap in those tartarous teeth. "Give me her file, boss. You can have half the reward."

"I'm very sorry. That's all finished. It's a new world."

"I've tested the water. He's got money. But we can get more − a lot more, I reckon."

"How much?" His eyes returned to his mother's face, the skin around the eyes and mouth folded over itself.

"Well, he's agreed on five thousand Marks. But I wasn't going to give him the file − just show him we've got it. What do you think, boss? What's it worth? What's a doctor in West Germany make? How much liquid will he have? He can scream and yell, but he's going to have to go back to his West German city and collect it."

"You're going to take five thousand Marks and not let him read the file?" He asked the question almost pedantically.

"That's the way of the world, boss. Wake up. Where've you been?"

Uwe had been put under pressure in his time, but he was a calm person. There was no stopping his outrage when it came. "You were always the scum of the earth. All you ever were was a nauseating little capitalist. Get out of my sight."

"Don't give me that, boss. I need the file. It's worth a lot of money."

"Piss off."

Between them rose another leathery gasp. Kresse looked down and there spilled out of his eyes, as from the containers that bring minerals up out of the mine, all the impurities of which he was host. "Just as well your mother's been unplugged, boss. Or I might have done it for you."

The curtain fell back. Gone. But their conversation had been too much for the body on the bed. Uwe held the inert wrist, knowing he squeezed it for the last time, and for some reason remembered a day on the Kulkwitzer See when he was seven, watching the sails. His mother standing on the bank – yelling to him, pulling him by his hand, ticking him off for going too near the water – and his father saying, "What makes you think he's going to listen? He's just like you."

After he had brushed her hair, he called the nurse. He stayed to sign a couple of pieces of paper and went home.

Uwe's apartment occupied half the basement of a nineteenth-century building in Rosentalgasse. It faced west and he had chosen it because of the ancient wine cellar at the back. He had got in touch with the security firm in Munich through a work contact, and had had a reinforced door and another very good door put in. The oldest files, like fine wines, were stored in the stone racks according to their dates.

Initially, he had taken the files for his freedom. But they were also his security, to protect him from people like Morneweg and Kresse. And maybe the time would come when he could do someone a favour. Those people who had been, for whatever reason, unreasonably arrested or tortured outrageously. Because that was not what it had been about, not what he had worked for at all.

He turned into his street and his hopes, his aspirations before he met Morneweg surged back to him. For an ardent moment he was twenty-four again. At night he would go rowing on bad-smelling canals, but in his imagination he was pulling towards the university in Dessau where he would teach the natural sciences. And then his father died. He remembered the curious old man at the funeral – the brown suit and the low cough, the card with the name on it, the glass of sweetish white wine in the Bodega. He had never been a Party animal, but he found it surprisingly easy to be loyal to a man like Morneweg who treated him in a paternal fashion, who allowed him to go on believing in the State with an only child's conviction. He had a sense – even in his grief – of being welcomed.

"We need scientists," Morneweg had said, taking off his glasses to reveal his owl's face and breathing on one lens and then the other. "Your doctorate, I'm told, is on the smelling senses."

The door to the street opened to Uwe's touch. Down the passage he could see his own front door ajar, and he wondered gloomily if his neighbour, who had a key, might have come in to borrow his new vacuum cleaner. He looked with unease into what should have been a neat entrance hall – the paddle against the wall, the boar's head supporting on one tusk an orange life jacket, the brush mat. His visitor had not paused to clean his feet. Across the carpet towards the bedroom door led a set of prints outlined in mud and melting grey ice.

His whole body alert, his eyes raced over the footprints into what had been a tidy room. Through the door, drawers upturned on the floor and papers everywhere. Kresse hadn't had to go far: Uwe stored the newest and less important documents in the filing cabinet beneath his desk.

Kresse sat on the bed, scowling into the telephone. A file in his hand. He wouldn't have had time to read it, just a postcard or two. "At the zoo. The giraffe compound," in his whining, bitter, disgusting voice. Then: "I have reddish hair, but anyway I'll recognise you."

Uwe retreated. The sound of the receiver being replaced and more drawers opening and Kresse humming "How will you ever forgive me?"

"Herr Uwe!"

His neighbour stood behind him, a burly ex-fruiterer with pink cheeks and teddy-bear eyes. "I heard a hideous noise. I thought maybe I should come in, but it sounds like a friend."

In the bedroom the humming had stopped.

Next to the door was a shelf. He found his service revolver behind a row of books. "I think I know who it is, Herr Hölderlin. I'll deal with it," and swiftly reached up and retrieved the silencer from the boar's throat.

The footprints petered out in a pair of black ankle boots white with salt. Kresse stood against the far wall, his gun levelled at Uwe's chest. "Where's this to, boss?" and jerked his thumb at the door behind him, anonymous and reinforced with steel.

"I've been thinking, Kresse. We'll cut a deal."

"I'm not that stupid, boss." He watched Uwe closely with his poisonous eyes. "Unlock it."

"Fifty-fifty – if you do the work."

"Unlock it, boss."

Their two guns pointed at each other. It seemed incredible they could have been colleagues. Swords and shields in the same battle.

"I'll need a key," decided Uwe.

"Then, get it," twitched the uneven, pantomime moustache. A Groucho Marx nose wouldn't have looked odd on him, but for the gun.

Still covering Kresse, Uwe dug his left hand into his pocket. "How are we going to do this?" He felt like giggling. "I know," and without raising his voice: "Herr Hölderlin?"

An intense silence was broken by the sound of feet dragging themselves into the room. "Herr Uwe?"

Uwe sensed his neighbour's eyes rolling between them, back and forth, like balls of brown wool trailing fear between two paws.

Kresse's gaze fell on the whisperer, who contracted away, and flicked back to Uwe, jetting venom. "Who the fuck are you?"

Uwe, his gun trained on Kresse's chest, held out the key. "Could you kindly open that door, Herr Hölderlin?"

The key was plucked from his hand. He was conscious of the burly figure going round the back of him and edging to the door and the grating of metal on metal. And so he waited, one arm out, watching the other man, the barrel of each gun mimicking their stare like the dark unclosing eyeball of a fish.

"It's open," came the tremulous voice and the teddy-bear face swivelled as if it had never seen two men pointing guns at each other in a basement room with socks and papers and muddy footprints all around.

Suddenly, Uwe threw his revolver onto the bed. "I mean it, Kresse. Fifty-fifty, as long as you do the work."

Kresse grinned vindictively. "Get in there. You too, whatever your name is." And went on grinning at the wall, the stone racks, the files stacked there. "Where is it?" looking about.

"What?"

"One of these is mine."

Uwe went over and took a file out. He went further along the wall and took out another. But Kresse still stood there, making his calculations. "All these files, boss . . ." his voice tinkling, his gaze no longer insulting.

Then in a move so unhurried and effortless that Kresse didn't comprehend until too late, Uwe put his hand to the wall and like someone tugging the night behind him he pulled across a shuttered metal door and locked it.

They could hardly hear the banging and crashing in the hallway. "I don't think it will last long," handing Hölderlin the revolver. "But perhaps you might wait until I get back."

"It will be my pleasure to do this, Herr Uwe. As always."

Alone in the precious cellar, Kresse could scream until he was blue in the face.

CHAPTER FORTY-ONE

"MY COLLEAGUE – WHAT HE was planning, it was insufferable."
Uwe turned his tired eyes to the giraffes. The female took the
calf's tail between her lips and licked it and rested her head on
its rump and butted gently with her horns. "It went over the limit.
Really, it went over the limit."

Peter waited for him to say more, not drawing breath. But he
seemed far away, on the scorched savannah, the sun fizzing through
the thorn trees.

"Not too near the rail!" A mother calling to her child brought
Uwe prowling back.

"Look," removing the magazine from his coat pocket and
unrolling it. Tucked between advertisements for harness straps
and depth sounders, a postcard. "This was in your file."

A giraffe photographed in Hamburg zoo. And Peter, as soon
as he saw it, understood the reason. He turned the postcard over.
Postmarked April 7, 1983. Addressed to "Snjólaug" at the department of psychiatry, Karl-Marx University.

Peter stared at the two crimson stamps, his handwriting legible
but changed beyond recognition. "Dearest Snowleg, How will you
ever forgive me? I must see you again. I love you, Peter. PS This
reminds me of you."

"How come you have this?"

"I was one of her case officers."

In the year his wife absconded to the West, Morneweg had recruited
Uwe. Where once he worked for the "prevention, disclosure and
combating of underground political activity", today Uwe sold bread-
machines. In 1982, Morneweg empowered him to set up a unit
whose task was to gather smell-samples of those critical of the
regime. Over the following months he was sensible of a deepening
in the old man's regard for his work. He was promoted and, because

of his excellent English, Morneweg used him on occasion to check the accuracy of certain transcripts. In March 1983, Morneweg asked Uwe to sit in on his interrogation of a young woman suspected of plotting an escape to the West with an Englishman.

"I can keep this?"

"Of course. It's yours."

Peter tucked it into his pocket. Who was this man? Was he going to lead him up the garden path? Uwe had given him a post-card, but was he now going to say, "I don't want money myself – however, for another five thousand Marks I can introduce you to someone who may have seen her four years ago"?

"Tell me – what did you do to her? What did you actually do? Did you hurt her?"

"Did I hurt her?" The question took Uwe by surprise. "No, I didn't hurt her."

Peter saw the surprise and having expected to be shaken down he felt a wave of relief. A memory of Malory on the shelf next to *L.A. Woman* and a fox-cheeked girl stirred in his memory. "Listen, you're very kind to have come here, to bring the file . . ." A wooden stall, water boiling in a mug, and beyond the tangerine curtain the names being called – "Leadley, Liptrot, Hithersay, Tweed . . ." He wanted to go as far as he could. "You see," expelling the words in the way he used to say *Sum*, "I did something really terrible and it's been haunting me."

"Yes, I know," said Uwe. "We heard everything."

"What are you talking about?"

"Let's stop playing word games," raising his red-rimmed eyes and looking Peter full in the face. "We've all been fucked around long enough. If we're going to talk, let's talk."

Peter was really frightened now. Clearly, something much worse had happened. He lowered his leg from the rail and pulled himself to his full height, feeling a hideous stab in his spine. "I really need to know who you are and why you're here and what you've got – and then we can talk. I've had a pretty long day."

"Have you? I've had a pretty long day myself."

The keeper started feeding: from the rail they could see him throwing branches from a barrow. Peter watched the giraffes eating with a sliding chew.

"I take it," came the voice, measured again, "that you did not go on to great things on the boards?"

"No, I'm a doctor. Actually, I'm a German doctor," and was conscious of Uwe looking at him with a little more interest. "I always hated the theatre."

"Me too." With strained jollity, Uwe said: "I didn't see your show, Herr Doktor, but I sent a couple of people along – including my colleague Kresse, who had been trying to stop it. Kresse maintained you were four prats from Hamburg who were going to put on a ludicrous theatrical performance. But Morneweg – that was our boss – overruled him. 'They may be something later in life.'

"Well, Kresse reported back that in the whole history of stage management he had never seen anything so incompetent. He referred to you in the department as the Pantyhose Four. The music was disgraceful, too. And I tell you, Herr Doktor, he didn't like you any more when you ripped out our camera in the Schreber garden. You see, because of her brother the hut was already bugged. You remember – just outside on the lawn – der Gnom?"

His mind switched away. It was blasted clear of some things – loyalty, pride, patriotism – but others poured back to fill the mother-sized hole. He thought of Morneweg whom he had served with filial obedience, almost until the end. He thought of Kresse, hurtling his ginger head against the walls of his basement cage. "I don't want your money," he said. "But I thought if there's something I can do to stop Kresse finding her, if not for your sake then for hers . . ."

He tapped the padded envelope. "I'm sorry I was late – I was having a quick look at these files. Before you see them, it's important you understand the context."

There was no reason Peter should have remembered this, but he had arrived in Leipzig in 1983 not long after the West Germans had done something to make the East Germans look foolish. "You never saw such a mess. They had a dead body and they pulled it through the minefield, and what could we do? You're bound to shoot – and when we got to it, it had no stomach. The episode was humiliating. We wanted our own back."

This was why Uwe had reacted with alacrity when Renate telephoned from the Astoria. "She asked: Did I know of someone – a young woman – planning to escape that night with a group of actors from Hamburg? I had an idea who she was talking about. I said, 'Let her in. I'll get authority for this. Meanwhile, we can set it up. While they're at dinner, we can organise things.' We didn't have long, but I thought we had a chance here of seriously embarrassing someone, in this case the West Germans and the English.

"I was about to speak to Morneweg when Kresse came in. He had been on her trail since that morning – in fact since I went with him to the Schreber garden. I said to him, 'This is your chance, Kresse. Take your dog down to the station. Get the cameras. Let that wicker basket go to opposite the last carriage. You're in charge of the detail that will arrest her.' We might have had a marvellous – not a propaganda victory, but a humiliation victory. But even as we were putting it in motion you threw your spanner in our wheel.

"My first thought – when I heard how you'd behaved in the hotel – was: Could it be a blind? I said to myself: Maybe she's going to go off miserable and then turn up on the platform. She's going to walk to the end of the train, kiss you goodbye and vanish. *Brief Encounter* all over again. And if she had tried to escape, we were primed. I don't know to this day how serious she was about getting into that basket. Probably she was. Anyway, I had to assume she was, which is why I brought her in. But if she had got into that basket – that would have been the end of her, and her brother too. We'd have rounded the whole lot up, father, grandmother – you as well.

"Instead of which all we get is this girl, who didn't seem like someone who wanted to turn the state upside down."

Between the metal cranes and mansard roof floated thinning packs of cumulus clouds. Uwe sniffed. The sun had brought out a whiff of giraffe droppings and urine-soaked hay. It reminded Uwe of the smell of Morneweg's Wartburg and his first sight of the woman outside the Astoria, the doorman bundling her into the car and Morneweg catching up behind. He remembered how she kept looking round at the entrance. How she was still staring through the back window when the car lurched off, its tyres honing away in the sludge.

"I said to her – this was in the car: 'If you will implicate this English student in his escape plan we will lift him at the station.' She didn't seem to understand what I was talking about. I repeated what Renate had overheard. 'I want to go in your dressing-up box. I will fold myself so small you will hardly recognise me. I can't spend one more night in this country.' At this, she laughed. She said we had got it wrong. It was a lover's joke. But Morneweg was sitting next to her and he was adamant. Because of what happened with his wife, it was his philosophy that everyone was running away. She might be 'a mother of the underground'. She might be working for Workers of Peace. Or in league with her brother. And if she wasn't a hostile negative force, a term we used, maybe she was an indigent. Whoever she was, we couldn't let her get away. Since I was already involved in her case, he wanted me to be there at the interrogation."

Peter put out a hand to the rail. His knuckles were like stems that had been lopped off. "Who was she? You did find out, didn't you?"

"Yes, of course."

"Do you mind me putting it to you like this? Would you tell me as thoroughly as you can what happened?" He was willing to get down on his knees for any last gritty hurtful detail with which to sandpaper his conscience. "I'm not afraid."

Uwe touched – for reassurance – the large envelope, tapping his fingers on the printed words "Guggenheim & Berberich – bread-machines" as if to slow down and make more deliberate his thoughts. And decided that he did want to help this man who insisted on hearing everything. It was comforting to talk to someone who would register his words: it would stop him thinking of a hollow hand clawing for a morsel of air. A quick look through the file and the case had come back to him. He hadn't thought of it in 19 years, but his memory was infectious. Since he had started remembering, he remembered more.

———

In no time they reach the Runde Ecke. Wordlessly, Uwe guides her across a frozen quadrangle. The snow falling in dark grains. A police car with its bonnet up, a rack of bicycles, dirty icicles hanging from the gutters in jagged free-fall.

He punches his number into a security box, shoves her up some steps and along a corridor to have her fingerprints taken. The policewoman – blue trouser and jacket uniform, short hair dyed red, bat ears – squirts ink into a mirrored glass. She seizes the girl's right hand and rocks her little finger in the ink. Then takes her into a bright-lit room with a basin and a pail in the corner. There is hardly any ventilation.

"I watched her on and off through the night – and other nights too. I see your point, Herr Doktor. I remember her sponging herself in the early hours. Lovely to look at – except for that burnmark. But you must see many naked people in your profession . . . For me – as I said – this was no degenerate. This was a classic situation, a girl in despair. We can use this, I thought. We'll pick her up, we'll put her back together, we'll tell her, 'Darling, they're not worth anything. They're not worth horsepiss. Who would join one of these bastards? Join us. Get your own back.' I've seen it happen a lot. They scream their heads off, and after a while they're turned very simply. Some take two minutes, some two hours. But most give up in the end, there's only one way to go. Well, with this one it wasn't quite as easy as we'd hoped. By the next morning I know that she's not like the others."

She stands before him in Morneweg's office. She has slept in the clothes she wore to the theatre, plus she has on a police-issue woollen pullover, olive green and on the back "MFS". Lipstick and mascara smears on the collar of her shirt.

Uwe sweeps her slowly with his eyes and remembers a dark hair on a sheet and immediately files the thought away. "Please," he says politely, indicating a chair in front of the larger desk.

She walks hesitantly across the grey carpet tiles and sits. Shadow of a lace curtain on the wall. A flag: "Germany – One Fatherland". On the desk an embossed-leather-framed photograph of a teenage boy standing on a yacht's deck. Morneweg's son. There is a folder, two glass jars, a book, a key, two telephones, a tape recorder.

"My colleague will be here very shortly."

Through a second door, half open, the drift of a male voice conferring with someone. Morneweg comes in, closes the door and goes behind his desk. Loose tan suit. Pink shirt. Thick black-framed glasses. An old man with round child-eyes taking her in.

He starts the tape recorder. "Your name?"

She gives it and he stops the machine, spooling back the tape. A hissing fills the room and over it her voice, composed and clear: "Marla Hedwig Berking."

He smiles and starts the tape again. "What is your date of birth?"

"February 17, 1960."

"You are twenty-three."

The machine is a grey-ribbed Uran with a green light like a spirit-level that snakes back and forth as they speak.

Assuming an expression of great solicitude, Morneweg adjusts the microphone and leans forward.

"To begin with," Uwe tells Peter, "it's small talk. When did she finish her studies, what music did she like to listen to, what did she think of the theatre?"

"This incident last night. Tell me in your own words what you think happened."

"I was invited."

"You were advised it was a formal dinner."

"Not by him." The machine snuffles up her answer.

"By the doorman," Morneweg reminds her.

"I'd had a drink. But I was invited."

After a silence, he says: "Would you accept that terrorism has to be countered?"

Puzzled, she concentrates on the Party button in his lapel. The metal oval stamped with the yellow, blue, red of the Sozialistische Einheitspartei Deutschlands.

"Yes. But what has that to do with last night?"

Timid, as if afraid to infect her, Morneweg suppresses another cough. "I have to speak with you about a serious problem." It has come to his knowledge that a Western secret service has been collecting information about her. He needs to find out for what reason. "It's important for your own security and for that of your family." He takes off his glasses and breathes on them. "You must tell us all about yourself and your friends and relations."

"I can see she's wary, but curious too," Uwe tells Peter. "Is Morneweg talking about you, she has to be asking herself. Have the British sent a student to spy on her?"

She says: "No-one would have any reason to spy on me. What sort of information?"

Morneweg polishes his glasses on his shirt and begins to speak about her life, her character, her family. He tells her how her grandfather started his bleaching business. How her parents met. Her childhood. He knows everything. The milk bar where she bought ice cream as a 14-year-old. The first Beatles record she'd exchanged. The origin of the scar on her back.

"We are here to help you," he says with a friendly smile, and holds up his glasses to the light like someone checking a tumbler for lipstick. "Maybe we could do something for you."

"Her face is puzzled, at the same time impressed. I can see her thinking: Who told you this?"

"Yes," she says after a while, "there is something you can help me with," and explains her problems with Sontowski.

"You want to become a psychiatrist? Maybe we can help, but first we have to get more information."

Morneweg puts his glasses back on and studies her with shrewd, unreflecting eyes. The Englishman – how long has she known him? How did she come to meet him? What did they talk about? What did he tell her about his work . . . ah, yes . . . What was he going to do after university? What did he tell her about his family? Why did he come to Leipzig, to the Fair?

The fusillade of questions unsettles her. Her eyes swing around and come to rest on the glass jars. She cocks her head, trying to read the labels.

"I'm confused. I want to know who she is, this young woman who has got under the skin of my boss. I ask myself: Is this a dissenter? Could this person possibly be a threat? She doesn't impress me as an oppositionist or as a deviant. Morneweg has shown me the file – all her reports for school and university say she's the star pupil. OK, she's belligerent. OK, she barges her way into an official dinner at the Astoria. OK, she reads forbidden novels. But isn't this what she is? Just a spirited girl who's fallen for a Westerner and wants to see him again. As far as I have been able to make out, she isn't involved in any organisation. She doesn't belong to the League of Evangelical Churches. She doesn't fit any familiar dissident pattern. The point is, there's no broad resistance to the regime. Morneweg starts from the position that they're everywhere, like stars in the sky. But there aren't many. Just what we called single ghosts. And this girl is a single ghost, if she's anything. As I say, the whole thing is confusing. And most confusing of all is the key."

Morneweg picks up the key from the desk. "You gave this to the doorman. Why?"

She turns her eyes from the jars. "I wanted to see Peter again." The light from the window emphasises the bumps of a necklace under the pullover.

"This key, where's it to?"

She shifts in her chair and Uwe catches her scent of dried sweat mingled with a French perfume.

"His room."

"In Leipzig?"

"In Hamburg."

"Morneweg thought that because she had given the key to the doorman, she might be willing to do other things for us. We had few unofficial employees who were female. The boss was always looking for more. This may seem odd to you, but she was suited to the role. Ambitious, adventurous – and with a sense of justice. We didn't like them to volunteer. We preferred to find them ourselves. And if they had a black spot in their lives, so much the better. And that's what you were, a black spot."

Morneweg opens the folder. "The idea is not to punish someone who makes an honest mistake. But I don't need to remind you of the penalty for degrading the state." To return to a point made earlier, he feels it unusual that Citizen Berking refused to take No for an answer. Why did she insist on going into the hotel when she had been told not to? "I'd like you to tell us."

"I'd like to have a shower," edgily. "There are lots of things I'd like."

"Fräulein Marla, you are not so naive as you seem. You have been living in Leipzig – what is it, 23 years? – and you must know what the habits are in this country. I ask you again, why?"

"I'm a young woman." It was nothing more than bravado, something decided on the spur of the moment. She had always wanted to see inside the Astoria. When this Englishman invited her, she thought it would be fun to go. "Look, we'd had a great talk. Going into the Astoria, I felt it was a normal thing to do. Is it forbidden?"

"No, it's not forbidden for invited guests. But this foreigner said he didn't know you. When asked if he knew you, he said No."

She chews the inside of her cheek. "That I can't explain. Because what I'm telling you is the truth. He did invite me."

"Well, there's something else to this story," Morneweg said.

"Like what? Like what?"

"Hadn't he promised to take you with him to Hamburg?" his voice toughening.

"No! He never did. That was a joke."

"Why did you follow him inside?"

"I'm not embarrassed by my emotions!"

Morneweg walks round his desk and leans over her. "Citizen Berking, whether you like it or not, your action connects you with this Westerner and the ideas he represents. You say you were fascinated by him. That he invited you. But this man from the West, this medical student, he said he didn't even know you." He is wearing sandals and gives a soft kick to her foot. "Now, why would he do that?"

"Don't," she whispers, her thoughts unspooling.

"Why?"

He kicks again, but not hard enough to cause the tears. She lifts a swollen eye. "What's my crime? What on earth is my crime? I've done nothing wrong!"

"I'd like to believe you, but this is not an isolated incident."

"What do you mean?" rubbing her eyes.

"Are you aware," with the careful watchfulness of a hunter approaching a thicket full of pheasants, "that the father of this Englishman was from the GDR?"

"He told me."

"Did he also tell you that his father was sentenced for trying to leave the GDR?"

"He did. But he never met his father. He doesn't even know if he's still alive."

Morneweg holds up a photograph. "Do you know this man?"

"Of course!"

"Who is he?"

"It's my brother."

"This morning, your brother left for West Germany on a UN visa."

"So? Article Ten, in the '49 constitution, isn't it? Everyone has the right to leave."

He returns to his desk and stares at her, solemn. "Tell me again, where did you meet?"

She sighs. Crosses her legs. Stares out of the window. Her expression declaring how bored she is with his questions, with repeating herself. "It was a chance meeting." She had met him at the theatre. "That's all there is to it. He invited me and I thought he was nice."

"Nice, nice," says Morneweg, his right shoulder hunched up. Under the desk two white socks wriggle in their sandals.

"I did. I wanted to go to his party."

"That's not true."

She looks him in the eye. "What are you talking about?"

Morneweg reaches for the book. He lifts it for her to see. The novel she stole from the Book Fair.

"Is this yours?"

"Yes."

He starts reading. The room is silent. Just the spools grubbing and rooting.

After a page, he looks up. "This book is illegal. You know that."

"Is there a list?"

"Is there a what?"

"Is there a list of books that are illegal?"

"No, there's no list."

"Then, why is this illegal?"

"It's not written according to socialist aesthetic criteria," he says stiffly.

"Then, I want to know the name of authors who are forbidden so I can avoid them."

He continues reading. She watches his eyes flick back and forth. He turns the last page and he might have come across the news of someone's death. Slowly, he reads out, "Peter Hithersay, 54 Feldstraße, Hamburg."

He closes the novel and pushes a photograph across the desk to her. She sees herself in black and white at Bruno's farewell party. Talking to Bruno.

"You have already appeared with him here."

"So? Can't I talk to my own brother?"

He pushes her another photograph. "You have also appeared here."

335

She sits in a café, obscured by an art deco lamp. A blurred figure stands over her. Looking down her throat.

"He told her every word she had said. He could tell her your whole sentences. How else do you think we learned about your father? That's why we knew you called her Snjólaug. Well, she didn't know what to think. Was it the waiter? Was it a microphone? Maybe it really was you!"

"And here."

Peter. Dancing. Holding her.

"And here."

Sitting beside Peter on the steps of her grandmother's Schröver garden. Her breasts loose inside a white shirt too big for her.

"You're like ants," she hisses. "You're everywhere."

Morneweg removes the spools without rewinding and inserts another tape. "So. You never met him until that night?" He looks up. Presses START.

"Do you think it's possible for swans to carry our weight?"

At the sound of Peter's voice, her face drains. Her hands come together over her nose and mouth. She closes her eyes and leans forward until her head rests on the edge of the desk as if in prayer.

Morneweg stops the tape. She's sobbing silently. "Fräulein Marla, you are illegal. You have illegal contacts. What shall we do with you? At the very least, we could charge you with communication with a foreigner. But maybe I can play you something else? This was recorded a few moments later . . ." He reaches towards his machine.

"NO!" A string of mucus sways from her nose. She tries to wipe it away, but it sticks to her hands and spreads.

His finger hovers above the tape recorder as if suddenly the machine disgusts him. As if there's no lie he hasn't heard it record, no blandishment, no cruelty. As if there's nothing he doesn't know about sexual weakness and carnal appetite. The pitchy humiliations. The false promises. The boredom. "Of course, there's no reason you can't see him again if you want," speaking so tenderly

336

he might have been taking her into a great confidence that he would give only to a relative. "You can still be a psychiatrist. You can still enjoy a happy life here."

She looks at him, not understanding.

"Maybe you're not meant to be a hero," he says in a sympathetic voice.

"Just like we were taught in Golm, he leaned on her, hinted at the advantages to be gained. A telephone for her grandmother, a job at Karl-Marx University, a promise of books and clothes. He wanted her to feel that she had special knowledge we might be interested in, but it quickly became clear what he was asking her to do and she refused. She could never keep a secret. She had a lot of friends who said things she knew they wouldn't mean. She wasn't the informer type."

Morneweg's voice hardens as he reads out paragraph 219 of the criminal code: "Anyone who has contact with organisations, institutions, or persons who have as their goal any activity that is against the laws of the GDR will be condemned to a sentence of imprisonment of up to five years." He looks up. "Naumburg. Five years. Think of it."

She stares back at him with contempt, not hiding her tears now. "He's no spy. He wants to be a doctor. His father was from the GDR."

"Sentenced for derogating the state," he reminds her. "You realise, we can charge you with the same crime?"

"Go ahead." She breathes in the air in great gulps. "Go ahead. But I want a lawyer." She's tired. She's uncomfortable. On the desk one of the telephones starts ringing. She's angry. She picks it up.

Morneweg's eyebrows embrace in horror. He twists in his chair as if he has a stitch, and reaches across the broad desk to seize the receiver from her hand. "Hello?" glowering at her. "Hello?"

She leaps to her feet. Blindly, she looks at him. "Have you never fallen for someone?" shouting now. "Don't you know how it feels?"

Morneweg calls for Uwe to take her away. The call is important. He shields his hand over his eyes, lowering his voice. "Yes,
Herr Hirzel . . ."

Her fist crashes on the desk. He tries to say something, but she
slaps the telephone – cutting the connection.

"What people don't realise," Uwe tells Peter, "is that if you refused
to work for the Stasi it rarely led to negative consequences. Of
course, Morneweg wanted to get a new informer. But if he couldn't
intimidate or embarrass her, there was little he could do."

She spends two more nights in the cell and is brought up to learn
her fate. Morneweg is in his redoubt at the Astoria: he has left it
to Uwe to inform her.

"I have spoken with the judge. The decision has been made to
release you." He opens a drawer and takes out a typewritten letter.
"Please read this and sign it."

The letter declares that she will never say a word about their
discussions.

She shakes her head. "No, I never sign."

"It's your duty. You must sign."

"No, I don't understand it. I don't know what kind of consequences it will have."

He snatches back the letter. "If you don't sign then it's your
duty to remain silent about what has been said."

From somewhere she musters a smile. "I'm not going to sign."

Uwe looks at her and he has the impression that he is back in
the hut in the Schreber garden. A cerise silk shirt stitched with
dragons, a man's scarf and a silverfish crushed on the worn
matting. He lowers his eyes to the book on his desk and says
neutrally, "You may go." He presses the intercom on his desk.
"Kresse, please escort Fräulein Marla outside."

The door opens. She gets up to leave.

"Wait." Uwe is holding the novel she stole. That she had asked
Peter to take with him. As she had asked him, a little while afterwards, to take her. The muscles soften around his eyes. "Keep it."

CHAPTER FORTY-TWO

AT THE SQUEAKING BELLOW, Uwe stiffened and looked at Peter as if the noise coming from the giraffe was directed at them. Obliged to speak louder, he suggested a meal. "Look, maybe it's too late for lunch, but watching the animals eat has made me hungry," and gathered up the envelope. He wasn't yet ready, it seemed, to hand over the contents.

A blackboard in a street not far from the zoo advertised a set lunch for 20 Marks. Inside the restaurant, a broad-shouldered man with the face of a bulldog watched CNN from the corner of a brown vinyl sofa.

"Can we eat?" Uwe asked, looking around at the deserted tables.

"Shhh." The face scowled at him without respect. Once, thought Peter, Uwe would have had this man in his paws. Now it was over, he couldn't frighten anyone any more.

The man barked out a woman's name and rotated his eyes to the screen. A plane had crashed in the Peruvian jungle.

"I can pay for myself," Uwe said, laying the envelope on the table between them. "I'm sorry I can't take you out. I could have done. Times were good, but now they are not." He eased himself into his seat. "Oh, before I forget," and from his pocket produced one of those plywood keyholders that Milo made in his carpentry class. "Remember this?"

Peter took it. "A key to where?"

"Isn't it yours?"

"Mine?"

"That's what she said it was. We even had a copy made so that our people in Hamburg could search your apartment."

"I don't remember losing a key," frowning.

"Well, it didn't fit. But that was why the doorman let her into the Astoria."

Peter turned it over, and in clear detail like a photographic negative he saw Snowleg standing outside the Astoria. Holding up the

339

key. Looking into the doorman's face with eyes full of meaning.

"The plane came down in a remote part of the Amazon near Iquitos."

He knew what it was. He had picked it off the floor in the church hall. After she had hurled it at Bruno.

Uwe was saying, "Morneweg tried to have everything destroyed – tapes, reports, smell-samples. But for some reason I kept this. No, you might as well have it. It's no use to me."

Overcome by gratitude, Peter said: "Listen, I'd like to buy lunch." It was barbarous what this man had done, the manner of his interference in the lives of his people. And yet something in the red-rimmed eyes touched him. This was a man who would make up his own mind, who would bear the consequences and let no-one else, who would dispose of the rest of his life exactly as he himself pleased. At school, they might have been friends.

"No," said Uwe with emphasis. "I am not Kresse."

"At least let me pay for the wine."

"Then I do the food. No argument."

A waitress charged out of the kitchen in a busty hurry to take their order.

"What is the set lunch?" asked Uwe.

"Grünkohl."

"That's for me."

"And a bottle of this wine."

"Not eating?" Uwe didn't conceal his relief.

"I'm not hungry." It was more a state of fast, though.

Uwe drew out his cuffs and said evenly, "So what have you been doing with your life since you left Leipzig?"

"As I told you, I work as a doctor."

"Never married?"

"No."

"Me neither. Except to my boat!" and his laugh hung like a slack sail from the corners of his mouth while the waitress waited, rubbing her hand on her apron, for him to taste the wine. "Ah, that's from the right bottle!" licking his lips and nodding for her to pour Peter's glass.

The meal arrived – brown cabbage, bacon and sausage cooked in a pot – and between mouthfuls Uwe talked freely. After the Change he had worked as a detective in a shopping mall and was unemployed for two years before securing a job with the bread-machine company. The position wasn't as technical as he would have liked. He had long ago given up his dream of teaching the natural sciences.

Uwe was friendly with the waitress. He ordered a second bottle.

There was still an aspect of his life that he wanted to put back together before he parted with the package on the table. "We can all identify with the victims, it's a national necessity. What about the perpetrators?" He swirled the wine around his glass and removed a speck of cork. "You don't need a history lesson, but all this," and made a vague gesture out of the window, over the passing cars, at the Leipzig skyline, "it was formed against fascists and extermination camps. And yes, it went wrong because our leaders themselves became outlaws in a certain way. But not in the beginning. I know this is hard to believe, but we felt we were in battle. We embraced life in the GDR as a true alternative to fascism and war crimes. But to keep our people safe we felt we had to know everything about them and to make this knowledge a respectable, responsible activity. And that's where we went wrong."

His hand flinched away and he looked with distaste at the envelope. "All this information, who cares about it today? Who cares that you go to the lavatory three times a day and drink one seventh of a bottle of vodka or whether you pick your ear or nose or rub your hands? It was a terror. A greed. A dementia. We didn't understand that those who know everything – smell everything, hear everything – know nothing. I regret that your Snjólaug fell into this category, and so, Herr Doktor, did you. Do you think I might have another glass? No, let me speak. I know what you're thinking. 'Why should I trust this man? Why is he telling me this?' Once an enemy . . . isn't that so?" and clinked Peter's glass with his own. "You know, I always thought the English cowards. Nothing personal. They won the war, they won both wars, but they didn't score many points over here. It was your treachery that landed us in the hands of the Russians. What you, Herr Doktor, did in the

Astoria made it easy for us . . . But you see, I know you better than I should. We have never met, and yet I recognise you so well from your voice."

Uwe had leafed through the Marla Berking file before coming to the zoo and its pages carried him back 19 years to a more innocent man than this exhausted, motherless figure blocking his ears to the thump, thump, thump of Kresse's frustration pounding through the wall. He recalled immediately the case of the English medical student and the recording of the Schreber garden in Aachener Straße. At Morneweg's instigation, he had played the tape over and over while she was in the cells. He knew what was fake. He had listened to other of Morneweg's recordings, was familiar with the repertoire of seduction and betrayal. The shrieks on the hotel beds. The lazy questions. The flattery. "The hours we wasted transcribing these shouting animals clambering over each other, slobbering into each other's ears night and day. You're lucky, Herr Doktor. You don't have to listen to that crap. I always thought you'd have to be colossally stupid to sleep with someone in East Germany. It meant either you hadn't been round the block or you'd been around the block and didn't give a shit. Very rarely did one hear anything interesting. Because, let's face it, what are you hearing? I tell you, the banality was indescribable."

But the tape of Peter Hithersay and Marla Berking wasn't fake. This love, in so far as Uwe had heard it spoken or made, belonged to another category.

"Maybe I'm a little intrigued? And, yes, why should I deny it – now that we're one nation and none of this is supposed to matter – maybe even a little jealous, hmm?"

His awkward confession stung Peter, as if his biology teacher had announced that he was jealous of Rosalind or his mother. He swallowed his glass and filled another, feeling a protective swell of desire. The past was running towards him. He knew he would get drunk. "After you let her go, what happened to her?"

Uwe shook his head. "That's not such a good story. I'll be absolutely direct with you, Herr Doktor. It was a disgusting thing Kresse did to your young lady – a thing you wouldn't do to your worst enemy, not even as a last resort."

"What thing?" And his voice, like a sick man wanting to be told everything, sounded less aggressive than pleading.

"Well, you must understand that after she left the Runde Ecke I didn't look for her. Because she wasn't a case any more. But that's not how Kresse saw it. There was something about her – you could even say it was intolerable to him. It was Kresse's idea, by the way, to stuff your basket with that rope. That was typical of Kresse. Every time you sent a letter he would show it round the department with great merriment. 'Look, another one of these – from the Hamburg ninny!' He had to invent enemies. Build them up. Provoke them so that Morneweg wouldn't be disappointed. You were one of his enemies – and at the other end was Marla Berking. And being Kresse, he started to invent things about her."

Uwe sat back, enjoying the wine. Talking had made him less sorrowful. In resuscitating Snowleg, he had pushed back the memory of his mother in Dösen Hospital. While Peter had taken on Uwe's mood of despair.

"Just imagine," said Uwe. "It's Monday morning. You've got five or six officers around this table. Men like Kresse who'd like to have a decoration. All weekend, they've had to sit in church at peace meetings, listening to the Beatitudes. They've been up drinking the night before and they have to write a report on these enemies of the state. They're bored. They're creative. They're diabolic. Suddenly, they have some ideas.

"Kresse's were the most inventive, I have to say. And vindictive. He's the son of a writer – he even went as a Stasi observer to his father's reading and reported that he was no fucking good! Well, it was Kresse who spread these malicious stories."

"You mean, her gonorrhoea – that was Kresse?"

"He thought he would send a summons to a pastor's wife. And it caught on. All these husbands asking their wives who they'd been with. I tell you, it planted great suspicion and caused a lot of emotional breakdown – which Kresse was able to exploit. Well, soon after I release her he decides to go to work on your Marla.

"I know nothing of this until one day he comes into my office. He's quiet and apologetic, which isn't Kresse at all. He behaves as though he's surprised himself in some unforgivable act. 'Uwe, you'll never guess. Remember that girl from the Schreber garden

– the one you sent me to arrest? Well, something strange has happened . . . She's disappeared.'

"When Kresse tells me what he's done, I'm disgusted. I want to apologise to her. You see, for the rest of us it's becoming more and more difficult to believe in what we do. It's becoming exactly how Kresse described your pantomime in his report. A ridiculous puppet play. Sometimes we have to will the stupidity to participate in this big joke. So many motivations, mixed messages, options. I don't know which one is correct. I feel I could choose and defend any one of them. Even as Morneweg was interrogating her, I felt this. She was a rare spark of spontaneity who'd floated up into my life at a time when I felt choked, worn out, frustrated.

"Now, I'm not saying she's necessarily the reason. What I am saying is that I'm noticing all sorts of things I'd never noticed before." Ever since, it had seemed to Uwe that the world, like Kresse's moustache, was out of plumb. "I'll never forget how Morneweg reacted when she cut off his telephone. But I think I was more shaken than he. And why? Because of this passionate girl. She wanted something and she was going to go after it. Even if she didn't get it, she wanted it. She reminded me of something I'd lost in myself.

"So I tell Kresse that I will take responsibility, and I go to her building. I remember it was in Menckestraße because the orphanage was round the corner. It turned out that her grandmother had recently been moved to an old people's home and someone else was occupying the apartment.

"What emerged from the statements I was able to get from her neighbours was that Marla Berking had married and left the district. They didn't know where she'd gone, didn't care. They just wanted that fucking bitch out of there! I tell you, it horrified me the way people spoke of her. From an old man, an expression I hadn't heard since I was a boy. That was Kresse's method. He'd cast her as a drunkard, a Stasi snoop, a whore.

"Well, I wasn't able to discover where she'd gone – and I had a look in the file. The only person who knew would be Morneweg, or her grandmother."

"What's her grandmother's name?"

"I don't know. I may never have known, but she's probably dead by now."

"And Morneweg?" — a low-tide cormorant darting at a fisherman's scrap.

Uwe made a violent gesture, knocking into his wineglass. "Drowned two years ago in the Kulkwitzer See."

"Dead? I thought he was in government."

"Not Morneweg," replenishing his glass. "I saw the body."

The memory of that day hadn't faded. One morning — it was the beginning of the asparagus season — a former colleague had telephoned Uwe and alerted him to be at the boathouse in 15 minutes, no longer. Since reunification, Uwe's friends had found their niches in collecting stamps or fishing for Rotbarsch or tending their allotments. Uwe preferred to lose himself on the water. In the evenings he sculled along the Karl Heine canal and at the weekends he sailed on the lake he had known since childhood. "There he was. Bloated. Enormous. Big as a boat."

The boat-keeper explained: in the early hours he had lowered his dinghy into the shallows and rowed along the southern shore, the sun misshapen in the clouds and the lights from Markranstädt winking. He had lifted his blades over the bones of earlier Saxons and hubcaps and was oaring through the shallows when the hull scrunched into what he took to be a log.

He twisted, shading his eyes. Morneweg in the oily water. He was floating 12 inches above the surface. His eyes were mongoloid and white like a fiercely peeled potato and he was floating on his back. From the muddy bottom numberless glass jars stared up through the rainbows and effluent. Uwe's smell-pantry.

Uwe's boss — with Kresse's help — had dumped the lot. But nothing in those jars was ever so potent as the stink coming off Morneweg.

"The smell was indescribable. I thought his back was covered in moss and then I realised the skin had turned green, like parsley. It took five of us to lift him. I felt if I pricked him all the voices of Leipzig would hiss out. A waterlogged Tower of Babel in the filth of the Kulkwitzer mud. Probably suicide. Or maybe not."

"What became of Kresse?"

"Ah, Kresse. There's a question," and stood uncertainly. "I need a slash. When I get back, we'll open that."

"*There are thought to be no survivors.*"

Peter sat there, dabbing a finger in the red wine that Uwe had spilled, he noticed, onto the envelope. He put up his hand to ask for a cloth and put it down again. The waitress was making for the kitchen with her apron half across her face. Transfixed, the owner of the restaurant remained where he was, steadfastly admiring the breasts of the grieving woman.

Uwe sat down heavily and from the envelope drew out a folder the colour of old brick. On the cover, a label with a typewritten name: Marla Hedwig Berking.

"I want to put a record straight. I want to apologise for the behaviour of people like Kresse. Because of the way the world was, you were separated from your girl. The idea of that monster relic coming to take money off you was the last straw. I came here to say: first of all, you can have her file – as I told you, it's no use to me. On the other hand, I don't think you're going to find the information you want. She's disappeared from the face of this earth, and because she was no longer in the frame we never looked into where she might have gone. Perhaps you're interested to see once more the letters you wrote to her. Otherwise, I've pretty much told you everything you're going to find here."

Peter stifled a lurch of appalling anguish, but Uwe was taking another folder from the envelope, more faded than the first. "I also found this. I had a lot of files at home – fewer now. Until Kresse jolted my memory I'd forgotten that I had stuff from as early as that. Anyway, there it was," and with the sense that he was clearing out an element of his life – tomorrow he would take his mother's clothes to the charity shop – Uwe handed it over.

The folder was exactly the colour of Rodney's anchovy paste. "What's this?" Peter felt Uwe's tired gaze on him.

"It's your mother's file."

CHAPTER FORTY-THREE

As soon as he came into the street he regretted leaving his coat behind. The wind had got up again and it licked his face like a dog's tongue. He hoisted his collar and headed along Jahnallee.

He was still searching for a quiet bar or café in which to read the file when he made out – above the scaffolded roofs – the Gothic spire of the Thomaskirche. Barely able to keep an eye open against the wind, he hugged Uwe's envelope closer to his chest – and, not looking for the place, he found it.

It wasn't until he was through the door that he recognised the wine bar. Stupefied, he gazed around. He had – for the briefest moment – the impression of having reached the mountain-top where the Emperor Barbarossa sat alone. Had time stopped? Had nothing happened at all? The little table looked as on the day when he seized a book from its glass surface and went in pursuit of Snowleg. Same coffee cups. Same ashtray. Same art deco lamp.

He pointed and the waiter nodded. "Yes, that table's free."

At the next table, a man with thinning hair gathered in a rubber band lectured a girl in a black waistcoat. "The best way for Europe is to be Belgian." Over the loudspeakers some sort of nature tape was playing that sounded like a recording of whales calling to each other. She lit a cigarette and swayed to the sound.

The waiter brought a wine list. Peter was nervous of opening Uwe's envelope without another drink to steady him. And why the hell not, he thought. A man has just made me a present of 5,000 Marks. In a fit of extravagance he ordered a whole bottle of claret from the year he was born.

He took out the grey file – he was surprised how thin it was – and smelled it: dust and the vegetable smell of old carbon paper. The true scent of the totalitarian regime. The waiter arrived and made a performance of uncorking the wine and pouring it. Peter put down the file and raised the glass to his lips, tasting the years in the bottle.

He intended to take a sip, but he drank a whole glass before picking up the file and opening it. There were only a few sheets of paper. He wiped the table to make sure there was no ash or wine and began to go over the pages terribly slowly. The signatures and countersignatures. The official accusations. Reading how Henrietta Potter, a British citizen on a temporary artist's visa (No: XP78U1957), had been accused of "exploiting her function" as a singer in the Bach competition on October 1, 1960. He could see the headstrong woman of twenty through the brisk shorthand notes of the interrogating officer.

Stapled to one page was a photograph, black and white, a young man. Typewritten below were the words: "Peter Brendel – following recapture at 18 Zieglerstraße, Dorna, 5.10.1960." The photograph was stapled to a GDR death certificate. Four years after he was taken back into custody, the prisoner Peter Brendel was shot trying to escape. Interred municipal cemetery, Dorna.

"Brendel," Peter muttered to himself. He said it again, louder. "Brendel. Peter Brendel." And experienced an almost ungovernable desire to jump up from his seat. He was forty and at last he knew his name.

He picked up the photograph. No-one had asked him to smile, and yet the expression recalled one of Rodney's early attempts at his own portrait. The light on the face flickering as though it was rising to the surface. As though it was still in the stage of being developed.

The face was so similar to Peter's own at that age – twenty-two or twenty-three – that he could have been looking at his younger self. The dark slanted eyes. The furrowed expression. For a few seconds he had the sensation that the two of them had exchanged places.

"Peter Brendel." At least he didn't know he had a son.

A table away, the girl in the black waistcoat looked round. Peter smelled her tobacco, instantly recognising the brand. "Doesn't matter how long you go without," the hypnotist at Ochsenzoll had told him, coughing. "One puff and you'll be back to sixty a day within four days." Warm air and cigarette smoke filled his lungs and the same dizziness came over him as when he left

Bettina's studio for the last time. He leaned over and asked the girl for a cigarette. His first in 13 years.

The sensation of the hot smoke hitting the back of his throat was furious, pleasant. Since breakfast he had only drunk wine, and inhaling again he felt a jolt of nausea. He pounded down his hunger and his nausea with another long draught, and the smoke went through him and around him until he was cloaked in it.

Another glass. He pulled out the brick-coloured folder.

Some time later the music stopped and the waiter went behind the bar and changed the whalesong into jungle frogs and parakeets.

Uwe had told Peter everything. It was impossible to resurrect Snowleg from these clinical reports on Marla Hedwig Berking. Only in Peter's letters – a dozen or so written over two years – did she seem to have existed.

He poured another glass.

I will fold myself so small you will hardly recognise me. I can't spend one more night in this country.

A slow flush crept over his face and he felt himself unstitching and the threads coming out of him. Little could he have dreamed that 19 years after saying No he would be looking for her again. Or that his way of saying No would have sent her spinning out into the universe irretrievably, to where not even the Stasi could find her. He had propelled her into oblivion by his cowardice and his father was dead.

"What saw you there?
Sir, I saw nothing but the waters wap and the waves wan.
Ah, traitor unto me."

"What did you say?" The girl looked over her shoulder. "Were you talking to me?"

"No, I was talking to King Arthur."

"You were what?" She threw him a sympathetic expression and turned back.

He inhaled again, the smoke fuming into his lungs and unpacking something. A coward dies a thousand deaths, a brave man once. That was the difference between Sir Bedevere and Arthur. He felt a choking and his eyes smarted, peppery with pain. He couldn't see the couple at the next table. Nor the light from the lamp, his father's photograph, his letters to Snowleg. All he could hear was the jungle static of frogs and parakeets and crickets. He was standing on a chalk cliff. A pilot in the cockpit of a blazing bomber. Spiralling into a rainforest. Branches and thorns slashed at his face. He breathed in. The air was thick with smoke. His ache kicked out and he felt a pain scrabbling up the wall of his stomach and falling back into its pit and rising again.

"Are you all right, sir?" The waiter leaned over him.

"I'm fine, absolutely fine."

The waiter lifted the bottle to pour more, but his life was empty.

What time was it? Looking in his pocket for his watch, he touched the key to the Schreber garden and its weight was heavier than a body. His father's watch said 7.30 p.m. He hadn't realised how much he had depended on finding him. On finding both of them.

He paid the exorbitant bill and fled with the folders. He had eaten nothing all day and he fed on his footsteps, walking faster and faster. Not since the reunion at the Garrick had he been so drunk.

Somehow he crossed Dittrichring in the direction of the Pension Neptune, and into the park. He followed a path through the trees to the river. Soon he was stumbling beside the bank. The river rising and a low linen moon catching ridges of foam and black serpents of water coiling.

A noise like applause rose from below, and he had the impression that people were clapping him. He looked down, his attention caught by a movement on a root exposed by the fast gargling water. And there floated to the surface, above the cheering and drumming of heels, Milo's excited voice: *Daddy, Daddy, have you seen Frau Weschke? She promised to catch me a river crab.*

Could that be a river crab clinging to the tree root? No, it was absurd. Again it moved, like a duster flicked on the water. He had no idea what river crabs looked like – whether they had a season, whether they still existed even. Milo's drawing was all he knew. But how hard could it be to catch one? The river must be teeming with them. To catch a river crab for his son seemed to Peter the absolute grail. He could picture Milo's delight. Yes, things were going to change.

He took off his shoes and socks, laid the envelope beside them, and slithered down the soft bank. It went very quiet after his legs hit the water. The cold took away his breath and the river rapidly filled his trouser legs. As stealthily as he was able, he inched towards the root.

You can only catch them from the back.

He saw a fleck of moonlight on a pearly shell and a fluttery movement — the crab manicuring itself. He hadn't frightened it away! With massive care, he stretched out his fingers: 6 inches. Remain unseen for only 6 more inches . . . He took a furtive breath and leaned forward, but even as he pushed out his hand he could see the texture was wrong.

The water hugged his knees. He threw the crisp packet back into the stream and clambered onto the bank.

He was careful not to make a sound as he stepped into the hall. But his shoe squelched on the first step of the staircase. A door cracked open and a shaft of light impaled him.

"Herr Doktor?" From behind the neon blade, Frau Hase's anxious voice. "Herr Doktor Hithersay, is that you?" She stood with her mouth open a little. "You're trembling." Peter caught sight of the calamity in the hall mirror and mumbled something and staggered on up the stairs.

He stood under the hot shower until he was warm again. Afterwards, he sat naked for a long while on the edge of the bath, looking out at the street and the sky, his heart going slop slop slop in his hollow body like someone beating a path towards him.

PART VII

Milsen, 2002

CHAPTER FORTY-FOUR

SEVEN KILOMETRES FROM THE Czech border, a car drives into the courtyard of an old stone-built house. A woman gets out and collects her suitcase from the boot. The handwritten label on the handle reads: "Metzel, Milsen."

In the middle of the courtyard was a water-pump. She paused beside it to exchange her grip, breathing in the still, early-morning air. She had never been gone so long. Her time in England had given her detachment. She looked up at the ancient house – the stork's nest in the chimney, the sun reflecting on the skylight of the brick dovecote, the neighbour's beehives – with the small shock of experiencing something both intimate and foreign, like the smell of her daughter's breath. She picked up the suitcase. "Katya!" she called once inside. "Katya!"

Her daughter, alerted by the whippet's barking, bounded down the wide, imposing staircase in a tracksuit and trainers

"How was London?" embracing her.

"Let me tell you over a cup of tea."

Katya pulled a face. "I'm trying to get in a run before Sören arrives." He was picking her up at noon, she explained excitedly, and taking her to a rock concert in Dresden.

They went into the kitchen, where Katya indulged her mother by sitting down rather primly to drink a glass of water.

"So, how did it go?"

"I sold all but two," filling the kettle.

"Mutti, fantastic!"

"Better than I expected." She switched on the kettle, chatting on about the opening night, the review in *The Times*, her days in England. She wanted to tell Katya that she had fulfilled a child-hood ambition to visit Hampstead Heath and the ravens in the Tower of London, but her daughter was elsewhere. "Listen, go for your run."

"Catch up later," said Katya, leaping to her feet and giving her mother another hug. "I'm sad for you about Oma" – and to the whippet: "You talk to Mutti."

She watched Katya walk from the kitchen – the pronounced way she had of springing on her heels – and felt rueful. I won't get you back, she thought, till I'm a grandmother.

Katya stopped at the door. "By the way," beginning – before she corrected herself – to speak in the tone in which she had addressed the dog, "a doctor rang from the city. He said he would ring again and talk to you about Oma's ashes. As a matter of fact, he's got the ashes himself. Does that make sense?"

"Did he leave a number?"

"No, but I said you'd be back this morning. If Soren arrives, I'll be ready in an hour."

She heard the door slam and thought, See you in ten years.

The number for the Lion's Manor was pinned to the cork board. She telephoned Sister Corinna. Yes, Frau Weschke's very special doctor had himself taken the ashes to Leipzig. His intention was to deliver these in person, together with a box containing her grandmother's things and a letter.

"I didn't mean you to go to this trouble."

"It's not a trouble," Sister Corinna said quickly. "The doctor needed to be in Leipzig anyway."

Grateful to be spared the journey to Berlin, she made a pot of tea. Glancing over the kitchen for a cup, she noticed Katya's efforts to tidy up and was moved, but it turned out to be a job unfinished. In the sink was a thick wool sweater that smelled of rain-soaked sheep. There was a pile of not very well washed plates and on the table in an untidy heap the mail of the past fortnight. Some circulars. Two bills. A note from Stefan to say that he would bring Kristjan back on Friday. An envelope with a Berlin postmark.

Her heart jumped. She couldn't help it – whenever she saw a letter with handwriting she didn't recognise, the superstition seized her that the author was a previous owner of the house who was writing to claim it back. Abandoning her quest for a teacup, she found a knife, butter still on the blade.

She breathed out. A letter of condolence. She wondered why there weren't more, before reminding herself that Oma had outlived everyone, even her century, her country too. "It's sad what I'm telling you, but true," had been her words in the ambulance that took them to Berlin. "In my long life I have seen Germany – my Germany – defeated, divided, reunited, vanish." There was no-one alive to mourn her. Save for Bruno, who would never mourn anybody – and the author of this letter.

"I only knew her for a short while . . ."

She read the past tense and let out a groan. It was different to be told something over the telephone than to see the cold dead fact of it in writing.

". . . indeed, my son had come to think of her as his own grandmother."

Her eyes flicked to the top of the page and when she saw the address she couldn't help thinking of the words of another doctor in another hospital where her grandmother had been admitted when she broke her leg. "There's little chance she'll get out of here," warned the solemn little man with a pointed chin.

And yet two months later there was a knock. Anne-Katrin from the corner shop. "Telephone!" In his wheedling voice she recognised the pointed chin. "Please collect her. She's walking like an athlete." And he conjured the spectacle of a fierce, petite old lady tapping her way along the crushed-marble corridor – "driving us crazy with her cane".

She went on reading, the memory returning of the afternoon she travelled to Dösen to fetch her grandmother. The heated look. The gruff voice: "What on earth's happened to you?" The pressure of those old palms on her face. As if she was able to tell by the simple gesture of squeezing her granddaughter's cheek all that had taken place while she lay there, her leg in plaster.

She turned over the page and saw the signature. Her free hand went up to her eyes. She shook her head. It must be a different doctor.

Twenty minutes later, he telephoned. "Frau Metzel?"

"Yes."

357

"Thank goodness." He introduced himself and she recognised the voice. "Did your daughter pass on my message?" He was being polite. He sounded tired, disheartened.

"Yes." She waited for him to go on, to say something more. The last time she had heard him speak – on Morneweg's tape recorder – he was talking about swans.

In his English-accented German he asked for directions to her house.

She must have given them because she heard herself saying: "It's five minutes by car – or half an hour if you walk . . ."

"When would be convenient?"

"Any time. I'm here all day." What can I say to keep him on the line? – but in the background his train was announced, he had to go.

She put down the receiver and spread her hands on either side of the letter. She leaned forward in order to reread the signature and when she realised with a spasm of understanding that there was no mistake her breath snorted out as if she were laughing. A successful doctor, then. She wasn't surprised. He had known that there was nothing wrong with her throat.

Once more she read his name and her eyes moved down her stomach to her legs. She went over to the sink and picked up a glass. She peered at it for dirt and filled it from the cold tap and drank.

Why are you coming? I can understand why then, she thought, but why now?

In two hours' time a dead man was going to walk into this house and she didn't know what he wanted, what she was going to say to him.

CHAPTER FORTY-FIVE

PETER WAS ANXIOUS TO look his best for Frau Weschke's grand-daughter, but apart from his twill overcoat and the shirt Frau Hase had washed, and which smelled of something like Dettol, he realised he had nothing to wear.

Glumly, he riffled through Renate's "hot new season" clothes, pulling out, one after another, a pair of black Rip-Off shorts, a pair of brown cowboy trousers stamped to resemble cow-hide, and a "J'adore Capri" shirt in the piercing green of Renate's dress. With a sense of deepening hostility he held them up against his body and it seemed he was being invited to try on pains of different colours. All at once he thought of the trousers that had been left in his room.

"But I haven't washed them," wailed Frau Hase. "Besides, they might not fit. Herr Mehring was a little smaller . . . Wait, I will fetch them and you will see."

Back in his room he tried them on. He had woken with a savage hangover and tiptoed across the floor in order to keep the pain at bay. At the same time he felt more stable and moderate in his thoughts than in weeks. Khaki corduroys, Herr Mehring's trousers smelled of cologne and pinched at the waist – but they would do.

When he had finished packing, Peter left Renate's clothes on the bed and wrote a note to Frau Hase to say that these were for her with his very best wishes and more lingerie was to come. Ten minutes later he carried his suitcase downstairs and settled the bill. "I will mail these back to you."

Frau Hase glanced with grave disdain from his trousers to the walking stick that seemed to have become the centre of his gravity. "Oh, whenever," in a strained voice. Then blurted out: "Herr Doktor, I am so sorry you didn't find your friend." She spoke as if she personally was to blame. "Will you be coming back?"

"No," and buttoned up his coat. He had been through the mill, the seven storeys of hell. He wanted to get out of Leipzig.

The horizon glowed pink through the deer-heads of blown trees. The warm wind had melted the snow from the branches and beside the railway tracks scales of watery skin glittered in puddles in the first sun. Alone in his compartment, Peter didn't shift his gaze from the window until an attendant with a trolley pulled open the door. He bought two bottles of mineral water and drank them one after the other as the train hurtled through the morning landscape. His head throbbed so violently that, to his relief, he no longer heard the lather and scratch of his memory. With every kilometre that the train put between him and Leipzig, Snowleg sank away from him until it seemed that he had left her safely behind. Snowleg, and the unbearable memory of his last sight of her.

The train crashed through a forest. Rank after rank of sea-green pine. The sun hurling black shafts through the mist into the dew-frosted grass. The trees not trees, but a king's company of pikes and halberds and lances, awaiting the order to advance. He settled back into his seat and nursed his queasy head. He wouldn't ever know the end of the story. He would discharge his undertaking to the old lady and go home, cultivate his garden, behave better.

CHAPTER FORTY-SIX

NOT UNTIL SHE CAME into the bedroom did she remember: Katya was jogging. Bed unmade. Lights on. Curtains drawn. The place was a mess. A litter of lipsticks, bottles and creams all over the chest of drawers and on the floor clothes everywhere in dark piles.

The confusion startled her. Normally, she shut the door on Katya's disarray, but this time she started to pick things up off the carpet. An application to university. A dry-cleaning bag. Nail-polish remover. She took stock of the dust, the unpaired socks, the empty teacups – so this was where they were – and felt a charge of protectiveness for her daughter.

She threw open the curtains and then the windows. She changed the sheets on the bed, put all the black clothes into a laundry basket for Katya to sort. And ended up sorting them herself.

Cleaning didn't require deliberation or discipline or the use of too many faculties. Cleaning took her back to herself. Back to her own days and months of drudgery after Katya was born. It gave her an oddly comforting feeling to think that anyone from that time who saw her dealing into separate heaps the black tube skirts, turtlenecks, Lycra shirts, would have to believe that her world had stood still.

Setting the room in order, she started to ward off the shock of recognition at Peter's voice. She pulled the bed away from the wall and worked her way around and under it with the vacuum cleaner. So her grandmother had ended her days in his care! She tried not to make sense of the information. But her efforts to keep it at bay were futile. She would spend the morning working alongside the coincidence, adjusting to it, until he arrived.

I thought it was dead and buried, she told herself. And now you're coming back.

She knelt beside the bed and hunted in the dust and the biscuit crumbs and the tiny balls of tissue paper. The room had a distinct smell – their daughter's smell.

"Afterwards – what happened to you afterwards?" Isn't that the first question Peter would ask? And she thought of her grandmother. "Men are so transparent," Oma used to say. "Men are such cowards. Very few try to taste courage. For women it's the opposite."

She switched off the cleaner. The room was neat at last, but she looked around it with apprehension. If only she could untangle her half-memories as easily as her daughter's clothes. What would Katya's room have been like if she had grown up with Peter, a doctor in the West? Would she have run in the fields?

The sun poured in through the six-paned window. Outside, a tractor ploughing the field and the distant figure of Katya picking her methodical and insistent way across the skyline. Did he even suspect he had a daughter?

She touched her short blonde-streaked hair, her face. With the same fingers, she tugged her jersey over the belt accentuating the fullness now of her body. This was the person she had become. But the younger woman, what about her?

She looked at her watch. His train would arrive in ten minutes.

CHAPTER FORTY-SEVEN

AT 9.26 THE TRAIN halted at a small country station of mauve brick. A geranium in a rusted paint tin. In the field, a little grey colt with a bald patch. Peter stared through the window and interrogated his reflection. He imagined that he saw his father. The nose slightly larger than he had pictured it. The eyes more slanted. The mouth like something started and abandoned.

His imagining disintegrated into a young man entering his compartment. He was dressed rather as Peter had once seen Johnny Rotten: Beuys-type waistcoat, legs shackled in ripped bondage jeans, stiff green hair, two rings in a nostril and wearing children's plastic sunglasses. "You're in my seat."

Peter got up and caught sight of the station sign. He stood motionless while the guard ambled along the platform calling out "Dorna! Dorna!"

CHAPTER FORTY-EIGHT

SHE LIT A FIRE in the kitchen and sat at the table and waited. The clock struck ten. She went into the corridor and stood before a low shelf. She brushed a finger along the spines and tugged out a book. Then returned to the kitchen.

Nervous, she hunted for her reading glasses. But she couldn't concentrate on the book. The slightest sound and she glanced up at the window.

If he had taken a taxi he would be here by now, she thought. He must be coming on foot.

The clock struck the half-hour. Maybe he's not coming! and savoured the last-minute reprieve.

At 10.45 a.m. she took off her glasses and stood up. She would go into town – after all, she needed to buy toilet paper, bread, milk. She started to put on her coat. But I told him I'd be in all day. What a stupid, stupid promise.

She looked out of the window. The only person in the lane was her daughter, running home. She watched Katya getting closer.

It was the morning she discovered the valley.

She had saved a little money from her scholarship and had permission once she graduated to work as a free artist. She informed Professor Kleist that she didn't want a studio in Leipzig – she preferred to be in the countryside to paint. He beamed at her. "That's marvellous!" Every other student had requested a studio in town. There were more artists than rats, he told her, and he had no space. "For you, I will write a letter tonight."

She spent the summer exploring empty lanes by bicycle. One day she met a shy but determined engineer who was putting up protection orders on old houses. He told her of a house near

Milsen, a twelfth-century fortress that belonged to a von something or other. He loaded her bicycle onto his van and drove her to the top of the valley.

They stopped to ask the way at a farm. Under the cherry trees a child lay asleep on a mattress while an old woman with a clerical hat tied under her chin threw tarnished *boules* into the dust. She pointed to a dilapidated orange-tiled roof. The park was overgrown and the trees had lost their formality. Beyond, open fields led to Czechoslovakia.

The rooms were derelict. Villagers had stolen the tiles. The ransack was complete. No doors. Windows smashed. Even the gatepost missing. Only birds lived inside.

The fortress dated from a time when Otto I was delivering Christianity to the East. In the 1960s, forty Czech families had occupied it, but for seven years now no-one had slept here save for a few hunters. There was a print of Landeburg on the principal staircase and some feathers where a pheasant had been slaughtered and, balanced across two ruined mahogany chairs, a slab of amber-coloured bacon.

"A good place to make music at night," Stefan had said, coming up from the cellar, when she took him there a week later.

There was no water, no electricity, no sewerage. In point of fact, the shy young engineer confided, the district government were hoping the house would collapse. They planned to cut it from history like a shame. Then along he had come to secure it with a protection order. And now there was a strange family who had official permission to live there. In the village, they didn't know what to make of it.

She handed Professor Kleist's letter to the mayor. He read it aloud, bemused: "Please give your support to this young artist. It's essential for our nation's cultural life that artists of her quality can live and work in the country. There are no more studios in Leipzig."

The village elders agreed to connect electricity to the old house, to enrol her children at the village school, to help with materials. They were too cowed to say No.

That summer the family slept in the village inn and she and Stefan laboured themselves to repair the roof. The next four months were the best they had together. They built an outside toilet with a black-market cistern and bricks. They glassed in the dining-room windows. They laid floorboards. And they discovered, with the help of the old lady at the farm, a water supply. She had remembered seeing a pump working in the courtyard before the war. They dug for many days and 4 feet down, far from where the old lady had thought it, they found a hand-pump and a well. Before the year's end, they had restored two rooms. Enough to abandon the inn.

In the late autumn evenings Stefan lit a bonfire and toasted garlic and bread. She could buy four loaves for an Ostmark and the bread was good. She looked at the fire then as her two children now watched television. Saying nothing, not even thinking.

The spacious dining room became her studio. She slept here with the children, surrounded by books and trays of nibs and rolls of thin brown paper – until she learned to make her own from hollyhocks – that a contact of the baker purloined from a mill in Dessau. No stranger came there – and Stefan only when he was drunk. She went out by day with a sheet torn from this paper and sat in the woodland and waited for a sound – a bird singing or a voice in the distance – and tried to repeat the noise with her nib until the nib was part of her, a finger.

These hieroglyphs were her notes. She also took Polaroid photographs. At the academy Professor Kleist had tried to coax her from painting to photography, and in particular to study the work of Sander and Cartier-Bresson. But though she used the camera incessantly, she ran into so few of Cartier-Bresson's "decisive moments" where she was now living that she had no appetite to seek them out. Her instinct was for self-effacement. Her short-term ambition to let a shy, mistrustful nature trust her. Make her its lightning rod.

When the children slept, she lit a lamp and settled at her table. She worked through the night, drawing after drawing, while her husband's electric guitar beat out from the cellar and over the abandoned park. Once she opened the shutters and the lamplight reflected in a squirrel's eye.

Nobody from the village came. They listened to the jagged

discord of Stefan's music and were friendly enough, but they never came.

"They're afraid we're Stasi," Stefan said.

A door slammed. She heard Katya panting along the corridor. "Soren not here?" called her daughter between heavy breaths.

"No, darling," and took off her coat. She had nothing of him. No photograph. No letter. Once there had been a blue hat and woollen scarf, but Stefan had taken to wearing these for his concerts until one night he didn't bring them home. All she had was condensed in a forgotten novel by an author whose name she had never heard uttered again.

Katya climbed the staircase and tramped along the corridor, creaking the beams.

She sat down and put her reading glasses back on.

The story had gone right out of her head but, her English revived by a fortnight in London, she was drawn in, and having understood one page she read another until she looked up at the window less and less.

In the early dawn, he walked to the canal that fed the lake. The birds knew him by his movements and advanced towards him in a silent cavalry. He tied one leg with string and then another. Soon they were ready.

CHAPTER FORTY-NINE

HE GOT OUT AT Milsen. Since the place appeared destitute, Peter, after waiting five minutes outside the station without any sign of a taxi, decided to proceed on foot according to Frau Metzel's directions. A walk might clear his head. Wheeling his suitcase behind him, he headed out of the village.

At first glance it was like any of the villages seen from the train. Buildings the colour of a horse-rug. Empty chairs on a veranda. A war memorial, its plaque cracked in half. A woman sat on her steps bare-legged in the sun and watched him go gingerly by. In a garage workshop, an aria from *La Traviata* – possibly Pavarotti, more likely a mechanic.

He passed a row of houses each with a small front yard and a wire gate, his progress punctuated by the snarl of locked-up dogs. Signs warned of their disposition to bite. An Alsatian stood still and shivered at him. At the next gate another dog lunged to the end of its chain, darkening as it growled.

The border was only kilometres away. Had these been guard dogs? Milo's mother in her article had written how trains stopped at the border for 15 minutes to let trained animals crawl under the carriages and sniff out anyone clinging to the underside. Reunification had made these dogs redundant, their former handlers compelled to sell them – or else to bring them home as pets, sometimes, Frieda said, with dreadful consequences for the community. The dogs attacked ducks, goats and cattle as well as villagers. "Were he to return from the dead," wrote Frieda with her usual woolly reprise, "not even Colonel Most would be guaranteed a safe reception."

An Alsatian in the last house choked at the end of its tether. Licked the spittle from its snout and crouched. Black eyes sparkling. Nostrils quivering in a low snarl.

"@ Schillerstraße, left, keep going > a crossroads."

The fields were covered with a blanket of snow and mud.

Hedges standing like yard-brushes. By the time he reached the crossroads the barking had died away.

He picked his slow way along the narrow road, his suitcase rattling behind him and the tap of his cane on the asphalt. He knew he must sound like a blind person. Stopping to rub his eyes, he focused on the sun bobbing out of the clouds like a fisherman's float. Impossible to know what the sun would do with the rest of the day. The sky that had been clear earlier on had the grey-white texture of freshly filleted cod, and was dotted here and there with scales of Prussian blue.

He followed the road through a line of poplars. Their trunks grey and the uppermost bark pinkish with the stripped patina of burnt skin. Along the roadside, white-painted crosses marked the scene of accidents.

The trees gave way again to open country. The road climbed steeply up a vast field. At each step he felt a recurrent pain in his back and neck. He slackened his pace, stopping once or twice to rub the sweat from his eyes. The field was furrowed in neat and specific rows and cropped as he used to imagine his father's head. The snow had shrunk back into the earth, but when he breathed in there was still a smell of cold in the air, like fur.

Over the brow, where a lane branched to the left, a shallow valley unfurled below him. "You'll see it to the left."

Frau Metzel's house was not at all what he was expecting. An old fortified manor-house that lifted its stone gaze above a court-yard and across fields that might have been landscaped. In contrast to the hostile uproar in Milsen the scene that met his eyes was tranquil and soothing. A tractor, its ancient plough-shares gouging open the soil, trundled out of sight behind a timber barn. Pigs lolled in a field, and in the distance a runner closed on the house. Long dark hair, black tracksuit, young.

He looked at his watch. What did she mean, half an hour? It had taken 50 minutes. Leaning on the cane, he stepped towards the house. When he had delivered Frau Weschke's ashes, he would ask her granddaughter if she could save his weary legs and drop him at the next village.

CHAPTER FIFTY

HOLLYHOCKS BRUSHED HIS KNEES as he approached the door. He pressed the bell. The buzzer whirred. Feeble, like a beetle on its back.

He took off his hat and mopped his brow and waited. Not a sound. He pressed the bell a second time and after long seconds stood back and looked through the window. A woman sat at a table. He had a fleeting image of simple black clothes, fair hair. She didn't turn. Didn't move.

Peter rapped at the glass with the silver horse-head. The corner of the window was stitched with cobwebs and there were honey jars and bottles along the sill.

"Yes?" The tone of a woman interrupted, but there was no-one else in the kitchen. She was reading.

The woman who opened the door was dressed in the sombre style of the newly bereaved. The dark clothes fitted loosely and he couldn't tell her age. She had a long, intense, slightly pale face and her skin was delicately netted as if someone had squeezed it hard between their palms and left the prints.

"Frau Metzel?" He smiled at her his professional smile and she smiled back, excited and then disappointed, and he wondered if she had expected him to be someone else. "Peter Hithersay," introducing himself. "I spoke to you from the station. I've brought your grandmother's things."

She went on looking at him and crossed and uncrossed her arms in a gesture of consternation. He hasn't recognised me, she thought. But why should he? We met for three days 19 years ago and I've changed. She was 10 kilos heavier now, with her long dark hair cut off and streaked; and she had steel-rimmed glasses through which she studied him with grey eyes that had no doubt lost their fire.

He peered back at her with an odd expression. She was about to take off her glasses, but stopped herself.

"I recognised you straight away," he said – and she thought with a pang, Here we go. "You look like your grandmother."

Frau Metzel didn't say a word. Finally, she stepped back. "Won't you come in?" her face in shadow.

He wanted to say, I must go, there's somewhere I've got to be, but the voice smouldering in his suitcase said, Don't you dare. "Well, perhaps for a minute."

Her long stride carried her away from him into a tall-ceilinged hall, passing a perfectly preserved stone staircase, a battered suitcase on the bottom step. The hall smelled of turpentine, maybe dogs as well, and half a dozen canvases were stacked against the left wall.

He ought, he knew, to ask about her art – Bettina would have shot Pericles for a show at the Whitechapel.

She went ahead into the kitchen. Long pine table with a book open. Large 1960s fridge stickered with photographs. Board pinned with telephone numbers and pictures cut from art books, and a door with coats and hats hanging on it leading to the garden.

"I see you're limping badly. What is it?"

"A knee."

"You had a rough weekend?"

"You don't know the half of it, Frau Metzel."

She looked at him enquiringly, but just then a black whippet emerged from under the table and sniffed his crotch. She made a quick gesture with her hands. "Shadow – please. For goodness' sake."

He patted the whippet away and the dog, as if they understood one another instantly, turned and went back to its basket.

"You're right to ignore him," and she stared at Peter, musing. The mud-spattered, not especially well-fitting trousers, the face a little exhausted. A man with a stick who smelled of snow and something antiseptic.

He lifted the stick and she thought, Any second now . . .

Peter wasn't prepared for the rush of emotion when he set the cane on the table. He felt – despite the violence of his hangover and the pain shooting down his spine – the liberation of someone dismounting having accomplished their knightly task. And yet he was reluctant to part with it. He caressed the tarnished handle and the extravagant thought flashed through him that his fingers weren't touching an inanimate mould but the haft of an infinitely precious weapon.

She waited tensely. "Do you want to take off your coat?"

He started to unbutton it, when he caught sight of something on the table. He had noticed the book! But it was his letter from the Hilfrich Klinik. She half turned her head and took frowning note of his face as he reread his words. This she hadn't foreseen. All morning she had composed herself for his coming. Her flare of disbelief that he hadn't recognised her gave way to a bolt of anger, swiftly leading to silence.

He straightened. Without his coat he appeared very thin, like something maltreated. She stared wonderingly at the trousers and his shirt with its faint reek of Sagrotan. He looked raw, defenceless, and more authentic somehow than the young man of her memory.

"Here – give that to me," and she added his coat to the garden door.

He went to open his suitcase. His walk unchanged and rocky, like a skater taking different glide steps. Unchanged, too, the way he swept his hair back from his eye.

Under the table, Shadow slept.

She went on watching him with her secret gaze, and as he delved around in his suitcase she had a disrupting sensation, as though time had stopped and she was resuming a conversation that could be heard across a vast expanse of ice. As though not an hour of the time they had spent apart had been endured.

He pulled out a white cardboard box and she was now afraid that he was going to recognise her after all.

"Sorry about the packaging. It's really meant for cakes," he said unnecessarily.

She looked at the words BÄCKEREI MEYER stamped on the side, the cellophane peeling from the lid. "I must say, I didn't expect this. Is it usual for doctors at the Lion's Manor to ferry their patients' ashes?"

"Your grandmother made us promise to bring them to you."

He smiled that odd smile again. "Anyway, I've been looking for a reason to revisit Leipzig."

She tore open the lid. In the muskrat sleeves was the burgundy container with Frau Weschke's ashes. She took it out and put it on the table.

"By the way," he said, "I was meant to give you this letter."

"She wrote a letter to go with her ashes? That's quite bizarre."

"She could be very insistent – well, you know that."

Trapped between him and the envelope with her name scrawled on it, she burbled on: "I've heard that doctors are more affected by some cases than others. Who would have thought that my grandmother would be the one to get such treatment? She's not an obvious candidate – you should have heard what the doctor in Dösen said as she was leaving! Nevertheless, I think I can understand why you did it."

But a vagueness had entered his eyes. Hidden behind his own gaze, he seemed not to see her – a motionless stooped figure whose spirit was indicated only by the hand that fretted with the walking stick.

"Of course you can," patting his borrowed steed. "She's your grandmother."

Her reflex of affront and frustration had vanished and now in place of relief a shyness paralysed her. She took a deep breath and resolved to confess herself. But her resolve faded as she looked at him. That's what attraction does, damn it. Anyway, what would she say? Tell him all that had happened? If you've had to stop telling stories, it's difficult to start up again. Besides, telling people your story doesn't tell them who you are.

She darted a hand inside the box. "Well, let's drink to the old battleaxe," and held up the bottle of white wine. The letter could wait.

They toasted Frau Weschke.

She said in a tight voice, "To Marla."

He brought the glass to his nose. "To Marla." Tipped it and swallowed.

She pushed at a log on the fire with her foot and took another sip. "This is really good," she said, surprised. It hadn't been chilled and it had been trundled over the hill from Milsen, but it was really good.

"Isn't it?" The wine made him feel better at once. The hair of the dog.

She read the label. "Saale-Unstrut, 1983." She laughed, and it occurred to him that the laugh was a bit nervous. "I bought it for her."

He looked at her again and put down to the wine a wave of extraordinary dizziness, similar to the one which had almost overwhelmed him at the zoo. When she opened the front door he had been mildly disappointed. At first sight, she had appeared quite neutral, severe even, but now, as she leaned back, he noticed a twist here, a touch there. A jewel at her neck that hadn't shown before, a good smell. He had mistaken simplicity for dowdiness and he saw that the cut of her black jersey and quilted trousers was rather elegant. Beside her he felt drab. "You know, you do take after your grandmother."

She turned her face, a gleam in her grey-green eyes. "People say so. It's hard for me to tell." Then, the wine making her flirtatious: "Who might your children take after?"

"Presuming I have children."

"Yes, presuming you have children."

He dug out his wallet and showed her a picture of Milo. She drew breath. She inspected it fiercely and returned it with a smile. "He's a nice-looking boy." And pointed. "That's my eldest." She walked over and removed a Polaroid photograph from under the fridge magnet. Handed it to him.

"God, they could be siblings," he said. "But most children look the same to me."

"You spoke to her – Katya." Her voice didn't stumble when she imitated her daughter. "'A man from the West is bringing Oma home.'" She moved away, giving him time to contemplate the girl, and looked out of the window at the studio converted now from the dovecote where she had discovered life could be joyful with not enough minutes in the day. In the black meadow pigs were up to their tails in slush. Beyond the hollyhocks and daphne that she had planted for making paper, she could see her neighbour's

374

beehives and the farmer still ploughing. Drilled down by circumstance, she had dissolved into that landscape. A long time had passed since she had felt the need to be articulate about herself.

Her eyes strayed to the book on the table, open where she had left it to answer the door. If she hadn't stolen that book, if Peter hadn't followed her out of the Book Fair, if she hadn't gone with him to the Astoria . . . She might not have had a child. She might not have had two children. She might today be a fully fledged psychiatrist.

Eyes lowered, he went on looking at the photograph of their daughter.

She stared at him, and her shyness returned. She had expected to confess herself and then, like someone who has forgotten to ask the name of the person they've been conversing with, it had become too late. They were too far in. He had to recognise her on his own or not at all.

"Yes, maybe you're right," she said. "Maybe all children do look alike."

He gave back the image of a girl with black hair cut level with her jaw as her mother's might have been. "Or maybe all photographers make them look alike."

"Where's Milo's mother?"

"We're not together. He's with her right now. Tell me, could I get to Dorna easily from here?"

"Dorna? Well, actually Katya's boyfriend is coming to pick her up. I'm sure they can drop you – as the crow flies, it's amazingly close. Why, do you know someone in Dorna?"

The idea, which had been forming ever since the train stopped at Dorna station, had crystallised on the walk to Frau Metzel's house. He thought, I can kill two birds before I return to Berlin. "My father's buried there."

"Your father." She nodded to herself.

"I've only just found out, as a matter of fact."

Now that he wanted to leave, she felt an urge to detain him. "Is that what you were doing in Leipzig – looking for him?"

"Well, not exactly."

"What were you doing?" and heard the false vagueness in her voice.

"Nothing much." Then: "Thinking. I don't get the chance at the hospital." But he sounded to her like a man on autopilot. He had discharged his duty and was on his way home. He was just being civil.

"Thinking?" in the rasping manner of her grandmother. "What about?"

He had been about to say that he wouldn't bother to wait for Katya's boyfriend and could he telephone for a taxi, but he heard the fired-up note in her voice, like a conversation he might have had with Frau Weschke, and this made him want to answer her question. "I was thinking about how you can do things, say things, that you don't mean – and how this can haunt you."

She raised her hand to slap something on her arm, but thought better of it. His failure to recognise her gave her room to move, a leverage. But what to do with her advantage? The ladybird landed on the table and she stared at it. "Gunter Schabowski said a sentence he didn't mean and it opened the Wall. What things are *you* talking about?"

They had been standing and now they sat down. He moved his chair forward. "I was wondering how you expiate a wrong that you've done – oh, years and years ago." His hand covered his brow. "When you're young, you do such stupid things. Things that when you look back make you aghast. When you're young, you *do* hurt people without thinking. I mean, you must be familiar with this feeling . . ." He wondered if he was embarrassing her, and then, himself embarrassed, shut up.

She turned to the window – he could see her cheeks moving where she bit them – and he was conscious of a constraint to her look.

He had been thinking about time, he went on – and immediately regretted saying it. It sounded pretentious and yet he had never felt more need to speak with honesty. "What happens when you do something awful and you're not forgiven for it, or you're not in a position to be able to ask for forgiveness. How do you get yourself forgiven?" But he was dissatisfied with what he was saying. He had never been good at philosophy. "I know that this sounds like nonsense out of context."

She lowered her gaze to the fire and twisted a strand of hair behind her ear, winding him in. "Did you reach a conclusion?"

He glanced downwards. "I don't think I did."

"Would you like another glass of wine?"

She got up and poured it.

This time the wine burned through him. How flippant he sounded. All of a sudden, he felt terrible.

She sat down again, her hands darting back to her lap. "You're speaking in abstractions."

"It's not important. I'm talking about something that's dead and buried."

She realised it wasn't going to happen. She was safe. She pushed the bottle forward. "Tell me."

He sat sideways in his chair, his mouth open and his hand fiddling with the cane. He began to talk, not seeing her, his eyes glistening. Speaking about a girl he had met when he was a medical student. The wine a truth serum.

"We were getting to know each other when I killed a promise."

"How so?" Her voice was soft, but he could see the tension in her hands. Under the table, Shadow quivered in sleep.

"It's not –"

"Go on," she said with a little smile that he couldn't interpret, and he was aware of the dramatic light on her cheeks and the darker hollows of her eyes. He noticed how dark her eyebrows were and saw refracted in her eyes – was it Frau Weschke? "Tell me," she said, again.

Peter had rehearsed over and over what he was going to say. He might as well say it to Frau Weschke's granddaughter as to anyone – it was Frau Weschke, after all, who had returned him to Leipzig. And there was a texture to this woman's listening that kept him needing to talk.

"Over the weekend I've come to realise it's far and away the worst thing I've ever done."

She opened the envelope, ripping the silence. "Let me read this, let me see what she's written," surprised to hear her voice so level. She unfolded Frau Weschke's letter and the seconds passed, the only sound the dog panting and the tap-tap-tap of his shoes on the blue and white circle pattern of the linoleum floor. When he glanced up, tears were running down her face.

Poor old thing, said Peter to himself. But he couldn't bear to look. He couldn't bear to be wept over today. It wasn't what he was here for.

"It was a terrific funeral." His voice light again, he picked up the earlier conversation. It had been a mistake to talk about himself when she had her own grieving to do. "The whole of the nursing-home staff came, every one of them. She was a very special lady. Everyone understood that you were taking care of your exhibition. And it's all right. It's a tremendous step to have – even I know that."

But it was no good. Whether encouraged by the contents of the letter or by what he had said or by the flow of wine, tears continued to stream from her eyes. She tried to laugh, tried to say something. All that came out was a sobbing wheeze.

He got up and stood behind her chair and rested his unsuspecting arm on her shoulder and listened to her crying. God knows, he had seen a lot of weeping women in his working life, but for once these tears seemed to be aimed at him.

His face wavered indistinct in front of her. She did nothing for a while. Then her hand reached slowly up and clung to his. "Sorry."

He lifted her hand – and, struck by an unexpected feeling of understanding for his mother, kissed it.

"I'm so sorry," with the back of her other hand wiping an eye, "I'll get over this in a second."

"Don't apologise." He said it kindly. He knew that those who go delivering ashes to the recently bereaved have to be prepared to accept a few tears. But he wasn't strong enough to cope with more of this. He had had an appalling weekend. The last thing he needed was for Frau Weschke's granddaughter – this perfectly nice, rather sad woman – to cave in on him.

Meanwhile, he had nowhere to fix his gaze. It wandered over the table. The window. The kitchen. The fridge made a singing noise and it was now that he made out all manner of snapshots magnetised to its door. The majority were Polaroids, probably taken with the large camera on the shelf above, and although he couldn't quite see what they were he had the impression of a lawn in winter, close-ups of leaves, furs. "Are these your preliminary photos –"

A car horn interrupted. Two at a time someone ran down the staircase and bounded with elephant's feet along the corridor. "Coming!"

A girl charged into the kitchen. About eighteen, her dark hair still damp. She retrieved her jacket from the door and was about to head straight back out when her mother stood up and grabbed her as she ran past.

"Hold on, slow down. I want you to meet someone. This is Peter. Peter, this is Katya."

She gave him a quick, unseeing glance. Tall, generous mouth, slanted eyes. "Hello."

"You spoke to him on the phone. He's brought Oma's ashes."

"Oh. Yes. Hi." Politely, she held out a hand, poised and distracted in the way that teenagers are. "Oh, Mutti, I forgot, the dentist called on Friday. He wants you to ring him – hey, are you all right?"

Frau Metzel tore off a strip of kitchen roll and blew her nose. "It's nothing, darling. Peter also brought a letter from Oma. It's made me very sad, I'm afraid."

There was no time to discuss it further because there was a knock that was not really a knock and a young man strolled into the kitchen.

"Sören!"

He was dressed in a tight red shirt and kissed Katya on the lips. "We're late," waving a car key on its chain and catching it. He was prematurely bald with a square, clean-shaven face, a turned-up nose and a long neck.

Flushed, Katya caught sight of the plastic urn on the table. "Are these Oma's? Gosh, they're heavy! But she looks good in a bottle." She put it down. Eager to leave.

"What direction are you heading?" Peter asked. He had no more time to waste.

"Why, where do you want to go?"

"Dorna," said Peter.

"Darling, could you run him there?" said her mother, agitated. "I did promise."

"I guess," said Katya, and looked at her boyfriend.

Sören compressed his lips. "How long will it take?"

"Ten minutes," said Frau Metzel. "Actually, the drive is longer, but if you go through the woods it's much quicker."

"Perhaps I could walk," said Peter.

"No, we'll give you a lift," said Sören.

She watched Peter tug his coat from the door, begin to put it on – and suddenly she wanted to give him something. But what?

He stooped to pick up his suitcase and through the window behind him she saw a movement in and out of the hollyhocks. "The honeybees are back! I don't believe it. Bees in March!" She touched his arm and pointed out two boxes in the adjoining field, corrugated at the side as in structures that measure rainfall. "Isn't it extraordinary, they find their way back every year to the same place – heaven knows where from." She continued talking in a babble. "I don't like bees myself. I mean, do you have bees in Berlin? Of course, you do. They're not everybody's cup of tea, but we do well by our neighbour. The children used to be fascinated by the honeycombs – remember, Katya? I tried to draw what they sounded like. You can tell what they're smelling from their sound. They see blue very well, ceanothus, lavender, blue mint, echium, crocus. Have you ever tried to draw?"

"Mutti!" said Katya briskly. "Stop it. We have to go!"

But she hadn't finished. "Why don't you leave your suitcase here? I'll run you to the station." And before he could reply: "Here, take this."

CHAPTER FIFTY-ONE

THE CAR WAS A renovated Trabi, painted a garish yellow. Peter sat in the back, Frau Weschke's cane across his knees. When Sören started the engine, the music came on very loud, *Fuck and Run* blaring from the windows. He fiddled to lower the volume, but turned it up – and off they drove, waving to Frau Metzel.

Peter saw her staring after them. She stood at the water-pump and waved what seemed a borrowed hand and then the Trabi turned into the lane, losing her, and all he could see of the house was the stork's nest on the roof.

They sped through the trees and the car as it filled with exhaust fumes smelled like warm goat's cheese. In front, Sören squeezed Katya's knee, then moved his hand to her thigh. Peter caught his breath and leaned forward to say something. But Katya was putting on her seat belt as if it was the most natural thing in the world to be driving along a narrow country lane at 100 kilometres an hour with the driver's hand between her legs.

Peter felt his hostility rising. Katya couldn't see what Sören was doing, but he could. He knew what this boy wanted, what his kneading hand was up to. And yet what could he say or do? It was none of his business. He was the interloper. He was the outsider.

Sören caught Peter's eye in the rear-view mirror. He shook his head and smiled and it unmanned Peter to see that the boy's smile was self-conscious, innocent even. He kept staring at Peter in the mirror and then whispered into Katya's ear.

Brushing the hand away, she glanced over her shoulder and said something to Peter.

"I'm sorry, I can't hear." He removed the cane from his lap and put it on the seat beside him. "What are you saying?" coming forward.

She turned down the music. "He asked if you were my uncle."

She swept the hair from her eye. "Are you?"

He thought she was teasing, but for the first time she was looking at him. "No, I don't think so," he said.

Still she went on looking, as he had seen babies look at their parents, as Milo had looked at him – a strange, concerned, ancient look that was almost not human nor sentimental. As though she was staring at him across years, even centuries.

"Sorry," he laughed.

Sören switched up the music and thumped his hand against the steering wheel. He accelerated down the avenue of poplars and Katya rested her arm on his shoulder.

Peter's laugh blew something away and he saw everything in dazzlingly clear outline. He had not had such clarity since he was a little boy bicycling along the road to Tisbury. Suddenly it was obvious. Soren was just a young man. He was behaving with Katya in the way that young people everywhere behave. The way he had once behaved himself.

Peter watched the couple, not hearing the music. The two of them unspoiled. Everything possible. As it was when Snowleg had taken him to her brother's party.

He was moved and it struck him that he was recovering the image of something that had been his before he defiled it. A kind of giddiness. A promise he had never tasted again.

In slightly more time than Frau Metzel had estimated, they reached Dorna.

"Where do you want to go?" said Katya.

"Over there. Could you drop me by the church?"

"Do you want us to wait?"

"No, I'll walk back."

"Are you sure?" said Sören.

"Yes, I'm sure. Without the suitcase I'll be fine."

"We can run you home," said Katya.

"It's very kind. But I'd like to do some thinking," and tried to climb out, but the door was locked from outside as though child-proofed and she had to come round and open it.

"Remember your stick," said Katya. She handed it to him, her arm exuding impatience and the satirical officiousness of the young when they are playing parent to the parent.

He felt impelled to kiss her on the forehead and she smiled as if it was her due. As if his kiss was part of the bounty of people's affection for her. She was in love. She had a boyfriend who loved her. Everyone wanted to kiss her. Why wouldn't he?

CHAPTER FIFTY-TWO

FEELING AN OBJECT TUCKED into one of the sleeves, she removed the Karlovy Vary mug and then lifted the muskrat coat from the box. The hem needed stitching, but Katya might like the coat. She smoothed out the arms and heard, *Once is never enough.*

She carried the plastic container with both hands to the garden and poured the contents over the hollyhocks. Shadow came running, but after a desultory sniff turned away.

Her grandmother had known. "An extraordinary thing, but there's a doctor here who has looked after me so sweetly and so kindly that if I could, I would commend him to you. In fact, dearest Snjólaug, I may send him with my ashes." She had discovered who Peter was and the old woman's last act on earth was to send him to her.

Out of habit and a sense that she needed to be among her tools she left Frau Weschke's letter on the table and walked along the brick path to her studio. Even as she put out a hand to open the door, she felt that something was not right. When she picked up a pencil it was heavy and lifeless and blunt. She began to draw, but she knew without having to try that nothing was going to come of it.

The sound of a bee blundering against the skylight made her get up from her desk. Listless, she returned to the kitchen and started to wipe the top of one of the jars on the sill. The jar had leaked and there were twigs and flies beached in the honey. As she rubbed the stickiness from the glass she could hear her daughter saying tartly, "Nice present, Mutti!"

No. On his own, or not at all.

CHAPTER FIFTY-THREE

THE CHURCH WAS PARTLY camouflaged by oaks, a building of unhealthy red brick the colour of a drinker's face. Of someone who had left their secrets in half-bottles under cushions and beds.

He searched among the older tombstones. They lay in short grass, slabs of black marble with gold lettering and snowdrops rubber-banded into jars. He didn't suppose it was a deliberate policy of the gardener, more like inattention, that the memorials of the Russian soldiers were overgrown. These were arranged in stiff ranks down the slope, cracked obelisks 2 feet high and each with a red star and a relief of once-gold bays. Some of the obelisks had names, others not. Most had died in 1945 and 1946.

He found his father's grave on the lower level: a perfunctory slab, about a foot square.

"Peter Brendel 1938–64".

The concrete was spattered with bird-droppings and on the ground before it was a burnt-looking circle of grass as if a rainbow had come and gone and all that was left was a scorchmark in the soil.

Peter found it hard to line up an emotion with the event. To feel it fully, he thought, I'll have to come back. He dropped to his knees and ran his fingertips over the chapped surface, outlining the indented letters and figures. The barrenness distressed him. No RIP. No biblical text. He twisted around for something to put on the grave.

In quite a short time he had collected a larch cone, a sprig of conifer needles, some berries and feathers. I will write to my mother, he thought. I will give her a report on this place. But what I would really like, after I've created a bouquet of feathers and leaves, is a photograph to send her. Something she can have which will resolve her obscure grief. Something which says: The man who was the father of my child is here in some way united with his son.

And there came back to him the image, under a fridge magnet, of a lawn in winter. Frau Metzel – that perfectly nice, rather sad woman – she had a camera, a Polaroid.

CHAPTER FIFTY-FOUR

SHE PARKED WHERE THE Trabi had left him an hour before.

"Don't get out," he said. "It will only take a second." At the house he had handed back the cane with the gesture of a man checking in his lance and breastplate, a man who had travelled as far as he could go.

"No, I want to come with you."

She walked in with him. The fragile bouquet was where he had left it. He knelt, thinking: This is it. I've failed in every other respect this weekend, but at least I am here. He arranged the bouquet on the slab and with his finger sketched an X on the concrete in the way that as a schoolboy he used to finish a Sunday letter home. "I'll just do this and then we can go."

She saw him fumbling with the camera. "Would you like me to take it?"

"Would you – since you're here – do me a terrific kindness? Could you take a photograph of me actually standing by the stone?"

He faced her. He was writing the letter in his head. Dearest Mummy and Dad and Ros, I'm sorry I haven't been in touch. I had various reasons for coming to Leipzig, but the most important was to see where my father is buried. As you always suspected, Mummy, he didn't make it to old bones. He was shot trying to escape (I would have been about three at the time). I'm going to make the grave cleaner and tidier –

"Look up."

He straightened his back. He took her honey out of his pocket and held it in front of him.

She was four, five paces away. She lifted the Polaroid to her eye. But the photographer, not the image, was taking shape before him. A hatch was lifting and he felt fresh air pouring in and down, drenching him, and all his past and present confusion, guilt, misery, loneliness, flooding out. Snowleg. But he cannot speak. He cannot move.

He sees her walk towards him.

She takes his arm. "Peter."

ACKNOWLEDGMENTS

THIS IS A WORK of fiction and not one of the characters is a real person. Many of the events described did take place. I am grateful to Katja Lange-Müller, Johanna Bartl, Bernhard Robben, Katharina Narbutovic, Bettina Schröder, Elmar Gehlen, Reinhard Jirgl, Ulrike Poppe, Sabine Moegelin, Gesine Udewald, Hans-Jürgen Hilfrich, Stefan Richter, Edda Fensch, Frank Berberich, Corinna Ziegler, Rachael Rose, Ulli Janetzki, Michael Hofmann, Matthew Kidd, Simon Cole, Tim Blackburn, Richard Lowe, Daniel Johnson, Jo-Ann Johnson, Patrick Hanly, Patricia Linders, Sharon Mar, Gillon Aitken, Clare Alexander; and most of all to Christopher MacLehose and Gillian Johnson. I am glad to pay tribute to *The Other Germans*: *Report from an East German town* (Pantheon, New York, 1970), by Hans Axel Holm. My thanks too to the Literarisches Colloquium in Berlin and to the Künstlerhaus Schloß Wiepersdorf, where parts of this novel were written.